Praise for Look Back with Longing
Book One of the Clearharbour Trilogy

by Fred Tarpley

After an absence of two decades, Houstonian Suzanne Morris returns with another distinctive work of romantic fiction, *Look Back with Longing,* the first segment of the *Clearharbour Trilogy.* In 2006, *Elizabeth's Legacy* and *Clearharbour* will conclude the multi-generational saga set primarily in Houston and England.

Morris continues her successes with intricate plots, sharp characterizations, manifold locales, and interwoven conflicts, found in *Galveston* (1976), *Keeping Secrets* (1979), and *Wives and Mistresses* (1986). In her latest work, the narrative unfolds in a quartet of two-year segments between 1914 and 1931.

Told with an omniscient point of view entering the consciousness of several provocative characters, the novel focuses on Geneva Sterling, a red-haired, green-eyed beauty with talent, resolve, and endurance. Orphaned shortly before her 16th birthday, when her parents die in an accident while traveling, Geneva remains in Houston as the ward of her mother's cousin. Victor Calais, the husband of the guardian, introduces Geneva to art photography as well as deep, human attachment in his studio behind the family home in Houston Heights. Her decision to model for him triggers lingering complications in her life.

Geneva's talent and classical training at Madame Linsky's dance studio in Houston attracts British variety dancer Tony Selby, and the pair tour the vaudeville circuit with their charismatic performances. The relationship off-stage is as intense as their dances on stages from the West Coast to the Palace in New York. Plans for marriage are obstructed, however, by Geneva's past, her new guardian, and a menacing banker who manages her trust fund. Their happiness is further threatened in England when Tony is subjected to the impending loss of his father's estate and the psychotic vengeance of his former lover.

Especially impressive in the novel are episodes demonstrating Morris' cinematic writing style, creating on the page what Hitchcock so brilliantly achieved on the screen. For example, the royal performance at the London Palladium by Geneva and Tony juxtaposes the movements of their dance, *Chimaera*, against excruciating tension in their personal lives. The scene intensifies the technical agony of the dance, the emotion of the performance, and the drama of the situation that has erupted in the plot.

Morris writes, "…turning…turning…turning. Tony's hands making a stirrup for her foot, then lifting her on his shoulder, and now in an arabesque, she was turning…turning…then swirling down Tony's body to the floor, falling in love expressed in a series of alluring pirouettes, ending in a swooning backbend over the collector's arm, and up and up, higher and higher, a windmill churning. As the collector with his outsized net romanced the butterfly, the police romanced Emelye's abductor with a London-sized net of trained professionals."

Meticulous research entertains and informs the reader with graphic and resonating excursions into the mores, fashions, and events of each era. If Morris reports that an unexpected snow chilled Houston or that a particular dance step was in vogue, her words mirror history with accuracy. With her large cast of characters, interest in art, dance, theater, photography, and finance, the representation is authentic. Research trips to England, tours of theaters, familiarity with historical events and daily life coinciding with the timeline, and interviews with vaudeville performers, dancers, and trust officers serve her fiction well.

Despite a dense population of characters, there is no wondering about who's who because each is named aptly, delineated uniquely, and described in broad but incisive strokes.

The plot constantly accelerates with stunningly unpredictable but plausible twists, misjudgments, and reversals. Readers trying to second-guess the next revelation will usually agree that alternate paths have been foreshadowed with subtlety. Recurring as a theme is the struggle of Geneva and others to understand and accept divine and human love in the adversity of an imperfect world. The book succeeds on numerous levels as mesmerizing fiction.

Mystery and suspense engage the reader at every turn, and more than one character is a likely perpetrator of each transgression. By the final page, major conflicts have been resolved, but enough strands of the plot remain to haunt the reader. The enticement will compel the curious to follow Geneva, Tony, et al, into *Elizabeth's Legacy* and *Clearharbour*.

Fred Tarpley is Professor Emeritus of Literature and Languages at Texas A&M University-Commerce, and director of literary criticism for the Texas University Interscholastic League contest.

ELIZABETH'S LEGACY

Also by Suzanne Morris

ELIZABETH'S LEGACY

Book Two of the *Clearharbour Trilogy*

A Novel

Suzanne Morris

iUniverse, Inc.

New York Lincoln Shanghai

Elizabeth's Legacy
Book Two of the *Clearharbour Trilogy*

iUniverse books may be ordered through booksellers or by contacting:

iUniverse
2021 Pine Lake Road, Suite 100
Lincoln, NE 68512
www.iuniverse.com
1-800-Authors (1-800-288-4677)

This is a work of fiction. All of the characters, names, incidents, organizations and dialogue in this novel are either the products of the author's imagination or are used fictitiously.

ISBN-13: 978-0-595-39899-7 (pbk)
ISBN-13: 978-0-595-67752-8 (cloth)
ISBN-13: 978-0-595-84296-4 (ebk)
ISBN-10: 0-595-39899-5 (pbk)
ISBN-10: 0-595-67752-5 (cloth)
ISBN-10: 0-595-84296-8 (ebk)

Printed in the United States of America

In memory of my mother,
Ruth McMickle Page

Acknowledgments

I am grateful to many people for assistance in writing this novel. Some are no longer living. I am pleased, nonetheless, to include their names here.

In the United States:

Susan Schwartz, for editing the manuscript; Karen Giesen, for proofreading and copyediting; Richard Plessala, M.D., for information on the symptoms and effects of severe respiratory distress in infants; Colonel Jake Wilk, Jr., USAAF (Retired) and Captain Fred Philips, USAAF-RES for providing information about their experiences as Air Force pilots in WWII; David Anderson, Crew Chief, for a guided tour of the Lone Star Flight Museum, Galveston, Texas, early in my research and for fact-checking and proofing more recently; and First Sergeant William J. Reineke, Army of the United States, for sharing memories of active service in WWII, in England, France, and Germany; Clayton and Elizabeth Lee, for sharing memories of growing up in the Houston Heights; and C. G. Javellana for the original promotional art.

In England:

Patrick Beaver, first, last and always, for answering my many research queries; Joyce Watts, Administrator, Bodmin Town Museum, Bodmin, Cornwall, for a guided tour of the museum and answers to numerous queries; Hazel James, life-long Bodmin resident, for information on Harleigh School and a variety of other local subjects; and the following residents of Bederkesa Court, Bodmin, for a lively roundtable interview: Marjorie Vine, Joyce Skea, Glenny Welch, Joyce Owen, Ann Minter, and Archie Burden; Neville Chapman, B.A., A.L.A., Bodmin Library, for arranging the interview and digging out answers to numerous queries; also, Kim Cooper, Librarian, Cornish Studies Library, Redruth, Cornwall; the Rev. Canon Ken Rogers, St. Petroc's Parish Church,

Bodmin, for acquainting me with customs of the Church during my story period;

Dr. Joyce Reynolds, Newnham College, Cambridge University, for a very helpful interview, and for searching out answers to my queries about life at Newnham College during WWII.

In France:

Bénédicte Lilamand, for her generous hospitality in Paris, for researching numerous queries about life in France before and during World War II, and for providing introductions for me at particular places that would form the backdrop of my novel; Valérie Dufournier for providing a guided tour of the fashion salon of Jean Patou and answering my queries; and Deborah Schocket, Associate Professor of French, Bowling Green State University, Ohio, for checking for errors in my use of the French language.

Last, but by no means least, I am indebted to Donna Bonner Garner for accompanying me on a month-long research journey in England and France in 1994, without which I could not have completed the *Clearharbour Trilogy*.

Contents

Wispy leaves of weeping willow,
  brush the ground about us
  like a widow's veil;
And hide our tears until time's weather
  dries them.

—Elizabeth Selby

Interlude

September 1, 1931

Dearest—

It's three o'clock in the morning, but I could not fall asleep if my life depended on it. A few hours from now the movers will arrive, and by nightfall Emelye and I will have closed the door behind us, and 1207 Heights Boulevard, Houston, Texas will be empty of all except our memories. Tonight and tomorrow night we will sleep across the street at the Youngers, while I—with the help of Willa's cleaning lady—spend all my waking hours scrubbing the baseboards, waxing the wood floors, polishing the windows, cleaning the light fixtures and fans, scrubbing the bathroom tiles, etc. I intend to leave this house sparkling clean. I admit this is not only out of my desire to help Rodney do his job, but also out of a sense of pride.

By the way, Rodney has found a buyer for my dancing school out on Milam, a dance instructor newly come to town about whom I know nothing, nor will I be around to discover if she is a worthy successor of Madame Linsky and me. (I expect Willa will keep me appraised of how Serena progresses with her, however.)

I find that in the seventeen years I've lived here I have become attached to this house, and have already shed an occasional tear about leaving. Will the new owners take good care of it? Will they keep up the gardens I spent so much time developing and nurturing? I hope so. Perhaps caring so much is foolish on my part, but then, I wonder if anyone ever really lets go of the past entirely. Our ability to remember binds us to it—the good and the bad. And there has been plenty of both here.

Well it's hardly out of a sudden burst of sentimentality that I sit down to write you in the wee hours of the morning. And if not for the two days we are to remain in Houston, plus the two-day trip by rail to NYC, and the four-day stop-over there before our ship sails, there would be no hope of this letter greeting you before we do. So, in the small hope you may have it in your hands before you leave for Southampton to meet our ship on the 18th, I now set about explaining a decision I've made while the impressions that brought it about are intense and clear in my mind, before events of the coming days are superimposed on them. Also, I know you dislike unpleasant surprises—which you may find this to be—and therefore I want you to have a little time to assimilate your thoughts, before we see each other.

The nude photographs that have been a blight on my life for years, and Emelye's life for too long, and on our relationship from the beginning; and that we anticipated my destroying at the earliest possible moment, arrived by registered mail shortly after I last wrote to you in August. However, I put off dealing with them until a few hours ago. While I dreaded the sight of those pictures and all they revealed about me, I knew full well that I must face down the foolish person who agreed to pose for them in spite of all reluctance.

Remarkably, as I viewed them carefully, one by one, I came to feel that I was not mistaken when I agreed to pose for them, as I had always believed. My aversion to them was based on the certainty that no matter what Victor claimed, they were harsh and burlesque in quality—how could they be otherwise, when they were born of my corruption? And to be fair, some narrow-minded people will always find with open eyes what I feared in my blindness: Victor's own daughters considered them 'vulgarities.'

Since returning the photographs to the envelope in which they arrived, I have reflected on all my actions through the years, arising from the worrisome knowledge they were out of my reach. I've come to realize my greatest error was my reasoning when I refused to accept them from Victor before he left me, after Anne's death. With no inkling that the photographs were examples of a great photographer's art, I viewed them as souvenirs of our time together, and desperately hoped they would remind him of all I meant to him and compel him to return to me. Of course I was wrong to believe my scheme would work, nor—it goes without saying—would it have been the best thing that could have happened to me.

Like Victor's *Maiden at the Window*, these four compositions are surrealistic in style, soft and dreamy in tone and, I think overall, provocative in nature. While they are undoubtedly suggestive of nudity, they are a good deal less revealing of my body than I imagined. And, if my instincts are correct, they will far outlast me. How humbling it was to be faced with reality: the fruits of Victor's talent transcended our relationship. Time's equilibrium will surely place me in a footnote in his body of work, if that. It occurs to me that he may have done additional art photographs, with other models, prior to his death in Singapore. If so, I'd be interested in seeing them. Yet obviously I won't have an opportunity to open the crates from Springfield to see what's there, before forwarding them to England.

As you will have guessed by now, I am determined to preserve the photographs, rather than to destroy them. I would like to think you might have a look at them sometime, but I realize what painful associations they hold for you, and therefore I won't be the first to suggest it. All I ask is that you understand my change of heart.

While I intend to donate Victor's entire photograph collection and all his equipment to an appropriate museum, please be assured that I am in no hurry to investigate the possibilities. Nothing will distract me from the official wedding and second honeymoon we have dreamed of for years, or from the important task of establishing our home at Clearharbour Farm and caring for Emelye and Elizabeth while your energies are focused on preparing for the reopening of the *William & Mary*. So in the meantime, perhaps you will suggest a safe place where the photographs can be stored.

Otherwise, dear Tony, I urge that we put this subject behind us once and for all, and let none but happy words be exchanged when we come face to face and the joy of life together anticipated by all our letters, written over the years, finally begins.

All my love,
Geneva

PART I

1931–1933

CHAPTER 1

It was too late to go down and slip in unnoticed, for they were here.

Elizabeth stood at the edge of her second-story bedroom window at Brookhurst and peered down below as her father's new pearl gray Rolls-Royce approached the circular drive, then cruised slowly round and came to a halt before the arched entrance way of the house. The luxury auto was Father's wedding surprise for Geneva. It moved with the speed and grace that one imagined of an ocean liner, in a picture advertising the White Star line.

Elizabeth could not imagine ever traveling on an ocean liner as Emelye and her mother had done, for that would mean leaving England when she was reluctant to so much as set foot outside the Brookhurst grounds; and she didn't much fancy the idea of riding in an auto now, after the drive with her mother through Dartmoor Forest, though—more was the pity—she didn't suppose she could go through her whole life avoiding it.

She may be forced to move to Clearharbour Farm, though she hoped not.

The weather had been cold and crisp this morning when the roses were brought in from the garden by the basketfuls—Grandmother ordered vases filled in all the downstairs rooms, in honor of Geneva and Emelye's arrival. But now the sun had vanished and a strong wind was blowing from the north. The air smelt pungent, and the sky was terraced with swiftly moving clouds. One could hear the sound of thunder in the distance, like the roll of a kettle drum leading up to a great clash of cymbals in an orchestra pit. Elizabeth used to love it when Father would take her to see a musical where dancers performed his routines. She always imagined that one day she would dance in musicals also. Often during rehearsals, he would have her brought to the theatre where he was working. He worked in all the West End theatres that were suited to musicals—the *Palace*, the *Coliseum*, the *Drury Lane*, for instance. He liked to introduce her to his theatrical friends, for he was proud of her. But gone were the days when she dreamt of growing up to be a dancer; the days when she happily burst through the auditorium doors and rushed down to the stage, where Father would wait in his dancing shoes, his sleeves rolled up to the elbows, his arms flung open. *"There's my Lizzie!"* he would say. Apart from the fact that she was no longer capable of dancing, or rushing anywhere, nor would she ever be, she could no longer bear for Father to call her by her special name. This she had told him. She had not told him the reason.

Elizabeth watched as her father opened the door on the driver's side and stepped out, gazing up at the troubled sky with his eyebrows hitched together, as if he regarded it as an ill omen. If Mummy told the truth in Dartmoor Forest, perhaps it was an omen that Father's marriage to Geneva would be unhappy. Of course, one could never be sure when Mummy was telling the truth, an unhappy fact that Elizabeth lived with every hour of every day.

Father opened Geneva's door and assisted her out on the pavement. Unlike Elizabeth's mother, whose figure was small and flat, Geneva had rounded hips and a full bosom. "Soon Geneva will become your new mother," said Father with satisfaction. What would it be like? She wondered. She remembered clinging to Geneva's skirt in fright on the day the man took Emelye away in London, remembered Geneva's gentle hands embracing her swiftly. Just now she had a fleeting wish that Geneva would draw her close and comfort her again.

Geneva was clad in a dark green dress of rather slinky material, with big shoulders and loose-fitting sleeves, the skirt knee-length in front and curving to a deep dip in back. Round her neck was a long figured scarf of green, gold and brown. The wind unfurled the scarf so that it looked like autumn leaves being whirled through the air. One brown-gloved hand flew up and grasped the scarf, and the other grasped the brim of her small green hat with the partridge feather, to keep it from blowing off. Geneva threw her head back in laughter, and her short red waves jiggled. How happy and carefree she looked. Father said something to her that Elizabeth could not hear, then he, too, laughed.

Now came Emelye, in a deep blue dress with smocking from the waist up to the round white collar. She wore black patent shoes with ankle straps and dainty white socks trimmed in lace. Her beautiful dark blond hair escaped the great blue ribbon bow on her head, and her skirt hem flew up, along with the white flounces of her petticoat. She pushed the hair back from her eyes with one hand, and modestly pressed down her skirt with the other, but not before

Elizabeth noted the perfect shape of her legs, with their suntan acquired in Texas. No one would ever feel repulsed upon glancing at Emelye's legs, as they would if they chanced to see hers. She felt a twinge of jealousy, though she knew she must struggle against it, for it was wrong.

Just as Grandmother and Grandfather hurried out on the steps to greet the new arrivals, with the dogs barking and circling, Father boldly caught Geneva in a hug and kissed her. Elizabeth had never once seen him touch her mother in an affectionate way.

"It drove me quite mad that he didn't love me, when I all but worshiped him...." And all the while the white Mercedes hurled along, Mummy's white-gloved hands on the steering wheel, her chin tilted, her steel blue eyes darting now at Elizabeth, now at the tangled road ahead....

Elizabeth dreaded going down and walking into the library, with all of them waiting, their eyes turned on her, whereas if she had gone down earlier, she could have been seated when they came into the room. She turned and viewed her figure in the full-length mirror. She wore a black velveteen pinafore and a white silk blouse with lace on the collar and sleeves. A pair of black stockings hid the scar on her left leg. There were a dozen pair in her dresser, sent down from a shop in London. She would never, ever leave her room unless she was wearing black stockings. Unfortunately, Father and her grandparents and Auntie Nell had already seen the ugly purplish-red streak that ran like a bolt of lightning down the back of her leg from the knee to the ankle, and that would never go away or even become less pronounced. But she would never allow Geneva or Emelye, or anyone else, to see it. That was why she must beg to be excused from moving to Clearharbour Farm.

"What do you think of when you hear the word, 'Clearharbour'?" Father asked one day, his mouth twitching into a smile under his neat brown moustache.

"I suppose one thinks of water that is clean and pure...and fresh."

"And...? Harbour?"

For a moment she thought of Ready Money Cove at Fowey, how the water crashed violently against the high slate boulders protecting it on either side, but was becalmed as it spilled into the cove. She ventured, "Safety, I suppose, and peacefulness?"

"Precisely! And that is what Clearharbour will be for our family: a place to begin afresh...a place where we will live in peace."

Elizabeth understood his meaning: without Mummy around, everyone could be at peace. Yet she did not believe she could ever begin afresh, or ever be at peace inside.

She and Emelye were to share the dormer attic room, high up under the steeply-pitched slate roof. Father was having it done up specially for them, with a small fireplace where one could burn either coal or wood, a window seat, and a bath put in next door. "Won't it be fun? The two of you way up there, in your own cozy hideaway!" he said, beaming. *No. I shall have no privacy at all*, Elizabeth thought with dread. She wished now that she had said so, but she'd been reluctant to injure Father's feelings. That was something else she had to live with, feeling guilty for treating Father cruelly behind his back, and hence being anxious to avoid hurting him to his face.

Still peering into the mirror, she pressed her fringe of dark bangs against the scar on her forehead. (Every day she checked to see if it was growing smaller as the doctor predicted, but she could see no change as yet.) Then she folded her hands behind her waist, stood straight, and wished it were possible to pose just so, always, and never have to walk about in front of people. One might be a girl in a painting, hanging in the National Gallery. People would pass by, some of them glancing her way, saying what a fine painting it was—one of Sir So-and-So's best—never guessing the model was crippled, let alone the reason why.

"Father, pray tell me, what made my mother the way she was?"

"I have no idea. But all that's in the past. It's best if we don't think about it any longer."

It would never be in the past for Elizabeth.

In the library—her favorite room at Brookhurst—the fragrance of Grandfather's cherry pipe tobacco mingled with the smell of leather book binding and seasoned wood. There were hundreds of books sitting on shelves behind glass doors, some of which she had looked through, all of which she intended to read one day when she knew enough words to understand them—there were few illustrations to assist one. And there was a wooden stand with spindled legs holding a huge lexicon. Sometimes she stood on a little stool and ran her eyes up and down the columns in fascination. It seemed to Elizabeth quite amazing that it required a volume that large to contain all the words in the English language. She knew ever so few. And at the rate of fifteen new vocabulary words per week, how would she ever learn that many? Grandfather said that his father collected most of the books after he built the house, not because he was a great reader of literature—"No more than I am myself," he admitted—but because he thought a great house should have a classical library. For the same reason he acquired plaster busts of Descartes and St. Augustine, which sat upon wooden pedestals on either side of the fireplace. One day she asked her friend Father Ogilvie if he knew about these two men. He told her that Descartes believed the idea of God could not have been thought up unless God existed. St. Augustine believed that all history was directed by God, and one must strive to be in mystical union with God. Elizabeth was determined to read the works of these two great thinkers one day.

The library walls were covered in dull gold wallpaper, and on the floor was a red medallion rug. The room was rather dark, for it was located on the north side of the house and had only two tall casement windows on one side to allow in the light. It was darker than usual today, with thunderclouds gathering.

Elizabeth paused in the doorway and pressed her fingers against her bangs—she felt so dreadfully exposed! Grandfather was sitting across from Grandmother by the fire in his favorite tweed jacket and riding jodhpurs and boots, lighting his pipe. He spent most of his days riding round the estate farms, looking after things with the help of a steward. Before the auto crash, she used to go riding on a pony along with him. Grandfather was quite tall, with keen blue-gray eyes and silver hair. He had the commanding but benevolent presence of a very wise king, one who always treated his subjects fairly, and was loved. When she was getting well from her injuries, he sat by her bed for hours. Sometimes he read stories to her; other times he told her tales of the days when the family owned a tin mining business. "Now, stop me if I've told you this one before," he would say, because he had been telling her stories for as long as she could remember. But she never would stop him because she loved his stories, and his voice which flowed smoothly and deeply as he reminisced. Now and again he would pause after uttering a certain word, and bring a finger to his chin thoughtfully, as if the word itself had snagged yet another memory along the deep shaft of his mind. "Where was I?" he would ask suddenly. She would tell him, and he would continue, "Oh yes, as I was saying...."

One day Grandfather brought up a large box with a hodgepodge of old photographs to show her. There were miners riding engines down into the dark, stratified earth, wearing hats with candles on the front like the one he kept behind glass in his study, alongside his old log book with brittle pages and stained leather binding. There were stone engine houses that looked like small churches, with gothic windows and towers, the kind she'd seen abandoned and overgrown with vines along the Cornish coast. There were men with smudged faces having their lunch of Cornish pasties, with meat and vegetables at one end, and fruit at the other, for dessert; grimy men, bare to the waist, washing in the change house at the end of the day. There was a photo of Grandfather and Uncle Morey, wearing suits and hats, and broad smiles, standing inside a vast steam cylinder of a pumping engine they had just acquired for a great deal of money.

After returning this photo to the box, he said, "All a part of the past."

"Why don't you open the tin mines again?" she asked, for it seemed to her that he regretted not working there any longer.

His eyes leveled on hers. "Because times change, my dear, and we can't bring back the past, even the good parts," he said. After a pause, he brightened and added, "The most important thing is, here we are, safe and happy at Brookhurst!"

"They were about to lose everything, even Brookhurst," said Mummy, her brow lifted as though she had just imparted a very wicked secret.

"It was good that Mummy saved Brookhurst, wasn't it?" Elizabeth asked sincerely. Yet as the color leapt to her grandfather's cheeks, she feared she had either spoken out of turn or somehow given away her treachery in Dartmoor Forest, or both. She waited with pounding heart for him to demand to be informed how she knew this. He did not, however. Suddenly she wanted to empty her heart out to Grandfather, to confess that she had betrayed his son. But before she did, he said in a low voice, "Yes, it was."

Abruptly he rose from his chair and picked up the box of photographs. "You'd better rest now," he said, then left the room.

Elizabeth was thankful she had not confessed to Grandfather. It was to her father she must gather the courage and confess one day, regardless of the fact that Father Ogilvie said she need confess her sin only to God.

She did not want Grandfather to know what she had done, for he would think ill of her, and she could not bear that. Elizabeth's love for her grandfather was as strong and clear of confusion as that she once felt for her father.

Grandmother held her chin high as she poured tea from a silver pot into a china cup. She wore a silk dress patterned in irregular shapes of red, yellow, and black, with a high neck and sleeves that reached to her slender wrists. Her dark hair, streaked with gray, was parted down the side and curled on the ends. Elizabeth was quite sure that Grandmother was the most poised of all women, and surely the most confident. Grandmother was kind and generous, and Elizabeth loved her. Yet sometimes she wished she had not returned to Brookhurst last summer, to live once again with Grandfather, for if not, perhaps Father would permit her to continue living here, as Grandfather's companion. This made her feel terribly guilty—she knew her grandparents were very happy to be together again—but she had not lived with Father since before the auto crash, and now she felt anxious at the thought of being around him every day. She hoped, if he insisted on her moving to Clearharbour Farm, he would stay in London most of the time. And this made her feel guilty, too. It seemed that one feeling of guilt led to another, like a vine creeping up the wall of an engine house.

Emelye was sitting on the sofa with her mother, while Father filled a plate from the pyramids of sandwiches and cakes on a tray. "And how about one of these, Emelye? Do you fancy egg salad?"

Just then, Geneva looked towards the door. At the sight of Elizabeth, her lips parted slightly. For a moment her green eyes were locked in a stare, making Elizabeth aware of her pale, sickly-looking skin, her dark eyes burning large in her face, and her crippled leg. How inferior she must seem to Geneva, whose own daughter was perfect.

"Here's Elizabeth now," Geneva cried abruptly, obviously recovering her surprise.

Emelye leapt to her feet. "Elizabeth!" She ran to her and took her hand, her brown eyes sparkling. "Are you glad to see me? Grandmother says you don't even have to use crutches any more, and Daddy says we're going to have a room together at Clearharbour Farm!"

Elizabeth was dancing round Emelye, kissing her fingers, rejoicing that her sister was delivered safely from the terrible man who took her away. Yet, Clearharbour—"Yes, I am very glad to see you, Emelye," she said, regretting that the words sounded false, in spite of her sincerity.

No, you aren't, Emelye thought uneasily, looking into Elizabeth's immobile face. Since she and her mother walked down the gangway from the ship this morning, Emelye had felt stranded because she realized just how far away from home she was, so far away that she might never see her neighbors James and Serena again. Immediately, she had begun to count more than ever on Elizabeth being her friend. Now, her mother's assurances aside, she feared that Elizabeth no longer adored her as she had when they were together in London last year, and would never again be like the person she remembered, who laughed so gaily and thought endlessly of ways to have fun. Desperate, she tried again. "Come and sit by me!" She tugged her hand.

Whenever Elizabeth sank down into the big overstuffed sofa, it was awkward getting to her feet again. Hard chairs were more manageable. She pulled her hand free. "No thank you, it's very kind of you, but I shall just sit there, by the library table, if you don't mind."

Crestfallen, Emelye returned to sit next to her mother. Geneva hugged Emelye close, as if to protect her. Elizabeth felt she'd had no right to wish Geneva might draw her close. She was going to ruin things for everyone.

As Elizabeth made what was—for her—a long journey across the room, she felt all eyes upon her. She tried ever so hard to keep her balance so that her limp would not be terribly noticeable, so that the others would not pity her. But of course, it was no good, it never was, no matter how many times she practiced. The limp was not to be concealed; its mark upon her body signified the mark upon her spirit. God's forgiveness, assured her by Father Ogilvie, did not spare her this outward sign of her inward corruption.

"Elizabeth, darling, we were just telling Emelye all about the plans for your room at Clearharbour," Father said brightly, handing Emelye her filled plate. "And what kind of sandwiches will you have? Water cress, cheese, olive, ham salad—?"

Elizabeth's stomach churned violently. "No, nothing for me, thank you," she said, taking her seat at last. *And I shan't be moving to Clearharbour.*

"We'll move there right after the wedding, won't we? Straight from here?" Emelye asked, always on the watch in case the grown-ups announced they must all go to London to be near Daddy's theatre. Her mother always kept her promises, but then, Emelye had learned from being around Serena and James, that when mothers talked to daddies about things, sometimes they changed their minds. "And till then, I can sleep with my mother, right?" she asked. The huge stone house—she had counted up three stories, and there were more windows across the front than she had ever seen except in a hotel, which meant it had a great many rooms—was terrifying. What if she got lost inside?

Geneva and Tony exchanged a glance.

Cynthia cleared her throat and said to her granddaughters, "Wait till you see the four dress designs under consideration for you to wear in the wedding procession. Samples are being sent down from Selfridge's tomorrow. The bride can choose her favorite."

Geneva smiled at Elizabeth. "Dear, did your father tell you that you and Emelye are to be flower girls?" she asked in an encouraging voice.

He did not. And surely they could not expect her to walk down the aisle, with everyone watching! Breathlessly, she said, "I—I'm sorry, but I shouldn't like to be in the wedding if you don't mind, and I—I have decided to go on living here at Brookhurst. I've grown accustomed to it, you see." She looked at her father imploringly. "That is, if it's alright." She could feel beads of perspiration gathering on her forehead and the ridge above her lip.

Father looked at her as she had often seen him look at Mummy, as if he were quite at pains to imagine her reasoning. "It certainly will not do for you to live at Brookhurst," he said firmly, "and as to the wedding—"

Just then, there came a great ripping sound of thunder. Elizabeth's shoulders jumped. Immediately the rain poured down.

Merton rushed in, in his uniform with stiff bow tie and black tailcoat. Hurriedly he closed the casement windows, the gauzy curtains swirling about his outstretched arms like ghostly fingers, the lightning reflecting dramatically on his face. Merton had thinning hair, combed straight across the crown of his head, and jug-like ears. He was now the full-fledged butler, his father Parker having retired last year. When he was finished, he asked Grandfather, "Shall I light another lamp, your Lordship?"

Grandfather was drawing on his pipe. He looked up. His eyes moved first to Elizabeth, then to her father. "Yes, I'm afraid it has become quite dark in here, suddenly."

Everyone remained silent until the lamp on the library table was lit and Merton left the room and shut the door. Now with soft light illuminating the tall glass-fronted shelves, Elizabeth imagined the books a gallery of friends gazing down upon her encouragingly.

Grandfather said agreeably to Geneva, "Fr. John Key—he's our new vicar, you know—tells me 'twas the first time the Bishop had ever been asked for permission to do a wedding in the old chapel ruin. 'I do hope you'll furnish umbrellas in case of rain,' the vicar said."

Elizabeth knew that Grandfather was being humorous. But from the fretful look on Geneva's face, she didn't understand. "Oh dear, Tony, what if it does rain?" she said.

"It wouldn't dare. The 17th of October is going to be the most perfect day of the year," he predicted. He winked at Geneva and smiled.

For the moment, everyone forgot about the awkwardness Elizabeth had created. But she knew she could not escape a talking-to by Father, later. She remembered how it used to be, that scarcely did she ask for anything he would not readily give. Sometimes she felt that he could see right through to her betrayal, and did not love her anymore.

CHAPTER 2

Geneva did not sleep much that night. Shortly after ten, feeling reasonably certain that Emelye was alright—she was quite sleepy, and yawning—she tucked her into the bed they shared and promised to be back soon. Whence she headed for Tony's room and knocked on the door. They fell into each other's arms and did their best to make up for eight years of being deprived of the pleasure of making love. When finally they released each other, every nerve in Geneva's body protested. And as she slipped ever so quietly back to her room, she hoped to find Emelye fast asleep so that she could return to Tony's arms for the remainder of the night.

To her despair, there she found her daughter not only awake but sobbing her heart out, pleading, "I want to go home! I don't like it here!"

After the exhausting weeks of packing for the move and getting the Heights house ready to put up for sale, all the while assuring Emelye that everyone in her family in England—and especially Elizabeth—could hardly wait for her to come and live over here; after all the high hopes that sustained her through eight straight days of her usual bout of seasickness aboard the ocean liner, Geneva felt utterly defeated and spent, though she could hardly say she was surprised.

As she took Emelye in her arms, the image that came to mind was that of her daughter sitting at the kitchen table for hours, week after week through last winter, drawing pictures to help cheer up the injured girl she had been taught to regard as her sister. While Geneva would never admit it to anyone, she was fighting down resentment toward Elizabeth. It didn't matter that the child was cool toward her, but her indifference to Emelye, followed by her shocking request to continue living at Brookhurst rather than to share a room with her at Clearharbour, was the cruelest blow that Emelye could have received. And Elizabeth spent the remainder of the afternoon till dinner behind the closed door of her room, claiming she needed to rest. Yes, the child had been through a great deal, and naturally she was not as lively as she used to be—Geneva had prepared Emelye for this. But nearly a full year had passed since the auto crash. Elizabeth had been loved and doted on every single day, and her friend Father Ogilvie had spent many hours at her side, in an effort to nurse her spirit back to health. In spite of all this, had her kindness and compassion—once a clear testament to her remarkable faith—been left at the bottom of the embankment in Dartmoor Forest?

Tony had his own theory. He had always believed that Elizabeth blamed him for failing to save her from her mother, and he was convinced—wrongly, of course, though there was no changing his mind—that he deserved the blame. Tonight as they wound up the evening with a drink together in the library, he said that while he must live with this, he would simply not allow her to take it out on Emelye and Geneva. He intended to have a talk with Elizabeth tomorrow, and "get her straightened out." For the moment this seemed as good as any other solution, and prompted Geneva to kiss her daughter and assure her that everything would be better tomorrow.

Yet, after she finally got Emelye settled down to sleep, her back nudged against her mother's in the big four-poster bed as if to be sure she wouldn't escape again, she lay there thinking. Whether or not Tony was right about what was going on in his daughter's mind, a stern talk at this point may well backfire and cause Elizabeth to retreat even further from her and Emelye, to consider them enemies. She must head him off, and talk with Elizabeth herself.

The next morning breakfast was laid out on the sideboard in the small dining room—a cheerful room with exposed rafters, wallpaper in a cornflower pattern, and pot plants thriving on the deep window ledge. There were fried eggs, sunny side up, sizzling in a chafing dish; plump sausages and meaty back bacon; grilled tomatoes, baked beans; toast triangles and currant scones, with jam and honey and butter. Geneva was grateful to find a pot of coffee as well as tea. As Tony pulled back her chair at the table, she managed to whisper: "Let me talk to Elizabeth." Their eyes met briefly, then he nodded.

During the meal, Geneva noticed that Elizabeth picked at her food in silence, occasionally stealing a worried glance at her father, then lowering her eyes to her plate. How she hated this! The sooner she got to the bottom of Elizabeth's troubles, the better it would be not only for Emelye, whose eyes were puffy from crying this morning and who had no more appetite than Elizabeth, but for everyone else. Finally, after emptying the last of her second cup of coffee, Geneva wiped her mouth with her crisp white napkin and said to Elizabeth in a friendly manner, "How about coming out into the walled garden with me? We'll have a talk, just the two of us."

Elizabeth looked at Tony as if for approval, or perhaps clarification. "Go along," he said, not unkindly. "And you will both need a sweater. It's chilly outdoors this morning."

Soon Geneva and Elizabeth were approaching the gate through a long trellis archway that Geneva didn't recall from her previous visit, though it was obviously not a recent addition. Now she remembered, the archway was virtually hidden by a cascade of deep blue morning-glories nestled in dark green leaves. It was summertime then. Today it was bare and gloomy, the vines having been cut back for the approaching winter.

Inside the gate, she and Elizabeth took their seats under the wooden pergola stretching along the far end of the garden. The wisteria vine that in summer sent pale purple blossoms like clumps of grapes through every opening in the lattice roof was now swiped back to its thick knobby trunk at one end. Last night's storm had passed over, leaving the sky a fresh-washed blue with a host of ballooning white clouds. Sunlight slanted down upon them through the pergola roof.

For the moment Geneva breathed in the sharp cold air, and looked around, remembering the blaze of color, the infinite variety of flowers that filled the beds and grew up the stone walls her first time here. All that remained in bloom this late in the season were the famed Brookhurst roses in the center of the garden, below the terrace, and last night's storm had stripped away many of their petals and scattered them along the ground. *I'll be here to see this garden come to life the next time around,* she thought with satisfaction, *it won't be like before, when everything blew up in our faces.*

And yet, weighing on her heart was this child nearby, sitting forward with her palms resting on the edge of her chair, as if she was hoping for an early escape. Geneva knew what she wanted to say to Elizabeth, more or less, but she was not quite sure how to begin and her mind felt fuzzy from the restless night. As she was gathering her thoughts, Elizabeth turned to her with a defensive look. "Did my father ask you to have a talk with me?"

"Not exactly," she said. "But we've both been concerned."

She looked off again, toward the terrace, took in a breath. "Why?"

Geneva despaired to notice a slight tremor in the child's thin arms. Elizabeth had been frightened for most of her life; the last thing Geneva wanted was for her to be frightened of her new mother. With an effort to sound reassuring, she answered, "Well, first of all, because you don't want to be in our wedding."

Abruptly Elizabeth raised her fingertips and pressed her bangs against her forehead, a panicked look crossing her face. Geneva thought of the scar concealed by the bangs. If ever a child needed patience—

"I really don't see why it is so important," she argued. "After all, you'll have Emelye."

As if Emelye were a commodity to be pawned off in exchange. Geneva took in a breath. "It's important for the same reason that it's important for you to live with us at Clearharbour: because we're going to be a family now, and our family will not be complete without you."

Elizabeth looked down and traced one finger along the wicker braid of her chair arm. "I doubt that you will find it agreeable, having me as part of the family. I know I shan't be happy at Clearharbour Farm," she said, then shrugged. "Not that it matters, since Father has decreed that I must move there."

"What makes you so sure you'll be unhappy?" Geneva implored.

Elizabeth went on looking down, tracing the wicker design. "Really, everyone is always saying, 'Elizabeth, we do *so* want you to be happy!' But one can't just be happy because everyone wishes it," she said practically.

"No, I suppose not," Geneva admitted. She observed Elizabeth's delicate hands, her upturned nose and dark lashes, her long dark hair swept behind her ears and rising in wisps at the nape of her neck. She was a beautiful child. How tragic for her to have such a fatalistic attitude about life.

"Does Emelye ever make you cross?" Elizabeth asked suddenly, turning to her with an earnest gaze, as if much depended upon the answer.

The reason for the question seemed obvious enough. Geneva was hopeful this was a sign that she regarded Emelye as her equal. "Well of course she does. But we have a long talk to work things out, then everything is alright again."

Elizabeth considered this momentarily, then she sighed and looked off in the distance again. Geneva found it disturbing that she repeatedly broke eye contact with her. Was it because of her loss of self-confidence, or was she hiding something? She decided to take a risk. "Are you jealous of me, Elizabeth? Unhappy that your father and I are getting married?"

Elizabeth threw her a quick glance.

So that's exactly what it is, thought Geneva. Why had this not occurred to her? When she and Emelye came to London to visit last year, and found Elizabeth so remarkably hospitable, there was no talk of their becoming a family.

Now they were both forcing her to share Tony for the first time in her life. "Don't think Emelye and I are trying to take your place in your father's heart," she assured her. "He loves you in a way he will never love anyone else. And that's as it should be."

Again Elizabeth was thoughtful. When she turned to her again, Geneva was surprised to find her eyes were glistening. And they seemed to reflect more love than any parent had a right to expect from a child. Yet, it was obvious that for some reason her love for Tony had become a source of pain. Geneva's instinct was to take Elizabeth in her arms: she desperately needed to empty her tears on a sympathetic shoulder. But even as she lifted her hands from her lap, over the child's face spread a calculating look that was thoroughly unnerving, for it was so like Jane. "Did you know my mother?" she asked, her eyes veering away.

Geneva had a sickening sensation that Jane was reaching out from the grave. "Not really. I met her once," she said.

Elizabeth grew more alert. "Where?"

"Here at Brookhurst...at a dinner party." She thought of Jane's tidy figure in a pink chemise and silver slave bracelets; her cold blue eyes and cruel mouth set in a pale, flat complexion. The saucy way she sat with feet tucked under her on the sofa in the drawing room—the most formal chamber in the house.

A considerable pause. A frown of concentration. "Then, was this *before* she married my father?" Elizabeth asked slowly.

"Yes. Why?"

Another pause. "So you knew my father *before* he married my mother."

"Yes," Geneva said. She would have thought this obvious, given that Emelye was Tony's child with her, and was several months older than Elizabeth. Then she realized it would be far beyond the ability of a child less than eight years old to piece that sort of information together.

Elizabeth pressed her bangs again, ran her tongue over her lips. Still avoiding looking at Geneva, she asked, "Was my mother...was she nice then?"

Then? Geneva decided it was time to put an end to this. Tony needed to talk with Elizabeth about her mother frankly, and soon. Obviously the child was confused, and only he could set things straight. She hedged, "As I say, I really didn't get to know her. And by the way, weren't we talking about the wedding?"

Elizabeth let out a quick breath of resignation. Her shoulders sagged. After some hesitation she looked at Geneva and said boldly, "Black stockings would be unsuitable for a wedding procession."

Luckily Cynthia had already thought of this. "Black stockings? But you won't need them. Your dress will be long. I assumed you knew that."

Elizabeth reflected on this, her countenance brightening. "No, I didn't. I've never worn a long dress before, except of course the Selby christening gown. There's a picture…."

And you're dying to wear a long dress again. Geneva was relieved to see just a hint of the enthusiasm Elizabeth used to have, before the auto crash aged her beyond her years—that's what she was, Geneva realized now, aged far beyond her years. *Oh Tony, we've got a lot of work to do here!*

Elizabeth's face soon clouded again. "Still, there's my limp, you know. People will notice, and…and—" Her voice broke off. Her nostrils flared. She squeezed the woven chair arm tightly. "No, I couldn't possibly."

Tony had used the term, 'cloistered at Brookhurst,' to describe Elizabeth's life since she came here to convalesce. Geneva felt torn between wishing to spare her a public appearance, and knowing that she must overcome this obstacle to her recovery, that it might well be vitally important in changing her attitude. After a moment she said, "You know, in a wedding procession, everyone walks at a very slow, deliberate pace. It's a sign of respect for the occasion, I suppose."

Elizabeth's eyes swept up to the pergola roof, then down to Geneva's face again. Solemnly she said, "Yes, when one gets married, it's—it's supposed to be forever."

Was the remark meant as a reprimand? Was she aware that a divorce was in the works when she and Tony moved out of No. 3 Wilton Place, leaving Jane behind? Geneva added one more item to the list of things she must report to Tony about this conversation. "Indeed it is," she agreed.

Thoughtfully Elizabeth said, "I suppose I could practice up in my room. Then if I think I can manage—but I shan't promise anything."

"Fair enough." Geneva smiled with pleasure. Again, she wished to hold Elizabeth in her arms. But perhaps it would be better at this point to respect the distance the child had placed between them.

Lowering her voice, Elizabeth said, "Oh, and I must ask this. You shan't expect me to show you the scar on my leg, or Emelye either. It's important to me that no one should ever see it except those who already have." She frowned. "Promise you won't force me."

The plea brought home to Geneva the sad fact of how often children struggle under the authority of adults, having very few rights of their own. And now she realized why Elizabeth was reluctant to share a room with Emelye. "I wouldn't dream of it. And I'll tell Emelye, too," she assured her. Surely one day

Elizabeth would overcome this obsession. "Emelye so wants to be with you," she could not help adding.

"And Mr. Bounds will be instructed to put a lock on the door to our bath."

"Of course. There's always a lock on a bathroom door."

"Just the same, please make absolutely certain he understands," she said, and with Geneva's nod of reassurance, she sank back in her chair, clearly relieved.

Geneva was grateful the conversation had accomplished a goal for the immediate future, but she was not much encouraged about the long term.

"Shall we go in now?" she said, longing to take Elizabeth's hand as they walked.

Yet just then the garden gate opened and Tony's sister Nell looked in. "I say, Geneva, could you spare me a few minutes, please?"

CHAPTER 3

As the day drew near when Nell would face Geneva, she had dreaded the ordeal more and more. At nights she tossed and turned, unable to stay asleep for more than a few minutes at a time. The night before last, in spite of her efforts to the contrary, she managed to disturb her husband's sleep. Morey raised up to find her pacing the bedroom floor. "What's got into you, Love? Come back to bed. I'll be on my way to Camborne at the crack of dawn tomorrow, and you know I can't sleep without you beside me." She returned to bed and he folded her in his arms and kissed her, his breath musty. "It's going to be alright. Geneva's not the big bad wolf, now is she?"

Morey is right. Geneva cannot take away what's most important in my life: Morey's love and forgiveness, and our strong, healthy son sleeping right across the hall. Yet, no sooner had Morey resumed snoring, with Nell cuddled against his broad hairy back, than she was going over her apology yet again, trying still new ways of putting it: *My family have always been very important to me. I should do anything for them. Them.* It sounded as if she were excluding Geneva from their future. *One felt so desperate.* Yes, that was better. *And I really didn't know you at all....* No, no! She might as well say, *I judged you to be beneath us.* Yet, wasn't it too obvious, when she believed Geneva and the child she was carrying could be bought off, persuaded to stay out of the way so that the Selby family fortune would be saved? *I'm so terribly sorry, for everything. For...for judging you. Do forgive me, and allow me to be—be—*But what could she possibly *be* to Geneva? Not a bosom friend, surely. They were too different from each other. Nell remembered the morning years ago when first they met, the two of them strolling through the Brookhurst walled garden: Geneva in her clingy sweater, shapely and attractive; and Nell, plain and stout, wearing a tweed jacket that would have cut off circulation had she fastened it across her bosom, and a skirt that was so tight round the waist, the button threatened to fly off.

But that's it, of course! she realized. And thus did the idea of a peace offering finally present itself. That is, if Geneva still longed for her own garden as she had claimed that day. Nell would ring up Tony to see if she was still keen. She hoped desperately that she was.

And now they were in the Brookhurst garden again, Elizabeth having kissed her Auntie Nell and repaired to the house. For a few moments, both women watched Elizabeth's slow, labored steps from behind, lost in separate, bittersweet memories of the child's liveliness before the crash. Then they looked into each other's eyes, Nell thinking that if not for Tony having married Jane, there would be no Elizabeth; Geneva thinking that if not for Jane, Elizabeth would be skipping away right now—each of their mental perambulations leading to a dead end. "Sit down, Nell," said Geneva, her tone of voice calm and unrevealing, like a doctor interviewing a new patient.

As Nell lowered herself into a garden chair, she was aware of an anxious thrumming in her ears. She soon found herself quietly rationalizing her thoughts, as if Geneva had read them: "That's the greatest tragedy of all. One really didn't imagine what Jane was capable of. If I had, I never should have—" This was not how she had intended to begin, and now she felt quite scattered.

"Well! I came here to offer my apologies," she blundered on, her voice tinny. "Tony has told you how things stood when I...I took it upon myself to ensure that nothing should prevent his marriage to Jane. Not that it's any excuse."

"Yes, he wrote to me about it."

Nell took in a breath. "I feel simply dreadful," she said. Then, her voice trembling with anxiety, words began rushing out, most of which she had not planned to say. "If you could see your way to forgive me—of course, I—I'm sure it seems a fresh wound to you, having just learnt of it lately. I can tell you that, living with it for all these years, waking up to it every single morning—well, I—"

"Was punishment enough, I guess," Geneva interrupted, not wanting to dredge it all up again. "I realize how much of your family's burden you were taking upon yourself back then. It must have been very hard."

Nell searched Geneva's eyes. Was she offering her forgiveness? Would she ever actually say the three words that Nell longed to hear? Or, would she always hold them a little out of reach? "I expect you've been over to Clearharbour

Farm by now," she said hopefully. That was where she had intended to begin, then Elizabeth diverted her—

"No. The weather got so bad after we arrived yesterday, we put it off. We plan to drive over today—but not for long. Tony has to go up to London this afternoon. He won't be back till a few days before the wedding."

Nell was disappointed. If Geneva had already seen the garden, it might be easier. Oh well. "I did a bit of tidying up there, and I planted some cyclamen and pansies in the curving stone plinth, and a couple of other things that won't mind the cold weather. I planted some roses in the little garden off the dining room. And—oh yes—I noticed, there's a small bed by the conservatory, in the crook of the drive. I took the liberty of planting a camellia bush there. I think it should do fine. Of course, if it grows too tall, you can cut it back. Or, you may not even want it...." Nell wrung her hands. She felt she was staggering backwards, down the side of a hill.

Yet Geneva was grateful, and told her so. "It will be a while before I can get around to the garden. There is so much to do!"

But do you understand, it's my peace offering? Especially the camellia, for my camellias are such a part of me? Nell could not bring herself to say this aloud. "I remember your saying to me long ago that you would like to learn about flowers. And even though—I understand from Tony—that you became quite the gardener back in Texas, the climate here will demand adjustments. I can teach you what little I know, if you like. Or, shall you be spending too much time in London?" *There will be all those glamourous nights at the theatre, my brother so handsome and successful, and you there on his arm, your beauty catching everyone's eye, the two of you making everyone think: aren't they just so lucky! Not knowing how you've both suffered from betrayal....*

"No. I'll be around here for the most part. Emelye doesn't feel safe in London—no surprise," Geneva said.

"I see." Nell rose to her feet, uncertain whether or not Geneva meant to accept her offer. "Well, I shan't keep you any longer this morning. Please, just know how very happy Morey and I are for you and Tony. You deserve your happiness. You've waited a fearfully long time." Perhaps she ought to add, *No small thanks to me.* But what would be the point?

"Thank you," said Geneva.

"If there's anything at all that I can do, for you or Emelye—"

A light went on in Geneva's mind. "There is one thing. I'd like you to make a special effort to make my daughter feel welcome here," she said, with a knot in her throat. "Elizabeth is…well…withdrawn these days. It may be awhile before she comes out of her shell. Meantime, Emelye feels stranded."

"Oh yes. I wouldn't have imposed, but I was hoping to get to know Emelye," Nell said, then added awkwardly, "I was only afraid, that is, I didn't know what you may have told her—"

"Emelye knows nothing about all that. And I don't want her to. She and Guy are close enough in age, I was hoping they might be playmates."

"Oh yes indeed! Guy is a sweet boy, a good lad!" she said with feeling, as if to assure Geneva that he had none of his mother's shortcomings. Geneva had not forgotten Nell's tragic loss of her son Gerry in the Spanish Influenza epidemic. "I'm sure he is," she said kindly.

"I shall bring him over in a day or two, if you like," she said. "Morey is at home today, just back from a trip to Camborne, so I left Guy with him."

"Yes, I would like that very much and I know Emelye would too. Meantime, why don't you come in and meet her now? She is upstairs with your mother, learning all about stage make-up in the old days."

Nell laughed. "Oh dear! I do hope she will leave out the ghastly part about performers dying from lead poison in the grease paint!"

The brightening in Nell's countenance brought home to Geneva just how hard these few minutes had been for her. She pitied her. Should she say, *"I forgive you"*? But that wasn't the same thing. She wasn't sure she felt forgiveness yet, wasn't sure if she ever would. "Thanks for everything," she said.

They took a long look at each other. Secretly Nell vowed she was going to be the very best aunt that Emelye could ever have. And if, through her friendship with Emelye, she could win Geneva's forgiveness and perhaps even her respect, all the better. Already she was imagining Emelye with Guy, running about among the ash trees and oaks and sweet chestnuts that shaded Camellia Cottage, climbing up into Guy's tree house, scampering down the hill to the shallow brook. As he and Elizabeth used to do, but no more. And what could she make specially for Emelye to eat? Oatmeal scones, perhaps….

No sooner had they walked through the garden gate than Geneva regretted not having extended her forgiveness to Nell. Now that the moment had passed, she could not imagine a future context in which it might happen without unbearable awkwardness on both sides. So now she, too, had a sense of guilt.

CHAPTER 4

❀

She was proceeding ever so slowly and perfectly down the aisle of the Chapel of St. Thomas Becket, wearing her long gown of dusty rose Crêpe de Chine, her head held high, a smile on her face as she scattered rose petals from her basket. Back and forth, up and down, Elizabeth paced, ankles trembling, from the corner of her bedroom towards the full-length mirror, wearing her long petticoat, scattering small folded papers along the floor from a basket borrowed from Mr. Malone the head gardener. Her final rehearsal.

It was the 17th of October, the morning of the wedding.

For days wedding gifts had been arriving in a constant succession, and inevitably the article was unwrapped and pronounced, 'perfect' by the bride or the groom: *"Look at this exquisite water color, sent by So-and-So. Won't it be perfect, hanging in the dining room!" "I say, what a splendid clock—antiqued brass! I should think it would be perfect on the chimneypiece in our bedroom, what do you say?"*

Three nights ago, the Younger family arrived from Houston, Texas—another of Father's surprises for Geneva. It seemed he could not do enough to make their wedding perfect. Mrs. Younger would serve as matron of honor; Emelye would be promoted to bridesmaid, and Serena would be a flower girl like Elizabeth, walking just ahead of her in the processional. James would carry the pillow with the ring. Lastly, Mr. Younger would accompany Geneva down the aisle. "Oh, it's going to be absolutely perfect!" Geneva cried.

Upon greeting her dear friends and former neighbors, Emelye burst into happy tears, which made Elizabeth feel guilty for her neglect. Yet, how could she keep up with her studies, practice for the wedding procession, and play with Emelye at the same time? Besides, Emelye was always skipping about, which made Elizabeth feel awkward. Then she insisted upon trying out the crutches that finally had been put away. As if using them were a lark. "They rub blisters on one's under-arms," Elizabeth warned.

Back and forth, up and down, she paced.

Surely the heavens shined down upon the wedding, for the weather this morning was perfect, too. Earlier, when Elizabeth rose from the bed and looked out her window, two of Mr. Malone's assistants were raking autumn leaves from the front grounds and the drive, for the third day in a row, as if not one shriveled leaf must be allowed to mar the perfection of the view. Far to the right, at the east end of the house, in front of the stable, the new Rolls-Royce was parked, the sunlight glancing off its silver radiator as two servants polished once again the already perfectly clean, shining honeymoon carriage. "*Our wedding? It was at the local registry in York, you know, just the two of us and somewhat rushed. I believe it rained that day, though I'm not sure,*" *said Mummy vaguely.*

Downstairs, the huge formal dining room dazzled with silver and sparkling crystal. Selby heirloom table linens provided the perfect setting for stately arrangements from Miss Pennett's Florist in Bodmin: white gladioli, chrysanthemums, day lilies, Michaelmas daisies and roses, banked with lacy green fern. All the floors were scrubbed and waxed; brass was polished and upholstery, cleaned. Mirrors and window glass glistened. The two Old English sheep dogs, Abraham and Sarah—successors of the late Angus and Kenegy who died of old age within weeks of each other last summer—were banished from the formal rooms so that not a single shaggy hair would be shed on the hardwood floors. Elizabeth paced up and down, up and down, scattering folded papers, wishing she had not agreed to be in the wedding party after all, for everyone except for her was going to be so *perfect.*

Then came a knock at the door and the voice of Mrs. Ivey, a cheerful woman with gray hair whom Merton had recently hired as housekeeper, with Grandmother's consent. "You're needed in the bride's room, Miss Elizabeth, where your gown is ready to put on, and Auntie Nell is fixing all the little girls' hair up in curls."

Elizabeth took one last imploring look in the mirror, then slipped into her house robe and opened the bedroom door. Already she could hear giggles and happy chatter coming from the bride's room down the hall.

Four o'clock. In the rosy autumnal sunlight, Elizabeth stood with the bridal party clustered at the foot of the Chapel of Thomas Becket, which was

approached by a flight of stone stairs, each worn down in the middle from cen-
turies of climbing feet. The chapel was roofless even before her father's
time—not even Grandfather knew what became of it—and its location on the
spacious grounds of St. Petroc's Church was so obscure, the path leading to it
so overgrown with bracken and thorny vines, that it had been long forgotten
by most people. Father had the path cleared for today, and marked with tall
stakes, linked with white satin ribbon.

Looking ahead, Elizabeth noted that with the chairs lined up in rows and
filled with wedding guests, the aisle seemed much longer than it had during
yesterday's walk-through. Apart from this, the width of the aisle was narrowed
by the odd ladies' skirts poking out here and there, and restless children moving about on the edges. *I shall trip and fall.* She imagined the people sitting
nearby staring down at her body heaped upon the stone floor.

Father had arranged for Miss Pennett's Florist to strip the chapel walls of
dead plants and sprig them with literally hundreds of fresh flowers and vines.
White blossoms cascaded like a bridal bouquet through the chancel window
opening, and candle flames sputtered in nests of flowers and ferns in the window sills down the sides of the chapel. A white carpet was rolled out for the
procession, at the foot of which stood the vicar, with Father to his left and his
friend Kenneth Owsley, the best man, beside him. With his thick brown hair
and widow's peak, sprinkled with gray, and his dark brown eyes set nobly in his
face, Father was the handsomest man Elizabeth had ever seen. And today,
every stitch of his wedding garment, designed for his nimble figure by a London Bond Street tailor, was perfectly pressed, the pleats in his trousers sharp as
knife blades. A sense of pride welled up in Elizabeth's breast, until she thought
how very much the elaborate wedding preparations seemed to bear out all that
her mother had told her about Father and Geneva.

Now the clear strains of Albinoni's *Adagio* from Opus 9, No. 2—one of
Father's favorite pieces—swelled into the open air from a shiny brass trumpet,
and a three-manual harpsichord which would barely fit into the corner of the
small chapel. Down the aisle swept Emelye, her steps springing, the role of
bridesmaid making her appear older and more self-assured. Then Mrs.
Younger processed, tall and slender, wearing a filmy dress of very soft green.
Elizabeth's breathing was more shallow with every moment. She simply
couldn't do it. *No, you must! Remain composed. Remember the hours of rehears-
ing.* Then Serena glided off, her posture perfect as that of a princess, flower
petals drifting from her basket. Even more glamourous than Emelye, Serena
had a mannerism of cutting her dark eyes provocatively at one, as if she were

savoring some deep forbidden secret. As she passed along the pews, her chin tilted upward, auburn ringlets flicking at the nape of her neck, Elizabeth was certain that all the guests were transfixed by her, and they were praising her beauty one to another in reverent tones. *I should have asked to process in front of Serena rather than to follow her. How could I have believed there would be an advantage in putting off the inevitable for as long as possible?*

Elizabeth advanced a few paces along the last row of seats. Her basket was shaking in her hands, and worse, her knees—she suddenly realized—were positively quaking. Now as she paused at the foot of the aisle, waiting for Serena to reach the head and turn off to the left, her feet were as inert as if they were two stones mortared in the floor beneath her. Soon she saw Father nod encouragingly: *And now!*

After a few more agonizing moments, she stepped off. And when she did her knees buckled with such immediacy, she hardly knew that she had fallen until she found herself sprawled clumsily in the white-carpeted aisle, her elbows poking out, her chin resting on the basket handle. *It is my punishment. I should have burnt to death with my mother....*

James was within moments of following Elizabeth in the procession, thankful for any excuse to be near her. Ever since he arrived at Brookhurst four days ago, he had been fascinated by her. She was different from any girl he knew, including his little sister, who was always showing off, talking big, and Emelye, who was always following him around and wanting to sit next to him. *"Good evening James, I am honored to meet you."* When Elizabeth spoke, it was like his teacher Miss Thompson reading a poem to the class: her voice flowing in a deep clear stream; her eyes closing when she read certain lines as if the beauty of them had put her in a trance. *Honored to meet you....* So quiet and dignified. Everyone said Elizabeth was a scholar. James was sure she knew exactly how to spell and pronounce every word in his spelling book. He would like to talk to her very much. But she probably wouldn't like hearing about baseball, or cub scouts. Might he impress her by reciting the refrain from the poem by Edgar Lee Masters that Miss Thompson read last year at Halloween, about all the dead people in the town? He liked that poem so much, he later checked out a book where it was included among other poems, from the Heights Library. As he read over the verses of *The Hill*, he could just see Miss Thompson tilting her head back, closing her eyes as she recited the refrain with just the right space between each word: *"All, all are sleeping, sleeping, sleeping on the hill."* He read it so many times, he memorized certain stanzas.

But no, he could never recite those words for Elizabeth. She would think he was crazy, liking a poem about dead people.

Since he lacked the courage to start a conversation with her, he had been trying to figure out a way to show her how he felt. Then, like a miracle, his chance came. He did not see Elizabeth fall, as at that moment he was testing the ribbon that was looped around the ring on the pillow, to be sure it would hold. But suddenly he felt a hand on his shoulder and glanced around to see his dad nod toward Elizabeth, a worried frown on his face.

In an instant James was speeding to her side. He arrived just as a gentleman from the congregation approached, and was panic-stricken—*no, stay back, she's mine!* Then he was leaning near, offering her his arm. Rising slowly to her feet, she was as beautiful to James as a water lily opening in the Japanese sunken gardens at Brackenridge Park. He knew without a doubt that he was in love.

Elizabeth looked into James's face. His eyes were deep brown, flecked with green, and slightly tilted, giving him a mysterious look. She would have given anything to hasten from the chapel, and find a place to hide. But the intensity of his gaze upon her face, and his gallantry in coming to her rescue, gave her the courage to fulfil her duty. Suddenly remembering her manners, she murmured her thanks, reclaimed her basket, and stepped off, quite forgetting her feet. The music never paused.

Despite her quaking knees and trembling hands, soon she had spanned the entire length of the aisle, and was passing to her place at the front. She saw her father gazing at her with the look of pride she used to see frequently on his face, but seldom did anymore. That she had pleased him on his wedding day temporarily took the sting from her guilt for betraying him. Then there was Mrs. Younger's reassuring smile, and finally Grandmother and Grandfather beaming at her from the front row, tears in Grandmother's eyes. *"Good show!"* she heard Grandfather say. Only as she came to a stop and peered up the aisle to watch for the bride, her heart beating hard as a fist in her breast, did she realize she had forgotten to scatter her rose petals.

Then Geneva appeared, on Mr. Younger's arm. The music paused. A hush came over the congregation. Geneva seemed to be not of this world at all, but rather a vision in ivory silk who had drifted down from the heavens, a bouquet of white roses and peonies in the crook of her arm. Grandmother's wedding lace of *rose point de gaze* lay lightly on her hair like morning mist upon a sleeping valley.

The music flared; the bride's procession began. When she and Mr. Younger were halfway down the aisle, Elizabeth looked at her father's face, fixed adoringly upon Geneva, as if nothing in the world existed apart from her. Elizabeth was quite sure she had never seen him look at her mother in that way.

CHAPTER 5

The plans for a second honeymoon, like those for the wedding, were left largely in Tony's hands. Though Geneva was open about the matter, at first he felt somehow compelled to return with her to the Lake District, for it would seem deeply symbolic—a sort of picking up where they left off. Yet he was wary. Looking back, the romanticism of that idyllic week had not derived solely from the sweet pleasures of expressing their love physically for the first time. Their sense of impending doom—off-limits for discussion by mutual consent, but nonetheless always lurking in their thoughts—made it seem as the days went by in the intoxicating mountain air that their love was watched over and protected by the beauty and majesty surrounding them. It made their leaving at the end all the more bittersweet. Perhaps if they went back now, the memories they treasured would recall other, painful memories of the disaster into which they were inevitably swept once they returned, and that they both endured for quite long enough—and especially him, for the nightmare of his marriage to Jane had lived on in spite of her death, in the injuries she inflicted upon Elizabeth both physically and emotionally. No, surely he and Geneva would be wise to put off returning to Lake Windermere until the bad memories had been placed in perspective by many new experiences of living together.

So to the seaside village of Lyme Regis in Dorset they were bound, hurrying from the Brookhurst steps round nine o'clock through a shower of wedding rice and good wishes, and stepping into the *Phantom II*. Marvelous machine! Tony thought with pride as the head lamps flashed on and the tires crunched on the gravel drive. He gathered Geneva was not too keen. Upon seeing it for the first time, she asked worriedly, "It's awfully extravagant, isn't it?" He had to admit it certainly was: a symbol of his optimism.

Life was looking rosy just now. The *William & Mary* was scheduled to reopen round the middle of February, with George Bernard Shaw's *Candida*. Reading the play, he had fallen in love with the heroine—and little wonder, for she was not only charming and provocative, she was also red-haired! The plot was intriguing, an inversion of Henrik Ibsen's *A Doll House*, which Tony also hoped to stage one day. Against his better judgment—for he was frightfully busy these days—he had elected to design the set for *Candida,* as he had done for several productions in the past, including his musical *The Baron and the Texas Girl* and the first annual production of *Pip 'N Pocket.* Blame it on the playwright, who provided the most delicious details, almost like a novelist building a scene. Tony could hardly wait to see the curtain open on the Reverend Morell's office, with its window looking out on Victoria Park; his long desk cluttered with everything from pamphlets and letters to postage scales; the crowded bookshelves in recess above the fireplace; and Miss Proserpine Garnett's little desk with its typewriter.

Fortunately, he had a highly capable house manager on staff—Bill Rutgers, whom he spirited away from the *Aldwych*—to take up the slack so that he could work on the set design, and Mrs. Fairfax, his secretary whom he hired last summer when the paint on the office walls was not yet dry, and was efficient beyond his greatest hopes in managing his schedule and correspondence. Tony believed that as play openings continued at the *William & Mary*—his own productions and those he booked with outside parties—the two of them would spare him becoming mired in the tedium of the business so that he could concentrate on the creative end.

And spend more time with his new family. Oh, how he anticipated the joy of opening night, with Geneva on his arm!

He'd reserved a third-floor room with a seaward view at the Alexandra—a small, tasteful hotel with a gabled roof that stood high above Lyme Bay, surrounded by terraced gardens. He'd stayed there on holiday several years ago, and was charmed by the cozy lobby with fireplace and easy chairs, seascapes on the walls, model ships in glass cases and a great bay window with a shiny brass telescope overlooking the sea. The Alexandra was a short walk from intriguing shops and galleries and tea rooms with thatched roofs, crowded along steeply slanting streets. It was, in short, the perfect place for relaxing on a second honeymoon.

Naturally what Tony wanted most over the next five days was to make love to his wife. After all the years of being married to Jane, with whom he could hardly bear to occupy the same residence, let alone the same bed, his gratitude when Geneva walked into his room that first night at Brookhurst moved him nearly to tears. Just to reach out and hold her, to feel the heat of her naked body next to his, to experience once again the joys of their physical union, and know there would never again be a door shut between them—well, it was worth the long and tortured period when he was prevented from doing so.

Unhappily he was off to London the very next day and did not return till he brought the Youngers.

Just before eleven o'clock they passed the road sign: Lyme Regis—2. Bracing, pungent air filled their nostrils, and the road grew more steep. Down below on the right, slivers of moonlight danced on the surface of the sea. Shortly they turned into the small cobbled yard of the Alexandra.

Tony switched off the engine and kissed his bride. "Let's go in and tell them that after a delay of *eight long years*, Mr. and Mrs. Anthony Edward Selby have finally arrived."

"Yes, do let's," she said, and Tony laughed out loud at her British phraseology, then kissed her again. Pretty soon they were mounting a set of winding, creaky stairs, giddy with happiness, feeling no older or more seasoned than when they mounted the stairs at the Ghyll Inn eight years ago, only twice as grateful.

Shortly after ten o'clock on Sunday morning, they rose from the bed and threw wide the draperies. Tony stood behind Geneva with his arms wrapped around her, and together they took in the view of their first morning as man and wife:

A pearl blue sky hung over the placid sea. Gulls flew high above, dipping down, soaring up again, carping noisily. Down below, scores of bright flowers bloomed in garden beds neatly sculpted on the sparkling green. People strolled along the garden paths, many with pet dogs on leads. Others sat out in striped lawn chairs, reading a book or a newspaper, or simply facing up to the sun as though to drink it in. An artist stood before her easel, facing the harbor, the wind whipping the sash on her sun bonnet as she applied her brush to the canvas. Tony kissed the nape of Geneva's neck. "Doesn't look as if there will be any rain on this honeymoon," he said wistfully.

Geneva nuzzled against him, but did not speak. After a few moments, she said pensively, "The Youngers will be leaving this morning."

"Yes, wasn't it grand that they could come? Even for little while."

Geneva let out a breath. "It's going to be hard on Emelye," she said, and he heard her voice catch on her daughter's name.

Pressing her closer, Tony sought to reassure her. "Well, she'll have plenty of attention, with Mother and Father and Nell and Guy. And I say, Elizabeth seems to be coming round remarkably—"

"Really? How do you mean?"

"Why, the way she carried on after taking a tumble last night. I've never been so proud of her. She could have easily refused to go on, you know. No one would have blamed her. I take it as a sign she's coming out of her shell, don't you?"

Geneva hated to cloud his optimism, but she could not ignore this opening to talk about Elizabeth. "I'm not so sure," she said. While she had told him of the positive side of her conversation with Elizabeth in the walled garden during their drive to Clearharbour later that day, she had not mentioned the darker side. For one thing, Emelye was in the car with them. And besides, she wanted to do some thinking on it first. Now she said, "There were things I didn't tell you about our little talk…things I found disturbing."

"Well…what?" he asked, guardedly.

"They had to do with her mother."

She felt his body stiffen. "Alright," he said coolly. He released her and sank down on the edge of the bed. So he was already put off. She just wanted to get this over with. She went and sat beside him, took his hand in hers. As she talked, she realized how much Elizabeth had conveyed through her gestures, which could not be described as well as she would like. She stopped short of mentioning the calculating look in the child's eyes at one point, a look that was chillingly reminiscent of her mother. She was reluctant to put too much weight on that in her own mind, and Tony might be inclined to make more of it than was necessary. Yet perhaps as a result, when she finished her report she was doubtful she had conveyed her reasons for being disturbed. "You need to talk to her frankly about Jane," she urged, "because I can't do it, and it's obvious she is confused about why her mother was so hateful.

"I think maybe she has the impression that I came between you and her mother."

"That's impossible!" Tony retorted. "As far as Jane knew we were never in touch after we broke up—I made sure of it."

"Yes, but when she came home from Ticehurst, Elizabeth may have told her about that time Emelye and I came to visit while she was away. And who knows what she concluded?"

Tony was shaking his head. "I was prepared for a scene, believe me, but Jane never even opened the subject. And remember, within a few days after she was released, Elizabeth and I moved out."

"But they may have talked about it during that drive through Dartmoor Forest. Jane might have said just about anything to Elizabeth—"

"Elizabeth remembers nothing at all except those last few words before the crash, when Jane told her they were about to take a trip to hell; I've questioned her time and again," Tony said, his voice becoming strident.

Geneva hesitated. If Tony was right, did it mean that she was wrong? Whatever the case, Elizabeth was troubled, that was clear. "Well somehow you've got to set her straight about her mother."

To her dismay Tony's face turned red. He withdrew his hand from hers. "What made Jane the way she was is something Elizabeth must never be told about, do you understand? Look here, I have already told her all she needs to know, that her mother was a very unhappy person, and made others unhappy consequently. Elizabeth needs to quit pitying herself, that's all. And I daresay she is trying to get back at me."

Geneva shook her head adamantly. "You're wrong. When I spoke of how much you loved her, tears filled her eyes—"

"And I know why: because she can't love me any longer after I let her down, and it hurts not having that anymore," Tony said, his voice raw. "'*Elizabeth,*' I must call her now, just like everyone else.

"It's been a year, Geneva, for Christ's sake. It's over and done with, and I shan't discuss Jane anymore. Not with her, and not with you."

Geneva was shaken. From the time Tony learned of Emelye's existence, their letters to each other were more concerned with issues involving their children than with the relationship between them. Now, just when they needed to be open with each other, he was shutting her out. "Excuse me, but I thought one of the purposes of our getting married was to finish raising our daughters together. Apparently you don't see it that way," she said hurtfully.

She started to rise from the bed, but Tony laid a hand on her back. She heard his shuddering breath. "Wait. Please understand. The only way to put Jane to rest is to quit letting her dominate our lives. A widower? Sometimes I feel I may as well be married to her ghost! Every time someone speaks her name, all those miserable years are resurrected. Every time I look into Elizabeth's eyes, I see my failure. Wouldn't Jane love to know that, since she failed to take Elizabeth's life, she has ruined our relationship forever? I wish I could have the whole bloody memory of her cut out from my brain, and Elizabeth's too. Damn her!"

Geneva turned around. The haunted look she saw on Tony's face reminded her all too well of those times during their first honeymoon when his troubles got the best of him. She had feared Elizabeth was forever scarred emotionally by the tragedy in Dartmoor Forest, but she had not fully appreciated the depth of Tony's injuries. She was still convinced he must talk to Elizabeth someday, but she should not have brought up the subject so soon, and certainly not during the only few days they would have to devote completely to each other. She thought of the wedding, so perfect in every detail—how Tony accomplished it with the *William & Mary* making so many demands on his time, she could hardly imagine. And this wonderful holiday he planned for them. She reached for his hand again. "I love you more than anything in the world...and I'm so sorry," she said helplessly, her voice breaking. "All you've done to make me happy, and now I've made you sad. I didn't mean to spoil everything."

Tony was amazed, and frightened. "Oh no, you didn't! I should not have been cross with you," he apologized. He urged her down beside him and closed his arms around her. He was trembling. She must make him feel safe again, to chase away his sorrowful memories. Soon they were making love as desperately as when they lay in their small room above Lake Windermere, when they sensed disaster looming.

CHAPTER 6

Emelye entered the standard three level at St. Michael's School on the Monday morning after her parents returned from their honeymoon. The weather was chilly and bleak, making the prospect of her first day at a new school—which she had been dreading—seem all the more frightening. Located in an isolated spot at the height of a steep street in Bodmin, the two-story squarish building stood out menacingly against the gray sky. Its front and sides were thickly covered with bright red leafy vines which gave way only around the square-paned windows and high fortress-like doors. A strong wind made the vines list and flutter like flames, as if the building were on fire.

As Emelye and Elizabeth approached the brick walk leading up to the school, Emelye paused, her heart beating hard and fast like a pair of running feet. "Come along," Elizabeth coaxed. "It will be alright." Elizabeth had been paying more attention to her since the wedding.

A crowd of boys and girls were standing around the entrance door with book satchels, most wearing jackets over their uniforms. Some were much bigger than she and Elizabeth. The boys and girls talked loudly among themselves as they waited for the bell to ring. Everyone spoke with a British accent. Everyone seemed to know everyone else. Regardless of Elizabeth's reassurance, Emelye felt a keen sense of foreboding. Recalling her mother's request, she turned to wave farewell at her parents, who were standing arm-in-arm at the curb, a few yards away. The sight of her mother's smiling face brought Emelye to the verge of tears. *Why did we have to move to England when we were so happy in the Heights?* she wondered mournfully. Earlier this morning, Mother took a picture of her and Elizabeth in the Brookhurst library, wearing their school uniforms: dark blue skirts and blazers, white shirts, black stockings and beanies. Elizabeth had told Emelye that she liked St. Michael's because of the regulation stockings. They did not wear uniforms at Queens Gate in London, she said, and had she returned there this year, her black stockings would have made her feel out of place.

The school bell rang. The students began lining up and filing into the building. Emelye's first day was beginning. Her knees began to shake. She wished with all her heart that she was back at Harvard Elementary, with Serena and James and all the kids she knew. She looked back at her mother once more. Tears threatened again.

Elizabeth had shown Emelye all the books for standard three, and the lessons they were doing: arithmetic, English, spelling, reading and writing. Elizabeth said that the lessons weren't very hard, but it seemed to Emelye that Elizabeth had learned a lot more in school than she had. And she'd heard people say that Elizabeth had a very good private tutor while recuperating from her injuries as well. Emelye had never heard the word 'tutor' before, and had to ask what it meant. Two days before the wedding, she had come here with her parents to meet the headmaster, Mr. Gempie. He had plump cheeks crisscrossed with purplish veins like bird's feet, and he wore round eyeglasses with steel frames. His breath smelled of peppermint. He turned to Emelye only once during the meeting, to warn that if she failed to keep up with the class she would be put back in standard two. Emelye dreaded this happening, for then she would truly be alone. She was determined to study harder than ever.

Soon the standard three pupils were seated in their room on the second floor. The teacher stood before the class wearing a gray flannel skirt and a white blouse with a high collar and long sleeves. Miss Sloane was tall and gaunt, and wore her ginger hair pulled into a knot at the back of her head. She had a long, severe face and small dark eyes. Her large front teeth protruded and overlapped, and occasionally when she was speaking, spit would fly from her mouth. As soon as she turned her back, pupils could be seen drawing in their bottom lips and making their front teeth stick out, to mimic her. Not Emelye or Elizabeth. Elizabeth had warned that if Miss Sloane caught you misbehaving, she would strike you hard on the back of your head, with her wooden pointer. Emelye had never gotten in trouble at school, and she was determined to keep it that way.

The day passed uneventfully, but by the end Emelye was so exhausted from concentrating that she barely had the energy to answer her parents' eager questions on the way home in the car: Were her classmates nice? Did she like her teacher? As soon as they arrived at Brookhurst, she went to her room where she fell asleep. She was still sleeping when her mother came to call her to dinner.

After a few days it was evident to Emelye that Elizabeth was the smartest person in the class. She sat on the front row, and Miss Sloane was always nice to her. Elizabeth usually made 100's on tests, and when Miss Sloane asked a question of the class, she was often the first to raise her hand. Unhappily, it was also evident that Miss Sloane did not like Emelye, because when the other kids made fun of her Texas drawl—and often they did—she never punished them. Frequently when Emelye raised her hand and asked a question, Miss Sloane would glance at her wristwatch and say stiffly, "I covered that earlier in the year, Miss Selby. I do not have time to stop and do so again. See me after class." Emelye learned to save most of her questions for Elizabeth to answer when they got home in the afternoons.

She did not tell her mother that her classmates made fun of her, or that Miss Sloane made her feel dumb. Elizabeth warned that if you tattled on Miss Sloane to your mother, and your mother came to the school, the teacher would be very hard on you from then on. Besides, Emelye was afraid her tattling might result in her being sent back to standard two. Her new classmates there would think she was dumb, and make fun of her more than ever.

So far Emelye was making average grades, and sometimes scoring as high as in the low 90's. Yet she was always afraid that when yesterday's assignment or—worse still—a test was returned, she would have failed. Every morning before school, her stomach roiled. To please her mother she would force down a few bites of toast. Every day began with assembly and prayers, and the headmaster made announcements. Then everyone had to write out a Scripture verse from memory, and a woman called Warden, who wore her hair in tight curls, would take them up. An award would be given at the end of the school year for the student who got the most verses correct. Then they went up to their classrooms, where Miss Sloane began by giving out graded assignments from yesterday. By ten o'clock, when the class went downstairs to the assembly room to sit around the pot-bellied stove and have their warm milk and biscuits, Emelye was always relieved that the part of the day when assignments were returned was over. She was so hungry that she gobbled the biscuit and drank all her milk.

Then came the first Friday of December, a rainy day like many others since she started at St. Michael's. This was two weeks after the family moved to Clearharbour and Daddy went back to London for the second time since Emelye moved to England—how could he be like her father when he was never around? She missed Rodney. He was more like her father. But when she told her mother this one day she almost cried, and said that was not fair to Daddy who would be here if he could, and anyway, maybe she would one day go to London. Emelye told her she would never go to London no matter what.

Friday was spelling test day, and this would be Emelye's fifth one. Though she had always been an especially good speller, and often won spelling bees at Harvard Elementary, now she had to relearn some words according to the British way—for instance, kerb, and neighbour. Sometimes there were two or three of these among the twenty-five test words. She was always glad when the spelling test was over because then she would anticipate the pleasure of sewing lessons with Miss Livingstone. These were only on Fridays, while the boys went outside for running, or high jumps, or something called "rounders." Miss Livingstone was very pretty, with blond hair braided in a coronet, and she was very sweet. Emelye wished she was their regular teacher, instead of Miss Sloane. Their first assignment was to hand stitch a bag with drawstrings, for sewing supplies. Though Emelye started late, she quickly caught up with the other girls. Her bag, made of cotton printed with tiny pink roses, was the neatest one of all, Mrs. Livingstone said, the stitches straight and uniform, and no pucker where the bottom joined to the sides. Yesterday Mother took her and Elizabeth to a shop called Bricknell's, where they purchased several colors of embroidery thread and small hoops. Today they would begin to learn cross stitch.

There was a boy with a heavily-freckled face and a hard slit of a mouth, whom everyone called Frompet. He was bigger than the others in her class, and he bullied people. That Friday, as they trooped downstairs for biscuits and milk, he pinched Emelye so hard on the back of her arm that she cried out and jerked around. He smirked at her. Miss Sloane stormed up from behind. "What's going on here, Miss Selby? Are you not familiar with the rule of silence on the stairs?"

"Yes, ma'am. Someone pinched me."

"Well? *Who*, might I ask?"

Emelye would have told on Frompet, but just in time she saw his threatening glare. She dropped her eyes. "I—I don't know, Miss Sloane."

"Well then, you can hardly expect me to discipline this person, can you? Come along, class. No more talking. And no more nonsense."

Soon they were sitting in a circle around the warm stove, rain streaking down the windows. Elizabeth whispered to Emelye, "Who pinched you?"

"Frompet," Emelye murmured.

"I thought so. Next time, tell Teacher. If you let him get by with it, he'll do it every chance he gets. You've got to stick up for yourself, Emelye."

If this had happened at home, she would have told James about Frompet, and James would have beat him up. Oh, how she missed James! *But this is home now, and James can't help me*, she thought. It was one of those dark moments of revelation when Emelye's entire body seemed fraught with homesickness, as if it had entered her bloodstream. She forced her mind away from this. Elizabeth was right. She must look out for herself.

During the test, Emelye clenched her pencil tightly. Her thoughts kept hastening back to Frompet. *Just let him try that again. I'll show him.* Only, had she failed to hear Miss Sloane give out number eighteen?

"Number eighteen, *prrractice*," said Miss Sloane with a flourish.

Relieved, Emelye recalled the sign above the long wall mirror in her mother's dancing studio: *"Practice, practice, practice!"* She ran her tongue over her lips and spelled the familiar word. By the end of the test, she was sure she had made 100.

Afterward, while the class worked quietly on their writing lesson, Miss Sloane graded the spelling tests. For weeks, she had been looking for a way to break Emelye, whom she despised on principle. How dare Mr. Gempie demand that she give the child preferential treatment. Not in so many words, of course. One afternoon while accompanying the boys outside to the sports field, she saw a fancy automobile pull up at the curb. The dashing widower Mr. Selby stepped out from the driver's side, wearing a smart tweed suit with a maroon scarf tucked jauntily inside his shirt collar. He opened the passenger door and offered his hand to the soon-to-be-Mrs. Selby—Miss Sloane had read the notice in the *Guardian*. She had short, shingled waves and an enviable figure. She wore black and white spectators and carried a matching handbag in her gloved hand. Now, the father reached into the car and out came a girl with dark blond braids, wearing a teal blue dress with long sleeves and frilly collar, and a matching ribbon tied in a perfect bow at the back of her head.

Half an hour later Mr. Gempie summoned Miss Sloane to his office and introduced the soon-to-be Mrs. Selby and her daughter Emelye, who was Elizabeth's sister and would be in her class—which for the moment Miss Sloane found rather confusing. After the threesome left, Mr. Gempie closed the door and explained to Miss Sloane in hushed tones that Mr. Selby and his fiancèe had been married once before, long ago, and divorced sometime after Emelye was born. She and Elizabeth were half-sisters. *Oh, what a touching tale,* thought Miss Sloane scornfully, *what do they take me for, an idiot?* The child would be placed in standard three after the couple returned from their honeymoon, said Mr. Gempie. They wished to be on hand to help Emelye adjust to her new school. Translated: Emelye, the illegitimate product of their adulterous affair, had been coddled and spoilt all her life. Now the couple were putting on a masquerade of respectability, even throwing a grand wedding celebration. Some people in this world got every happy ending they could desire, regardless of their low morals and irresponsible behavior.

Mr. Gempie cautioned Miss Sloane to be sure Emelye's classmates did not speak ill of her. Translated: there was always the possibility down the way of a sizable donation to the school, so let's be sure Mr. and Mrs. Selby were happy with St. Michael's. Miss Sloane had never received preferential treatment in her life. Packed off to boarding school as soon as she was old enough, she was the butt of every school yard joke, with her protruding teeth and skinny legs, and the teachers—as often as not, cruel themselves—never intervened. *I shall have my day of vindication,* she had told herself, year after year.

"Oh yes, Mr. Gempie, I understand perfectly," she said. She would obey his instructions to the letter, that is, to the degree her doing so was verifiable, but she would not give Emelye a fraction of an inch more. With the child entering late, it would not take long to weed her out and despatch her to standard two, so demoralized that the children there would find her easy prey.

Once Emelye began, however, her apparent determination to prove equal to standard three quite frustrated Miss Sloane. It would take a bit of doing to break her down. Now, with today's spelling test came the first opportunity.

She rose from her chair, Emelye's spelling test in hand. "Alright children, close your notebooks."

Emelye had not been paying attention to her writing lesson at all, so absorbed was she in thinking of how she must stand up to Frompet in the future. "Miss Selby, rise, if you please, and tell us how to correctly spell the word, *practice.*"

Emelye could hardly believe she was the only person in the room who spelled the word correctly, but it must be true or she would not have been singled out. Even Elizabeth must have misspelled it. She stood tall. Her voice ringing with the sense of confidence left behind in Texas until today, she spelled aloud, "P-r-a-c-t-i-c-e."

Elizabeth's stomach began to churn as soon as Emelye misspelled the word, for she realized that Teacher had decided to make an example of her.

Miss Sloane's beady eyes widened. "Oh? Is that so, Miss Selby? Are you quite sure?" she said grandly.

Emelye's field of vision began to blur. Was she wrong? But no. She knew that she was right. "Yes, Miss Sloane. My mother taught me the word."

"Oh, *really?* Tell her, class, how do we spell *practice?*"

The class rallied. "P-R-A-C-T-I-S-E!"

'S'. Oh yes, now Emelye remembered, with a sinking feeling. It was just that, thinking of Frompet had made her forget all about it being one of those special words.

"Now, what was the consonant just before the final vowel, class?" the teacher asked, the question oozing from her lips, her hand cupped around her ear.

"'S'!"

She smiled in approval. "You see, Emelye? Now, I suggest that in order to empty your mind of the *incorrect* spelling that *your mother* taught you, you proceed to the blackboard and write the word correctly 100 times. March!"

Emelye heard a voice mutter, "Emelye must have the dumbest mother in the world!" Titters went around the room. Miss Sloane did not seem to hear.

Emelye nearly broke down in tears at this slight against her mother. She must come to her defense, yet she feared the consequences of being disrespectful to her teacher. Forcing composure into her voice, she said, "Excuse me, Miss Sloane, but my mother was not incorrect. It's the way we spell *practice* in America."

Elizabeth's pained look, and the warning signal she was trying to convey with the quick shaking of her head, failed to register with Emelye.

Miss Sloane's throat and cheeks reddened. Aware she must keep the look of heightened pleasure from her face—this was going to be even more gratifying than she had imagined—she drew her head back like a snake preparing to strike. "Miss Selby, I do not care how the word *prrractice* is spelt in America, but your insubordination is of great interest to me." Emelye braced herself for Miss Sloane to reach for her wooden pointer. She had never been struck in her life, and she was terrified. Instead, the teacher looked out over the class. "Tell me, boys and girls, what is the punishment for insubordination?"

"You have to be locked in the attic!"

The words brought Emelye to the edge of panic. The blood was pounding so hard in her temples, she could barely hear her voice, "No, please Miss Sloane, I didn't mean to be insub—insub—"

But Miss Sloane was glaring at her, pointing one long, scarecrow finger toward the door. Emelye looked helplessly at Elizabeth, whose face was drained of color.

Elizabeth knew she must save Emelye from being locked up. But how?

"You will come with me at once Miss Selby, or I shall call the headmaster, and believe me, he will deal with you much more severely."

Emelye moved toward the door, her legs rubbery. She began to sob. "Miss Sloane, please," she begged, "please! Call my mother and tell her to come and get me, oh please! I want to go home!"

The adrenaline coursing joyously through her veins, Miss Sloane grabbed Emelye's arm and shoved her out into the hallway. As soon as the door closed behind them, the class began to jeer and Elizabeth began to sob, her hands covering her face. Just as Miss Sloane reopened the door to call the class to order, Frompet croaked, "When they take her from the attic in a week or so, they'll put her in the Barclay Home. And they'll never let her out!" One hand gripping Emelye's shoulder, Miss Sloane thundered, "Not another word, from you or anyone else, Frompet, or you shall all be disciplined when I return!"

What was the Barclay Home? Emelye wondered in panic as Miss Sloane opened a door on the stair landing and pulled a light chain. Where was it? How many times had her mother said she didn't know her way around Bodmin yet? She might not be able to find her there. "Please, please!" She begged, her feet stumbling up a flight of narrow wooden stairs.

It had not occurred to Miss Sloane that Emelye would become hysterical. Fleetingly she thought of Mr. Gempie's admonishment. Still, upon joining the faculty five years ago and discovering the suitability of the attic as a disciplinary tool, she had sought and won his approval. So she was well within her rights.

"Be careful, or you'll have both of us falling to our deaths. I must warn you, punishment for those who resist is much longer than for those who cooperate. There!" She opened a door and shoved Emelye inside a room the size of a clothes closet.

The door slammed shut behind Emelye. She stood trembling in the darkness. She heard the click of the door lock. Then the sound of retreating steps, and the rain beating down on the roof just above her head. Until today she had thought that only people you didn't know would do bad things to you. *Miss Sloane will come back and tie my hands and stuff my mouth full so that I can't scream, and then take me to the Barclay Home.* Emelye sank down in the floor, sobbing.

Abruptly her stomach rebelled. Biscuit and milk spewed from her mouth and down the front of her uniform.

Returning to her room, a little out of breath from exertion, Miss Sloane looked out over the class. With consternation she noted that Elizabeth was missing from her chair.

CHAPTER 7

Upon returning from their honeymoon, Tony began teaching Geneva to drive the English way, behind the wheel of his four-year-old Rover. Operating a vehicle from the right-hand side, rather than the left, was disorienting in itself, but in addition there was the confusing fact that left turns were the easy ones; right turns, risky, as you faced oncoming traffic. She started out in the countryside, using the narrow roads that wound through small villages in Cornwall and Devon. These presented no significant challenge except when one of the numerous harvest festivals was going on and autos were parked along both sides of the road through a village. Only one car could pass through at a time, barely squeezing by while a car from the opposite direction pulled over and waited. Unfortunately there was no clear rule as to who was to wait upon whom. Traffic roundabouts between towns, where several roads converged, presented an even more complicated problem. Sometimes there were only a couple of autos in the circle when Geneva approached, but other times there were at least a dozen, entering and exiting with aplomb at those odd-looking road signs pointing in all directions. Her every muscle tensed, her mouth dry with fear, Geneva would watch while speeding autos merged before her, waiting for Tony to say, "Go!" Whence, the Rover plunged into a gap between autos. No sooner was she inside the circle, trying to catch her breath, than Tony was hastening her to move into the exit lane. "Good show!" he would say when she was out on the open road again, no doubt grateful they had survived. Her heart pounding, she would pray they would not encounter another roundabout for a hundred miles.

Eventually Geneva worked her way up to the slanted streets of Bodmin, lined with stone buildings with high slate roofs. Though there were not a great many other vehicles—most people walked or rode bicycles, and there were a few horse-drawn conveyances—it was scary because often you had to brake at a crossing just before the crest of a hill, say in Fore Street turning onto Crockwell or Bell, then when it was time to go, press the accelerator and ease out on the clutch just so, to avoid sliding backward. Once when Geneva was precariously perched at the top of a hill, she noticed a solemn black-uniformed police officer waiting behind her on a motorcycle. What if she slid back and ran over him?

Geneva came to realize that Bodmin proper was at the bottom of a bowl-shaped terrain, with cross streets heading off the major thoroughfare of Fore Street. Much of the commerce seemed to be located down on the south end—on the way to the rail station and the military barracks and eventually to Clearharbour. Bodmin was a Crown Court town, and the court house and other public buildings were neighbored by butchers, bakers, grocers and chemists; stationers, photographers; wine and spirits shops; drapers and jewelers and confectionaries; professional offices, banks and hotels. The tall clock tower rose at an odd angle above leafy Mount Folly Square. On market day, when farmers brought in their fresh produce and dairy products, and clothing and flowers and other items were for sale on the square, there was barely room to walk around the narrow angling streets, much less drive a car.

By the time they moved into Clearharbour at last, and Tony kissed Geneva goodbye and returned to London, he was convinced of her proficiency behind the wheel. Yet each time she made her way down the long driveway, lined with sycamore trees, pulled out and crossed to the left-hand lane of Castle Canyke Road—a major two-way thoroughfare—she still struggled to reverse most of the principles she had followed for all her driving life.

On weekday mornings, after dropping off the girls at St. Michael's high up on the north end of town—or "up top town" as the locals called it—she would double back as far south as St. Petroc's Church, for daily prayers. She liked the new vicar, John Key, and she had come to feel at home at Sunday worship when the whole family filed into the pew with Cynthia and Edward at the lead, the pipe organ music swelling to the rafters, and the boys' choir singing like a band of angels. Yet she still liked it best when she arrived shortly after Matins, entered the nave and sank down on a prayer cushion, alone under the towering arches with light slanting benevolently through stained glass. There she felt a sense of peace, and a unity with all that was here and now and had ever gone before; and she sensed, somehow, that unity with God was really unity with all of life: a trinity of past, present and future.

Watching Emelye pick at her breakfast, then seeing her solemn face when they kissed goodbye at St. Michael's, Geneva was sharply reminded that this was a different child than the one who used to clean her plate at breakfast, then skip off to school with Serena and James. Therefore, after offering thanksgiving for her many blessings, she always began by praying that God would help Emelye find happiness. She prayed that Tony would one day feel equal to talking to Elizabeth about her mother, if that would enable them both to break out of the shackles of the past. *And please let me be helpful. Amen.*

On the first Friday in December, Geneva returned home just before ten o'clock, stopping outside to shake out her umbrella, then walking through the small conservatory with its shelves of pot plants, entering the front hall just as the longcase clock struck the hour. She remembered her father setting his pocket watch by this very same clock, long ago, and suddenly it was as if he was right there in the room with her. She stood listening until the clock was silent again. *Welcome to Clearharbour, Daddy,* she thought, her eyes stinging. Hard to believe he and her mother had been dead for seventeen years. She hung her raincoat on a peg, thinking that a cup of tea would be nice before she got busy. Lately she'd switched to drinking tea, for coffee had lost its appeal: a symptom of pregnancy, she hoped. She had not yet made an appointment with a specialist, but at Tony's urging, she stopped by the *Bodmin Guardian* office, across from the church, and placed an ad for a housekeeper. She must be careful not to overexert.

The telephone was ringing. She went to the little table by the stairway and lifted the receiver. "Hullo Geneva—Nell here! I should like to motor over for a few minutes, if I may."

Geneva felt reluctant. She and Nell continued to feel uncomfortable around each other, though whether because of the eight years Nell had cost her and Tony, or merely because of the difference in their personalities, she could not say. However, she owed Nell a courtesy. She had been very kind to Emelye. She'd taken her on long walks on the Brookhurst estate, taught her to identify several species of butterflies and wild flower varieties in the wood, and familiarized her with all the trees. Several times she had invited her to Camellia Cottage to spend the day with Guy. To Geneva, Guy looked like a miniature Morey, with a stocky build, dark hair and blue eyes; and he had his father's affable nature. He, too, was very nice to Emelye though she was a little shy around him as yet. "Good, come on, we'll have a cup of tea. But I must warn you, things are in kind of a mess," she said.

"I shouldn't mind in the least. See you in half an hour. Cheerio."

Geneva was holding the conservatory door open when Nell approached the small porch. Her stout figure shielded by a huge umbrella, she toted a large gift box wrapped around with blue ribbon. "Here, this is for you and Tony—a little housewarming," she said shyly, handing Geneva the gift box and dispensing with the umbrella. "How kind of you," Geneva said. She braced herself to pretend to like the present, whatever it was, but she hoped it wasn't an article for exhibit. Camellia Cottage was a bit fussy for Geneva's taste, with its many art prints on sugary themes lining the walls and stairwell, and its what-not shelves with ceramic birds and figurines.

This was Nell's first time to see the house since the renovations were completed. She peeked inside the beveled glass door to the sitting room, then glanced into the dining room, ignoring all the boxes and crates, and admiring the new cream-colored wallpaper, the highly varnished woodwork and sheer window curtains, and the plush figured rugs. Then they went upstairs to the attic bedroom. This was the only room completely in order—a product of Geneva's urgent desire to make Emelye and Elizabeth feel happy in their new home. Upon seeing the cozy hipped ceiling, the pink and green floral bedspreads, the ruffled dressing table skirt, and frilly window curtains—most decorating decisions having been made by Emelye, for Elizabeth claimed to have no preferences—Nell gave her a sidelong glance and said quietly, "It does make one long for a little girl…."

Tony had told Geneva that Nell could not have any more children after Guy. She felt sad for her now, and knew she'd feel awkward when her pregnancy was confirmed and she and Tony announced it.

Geneva never walked into this room without gazing up at Madame Linsky's wooden crucifix, mounted above Emelye's bed. She had told Emelye the story of rescuing it from the trash heap after her beloved teacher's death, and told her she hoped it would be a daily reminder that wherever she went, God was there, loving her. She overcame the temptation to embroider that with more comforting reassurances, because she knew from experience they were unreliable. In any case, Emelye seemed indifferent to the crucifix. Geneva would like to have it in her room, but she never could quite bring herself to reclaim it. She told Nell to come on down to the kitchen for a cup of tea. "I'm dying to see what's in that box."

"Oh, it really isn't much," Nell said deferentially.

Pretty soon they were sitting at the kitchen table and Geneva was removing the ribbon and lifting the box lid. Inside she was amazed to discover a handsome wreath of dried camellias nestling in their leaves, around eighteen inches in diameter. Worked into the design were clusters of tiny pine cones, dried berries, pomegranates and rosebuds, chestnuts and Michaelmas daisies and heather. "How lovely!" she cried. Carefully she removed the wreath and held it before her. "Did you make this?" she asked admiringly, glancing at Nell.

"It isn't terribly hard, just takes a bit of time—I finished last night," Nell said. "Everything in it is from the garden and grounds at Camellia Cottage."

Geneva felt humbled by the highly personal gift, ashamed of herself for doubting she would like it. She smiled. "I'm going to hang it in the dining room, above the sideboard," she said impulsively. That was where her parents' painting from Geneva, Switzerland, was to hang, but never mind. It would look fine above one of the glass-fronted bookcases that flanked the fireplace in the sitting room. "Tony will love it too—oh, thank you so much!"

Nell beamed with pleasure. Geneva rose to brew the tea.

"Tony's back in London, I gather," Nell said from behind.

"Yes," Geneva said. A sad parting. *"Ten days late?" Tony said wonderingly, his hand closing tenderly on her abdomen.* Then before they knew it they were kissing goodbye and he was speeding away in the Rolls-Royce. She stood alone on the drive for some time. Her eyes swept up to the tallest peak of the stone house, which shimmered against the hard blue sky; then she pivoted around and her gaze took in the double sycamore tree—its leaves curled up and scattered on the ground beneath it; she wondered if there was a rake somewhere—and the broad patchwork of meadows that lay beyond their property as far as the eye could see. This was the home for which they had waited so long, she thought, checking her sadness. She added with bravado to Nell, "He calls every evening at five o'clock, and he'll be home for Christmas. White or black?"

"Black for me. Cream is so fattening, though I adore it…."

With that remark Geneva was saved from locating the tin of biscuits in the hodgepodge that lined the counters. She brought their tea to the table. "Oh, by the way, I noticed the handsome new sign at the foot of the drive," said Nell.

"Yes—we felt just the name 'Clearharbour' would be more appropriate, since obviously we won't be doing any farming."

"Quite. Will the two of you keep the flat in Bloomsbury?" Nell asked.

"For the moment," Geneva told her, then explained they'd made an offer on a townhouse for sale on Norfolk Square, near Paddington Station, which they looked at on their way back from Lyme Regis. Built in 1890, when the area was considered far out on the fringes of London, it was three stories high with servants' quarters above, and had a splendid stairway of carved walnut, and ornate chandeliers with frosted glass. And, as luck would have it, there was a lift with a fancy brass cage, so one could avoid the stairs which Geneva would need to do. She was to spend the latter part of all her pregnancies in London. She and Tony had made a pact never again to be apart for the birth of their children. "I sure hope we get it," she said of the townhouse, thinking of the lift in particular.

"My, my, two homes, plus Brookhurst eventually," said Nell, raising her brow. She took a sip of tea.

Was she jealous? Or, chiding them for all the expense? Not that they could avoid it. Was this what it was like to have a sister? Giving her opinion on things that were none of her business? How she missed Willa!

After a pause, Nell asked with feeling, "By the way, how is our Emelye getting on at St. Michael's?"

"Fair enough. Elizabeth helps her with her studies," Geneva said, thinking of the quiet distance Elizabeth continued to maintain, otherwise. Well at least her helpfulness was a start, and Geneva was trying to be patient. She added with diplomacy, "I'm hoping that in time the girls will grow closer."

"Elizabeth is quite the scholar. It's a blessing all round, too," said Nell.

Noting that Nell had ignored the second, more important part of her statement, she echoed, "A blessing?"

Nell shrugged. "Well, as things are now, one must imagine that her only real chance at a rewarding future will be to surround herself with books."

"But why?"

Nell smiled with forbearance. Of course, Geneva had never experienced the quick glances from boys, conveying: *"Never mind. Her figure is not up to scratch."* A stout body, or any kind of disfigurement, made a girl undesirable, and often an object of scorn. "Well really, one can hardly imagine Elizabeth being popular with boys when she grows up. Take it from me, looks count for more than anything else in this world," she said sagely.

Geneva refused to accept the notion that Elizabeth must be resigned to a life of limitations. Still, there was no use trying to change Nell's narrow opinion. "One thing I've learned in life, you never know what's in store," Geneva remarked pointedly, and took a sip of tea. She felt a strained place at the nape of her neck. Conversing with Nell was like riding a roller coaster.

Nell feared she had put things awkwardly. It was just that she was anxious that Geneva be prepared to help Elizabeth with all the difficulties ahead as she grew into a young woman. Still, perhaps one ought not to have gone overboard.

Just as Nell opened her mouth to balance her remark by speaking of her own good fortune in meeting Morey, the telephone rang and Geneva excused herself to answer.

Mr. Gempie was calling. "Mrs. Selby, I must inform you that your daughter Emelye left the school without permission a few minutes ago...."

CHAPTER 8

Geneva and Nell were in Nell's auto, speeding toward Bodmin in the rain, with high stone embankments on the left side of the road that fronted higher-still gabled roofs and great vaulting cedars; and down on the right, along low fence lines, red and yellow nasturtiums and fuschias and, in between these natural obstructions, snapshot glimpses of the meadows and hedgerows beyond. Geneva's eyes were darting from one side of the road to the other. She was painfully aware that while the view was pretty clear beyond the low fences on the right, up on the left there were high roads running parallel with Castle Canyke, where stately old homes were hidden by the bank of cedars. Could Emelye be up there somewhere? She felt overwhelmed suddenly. Bodmin was a pretty big place when you came right down to it.

Whatever Mr. Gempie's explanation—something about Emelye being punished for insubordination—Geneva barely listened. All those mornings of seeing Emelye's unhappy face haunted her. Perhaps she was running away not only from school, but from home. If so, there was no telling what direction she had taken.

The mystery was soon solved. They intercepted Emelye heading toward home, passing Barclay's Bank on the right side of the street at the southern edge of town. *Thank God!* Emelye was without coat or beanie, drenched from head to toe. Her knees were bleeding and her eyes were wild. Nell lowered the window and they both began calling out, "Emelye, stop! Stay where you are! Mummy's coming!" She paused and looked around, puzzled. Nell wheeled across the street and pulled into a bank parking space. Geneva opened the door and leapt out on the pavement. "Baby!"

When Emelye slammed into her waist, the stench of soured milk all but took her breath away.

During the short drive back home, Emelye sat with her mother's arm wrapped around her, recounting through tears the incident from which she fled—remarkably, all the way from one side of Bodmin to the other. "When Miss Sloane opened the attic door, I ran past her and down the stairs. Warden tried to stop me, but I bit her finger as hard as I could. I—I fell down by the fountain on Mount Folly Square, and a man tried to grab me, but I got away. I won't go back there again! No one can make me!" The declaration ended in a shriek.

"There now, it's going to be alright," Geneva said, her own composure threatened from shock at Emelye's story.

Back at home, they all three huddled under Nell's umbrella and hurried into the house. Nell said calmly, "Now Geneva, you must give Emelye a good hot bath—have you some medicine for her knees?"

"I—yes, I think so—in a box up in my bathroom," Geneva stammered.

"Good. Meantime, I shall contact the school, tell them Emelye is safe, and demand an explanation. Have you the number handy?"

"It's in the black binder on the shelf under the telephone."

Geneva put her arm around Emelye's quaking body and they headed upstairs. As they reached the landing halfway to the top, Geneva glanced through the large window overlooking the drive and the double sycamore tree, and the meadows beyond. You could not see a thing. Rain was coming down in sheets. Thank goodness Emelye was home safe. But then with a pang of remorse, she remembered Elizabeth. "Where is your sister?"

"At school."

Well, she won't be after today, Geneva thought furiously.

"I'll run away if you and Daddy try and make me go back!"

"Don't worry, darling, we'll find another school."

"I want to go home, Mom, please let's don't live here anymore!"

Perhaps the plea was understandable, but it hurt. Geneva recalled Willa's offer, just before they moved, that Emelye may come back and live with her, if she didn't like it here. But Geneva had no doubt she and Tony could make Emelye happy in England. Now—but no. Somehow Emelye had to get over this and go on. "I'm afraid that's impossible," she said with quiet firmness.

The dormer attic room was chilly. Geneva paused to start a coal fire in the small fireplace, her fingers trembling as she struck the match. Then she helped her daughter out of her foul-smelling clothing.

Later, with Emelye in a clean gown, her wounds dressed, Geneva tucked the bed covers around her shivering body, then sat on the edge of the bed, toweling off her wet hair. The child's face was blotchy and swollen from crying. Her breath was still coming in gulps. Geneva felt she ought to have anticipated something like this. She had been told that discipline was harsh in English schools, but she always assumed that was true of boarding schools only, where parents were too far away to intervene. It never occurred to her that children could be terrorized practically right under their parents' noses.

Geneva glanced up at the crucifix, then quickly looked away. How could Emelye believe in God's love when so many terrible things happened to her? Right now she was having a hard time herself.

Presently Nell brought a steaming cup of hot chocolate. "I thought you could use this," she told Emelye. She put the cup on the table beside the bed and kissed her forehead. "Better now?" she asked, her voice gentle.

"Yes, ma'am, Mother says we'll find another school," she told her aunt, then added as though with a spasm of misery, "But I wish we could move back home. There are so many bad people in England! They make you be locked up and won't let you go. But I got away!"

The words brought home to Geneva how little Emelye really understood about what befell her that day in London last year. In any case, the thought that she had once again been snatched away and locked up sent a charge of anger through Geneva.

Nell was saying, "Poor Emelye, there are lots of nice people in England, though I'm sure it mustn't seem so today. But if you moved away, what ever would your father do, he'd be so broken-hearted? And your sister, and your grandparents, and Auntie Nell and Guy would miss you so much! Everything will come right in the end, you'll see." She hugged her close.

Nell's words and her manner, surely twice as reassuring to Emelye as Geneva's, nearly brought her to tears. Suddenly she was so grateful for Nell's many acts of kindness toward Emelye, and for her steadiness in the current crisis, she wished with all her heart to say, *I forgive you everything.* It was, of course, the wrong moment.

"Now. May I borrow your mother just for a bit?" Nell asked.

"I guess so," Emelye said reluctantly. Yet when they started out the door she said, "Wait, Aunt Nellie, what is the Barclay Home?"

Geneva looked blankly at Nell. Nell said haltingly, "Why, it's—it's a place where…girls…go to live sometimes. Why?"

Emelye's eyes screwed up again. "Frompet said that they would take me there from the attic, and that I'd never get out. But I got away!"

"Good heavens!" said Nell, lifting her eyes to the ceiling. "He just made that up, to be cruel," she assured her. Emelye sank back on the pillows.

Nell spoke quietly as she and Geneva walked downstairs. "It's in Pound Street; the Elizabeth Barclay Home, it's called. Some of the wealthy gentry hereabouts send their daughters to be raised there, when they're...well...I think the term is *defective*."

Geneva looked at her uncomprehendingly. "You've seen them round town, probably, wearing white overalls and tri-cornered hats trimmed in green. As far as I know, they're treated decently enough. They operate a laundry."

In fact, she had seen them, she realized now. They worshiped at St. Petroc's. She had assumed they were from St. Lawrence's Mental Hospital. *My God, what have I brought my daughter into?* "I thought England was supposed to be a *civilized* country," she moaned.

"Yes, well...." Nell said vaguely. "I came to tell you that Elizabeth went to Mr. Gempie's office, to intervene on Emelye's behalf. It backfired. For punishment, she is sitting in a chair in his office, facing the corner."

Geneva closed a hand around her arm. She felt she was ready to explode.

"I should be happy to go and fetch her, if you like. I just need to telephone Guy's school and warn them that I'll be late picking him up today."

"Oh, Nell, could you? Wait! No. You stay with Emelye. I'll go."

In minutes Geneva was throwing on her raincoat and heading for the door.

Nell stood watching. "Geneva, one thing that I've come to grips with over my life: beastly as it seems, the discipline in English schools does perhaps toughen children up; prepares them for the injustices of life."

If there was any wisdom in that remark, Geneva was too sick at heart and distracted to examine it. She raised her umbrella and raced to the garage, dodging puddles. Backing down the driveway, she glanced up at the dormer window of Emelye's room. It bolstered her some to think of her up there in that cozy attic room, with soft lamp light and a cheerful fire burning in the grate; safe and warm with her Aunt Nellie. But poor Elizabeth....

Minutes later she was doubling back down Castle Canyke towards the point where it converged with St. Nicholas Street then wound into town, the wipers making clear arcs in the rain-pummeled windscreen. All she could think of was confronting Mr. Gempie. *I thought you ran a school, not a prison. You ought to have your license pulled. Or better still, spend a little time locked in a closet where there is no light and very little air. It would do wonders in building your character. Miss Sloane has no business in the classroom, and you are the poorest excuse for an administrator I've ever seen. I intend to tell everyone I see what goes on here—*

Up ahead, through the veil of rain, the two head lamps of another auto flashed into view. A second later, Geneva realized that the auto was in her lane, speeding towards her. Her hands froze on the wheel as she comprehended that she was driving down the wrong side of the street. The driver in the oncoming car honked his horn frantically, his brakes squealing. Geneva's mind convulsed in an overload of conflicting signals. Then she was turning the wheel hard to the left and heading toward the stone embankment. When she pressed the brake, the Rover spun around, then blessedly stopped at a right angle on the shoulder, its bonnet pointed at the road. When the other car safely passed, the driver was shouting epithets at Geneva through his open window, rain hitting his face. She lowered her head on the steering wheel, her breath coming in gasps, the hair-raising night of Emelye's birth replaying in her mind. Her distraction could have cost her life and that of her unborn child today. All she wanted was to get out of the Rover and leave it sitting there, and never, ever get behind the wheel again.

Elizabeth needed her. She put the car back into gear, looked both ways up the street, released the clutch and pressed the accelerator, her feet shaking so hard they seemed to be dancing on the pedals.

As Geneva arrived at St. Michael's, the obvious struck her: there was nothing she could say to Mr. Gempie that would change the policies of the school. The system by which it operated was thoroughly entrenched all over England. She may as well save her breath.

She walked through Mr. Gempie's office door without knocking. "Now, see here, Mrs. Selby!" he cried, looking up wide-eyed from the papers before him, half-rising. Her heart broke at the sight of Elizabeth, sitting with her back straight and her ankles crossed, her face to the wall. When the child turned to look at Geneva, her eyes were red and swollen.

"Come Elizabeth, let's go home," Geneva said, with a murderous glance at Mr. Gempie.

"We do not tolerate insubordination, Mrs. Selby. Nor do we allow children to leave the classroom without permission," warned the headmaster.

Again, she was tempted to unleash her anger. However, she did not want Elizabeth to witness it, nor would continuing to be upset be good for her unborn child. She informed Mr. Gempie that she was withdrawing her daughters from the school, and walked out, her arm around Elizabeth's shoulder.

On the way home, Elizabeth said gloomily, "Miss Sloane has her favorite pupils—I expect I was one. Then, she is mean to people she doesn't fancy."

"So I gather," said Geneva dourly. "Why didn't you tell me, before this happened?" she asked.

"Some parents don't mind. And besides, it makes things worse when one tells," she said simply.

The statement made Geneva almost sick with revulsion. She immediately anticipated the warning she would give the headmaster at the next school. Yet, what if he scoffed at her, or worse, ignored her? Would she wind up putting her children's education in the hands of a full-time tutor, depriving them of the society that would help prepare them for adulthood?

They drove on in silence for a bit, then suddenly Elizabeth cried desperately, "Oh, what do you think makes people so dreadfully mean, Geneva? Is it from someone's being mean to them?"

Geneva glanced her way. "Perhaps so," she answered quietly, realizing Elizabeth was comparing Miss Sloane to her mother Jane.

"I suppose I ought to pray for Miss Sloane. Fr. Ogilvie would say so," she reflected.

Sometimes Elizabeth exhibited remarkable maturity. "Yes, I suppose so."

Elizabeth took a shivering breath. "When I was sitting in Mr. Gempie's office, I saw Emelye flash by out the corner of my eye. 'Run, Emelye, run as fast as you can!' I thought. I should have run away too, but I wouldn't have got very far, would I?" she said bitterly. "Oh, Geneva, do you think Emelye will hate me now, because I didn't help her?"

Geneva was so touched by Elizabeth's desperation, she very nearly lost all composure. There would be no more doubting her feelings toward Emelye. "No, Emelye could never hate you, my dear. Besides, you tried to help, that's what is important. I know she's going to appreciate that when she hears about it."

Elizabeth stared through the window at the relentless rain. "I shall always do everything in my power for her," she said with gravity. Then she added woefully, "Poor Emelye. She hates London, and now she'll hate Bodmin, too."

CHAPTER 9

Tony sat in his office at the *William & Mary*, the woman's letter and its enclosure lined up before him on his broad, leather-topped desk.

It was shortly after three o'clock on the 12th of February, 1932—less than five hours before the house lights would go down, a hush would come over the audience, and the curtain would rise on the *William & Mary* stage for the first time in nearly twenty years. It was the realization of all his dreams; the fruition of all his labors. It was the beginning of the return on an investment that had far surpassed his earliest calculations—*a settlement of £5,000? What does she take me for? She won't get a penny*—but that he knew had been worth it when the last tips of gold leaf had dried on the letters *W & M* intertwined, with a crown on top, above the proscenium; the carpet runners had been laid along the hardwood floor; the red velvet plush seats were in place and the opera glasses with mother-of-pearl handles had been fitted in their brackets. Two dozen ushers were trained and ready; they would look sharp in royal blue uniforms, brass buttons with raised letters *W & M*, gold stripes on the trouser legs, and white gloves. Special souvenir programmes in blue binders, with the *W & M* insignia on the front, and gold tassels, were stacked behind the stalls. The box office had been humming—performances were sold out for well into the next three weeks.

Late last night before leaving, he walked out in the entranceway and stood once again upon the *W & M* insignia—splendidly restored—of shiny golden tiles set in a polished marble crest. When first he came here, two years ago, many of the tiles were missing, and those that remained were broken. He'd stood looking with his lantern raised high above, knowing instinctively in that moment that the *William & Mary* had somehow been held in a sacred trust for the day he would chance upon it. Then last night, his eyes stinging with pride, he gazed up at the bright lights—ostensibly checking to be sure not one globe was unlit, though really just for the thrill of it, which didn't disappoint; his whole body seemed to be glowing! Then he focused on the bow-shaped entrance, his eyes traveling from one end to the other of the wood-framed doors inset with frosted glass, their brass handles shining.

The office in which Tony now sat had been a happy discovery. It had three floor-to-ceiling windows overlooking Trafalgar Square and the National Gallery, a barrel ceiling with exposed rafters, paneled walls and a huge marble fireplace in which a log fire was now briskly burning. Through a hidden door just beside the fireplace was a small corridor accessing the railed gallery that surrounded the rotunda above the lobby.

Tony had furnished this room appropriately, with leather chairs and mahogany tables and brass lamp stands, and several glass-enclosed book cases. In one corner he'd placed a small drafting table, and so far he'd spent more time there than he'd spent behind his desk. How he used to regret all those years of studying engineering at Oxford, considering it a waste of time to serve his family tradition! He couldn't have got through these last two years without the education he gained, could not have dealt intelligently with the architect, or all those many subcontractors that he paid so handsomely, much less designed his own stage sets.

But now he was anchored behind his desk by the allegations from Paris. *"I thought you'd want to have a look at these straightaway," said Mrs. Fairfax, placing the two articles at the top of the stack.* One quick glance and he'd felt his blood curdling from the sides of his neck down to his knees. Preposterous, of course. The woman had no claim on him whatsoever. And this lawyer—M. Bolard, at 17, *rue du Bois*—was obviously engaged to intimidate him. But it wouldn't work. It was all instigated by Jane herself, no doubt. Just the kind of twisted scheme she'd dream up to avenge herself—oh, he had to hand it to her; she was clever to the end!

He picked up the enclosure—a photostatic copy of a note in Jane's familiar, spidery, hand. How dare she! Thing to do was toss the whole business on the fire, he thought, sweeping them up and walking to the fireplace. Yet, just at the point of tossing the pages into the flames, he thought better of it. He returned them to his desktop, realizing only then that his hand was shaking. This he resented most of all. Damn and blast Jane. And wouldn't this just happen on one of the most important days of his life?

He forced his mind away, thinking again of tonight's opening. The director had assembled a capable, if not star-studded, cast—Miss Vivien Leigh was perfect as the beautiful Candida, oozing charm on the outside as she used her considerable intelligence to keep the props from collapsing under her pompous husband Morell; and Michael Redgrave portrayed the arrogant clergyman in all his dimensions, even gaining a little sympathy for the poor old deluded chap; John Gielgud did a credible job as the melancholy cad, Marchbanks, never letting the audience forget the danger he posed to Morell's fragile universe. The set that Tony designed could not have come out better. The couch and tables, lamps, and paintings, were borrowed from his and Geneva's townhouse on Norfolk Square. Otherwise the props department outdid themselves. The inventory of small props alone numbered more than 350, from Morell's letter opener, ink pen and blotter, magazines and pamphlets and postage stamps and postal scales, to the complete set of Browning's poems in the bookshelves above the fireplace.

There would be just one performance tonight, at 8 p.m. When he and Geneva made their entrance, she would be clad in a spectacular floor-length gown and evening cape of emerald green velvet—a Jean Patou original—and he would wear white tie and tails. His parents were due to arrive this afternoon for the affair. Elizabeth and Emelye were left at home in the capable hands of Mrs. Greaves, the housekeeper—out of a streak of loyalty to Emelye, Elizabeth had declined to come to London for the opening.

After the performance there would be a champagne reception beneath the oval-shaped glass rotunda, for the cast and members of the press, and around a hundred other invited guests. The front cover of the invitation was from an original engraving of the *William & Mary* facade, dated 1896—the year it reopened after a major fire in 1893. Artist unknown. He'd found it in the one box of documents that was stored in the attic along with crates containing props, trunks of faded, papery costumes and discarded stage sets. Also inside the box were assorted newspaper clippings, one announcing that as of 28 December, 1881, the *William & Mary* stage would for the first time be lit by electric lamps, and assuring the public there was no danger of fire. There was a detailed guide for maintaining the hydraulic stage elevators, installed in 1858, that were operating yet today. Otherwise there was a file with some preliminary pen and ink sketches of a rather ornate garden scene for a hand-painted curtain. The hand-painted curtain was no more.

Today Tony felt as if the proud history of the *William & Mary* was finally converging with present and future. As Geneva put it once, he was the theatre's only hope of salvation. Well, he wasn't going to let anything ruin this night of celebration. And he certainly wasn't going to tell Geneva about it. His beloved Geneva, in whose womb their child was growing…

…still…perhaps he'd better contact his solicitor, just in case.

He sat down again, glancing at his desk clock: going on four. In a few minutes, the chap from the *Illustrated Daily News* would arrive. There was to be a huge feature story and photograph spread in Sunday's edition. Feeling more impatient than anything else at this point, he pressed the buzzer for Mrs. Fairfax. When she answered he said, "Get Craig Muggeridge on the line, will you? Let's have him have a look at this thing."

CHAPTER 10

On the first of September, 1933, Elizabeth embarked with her parents and her sister Emelye on a holiday in France. Journeying by rail on the Golden Arrow from London to Portsmouth, they ferried across the channel on board the *Canterbury*, Geneva's Rover below deck in the cargo hold. Father would have much preferred driving his Rolls-Royce, for which he had so few opportunities that it still looked and smelt brand new. However, he was not willing to risk having it lifted high in the air by a crane and set down on its wheels again in order to be transported to their destination. The itinerary included a week of motoring through the French countryside, traveling as far as the Normandy coast, then a few days in Paris at the end.

There were several reasons for this holiday, not least of which was that Father needed a break from the demands of work. He and his colleague, Kenneth Owsley, were co-producing a musical comedy about a group of contentious literary ghosts, entitled, *Of Rhyme and Reason.* It was written by a new playwright whom Father had discovered, and he was very enthusiastic. Helena Magden, who was married to Mr. Owsley, was to play the leading role of Pamela Bunch, a scruffy-looking night maid at the British Museum. Elizabeth rather liked Mr. Owsley. He was a jolly Irishman with a freckled face, red hair and a balding pate, and large round eyes the color of topaz. He was always getting people on, and making them laugh. Miss Magden was very different, both in looks and temperament. She had lustrous light brown hair and an olive complexion, and her eyes were very dark and exotic. Her figure was so fair, with large breasts, a narrow waist, and shapely long legs, she made one think of the Grecian statues carved into the ceiling of the *Queen's* theatre. Of the many people Elizabeth had come to know in the theatre, Miss Magden was among the few who didn't seem to get on very well with other people, least of all her husband. While driving along, Father complained to Geneva that the couple had one row after another during the pre-rehearsal stage of the new musical, putting everyone else on edge, and on the day before they left on holiday, he'd had a word with Kenneth. "On the brink of separation again, I shouldn't wonder."

Geneva was stroking the nape of Father's neck, in an effort to help him relax. His secretary Mrs. Fairfax had their itinerary so tightly organized that he seemed constantly worried about being able to reach the villages and locate the lodgings she'd arranged, before darkness fell. "Why don't they just divorce, and be done with it?" Geneva said. "I'm sure poor little Jerome would be better off."

Did Geneva condone divorce? Elizabeth wondered then. If so, it seemed to bear out Mummy's claim that she was in large part responsible for Father's divorcing her.

In the months following the reopening of the *William & Mary* last year, Geneva had grown quite large. In June Father took her away to London, to stay for a long while. When they returned to Clearharbour in August, they brought their new baby daughter—named Elvira Christina, after Geneva's beloved dance mistress, the late Elvira Linsky. "Where do babies come from?" Elizabeth asked Geneva shortly after. "From love between a mummy and daddy," she said. So then, perhaps this was why Elizabeth had no brothers or sisters while her mother was alive: *"It drove me quite mad that your father didn't love me..."* Well then, where had she come from? Yet: *"...when I all but worshiped him...."* Perhaps if a mummy loved a daddy enough, even if he did not love her in return, a baby would come. Perhaps when mummies and daddies had lots of children, it was because they loved each other very much. After all, Geneva and Father were now expecting still another child, in the spring of next year. And this was an additional reason for the holiday in France: Geneva would soon be prevented from long motor trips, until after the baby was born. As if to confirm Elizabeth's reasoning, her father raised Geneva's fingers to his lips and kissed them, then asked tenderly, "Feeling alright, Darling? Need anything?"

"I'm fine...but I miss our baby, don't you?" she said longingly.

Father murmured his agreement. Elvira was staying with her grandparents at Brookhurst, for she was too little to enjoy a motor trip. Truly Elizabeth was glad they had left her behind. She had quite the loudest voice imaginable for such a wee one, and she employed it relentlessly whenever she was displeased, prompting everyone to scatter as far away as possible and shut the door behind them. Mrs. Greaves the housekeeper was the only one who did not cringe at Elvira's outbursts, being a bit hard of hearing. Father was fond of predicting that when Elvira grew up she would either become a stage actor or a great orator. Elvira adored her father, and if she were here now, she would be constantly struggling to climb into his lap as he drove, and protesting loudly at being prevented from doing so.

The final reason for the motor trip was to cheer Emelye, who always became cross just before Michaelmas term in the fall. After the unfortunate incident at St. Michael's, the two of them were enrolled in Bodmin Primary School, which Auntie Nell had attended as a young girl. And, perhaps owing to Geneva's stern instructions to the headmaster, so far neither of them had been ill-treated there. Still, Emelye dreaded school, and while Elizabeth helped her with her studies, she no longer tried very hard.

For a long time, at nights when they lay in their beds, side by side, Emelye would weep from homesickness. Elizabeth would reach across and hold her hand, and secretly pray that one day she might come to love England. Then, starting last Christmas, there was a long period when she believed her prayers were being answered. Early in December, Geneva told them that Father would be too busy putting on *Pip 'N Pocket* to come to Clearharbour for more than a day or so, for the holiday. She asked if Emelye might consent to spending the long vacation in London, so that they could all be together, but promised they would not force her. When Emelye shrugged and said alright, Geneva was obviously amazed. She hugged her daughter close and said she was very proud, tears standing in her eyes. Elizabeth was grateful. Out of a sense of loyalty, she had not been to London since Emelye came to live in England, and she did so like it there. There were numerous museums to visit, as well as the London Zoo. There were puppet shows and plays, and tea at the Ritz, and riding the underground, and shopping at Harrod's where one could find positively anything one wanted. Best of all, she could have luncheon or tea with her great friend Father Ogilvie, with whom she corresponded regularly. Father Ogilvie was now retired and living with his daughter in Kensington.

What fun they had at Christmas! It snowed for days, and on Christmas Eve Father helped them build a snowman on Norfolk Square, contributing his cap and woolen muffler. When they finished, Mrs. Briscoe took their picture, then they all went inside and upstairs to Geneva and Father's sitting room with its high ceiling and ornate frieze, and tall windows overlooking the square. There they drank hot chocolate and ate raspberry scones by the fireside. After the holiday, Elizabeth overheard Geneva telling Father: "I think Emelye has turned a corner." Father said, "Pretty soon she'll forget all about going back to Texas."

It seemed to Elizabeth that since that time, Emelye was more often in a happy mood than she used to be.

Yet, a few nights before they left on this journey, she stood behind Emelye at their dressing table, brushing her hair and admiring the long silky locks, with highlights like spun gold. "What are you going to do when you grow up?" Emelye asked.

"I suppose I shall enter a convent," she said, for leading a secluded life, not to mention wearing long habits that would conceal her scar, appealed to her.

Emelye's eyes widened in the dressing table mirror. "You mean, you're going to become a *Catholic*?"

"Oh no. The Church of England has convents too. The Community of the Holy Name in Malvern, for instance, and St. Mary's in Oxfordshire," she told her. Then she asked, "What will you do when you grow up?"

"I'm going to marry James Younger. He is my true love," Emelye said with ardor.

This seemed reasonable, for Emelye and James were both handsome-looking, and agile. Still, she asked, "How can you, when he lives so far away?"

"He will come and take me away with him, like Prince Charming and Cinderella."

Elizabeth was crushed. She glanced at the happy picture taken with the snowman last Christmas, which now stood upon their dressing-table in a silver frame. Emelye looked so happy, and yet still she was determined to go away....

Over the rolling country roads of France they sped, past broad fields of golden maize, and green pastures where cattle and sheep grazed. They crossed low stone bridges and tunneled down through tiny villages, with small apple orchards on the edge and rude houses and barns situated so close to the road one could practically reach out and touch them. So quickly did these hamlets vanish behind them, Elizabeth was compelled to swivel round and peer through the rear auto window for one final glimpse. She was intrigued that people might be born in such a place and live out their lives without venturing past its boundaries. Somehow this evoked in her a rare feeling of tranquility.

Occasionally they passed a great white crucifix along the side of the highway, anchored in a pile of stones. Each time Elizabeth saw one of these, she felt torn. Women who entered convents never married. Their lives were devoted to that figure on the cross. Was this really what she wanted? Mightn't it be fun to fall in love like Emelye? Yet of course, it could only be fun if the one she fell in love with loved her in return, and that would never happen.

One afternoon, the sunny sky abruptly became black as night, from an approaching storm. Soon the rain beat down with such violence that Father was forced to pull off the road. After a few minutes of sitting there, waiting, they were startled to see a dark hulking figure appear at Elizabeth's window, knocking desperately upon the glass.

Elizabeth's heart froze. "Let the poor fellow in," Father urged. Feeling uncertain, she unlatched her door. As she slid across the seat towards Emelye, the man tossed his wet kit bag on the floor then stepped inside, shedding water as if he were a huge wet dog. Apparently he had not washed lately, for the stench of his body was overpowering.

He sank down and removed his soaked felt hat, revealing a head of dark, matted hair. *"Merci beaucoup!"* Elizabeth and Emelye exchanged a glance, and Emelye pressed her nose against her shoulder, defending against the man's odor. He wore a dark plaid cape which was very long, and a pair of old boots with wide bands round the tops, their leather scuffed and cracked, and their toes curled up.

He spoke rapidly to Father, *"Parlez-vous français?"* So profuse was his facial hair, one could barely see his mouth moving.

"Oui, je parle en peu français," Father replied modestly. He was actually quite fluent in the language; but he had trouble understanding when it was spoken too rapidly. Briefly the two conversed, then all was quiet. Slowly, Elizabeth's eyes were drawn to the stranger's profile. She had never seen anyone like him, except perhaps upon the stage. His figure seemed to charge his surroundings with energy. His nose was large and prominent. His long beard, resting on his chest, was thick as moss, and matted like the hair on his head. Abruptly he glanced round at her. His eyes widened, the black pupils piercing her through. The color leapt to her cheeks. He blinked and smiled slightly, as if contrite, then faced forward again.

Reluctantly she looked away, his piercing gaze still imprinted on her mind rather like an image that lingers inside the eye after a camera flashes directly into one's face. What thoughts were concealed behind the Frenchman's fathomless eyes? she wondered. While she could not have put it into words, she sensed something deeply mysterious about him, that he knew something that others did not know. Not that he would use this special knowledge against others; no, he was kind, she was sure because of his smile which seemed to say: *I didn't mean to frighten you.*

As though prompted by the flick of a maestro's baton, the rain abruptly ceased. Late afternoon sun rays burst through the clouds and made a sudden, breathtaking rainbow. The man put on his hat and smiled all round. *"Merci beaucoup! Au revoir."* The door swung open and he stepped out and reached for his kit bag. In moments he had mounted his bicycle nearby, and wheeled away, his cape flapping behind him. *Where are you going?* Elizabeth wondered dreamily, her heart beating hard and fast.

"Ooh, I'm glad he's gone," said Emelye, "he stinks!"

Father and Geneva began to laugh. When Elizabeth moved back to her place, she noticed that in the place where the man had been sitting was a piece of soft wood, apparently in the process of being carved. She lifted it up—it was not much bigger than her hand, with her fingers included—wondering what it was to be. Then she realized it was in the shape of a cross. But the wood was humped high in the center, like a mountain. Was the figure of Christ to be carved there?

"Here, look what the man left behind!" she cried, handing it over Geneva's shoulder.

Geneva ceased giggling, took it from her and examined it. "Oh dear, maybe we should try and catch up with him," she said. Father was just pulling out onto the road.

"I suppose," he said, regretfully. They were far from the village of Falaise, where they were to spend the night, and it was nearly five o'clock.

As Geneva handed the cross back to Elizabeth, Emelye said, "It's just an ugly old piece of wood."

"Yes, but only think of what it was becoming!" said Elizabeth. "Perhaps it was to be his great masterpiece."

Now they drove on for some distance through the French countryside, the main highway intersected again and again by narrow lanes which presumably led to tiny villages dotting the landscape. They saw no sign of the Frenchman. "He could be anywhere by now," said Father, frustrated.

"Perhaps he meant to leave the cross, as a gift," Elizabeth mused.

"Why would he leave something that isn't even finished?" Emelye asked.

"I don't know," said Elizabeth, remembering her sense that he had some secret knowledge. It was almost as if he somehow knew her, in a way that no one else did, or ever would. *He wanted me to have this cross.*

Finally, they encountered a long caravan of hay wagons ahead. Young men and women sat in a row in caps and kerchiefs, with their feet dangling off the back, singing merrily. One could not see round the caravan, and despite much horn-honking they would not allow Father to pass, which annoyed him very much for he was afraid he may have missed the road to Vire, where he was supposed to have made his turn. Geneva unfolded the Michelin map, to see if she could pinpoint where they were. Emelye held the torch for her to read by.

"Father, if we do not find the man, may I keep the cross for my own?" Elizabeth asked.

"I don't see why not," he said, absently.

As they drove on, Elizabeth was convinced that a kind of miracle had taken place, that through the Frenchman she had received a sign post to guide her towards her future, much like the white crucifixes guided pilgrims along their way through France. Perhaps her life had been spared for a purpose, and in fulfilling that purpose she would be redeemed of her sin.

She stroked the soft wood of the unfinished work of art. How warm it was as she held it, as though alive, and waiting....

CHAPTER 11

Francine Tremont stepped out of the lift on the fourth floor of *Hôtel Le Bristol* and made her way down the long corridor, checking the numbers posted on the doors, the press of her feet upon the deep blue plush carpet as soundless as cat paws. She had long since learned to survive by her wits, and today her instinct told her that in a few minutes from now she would come away from Monsieur Selby's luxurious hotel suite with a check in her hand. Having denied through his solicitor that he possessed her jewelry, the astute business-man would surely recognize the benefit of helping her: after all, the investment would be no more than what her jewelry was worth, and in the long term, he would become a little richer.

After all, Jane would not have lied to her mother, not after she got her acquitted of the charge of murdering her father William, in 1918. Following the trial, Jane said, *"I'm sure I could never repay you for all you've done, Mummy."* Francine suggested she share some of the wealth she inherited. *Mais non!* Jane only smiled vaguely. *"Well then, perhaps you could return to me the jewelry locked up in William's safe, when I divorced him,"* she said. As she described the necklace of seven matched pearls linked with diamond scallops, and the earrings with diamond clusters and pearl drops, Jane shook her head doubtfully. *"Ah, surely you could not forget how dramatically they stood out when I wore them with my black velvet gown?"* *"No, Mummy, I remember you best wearing white. The effect was positively shattering."* Francine did not know what Jane meant by the remark, or the way her eyes burned when she uttered it. She would not degrade herself by begging. Besides, she was not desperate for money in those days, with Paul Silva her companion. She was desperate now, *incontestablement!* But wasn't it lucky? She still had Jane's letter:"Good news: I have discovered your jewelry! It must be quite valuable by now. I shall return it to you, only please verify your address."

William Tremont did not marry a penniless waif, *pas du tout!* Francine had her own money, set aside, beyond the reach of his greedy hands when she divorced him, except of course for her jewelry that was, unfortunately, locked in the wall safe to which only he knew the combination. Just as she was about to spend the last of her inheritance, she discovered Paul. For many years they were inseparable. An economist by training, and well-versed in European law, Paul enjoyed *une alliance* with members high up in the Italian Socialist Party, and after Mussolini came into power and they wisely fled to Paris, he quickly cultivated friends who were well-placed in the French Parliament. He always had money and they lived very well—he owned a lovely villa, surrounded by gardens and an olive grove, in Diano San Pietro; and later in Paris he had an apartment in *La Montparnasse*. Silva had a passion for expensive automobiles: Mercedes, Daimlers, Fiats—he would drive one until he was bored, then sell it and buy another. Even now, if she closed her eyes she could see him behind the wheel of his sleek automobile, tearing down the road as though he owned it, and woe be to the person unlucky enough to get in his way! He would wear a red silk scarf knotted at his throat and a black hat with a wide brim slanted forward on his head, his dark hair curling round the nape of his neck. She would sit beside him, savoring the wind on her face and the envious looks on the faces of others they sped past. And travel! Lucerne, Monte Carlo, Venice, Barbados—they were always going somewhere stylish, with gay parties of friends. Coco Chanel taught her how to dress. She purchased hundreds of frocks; and as to hats, gloves, handbags and jewelry, there was no end. Paul paid all the bills. *Ah, c'était le bon temps!*

Francine never knew precisely where Paul's money came from, but what did it matter as long as it continued to flow freely? She should have insisted they marry, for then she would have had some leverage when eventually Paul lost interest. More and more, she heard rumors of other women, and once or twice she caught him in lies. She clawed his face until it bled, beat him about the head, then took him back when he begged her. How she adored being begged...and Paul did it so charmingly! Finally, when the stock market collapsed, he married a woman half his age, with a secure fortune. What a shock! She spat in his face and walked away. To get by, she sold most of her beautiful clothes. Meantime, she was forced to find a job.

She went to work for Monsieur Zachary, waiting on wealthy customers in his small *boutique de mode*. There she was working when word came that her daughter had died in an auto crash. If only she'd had Jane's letter in her hand when she attended her funeral! But by then she had moved from Milan to Paris, and again, from Paul's apartment in *La Montparnasse* to a tiny street off *rue St. Germain*, and it took months for Jane's letter, posted shortly before her death, to reach her. Then she had to scrimp and save from her small earnings to hire *un avocat* to write to Tony Selby and demand he fulfil Jane's promise. Finally in February of 1932 an inquiry was despatched, including a copy of Jane's letter. The answer soon arrived, not from M. Selby but from his solicitor: No record was found of the existence of her jewelry. A lie! Having acquired all her daughter's wealth, was Tony Selby not rich enough, without stealing from her?

But what could she do about it? Then this summer, Monsieur Zachary said, "One must think ahead, eh? Times are getting hard. A little less business this year than last, and who knows about the future? So! I will find a buyer for the shop while I can, and emigrate to America. I have relatives there. I am afraid you must find other employment, Madame Tremont." He shrugged helplessly.

You are a Jew, and you are afraid of what that Jew-hater in Germany will do with all the power he is accruing, Francine reasoned. Quickly she thought ahead. With herself alone to support, the shop could survive until the economy improved. "I know someone—*un homme d'affaires, très riche…anglais*—he may be willing to set me up to buy the shop. Just give me a little time, eh?"

Through Paul she had made the acquaintance of many people with connections, even in London. Someone would give her a room for a couple of days, so that she could call on Tony Selby.

Magnifique! She had observed, walking through the lobby of the *William & Mary* with its dark polished wood floor and scarlet and gold carpet runners, its richly carved wainscoting and doorways. A huge oriental urn holding fresh flowers sat on an onyx table in the center, and high above was a splendid glass rotunda. *Mon Dieu!* Everything Tony Selby touched turned into money. *Even when others are in want, he is not. He owes me, and he can afford to pay.*

She found her way to his office and waited at his secretary's desk while she finished talking on the telephone. On the wall behind her desk was a large framed photograph, taken in the theatre lobby: Tony Selby in a tuxedo, an attractive wavy-haired woman on his arm in an evening gown, an orchid corsage, and a wedding band; a tall, affable-looking man wearing eyeglasses, and the bird-like secretary in a dark lace gown and a string of pearls, her hair swept up in curls. At the bottom was a plaque which read: *Opening Night at the* William & Mary–*February 12, 1932.* Little more than a year after Jane's death, and

Monsieur Selby was already remarried. "May I help you?" the secretary was saying now.

Unfortunately the tiresome woman recognized her name. Mr. Selby was out, she said, handing her his solicitor's card. But Francine concealed herself and waited for the inevitability of the secretary's lunch hour, and when she saw the tidy woman pass by in her hat and gloves, she slipped back into the office and scanned the appointment diary on her desk. *Voila!* A motor trip through France beginning the first of September, from Le Havre: Caen...Cherbourg...St. Lo...Falaise...Alencon...Chartres.... Then at last: "Paris on the 7th...return on the 10th." Francine looked up with a smile. She had only to locate M. Selby in Paris—a small matter if one was familiar with the habits of wealthy people....

It was their last full day in Paris, a beautiful autumn day under a blue sky marbled with thin white clouds. The trees were turning red and golden, and a chilly wind sent curly dried leaves swirling in the air and banking against the curbs and lampposts. While Tony and Elizabeth and Emelye went shopping and sightseeing, Geneva kept an appointment at Jean Patou's fashion salon on *rue Saint-Florentin*, where dress models, tall and wispy as poplars, streamed across oriental rugs, their images reflected in full-length mirrors with lavishly carved gilt frames. Today she was to have her first fitting for an elegant cerise-colored silk velvet gown, with beaded bodice and hem. The gown was for a mid-January opening and cast party. It was discreetly designed to accommodate her pregnancy.

Beautiful gowns were part of the life Geneva and Tony led in London—the cost of doing business in a very glamourous profession. Thanks to the large household staff at No. 12 Norfolk Square, with Mrs. Briscoe at the head, they hosted elegant dinner parties in the dining room, and musical evenings in the drawing room with its elegant crystal chandelier, sumptuous frieze and white marble floor. They had small groups of friends over for Sunday brunch in the narrow strip of garden behind the townhouse, seated around a wicker table in the pleasant shade of a cherry tree. On evenings when they weren't attending a play at one theatre or another, they dined leisurely at a fine restaurant, and often went dancing till two in the morning—what used to be their work had become their pleasure.

Most of Geneva's visits to London were brief. After three or four days she would kiss her husband goodbye at Paddington Station and board the train for Bodmin, feeling an almost physical loss as she was forced outside the radius of his vitality and the warmth of his love. Yet within hours she would be kissing her children hello, basking in their love, and slowing down to the rhythms of country life, clad in a well-worn skirt and blouse, and comfortable shoes. Always she thought of changing her clothes as an act of changing her perspective. Life in London was exciting alright—while there, she was as intoxicated with it as anyone else, and she would do everything in her power to help Tony succeed in his career. But it was here at Clearharbour that her life was *real*; here was the fulfilment of all her dreams. Her greatest thrill was when Tony walked up the drive with his suitcase.

Upon the conclusion of her dress fitting, Geneva returned to their suite at *Hôtel Le Bristol* where she took a long soaking bath in the deep white marble tub, and dressed for the evening—they were to dine at *La Coupole*. Having ordered a carafe of coffee for her and Tony, and one of chocolate for the children, she filled her cup and stood before one of the tall, sunny windows in the sitting room, admiring the colorful garden below with its splashing fountain, columned arbor and winding gravel path—But someone was at the door. She put down her coffee and went through the small vestibule to answer.

Only a moment lapsed before Geneva realized that the slight woman with blond hair and steel blue eyes was Francine Tremont: Tony had not exaggerated when he said she looked remarkably like Jane. Geneva felt a little wary, as you would feel if a shady relative whom you rarely encountered and who had no known address, appeared on your doorstep unannounced. How did Francine find out they were in Paris, and where they were staying? More to the point: What did she want from them?

Francine recognized the woman from the photograph she had seen in M. Selby's office. Her eyes ranged over her figure clad in a slim lime green dress with a high neckline, long dolman sleeves and a calf-length skirt with pleated inserts—a Jean Patou design, she was pretty sure. And the scent of her perfume confirmed it: Patou's exquisite *Joy*. So this was Madame Selby—and redhaired! Unfortunately redheads were often difficult. But time would tell. "I am Francine Tremont," she said. "I wish to see Monsieur Tony Selby."

"I'm afraid my husband is out at the moment," the woman said with a strained look.

So—*une americaine*. "Then I shall come in and wait, *s'il vous plait*. There is a matter I wish to discuss with him."

Whatever Francine wanted, Geneva knew that Tony would resent her intrusion. Yet perhaps it would be better to let him deal with her. Reluctantly she moved aside. Francine stepped in.

CHAPTER 12

Geneva watched as Francine swept by with the poise and confidence of a dress model, her head held high and her shoulders erect, her hips thrust slightly forward. Her ensemble was very chic—a deep blue suit with a straight skirt, a double-breasted jacket with padded shoulders, large gold buttons and a stand-up collar; and a small dark blue hat with a narrow brim. The seams of her stockings were perfectly straight on legs that were thin and boyish, like Jane's. Yet her black suede pumps were badly rundown, as if they had trudged for many miles. How very odd, thought Geneva, when she had taken such care to dress smartly.

Geneva wondered if Francine was aware Tony despised her. And, for that matter, how would Elizabeth react toward the grandmother who had not bothered to visit her while she lay in critical condition after the auto crash? Or did Elizabeth know about that?

Now Francine paused in the center of the sitting room, winking up at the small crystal chandelier. Slowly she pivoted around, her eyes taking in the elegant damask drapes in a floral print, the period tables and chairs arranged on an oriental rug, and finally resting on the Dresden urn filled with roses, peonies and irises, sitting on an ornate hand-painted console. She turned to Geneva. *"Elle est très belle, la chambre! Et chère, n'est-ce pas?"* she said with one eyebrow hiked. Her voice was low and gravelly, and her breathing sounded wheezy. Geneva had a fleeting thought that she was in need of expensive medical treatment, and had come begging for money.

"I'm afraid I don't speak French," she said. Well, they could not just stand here till Tony returned. She gestured toward one of two damask chairs with a low table between them, and sat down in the other.

Francine lowered herself gracefully into her chair, clasped her ankles demurely to one side and removed her gloves, placing them inside the envelope-style handbag on her lap. She looked up, her cold blue eyes meeting and holding Geneva's—Jane's eyes precisely; Geneva would never forget being fixed in that haughty gaze, the night they met.

Now Francine spied the beverage tray, placed on a small dining table. A silver coffee urn, porcelain chocolate pot, and fine china cups and saucers sat on a starched white doily along with four goblets of water. A cut crystal bud vase with a fresh pink rose completed the exquisite array. She looked at Geneva out the corner of her eye. "I'm sure you won't mind my imposing, but a little something to drink would be very nice," she said.

Geneva did mind. Still, at least it would help pass a little time until Tony got here. "Some water? Coffee?"

Ah, but no! Francine would see how far she could push Madame Selby. With a girlishly wicked look, she asked, "What is in the porcelain pot?"

"Chocolate."

Francine clasped her hands in delight. *"Oh, j'adore le chocolat!* May I?"

Reluctantly Geneva rose and poured a cup for her, feeling Francine's eyes upon her, despising herself for not having refused on principle. As she turned from the tray, the steaming cup of chocolate in her hand, Francine withdrew her cigarette case from her handbag. "I'd prefer that you not smoke," she said sharply. The only thing she didn't like about Paris was the unremitting cigarette smoke in every public thoroughfare. Not that London was much better. She wasn't about to put up with Francine puffing away in her face.

It was demeaning to be rebuffed, like receiving one of William's sudden and unexpected blows, and for a moment Francine indulged in the fantasy of Madame Selby being thrown back against the table as a bullet pierced her forehead, the cup of chocolate spilling to the floor. "Very well," she said agreeably, returning the case to her handbag. Accepting the steaming cup, she looking chummily into Geneva's face, then took a long savoring sip, her eyelids fluttering. She daintily replaced the cup in its saucer.

A glimpse of the bright red lipstick stain on the rim of Francine's cup recalled to Geneva's mind the sickening image of Jane imprinting her red-stained lips upon the mirror in her room the day she committed suicide: a narcissistic kiss goodbye. How much of Jane's evil was inherited not from her father but from the woman who had now barged in on their lives?

When Geneva sat down, Francine leaned near, her eyes mirthful. "You may be curious—how I managed to find you here."

Geneva waited.

Francine took another sip of chocolate, then placed the cup and saucer on the small table. "*Le Café des Etoiles*—just as the name suggests—is a favorite place for *les célébrités*." She drew her chin back. "Why, do you know? One night several years ago I saw your American film star Joan Crawford arrive in a red Lagonda, and step out, thin as a reed, dressed in white from head to toe," she said, one hand sweeping dramatically from the top of her head to her feet. She kissed her fingers. "*Très élégante!*" She waited, her eyes bright, like a child watching a circus parade.

Le Café des Etoiles was the place where Tony first saw acrobatic exhibition dancing performed years ago, though it was now strictly a restaurant—and a pricey one—with no floor shows. Geneva and Tony and the girls had dined there on Thursday night. They sat outside to lessen the impact of the cigarette smoke, and so that Elizabeth and Emelye could watch the *Citroën* light show on the Eiffel Tower, within view of their table. Had Francine been there also, spying on them? "And you saw us there?"

She shook her head, frowning. "*Non! Pas du tout!* I never go there anymore. It is much too expensive for me. Wasn't it lucky? Society columnists are always looking for tidbits of news—you know what I mean. A successful producer like your husband—" She shrugged. "Just look what I found yesterday!" she said, reaching inside her handbag. She handed a small newspaper clipping to Geneva. She watched her face anxiously.

Geneva had only just located Tony's name among the mystifying French words, and the name of the restaurant, when a key turned in the door. Both women turned to look. Whistling a cheery tune, Tony pushed it open. Geneva's heart contracted. He had needed this holiday badly, and all week he had felt happy and carefree. Now Francine would spoil it by making a scene. Why had she let her in? At least she could spare their daughters. She would retire to her bedroom and take them with her.

Emelye was the first to pass through the small vestibule. "Mom, we're back," she called out. "We brought presents for Grandmother and Grandfather, and Aunt Nellie and—" Her voice broke off when she spotted the stranger. Francine fixed the child in the pink corduroy pinafore and long stockings with a curious gaze, then she turned to Geneva with a look of cunning that immediately aroused Geneva's protective instinct. "This is our daughter Emelye," she said, "Emelye, dear, this is"—hesitating, "—Madame Tremont."

Just then Elizabeth entered the room. At the sight of her grandmother, she froze in her steps, her mouth slightly open. Francine affected an innocent smile, stumped for the moment: What was the little girl's name?

Tony was behind Elizabeth, toting two shopping bags. Seeing Francine, he put the bags down. "How dare you barge in on my family," he said icily. "My solicitor made things quite clear, I'm sure."

Tony had contacted Craig Muggeridge about Francine? thought Geneva, alarmed.

But just in time, Francine remembered her granddaughter's name. One must make a good impression. She was glancing at Tony, her finger raised. "*Pardon, s'il vous plait*, but I have come on another matter—Elizabeth? Is it my granddaughter? What a surprise! *Viens-tu, ma chère!*" She said to the child, her voice a caress. She held out her arms.

Elizabeth glanced at Tony, then at Francine, her cheeks bright, her eyes luminous.

"Never mind," said Tony, "now, you and Emelye go to your room, please, and close the door."

Elizabeth stood rooted to the floor, looking from one to the other. "Go along," he said, his voice edgy.

"Let's play with our new dolls," Emelye urged. While in Alençon, they had purchased Brittany dolls with fancy *coiffes* and colorful dresses and aprons, for all three daughters. Emelye pulled hers out of its box every chance she got.

Reluctantly, Elizabeth followed Emelye toward their bedroom, looking over her shoulder at her grandmother as if she could not force her eyes away. Geneva now felt reluctant to abandon Tony, and besides, she was eager to find out the nature of Francine's business. As her daughters passed by, she watched Francine's face: Her eyes followed Elizabeth's uneven pace and black stockings, her upper lip crimped in revulsion as if she beheld a freak. Recovering herself, she looked at Geneva, flashing a smile. The smile was so sudden, so false, it was as if her brightly painted mouth had been slit open. This was the woman who abandoned her child, like an animal abandons the sickly among her young.

At last the door closed. Francine opened her handbag and reached inside, then glanced toward Geneva, pursed her lips, and shut it again. Her fingers were shaking. How old was she? Geneva wondered. Close to fifty? Probably no older.

"Well then, what *do* you want?" Tony demanded.

Francine fluttered her fingers dismissively. With a glance at Geneva, she said, "Ah, perhaps my jewelry will turn up one day, *d'accord?* But, in the meantime, I have come to propose a business opportunity. I've a chance to buy a little boutique on *La Rive Gauche...*" As she talked, her eyes lit up, her words rushed out; the color in her cheeks heightened. "...the owner is eager to sell and would like for me to have it. I know all of his customers. A few thousand francs—what would that be to you? I could repay you, with interest.

"What do you say?"

Geneva was startled to learn that Francine apparently had the crazy notion Tony was concealing some jewelry that belonged to her. And Tony had taken her seriously enough to notify his solicitor. She found herself hoping Tony would consider Francine's business proposal, for she had a very strong intuition that it would be a mistake to further antagonize her.

She was dismayed to hear him respond without a pause, "I am not interested." Even more than the words, the glacial look on his face told her there would be no negotiating.

CHAPTER 13

Francine was retracing her steps down the plush blue carpet edged in gold fili-
gree that lined the hallway, her face burning with rage, ashes dropping from
her cigarette. *Quelle arrogance!* Tony Selby hardly listened to her proposal.

"But I would think you would see that you owe me some help—at least,
until my jewelry is recovered," she pointed out. "I got nothing from my marriage to William, you know, he saw to that. And when Jane died—"

"Took her life and tried to take Elizabeth's along with it," he interrupted
rudely. "I owe you nothing. Now get out, or I shall call the *concierge*."

At the door she turned and said defiantly, "I assure you, Monsieur Selby, I
will find other resources."

She despised him no less than William, who had made ridiculous accusa-
tions just for the pleasure of striking her so hard that she flew across the floor,
her face bruised for days. And Paul, changing the lock on the door of their
Paris apartment when he replaced her with his new wife. *Mon dieu!* Tony Selby
had extorted all she had left that was valuable, then kicked her out of his way as
if she were a dog. She took a drag off her cigarette, threw back her head and
exhaled. *Laisse tomber, merde!* Just as she informed him, she would find other
resources. Already there was a change in the air, eh? *Le vent a tourné!* She could
feel it in her bones. A new set of friends. New opportunities if one took care to
be in the right place at the right time. Oh yes, one day she would spit in the
face of Tony Selby and his wife, and his crippled daughter—ach—*répugnant!*
And the other one, the blond. How long was Tony married to Jane before he
was bedding his current wife? Not long, from the looks of the girl. Francine
stepped up to the ornamental lift made of wrought iron and brass, and pressed
the button so hard she could feel its imprint in her thumb.

No sooner had Tony shut the door and returned to the sitting room than Elizabeth hurried in from her bedroom. She had been eavesdropping. Her flaming cheeks gave her away. "Has she gone?"

Tony frowned. "As you see."

"Did you tell her to go?"

"Yes," he said firmly.

Elizabeth stared at the door, her mouth quavering. "You had no right. She is my grandmother. I shall go and find her."

"You'll do nothing of the sort. You are being very insolent. Perhaps you ought to go back to your room and think this over."

Elizabeth looked at the door again, miserably, for all the while, her grandmother was getting farther and farther away. *"My mother walked out on me when I was not much older than you are...."* She had so many questions to which her grandmother may have answers. Yet she could not run fast enough to catch her. She could not run at all. She turned back to her father, glaring, her hands drawn into tight fists at her sides. "Sometimes I—I *hate* you!" she cried. She fled to her bedroom and shut the door.

Tony stood staring after her, his heart pounding. Vaguely he wondered why Elizabeth was so adamant about speaking to her grandmother, whom she had never even met, but what astonished him was how quickly and violently her bitterness towards him had rushed from her lips. It was just as he had always believed: she had hated him since the day of the auto crash. And finally he had crossed her about something important, forcing her feelings out in the open. Yet—he rallied slightly—perhaps finally uttering the words would wrench her from the past so that she could move on. Not that it made him feel any less diminished....

Geneva leaned her head back against her chair and brought a trembling hand to her forehead, a moan escaping her lips. She could hardly believe that Elizabeth was capable of such cruelty.

Tony glanced at her. Forgetting all else for the moment, he hastened to her side. He touched her shoulder gently. "Are you alright?"

His voice was trembling. Geneva could have wept for him. She nodded. "I'm so sorry. This is partly my fault—I should not have let Francine through the door."

"Never mind," he said sweetly. "Please, please, don't let anything upset you. Just forget it." He knelt down and pressed her belly with a kiss, then laid his head against her breast and slipped his arms around her waist. She could feel his swift heartbeat against her.

"Elizabeth didn't mean what she said," she told him softly.

Tony did not look up. She wondered if there were tears in his eyes. She kissed the nape of his neck. The hair had grown out a little there. It was time for a hair cut, she thought, wishing to recapture the simple day-to-day things, the normalcy of their lives. "I love you," she said.

For a while Tony went on holding Geneva, silently. The very sound of her heartbeat was encouraging. They were together; that was what really counted. Finally he said, "You know what I think of, every time I put my arms around you and hold you like this? I think of your coming to London again, to have the baby. Oh, I can hardly wait!"

Geneva knew he was trying to revive his spirits, and perhaps hers as well.

The period surrounding the birth of Elvira had been the very best time of their marriage. Night after night as her time of delivery approached, they slept cuddled as close to each other as her growing size and increasing discomfort would allow. Geneva went into labor at noon on a Saturday, and Tony held her hand anxiously in the taxi, all the way to the hospital. She was not a bit worried, in spite of her difficult pregnancy with Emelye. Elvira was born with no complications, shortly after six p.m., and by seven Tony was holding his tiny daughter in his arms, his eyes moist with gratitude, then handing her into Geneva's arms to nurse at her breast. They could barely contain their joy that what they had been denied at the birth of Emelye was finally given them. And now they dreamed of another such time of sharing.

Tony looked up into her face. "When will you come?"

"Early in February," she promised. The baby was due in March. Emelye and Elizabeth would stay with their grandparents as before; Elvira would come to London with her mother.

He laid his head against her breast again. "Mmm...good," he said.

Delicately, Geneva returned to the subject uppermost in their minds. "I know that Elizabeth loves you with all her heart," she insisted, and her voice caught, "but something is eating away at her. I suspect—after what just happened—she believes Francine can help make sense of it."

Tony looked up in surprise. "Well, she is mistaken, that's all," he said and rose to his feet, his defenses up.

In the two years since their honeymoon, Geneva had put off renewing her plea that he talk to Elizabeth about Jane. She knew he would resist, and besides, nothing had occurred to provoke her. Tony and Elizabeth seemed to get on just fine together, and she had begun to believe the passage of time might solve their problems, if she just let them alone.

Yet now she admitted to herself that was wishful thinking. "But I bet you can say something that will at least let her know you care about how she feels. She needs that most of all, I imagine," she urged, "and that may just help to put an end to this—this friction between you."

He shrugged. "I doubt it. But alright, I shall give it a try. First, though, I think I can use a gin and tonic. How about you—glass of sherry, perhaps?"

She shook her head.

After he placed the order with room service, she asked, "What's all this about Francine's jewelry?"

He came and sat down in the chair beside hers, and let out a breath. "On the day the *William & Mary* opened, I received a letter from her attorney enclosing a reproduction of a letter to her from Jane, dated shortly before Jane's suicide. In it she claimed to have found some jewelry that Francine left behind when she divorced William, and that he swore was not in his possession when she tried to retrieve it through a legal process. Francine described the jewelry in detail, but I had never seen it. I contacted Craig Muggeridge—he has all the documents from William's estate—"

"But why didn't you tell me?" she demanded, an uneasy memory of the crisis that drove them apart years ago taking hold.

"I didn't want to spoil the evening for you. In any case, Craig soon put Francine's attorney on notice that there was no such jewelry listed in an inventory of William's estate."

Geneva wondered what effect the receipt of that letter had on Tony's enjoyment of one of the biggest nights of his life. "Do you think Jane was lying?"

"I don't know. But it would seem more likely, if the jewelry ever existed, William sold it and pocketed the money."

"How much was it supposed to be worth?"

"Francine said it had once been appraised at £5,000—though the document also had been left behind. Said she would settle for that amount, though by now the jewelry was surely worth a great deal more."

Geneva blew out her breath. "And Jane wrote her mother—"

"—Right after I served her with divorce papers."

Their eyes met. "So you think Jane had made up her mind to take her life, and she was just trying to leave a little more trouble behind."

"It wouldn't surprise me."

"God, will we ever be through with her?" Geneva moaned.

Tony caught her hand. "Sh, now, don't upset yourself. Regardless of what Jane intended, her mother is powerless to do anything more than annoy us," he assured her.

Geneva was not so sure. "You don't think it would be a good idea to give Francine a little help—I mean, just to get rid of her?" she asked.

Tony released her hand. His jaw stiffened. "Look, apart from the fact that I refuse to be bullied by that disgusting woman, I have no idea who she's involved with politically. I don't want our names linked with hers, don't want our check going through her hands. The way things are developing in Europe, it's too risky."

"You mean, because of Hitler and the Nazi party?" Geneva asked, a hollow feeling at the pit of her stomach.

"And his crony Mussolini—you will remember, all those years when Francine lived with her boyfriend in Italy, then fled when Mussolini came into power—I should think it likely that he had political friends. And where is he now? He must have had money. Otherwise, what has she been living on, for all these years? Perhaps he ditched her at some point. On the other hand, perhaps he got into some sort of trouble. One cannot be sure."

It was the first time Geneva had been forced to entertain the possibility that the intrigue stirring in Europe could eventually involve England. She felt very unsafe, and was thankful they were going home tomorrow. She had the mother's instinct to gather her flock around her.

Emelye soon grew bored playing with her new doll and returned to the parlor. Elizabeth had not joined her in her play. She was too upset, and besides, she thought playing with dolls, making up conversations between them, was rather silly. She lay in bed, staring at the ceiling. How she dreaded the moment when she would face her father again! How could she have told him that she hated him? Perhaps he would never speak to her again. Perhaps he would send her away to a boarding school, to banish her from his sight.

When, after a long while, he tapped on the door and opened it, her heart raced with dread. He came in and sat across from her, on the edge of Emelye's bed. Immediately she began to sob. "I'm sorry, Father! I didn't mean what I said, truly I didn't. Forgive me, please!" She bit her lip.

Tony wished he could fully believe her. "It's alright," he said, his voice tender. "Look, you need to understand that your grandmother does not care a bit for you. When you were in hospital, and she came to Bodmin for your mother's burial, she did not even visit you. You don't want anything to do with that woman, ever. She is no good, remember that."

But it wasn't her love Elizabeth was seeking. She raised up on the pillows. "Why did my grandmother leave my mother, when she was just a little girl? Was it because my mother was bad, and she wanted to punish her?"

Tony was aware that Elizabeth had done a great deal of thinking about her mother's hatefulness. But why this particular question? Remembering Geneva's advice, he said patiently, "I don't know much of anything about Francine, and little more about your mother, when she was young. She was nearly grown before I really got to know her, for I was away at school. I gather Francine went away because she was too miserable to stay with her husband, even for Jane's sake." He reached out a hand and gently smoothed the hair back from Elizabeth's forehead.

She remembered how he would do that when her mother had been cruel to her, saying that she mustn't be upset at anything her mother said or did, for he loved her more than anything, that she was the most special person in all the world, and that was what counted. Again she was seized with guilt for lashing out at him. She bit her lip again. "But why was she miserable? Because he didn't love her?"

Tony hesitated. Here they were, already at the point in conversation beyond which he must not go. "Perhaps. William was a dreadful man. No one liked him. And that's all I know," he said in a tone of finality that had become very familiar to Elizabeth since her mother died.

Still, she was emboldened by the unusual amount of patience that he had shown since they began talking. "Dreadful—how?" she persisted.

He shrugged. "Mean. Possessive," he said, then wished he had left off the second descriptive word. Thankfully, Elizabeth did not beg him to explain.

"Alright," she said at last. He kissed her forehead, looked longingly into her eyes for a moment, then rose from the bed and walked out.

As he shut the door behind him she thought: it was not really alright at all, for she was no closer to understanding what made her mother so hateful, or when, than ever she had been. She was still trapped in Dartmoor Forest. Perhaps she would be always.

PART II

1936–1940

CHAPTER 14

One fine spring morning Geneva answered the door at Clearharbour to find Cynthia waiting on the other side. "I'm on my way to luncheon at Lanhydrock, and I thought I'd stop by for a little chat, if you aren't terribly busy," she said breezily. Cynthia had become friends with Lady Robartes as they served together on various charitable committees. Their current project was aid for Cornish children whose families—like many all over England—were queuing up in bread lines these days. They needed not only food, but clothing, medical care, optical care and even school supplies.

Geneva was intrigued. Cynthia wasn't inclined to stop by for a round of idle chit-chat. Shifting baby Chris a little further up on her shoulder, she invited her mother-in-law into the sitting room and asked Mrs. Greaves to bring them a cup of tea.

The years had accrued handsomely on Cynthia. If she had grown more matronly, her silver hair, high cheekbones and dignified bearing commanded respect as surely as in the days when she was a sleek brunette, negotiating deals with Broadway producers for her talented clients. She looked radiant today in a chic black dress, cut on the bias, a black silk scarf with a bright yellow and red geometric design draped around her neck, and a black straw hat with a broad brim and a cluster of bright red cherries on the side. All of which made Geneva feel especially frumpy in her button down gingham dress. Happily, she and Tony were realizing their dream of filling the house with children. Elvira was now three, and Andy—Tony's namesake and heir—was two years old. Christiaan Sterling, the baby, was born last November. Yet in spite of all the hours Geneva spent out in the studio that Tony had converted from an old farm building, exercising and giving Emelye and Elvira dance lessons, she was still carrying a good ten pounds of excess weight from her last pregnancy. Losing the weight became a little harder with each new child.

Sitting down in a wingback chair by the fireplace, Cynthia held out her arms. Geneva handed Chris to her, hastening to remove the flannel blanket from her shoulder and drape it on Cynthia's. She would die of embarrassment if Chris spit up on Cynthia's garment just when she was on her way to luncheon in the grandest house in the county. "There we are, my sweet," Cynthia cooed, looking fondly into her grandson's eyes. Chris stared in apparent fascination at the bright red cherries on his grandmother's hat brim. Geneva sat down across from Cynthia.

"You'll never believe it!" Cynthia told her. "I've convinced Edward to sail to the States with me. We'll travel around for the whole summer, pay a visit to my brother and his family." Her eyes glowed victoriously, as they used to do when she had just booked a tour for *Sterling & Selby*. Settling into a life in the country, where her roles of wife, mother and grandmother finally coalesced, had mellowed Cynthia to some degree, and smoothed the edges of her personality like those of her figure. However, a part of her still lived for the next obstacle overcome, the next triumph, large or small.

Geneva was amazed as Cynthia went on to describe the busy itinerary in store. Edward was not inclined to do much traveling, and was very fussy when he did. Even a brief jaunt to London required Merton to develop exhaustive lists, and pack two portmanteaus and an assortment of smaller pieces of luggage.

"I'd like to take Emelye and Elizabeth with us," Cynthia said finally, and pecked her grandson's cheek with a decisive kiss. Chris made a grab for the cherries. She stilled his hand and looked at Geneva, her brow lifted in anticipation.

Geneva was taken by surprise, and she felt immediately reluctant. Tony had more leisure in summer than in other seasons, so he spent a lot of time at Clearharbour. Granted, it wasn't all play—he worked out dance routines in the studio, and caught up on paper work in his small home office upstairs. Still, they always took several motor trips, and these drew them closer as a family. Besides, though she didn't like bringing up the subject with Cynthia—she felt like such a failure!—summer was the only time the pressure was off between her and Emelye. All through the school year they battled over Emelye's stubborn refusal to try and improve her grades, which completely baffled Geneva. She was torn between the logical assumption that Emelye would be happier in England if she just applied herself, and the fear that her discontentment was paralyzing her natural abilities. By the time school was out, they both felt bruised and exhausted, and Geneva missed Emelye as if she had been miles away. The long vacation was the only time that she felt her daughter was really present, the only time when they were completely at ease around each other, as they had been when they lived in the Heights. Maybe it was wrong to have so much and yet still long to recapture those days when they lived just for each other, but Geneva often did.

"It's really kind of you, but we've already made plans for several motor trips this summer," she told Cynthia, realizing suddenly that with her in-laws overseas, their plans would change. She had anticipated weaning Chris by the end of May so that she could leave him with them for a few days at a time. Well, they would manage, and frankly she was in no rush to wean Chris. At age five months, both Andy and Elvira seemed impatient to be weaned, straining for independence. However, somehow she and Chris still seemed as one, as if the umbilical cord had not quite been severed.

Noting Cynthia's piqued expression—she still liked organizing affairs as she saw fit—she hastened to assure her, "Tony and I plan to take the whole family overseas one day, when our little ones are older."

Cynthia stroked the back of her grandson's head, covered with dark downy hair. To her delight, Chris showed every early sign that he would resemble the Fournier side of the family. "That's all well and good," she told Geneva, "and yet how soon will 'one day' be? Five, six years? Longer?

"Assuming, that is, we don't wind up in another war."

Geneva did not need reminding of this frightening possibility. More and more, the newspaper headlines loomed like thunderclouds: The League of Nations sanctions against Italy had now driven it into a liaison with Germany, and Mussolini was on the verge of invading Abyssinia. Unfortunately, without the support of the United States, the League seemed ineffectual in halting acts of aggression. Tony had suggested that, if war came, she should go to America and take the children. She flatly refused. The idea of leaving his side—especially during a war—was unthinkable.

Chris began to whimper. To Cynthia he had a way of sounding somewhat panicked whenever he did so, as if he was afraid his mother had vanished off the face of the earth. She handed him back to Geneva, whereupon he was immediately content.

Mrs. Greaves was placing the tea tray on the gate-legged table between them. A widow in her sixties, she had a shock of kinky iron gray hair, round eyes that protruded behind her spectacles, and a fulsome breast behind which beat a generous heart. She had adopted the Selby family as her own brood. "An' I've got some 'thonder and lightnin' too. Why, passin' by Adrian and Dawe's on the way to work this mornin', the smell of 'em waftin' out brought me feet to stand still." Geneva thought with longing of the soft warm bread rolls, filled with cream and drizzled with syrup. The last thing she needed at this point. Luckily the children loved them, so they would soon vanish. Cynthia shook her head, and Geneva asked Mrs. Greaves to save one for Tony, who was coming home tonight.

Heading for the door, Mrs. Greaves rejoined, "I've already put them where Mahster Andy can't reach; he'd rot 'is every last tooth with sweets, given chance." Abruptly she turned. "Oh yes," she began and threw up her hands as if in surprise—this she had a habit of doing whenever a new thought struck her—"Clifton said tell ye he will be here at three with some lomber to replace that rottin' board on the door frame of Mr. Selby's studio." Mrs. Greaves's bachelor son, with whom she lived 'up top town,' in Higher Bore Street, was very much in demand around Bodmin as a carpenter and handyman. He performed any number of small jobs for Geneva, and also served as an occasional chauffeur.

"Alright, thanks Mrs. Greaves," said Geneva.

"Mrs. Greaves is bad about interrupting," Cynthia fumed when the woman was gone.

It's none of your business, thought Geneva. "I know, but she means well," she said. Cynthia was astute at dealing with servants, but Geneva was not. In all her adult life before marrying Tony, she'd never had more help than an occasional cleaning woman one morning a week. She must have gone through half a dozen, none of them lasting very long, for various reasons. If Mrs. Greaves overstepped herself sometimes, well, she also did far more than was expected of her, especially when it came to looking out for the welfare of the children. Geneva adored her. "Besides, she's more like one of the family," she added, and cuddled Chris a little closer.

Cynthia looked fondly at her daughter-in-law now. Her cheeks were rosy and her expression serene as she peered lovingly into the eyes of her child. Geneva was the most devoted mother Cynthia had ever known. She positively radiated with joy in her demanding role of raising three little ones. In a way Cynthia envied her freedom to dote on her young. It wasn't that way for her, unfortunately. But times were different then. Edward was different then….

What Geneva overlooked was that Emelye and Elizabeth had a different set of needs, and—whether or not she would admit it—she could not stretch herself far enough to meet them all. A few motor trips this summer, piled into the car with three babies all demanding attention at once? What could possibly be of less interest to two twelve-year-old girls? She glanced at her watch—time was running out, and besides, she was not given to drawn-out discourse when she knew what was best. Delicately, she pointed out, "My dear, just think how broadening a summer overseas would be for the girls. Elizabeth has never traveled outside the U.K., and Emelye has seen very little of her native country. Nor has she met my brother and his family."

Geneva opened her mouth to protest, but Cynthia continued, "And I'll let you in on a little secret: Edward will enjoy the trip much more if the girls come along, be more open to adventure. So, you see? You'll be doing both of us a great favor. Check with Tony, see what he thinks, promise?"

Even as Cynthia kissed both her cheeks, then sailed out the door, Geneva recognized defeat. She knew Tony would be all for the idea, and besides, Cynthia had managed to make her feel selfish.

As time passed, Emelye's dream of marrying James Younger grew ever more consoling. Many nights when Elizabeth was asleep, she lay there in the dark, kept awake by the wind howling outside as it cut around the high attic room. She hated this sound because it was so creepy, like a haunted house. It wouldn't be so loud if she could shut the window all the way, but Mother said you had to leave a crack because the walls were so thick, and mold would be a problem. Emelye would plug up her ears with her fingers, and imagine herself radiant in her bridal gown, her arm resting on James's, just like her parents on their wedding day. And of course she and James would live in Houston.

"We're so proud of you!" her parents said when she agreed to return to London the first time. They believed she had finally overcome her fears. In truth, the incident at St. Michael's School had taught her she was not safe anywhere in England unless grown-ups she could trust were nearby. When Emelye and her mother and sisters arrived in London on that snowy December day in their heavy coats and mufflers and woolen gloves, Daddy reminded her even before they emerged from Paddington Station that the strange man who forced her to go away with him was no longer in London. Then, patting her arm reassuringly, he said, "Now during the next two weeks, if we should happen to go to a place where you feel frightened, all you have to do is tell us, and we'll leave at once." Even though Emelye knew Daddy was telling the truth about the man's whereabouts, she could never, ever be completely sure that he would not appear. Yet, Daddy's promise made her feel easier, for while she could not put names on any of the places the man had taken her, she knew she would recognize them if she saw them again, and that would be as terrifying as the nightmares she still had on occasion. She was thankful their new London townhouse and all that surrounded it looked very different from Daddy's house in Wilton Place. There were little shops clustered in the corners of Norfolk Square: a newsstand, a greengrocer, a sweet shop, a tobacconist, a place called, "estate agent" with photographs of houses posted in the plate glass windows, and in one corner, a place called a "pub," that she and Elizabeth were not allowed to enter. All the shopkeepers knew her parents and they soon knew her and Elizabeth as well. No one could snatch either of them away from Norfolk Square without being noticed. But just to be sure, at least one of her parents or grandparents, or Mrs. Briscoe, the housekeeper, was always with them when they left the townhouse. Mrs. Briscoe had faded hair, a beak nose, and a plump figure like Aunt Nellie, and she was very kind.

Over the holiday, Emelye saw how happy Elizabeth was in London—almost like her old self, before the auto crash—and she realized how nice her sister had been not to go there until she consented to go.

In Bodmin, whenever Emelye saw the girls from the Barclay Home trouping down the street in their odd-looking hats, with their matron at the rear, or in the pew of St. Petroc's Church on Sundays, she would feel as if a hand were gripping her throat. Their faces wore vacant expressions, but now and then one would smile for some mysterious reason, which was a little scary. Elizabeth said their parents considered them *defective*—like a Christmas toy that didn't work, Emelye thought at once—and sent them away to live like orphans. Mother had told her long ago that after her parents died in a train wreck, she was an orphan, and it was the loneliest time in her life. How could any parent send a child away?

One Saturday in Northey's Pharmacy, long after that frightening day at St. Michael's, Emelye recognized Miss Sloane from behind—the memory of watching her teacher write on the blackboard was still vivid. Her heart shivered then grew hard at the sight of the woman's long, rigid spine, and the tight knot of hair at the back of her head. Sometimes in Emelye's nightmares, the strange man in London became Miss Sloane, forcing her to go up to the attic, spit flying from between her rodent teeth. She did not want to catch sight of Miss Sloane's cruel face in the pharmacy. Mother did not see Miss Sloane, for she was listening to Mr. Northey tell her about a medicine he recommended for Andy's stomachache. Emelye moved close so she could feel her mother's comforting warmth. Presently the teacher walked out, the bell tinkling above the door as though even it was glad that Miss Sloane was gone.

Life at Bodmin Primary School was very different from that at St. Michael's, for both Emelye and Elizabeth. The teachers dare not raise a hand to either of them, for they knew that if they did, their mother would storm up to the school and "make a nasty scene," as Elizabeth put it. Everyone thought this strange, though it was not the only reason she and Elizabeth were set apart. Emelye was unfriendly to her classmates, and if anyone said a cross word to her, she reported it immediately. Therefore, no one trusted her. And Elizabeth was so much further ahead than all the other pupils, and growing more so all the time, only the teachers really knew how to talk to her. Elizabeth read books that other kids her age could not understand. Though she admitted she did not fully grasp the meaning in the big books on philosophy borrowed from Fr. Ogilvie, she read until all hours, and made lists of questions to take along whenever they went to London. Elizabeth once invited Emelye to go with her to visit Fr. Ogilvie. "He'll be your friend, too," she promised. Yet Emelye could not follow their conversation. She wasn't smart enough for Fr. Ogilvie to be her friend.

Emelye's cousin Guy was her only friend in England, and she did not see him as often as she used to, when they were little and she'd sometimes spend the day at Camellia Cottage. In good weather they rode bicycles and flew kites. They picked berries from the many vines along the edge of the shallow brook at the bottom of the hill behind Camellia Cottage, delivering pails of them to Aunt Nellie's kitchen. They climbed up into Guy's tree house where the tiny cabin became a lifeboat sent to rescue someone from drowning, or a fire wagon speeding to save people in a burning house, or an ambulance rushing someone to a hospital. On snowy days they rode sleds down the hill and tugged them back to the top again and again, until Aunt Nellie called them inside to warm up in her cluttered, spicy-smelling kitchen. Even though Guy was several years older than Emelye, he always played with her and he was always kind, like James. And Aunt Nellie made them delicious things to eat, such as the fat, golden brown Cornish pasties that miners carried in their lunch pails.

Now that Guy was on the cricket team and going out with girls in Launceston, he didn't have much spare time. Emelye poured out her heart in letters to Serena and James. If she did not have their letters to look forward to, she would have nothing.

Then one Friday after school, as she and Elizabeth were eating "thunder and lightnings" at the kitchen table, her mother announced they'd been invited to go to America with their grandparents.

"You'll be gone for two months, though, and you will miss out on our vacations together," her mother said discouragingly.

"I don't care. Can we go to Houston and see the Youngers?"

Geneva hesitated for a moment. "I believe Houston is on the itinerary."

Emelye could hardly believe her ears. She flung her arms around her mother's neck, then danced around Elizabeth, clutching her hands. "Oh, you will love it in the Heights! I'll show you where we used to live, and the school I used to go to. And Serena and James live in a great big house with lots of stairs, and a tiny room up in a tower where Serena and I play dolls. And I'm sure we'll go to Studewood Park and Galveston, and Lake Astoria...."

Geneva had not the heart to tell Emelye they would probably not be in Houston long enough to do all the things she was counting on. Perhaps she had no right to feel hurt that their family vacations obviously meant so little to Emelye, but she was. It seemed that as hard as she and Tony tried, they had accomplished little if anything in helping her adjust to life in England. Right now Geneva had an uneasy feeling that sending Emelye on a trip to America would not help matters at all.

CHAPTER 15

It was July 14th. As Emelye stepped off the train, into the sun's glare, she felt the Houston heat and humidity engulf her, but she didn't mind at all.

In moments she was surrounded by her best friends with their healthy summer tans. She listened with delight to their familiar Texas drawls. When Serena hugged her she could feel the soft plump curves of her breasts. Her letters had not exaggerated! Emelye was as flat as the day she was born. She was jealous now, convinced that living in England was stunting her natural development. James was much taller and more handsome than he looked in all those snapshots Willa sent to Mother. He was nearly fifteen years old, practically a man! Emelye drew hearts and flowers in the margins of the letters she wrote him. She always signed them, "Love, Emelye." James didn't answer every letter, and when he did, he wrote only a few lines, signed simply, "James." Would he ever care as much for her as she cared for him? Could she make him? Now he reached out his hand and grinned. "Hey, Emelye, good to see ya!" he said, his teeth bright in his bronzed face. His voice had deepened. It stirred her in a way that was disconcerting, and made her blush. Flinging modesty aside, she threw her arms around his neck. As his arms closed around her, she lay her head against his chest. She heard the strong ticking of his heart. *James will always protect me.* She wished to burrow into him forever.

Willa was holding out her arms. "Save some of that sugar for us!" She had not changed from the way Emelye remembered her. She was still very slender. She wore her hair parted down the side and shorter in back than in front. Emelye hugged Willa tightly, breathing in her familiar gardenia fragrance. Then Rodney was hugging her, lifting her feet right off the pavement. His perspiration bathed her cheek. "Hey, hey! Sweetheart, it's about time you came to see us!" Happy tears filled Emelye's eyes. She was *home.*

Within a few minutes they were squeezing eight people into a six-passenger car. Without argument, Serena sat on James's lap in the back seat. Willa must have set this up beforehand. Emelye wished she could sit on James's lap, but at least she managed to sit right next to him. Elizabeth sat next to her, then Willa.

Grandmother remarked that she had not seen Houston since she moved away in 1924, and she was amazed at the many tall buildings in the skyline. This prompted Rodney—who was proud of Houston and knew everything about it—to say it had changed dramatically in the second half of the 1920's. He drove them around a bit, showing the city off. Emelye was eager to get to the Heights, but she politely kept quiet as Rodney drove up and down the wide thoroughfares, pointing out a stream of buildings starting with the luxurious Sam Houston Hotel near the station, where every room was air conditioned. On Main there was the thirty-seven story Gulf Building that cost six-and-a-half million dollars. The bottom floors were now occupied by the National Bank of Commerce and Sakowitz dry goods store. It looked to Emelye like a great high gift box, with two smaller boxes growing out of it. There was the thirty-two story Neils Esperson Building on Travis, with 214,000 square feet of office space. "Splendid!" Grandfather kept saying. He had never been in a city as new as this, he said. Rodney told him, "The skyline has changed completely from when I was a boy. Of course, there isn't much construction going on nowadays, with the economy so bad, but Houston will spring back again." He made the city sound like a person who is ill and bedridden, but expected to fully recover. They drove past the Houston Public Library on McKinney Avenue, built in the Spanish-Renaissance style, with a tile roof. It was situated far back from the street, with a deep lawn and shade trees in front of it. People were walking in and out the doors, carrying books. Others sat on benches on the lawn, reading. At this point Emelye felt compelled to boast, "The Heights has a library, too. Mother and I used to check out books there."

"That we do," said Rodney, "and—let's see—there's Heights Hospital, over on Ashland Street, and a great big high school with a nice campus—you know, Heights High burned down. Believe it was the year Cynthia moved away."

"I'll be going to Reagan High one day," Serena boasted. "I can't decide if I want to go out for yell leader or be in the Reagan Red Coats—that's the drill team. They perform at half-time at the football games, and march in parades."

"If you don't start studying, you'll never get out of Hamilton," said James, who would enter Reagan as a sophomore this fall.

Willa was leaning toward them, a frown on her face, a finger on her lips.

Emelye wished she could go to Reagan one day. She felt the whole world was passing her by while she was stuck in Bodmin. Bodmin! What a dumb name for a town. She would be ashamed to say that's where she lived to anyone in Houston.

Elizabeth wanted to know if Houston had an art museum. Rodney said it surely did, located a little further south. "May we go there?" she asked, "I do so enjoy art museums! There are many in London and Paris, you know."

Grandmother said that would be fun, and also she'd promised Daddy they would go to the Majestic Theatre where he and Mother performed at the opening in 1923, just so Grandfather and Elizabeth could see the spectacular atmospheric ceiling. Rodney said the Majestic showed high-quality motion pictures now. "Yes, I know," said Grandmother. Emelye wondered why there was a note of sadness in her voice. What could be nicer than going to the picture show?

Then they were turning on to Texas Avenue, and Rodney was pointing out the twenty-two story Petroleum Building, where many oil companies had their offices. Emelye knew the story of the Spindletop oil strike in 1901, right here in Texas. That was what started all the oil companies. She was quite sure nothing that exciting and dramatic had ever happened in England.

Suddenly they were pulling up at the curb of the Rice Hotel, where her grandparents were to stay. While Willa had written to invite them to stay at their house, Grandmother declined, explaining that there were many things in downtown Houston that she remembered from her girlhood, and she wanted to show them to Grandfather. It would be more convenient if they were within walking distance. Emelye overheard Grandmother telling Daddy later, "Edward is too fussy to be a guest in a home without a staff of servants—he'll keep the hotel valet service busy constantly." They stepped out under the lacy black iron arcade that stretched around the hotel, and a porter came to take their many suitcases inside. Emelye was secretly happy that now she would have more of Willa and Rodney's attention. Whenever there were a lot of grown-ups around, all they wanted to do was talk among themselves.

Now they had crossed White Oak Bayou and were driving down Heights Boulevard. A streetcar trundled toward them on the other side of the esplanade, with the number 206 emblazoned on the front. Rodney said there weren't as many streetcar lines as there used to be, and he wasn't sure how much longer they would last. More and more, people relied on buses or owned automobiles. Emelye gazed out the open window through the summer haze, taking in the sight of every familiar house and yard and fence as eagerly as a swimmer who has been under water for a long while emerges and takes in a much-needed, delicious breath of air. Everything was just the same as she remembered—except she had forgotten how big the front porches were. Some stretched from one end of the house front to the other; some wrapped far around the sides. Some had lattice work above, and pots of ferns hanging from them; some had thick columns and rails. In England she never saw front porches like these, where children could sit on the wood floor with their friends playing JAX or tic-tac-toe, or paper dolls, as she and Serena had done; porches that seemed to say, "Welcome to our house!"

Neighbors who used to wave at her and Serena and James as they passed by, and happened to be outside today, waved toward Rodney's familiar blue Oldsmobile. There was Mrs. Myer in her sun hat, a basket on her arm, gathering roses from the bushes along her wood fence. Mrs. Cooley, having paused in her stroll to chat with Mrs. Myer, turned around to wave; up there on his high gallery was Mr. Paine, and there on her tall front steps was Miss Milroy. Emelye grinned and waved "Hello" from the car window; in her heart, she was throwing kisses. "You think they know it's me?" she asked Serena desperately.

"Sure, Sis, course they do," said Serena.

Emelye fell silent for a few moments, letting it all sink in. Then a feeling of tranquility rose from deep inside her: *Here, I was never afraid.*

As Rodney turned into their driveway, Emelye took a long look across the broad, leafy esplanade at the house where she and her mother once lived. A Mr. Gillespie and his invalid wife lived there now. Heavy drapes darkened all the windows except for the oval window in the middle of the second story. A wheelchair ramp led down from the side of the porch, and all the flower beds were gone. Emelye blinked, then looked again. The wide beds of colorful blooming plants and shrubs that used to look so pretty around the porch; the rose garden in the side yard—her mother's pride and joy—all were gone, as if they never existed! She felt a surge of resentment like that she had felt when Miss Sloane made fun of her mother's spelling of the word, "practice." Then she remembered how happy she and her mother were when they lived there. Sure, Mother was happier now that she and Daddy were together in England and had lots of children, but it wasn't fair that she had to give up her happiness for them. She thought of her mother's warm hug and tearful eyes, just before she and Elizabeth and their grandparents sailed away. She felt guilty.

Thankfully, the huge three-story Younger home appeared exactly as Emelye remembered, as though waiting for her return: The long walk leading to the big porch enclosed in lattice work; the pitched roof—even higher than she remembered—with turrets and pointed gables; the water hose, always coiled up in summer, that Emelye and Serena and James once used for squirting contests. The smell of magnolia blossoms from the big tree in the side yard—oh, look how much taller it was, and its branches were broader, like long outstretched arms! She wondered if the pecan tree in back had grown as much.

Inside, there was the peculiar way it always smelled in summer, with the windows open and the breeze ruffling the net curtains: of freshly-cut grass, mingled with the faint musty odor of old wood and leafy, moss-hung trees. As she carried her suitcase upstairs, the same stairs creaked that she remembered, and just as she remembered, the finial at the top of the post on the first landing felt smooth with wear when she closed the palm of her hand around it. She let her hand linger there for a few moments, thinking: time had passed, but her fingerprints from long ago were still buried there, like a fossil in a deep layer of earth.

Continuing up the stairs, Emelye felt more at home here than ever she had felt at Clearharbour or Norfolk Square, and she realized it wasn't just because she loved the house, or even that she wished to be near James. Though it seemed wrong, and it made her feel guilty to think of it, Willa and Rodney had always been as much a mother and father to her as her parents. And while she had been away in England, their lives had stayed exactly the same. Rodney worked just a few blocks from home—they had passed his office on the way—instead of being more than 200 miles away most of the time. Like Mother, Willa was home all day, but she was not busy with little babies. She'd have time to talk to you.

There is plenty of room in this house. Why can't I live here? she thought.

After three days, the travelers were due to go up into the northeast for more sightseeing, then spend the last week of their vacation at the Fournier place on Oyster Bay. Before dawn on the Sunday they were to leave, a storm came. The thunder was so loud it rattled the window panes and startled Willa from her sleep. The window by her bed was raised halfway up; the curtains were ballooning in the rain-soaked breeze. Quickly she got up and lowered the window. She'd just gotten back into bed and snuggled up to Rodney when she heard the door open and looked up to see Emelye coming in, her hair braids dangling down her chest, tears in her eyes. "Willa, I need to talk to you, please!" she begged.

Willa gently put a finger on Emelye's mouth, and glanced at the clock: 4:30. "Alright. Sh, don't wake up Rodney." She reached for her house robe looped over the brass rail at the foot of the bed, and put on her house slippers. Willa was so exhausted that her whole body ached. She had been up till midnight cooking for today's lunch. She'd made a batch of chicken fricasee, tomato aspic, and a pineapple upside down cake for dessert. At eight-thirty they would leave for worship at Christ Church, picking up Cynthia and Edward on the way. Afterward they were to have lunch here—she still needed to set the dining room table with her Spode china and good silver; she wanted it to be especially nice for the Selbys. Admittedly it was a little intimidating to reciprocate as hosts, when they lived in a mansion. She had been relieved to learn they had booked a reservation at the Rice Hotel during their stop here. After lunch they would all visit the Museum of Fine Arts, then head to Union Station. It was going to be a long day. She put an arm around Emelye's shoulders, and they quietly walked down the hall and into the kitchen.

Willa paused to put the coffee pot on the stove and turn on the burner. Through the window above the sink, she could see lightning pierce the sky in a jagged line. The light brought the big old pecan tree with its shaggy green limbs into sudden, sharp focus. There came a great thunder clap and then a long low rumble, like cannon fire. Umbrellas. They'd need several if this kept up. There were two in the front hall, she thought. Someone would have to hunt down another one in case Lord Edward and Cynthia needed one.

Emelye sat down at the table and folded her hands on top. She had always loved Willa's kitchen, with its high bead board ceiling, the square glass panes in the cabinet doors, the black and white tiles on the counters, and this porcelain table where she had eaten hundreds of times. Bananas and peaches were ripening in the wooden fruit bowl in the center. And nearby was the cookbook with the green cover that Willa had been using last night, *Sugar N' Spice*.

Willa sat down across from Emelye and took her hands. "Now, what's the trouble, Sweetie?"

The question returned Emelye's tears. She poured out her heart about her unhappiness in England, starting with the details of what happened at St. Michael's School. Geneva had written to Willa of the incident—though with fewer details—shortly after it happened. From the letter, things turned out alright when Emelye and Elizabeth changed schools. Willa was startled by the degree of Emelye's bitterness, even after all this time. She said that since then she had hated school, and never felt safe no matter where she was. Geneva had written how proud she was when Emelye finally 'overcame her fear of London,' and after that her letters frequently reported the whole family being at Norfolk Square, having a wonderful time. So Geneva had painted a pretty picture for her. It was not like her to be less than truthful, and Willa felt a little hurt. Yet—

"Have you told your mother all this?" she asked.

Emelye shrugged. "Mother just keeps saying that if I'd apply myself in school, and make better grades, I'd be much happier. But I'm so unhappy I can't concentrate, Willa," she said, her voice trembling. "I feel all the time like something is pushing down on my chest…do you know what I mean?" She crossed her hands over her chest and pressed in.

Willa nodded. She knew from her own tortured childhood that feeling of pressure in the diaphragm, remembered waking up with it every morning and going to bed with it every night. That feeling of being stranded in a foreign land—oh yes, there was more than one meaning for that term! She could not help feeling just a little angry at Geneva for her simplistic response to Emelye. It was like being told as a child that she had no right to long for her real parents, wonder who they were, and where they were, that she ought to just be grateful for all she had. *One day Emelye will rebel just as I did,* she realized with alarm.

"But you know what, Willa?" Emelye said, her face brightening, "when I got here on Tuesday, I felt so good inside, just like I used to! Even if I started to school here tomorrow, I'd be the happiest person in the world." Her brown eyes filled again. "But now we have to leave. Oh Willa, can't I stay here and live with you? I promise I won't be any trouble!"

Willa was taken aback. She needed to put her thoughts in order. She released Emelye's hands and rose to pour a cup of coffee. Oh, what she would give to have her live here! She had always felt partial to Emelye. One reason, no doubt, was her closeness to Geneva. But apart from that, Emelye seemed to have a deeper need than Serena for her affection. And that tiny wish that Emelye might grow up and marry James one day still emerged in Willa's thoughts now and then. Whether or not this ever came to be, wouldn't it be wonderful to know Emelye was happy growing up, in a way Willa herself was not? She recalled telling Geneva before they moved to England that if Emelye didn't like living there, she could come back and live with them. Dare she write and ask Geneva? But then Geneva had not really seemed open to the idea at the time. How could she put such a proposal in a letter now? She could imagine the horror on Geneva's face as she read it.

Willa could hardly bear to face Emelye when she returned to the table. "Honey, your mom and dad love you so much, it wouldn't be right for me to ask them to let you live with us. But one day when you're grown up, you can live anywhere you choose." Even as she uttered the last sentence, she regretted it. For Emelye, to wait till she was grown would seem like waiting an eternity.

Emelye had thought she could count on Willa. Serena thought so too, which was why, after they talked all night in their beds, she urged her to go to Willa for help. But Willa didn't want her here. Emelye felt humiliated. She knew she would feel guilty when she saw her parents again and they hugged her and kissed her and said how glad they were that she was home....

"However, I don't see why you couldn't stay with us for the rest of the summer," Willa was saying now.

Emelye was thrilled. She had no idea how she would meet up with her grandparents to sail home, nor did she care. Then she remembered Elizabeth, who had never left her behind. "Can Elizabeth stay, too?"

"Sure, if she wants to," Willa said, but in truth she hoped the child would refuse. Elizabeth was polite, of course, but she had little to say to anyone, and she often went off alone as if she were bored by being around the rest of them. And probably she was bored. She talked like someone much older than herself. Curiously, from Geneva's letters, she had come to feel close to Elizabeth. Willa was sure she never could get close to her.

"How about helping me with breakfast? Bacon and eggs and biscuits."

"Yes, ma'am," Emelye said, beaming.

"Oh, and don't say anything yet. Let me speak with your grandmother first."

All morning long, Willa was troubled. She knew it was right to invite Emelye to stay, but there would be some expense involved. The real estate market was slow, and money was tight. Her family had not taken a vacation in three years. She ought to have checked with Rodney first.

While they were behind the closed door of their bedroom, dressing for church, she told him what she had offered Emelye. "It just came out—she was so unhappy," she said. "Still, with train tickets and a hotel, it won't be cheap."

Rodney was frowning into the tilted mirror on top of the chest of drawers, as he unknotted his tie for the second time. Finally he said, "I guess we can take it from savings. I've got a deal or two cooking. We won't starve."

Willa was sitting on the cedar chest lid, putting on her stockings. She rose up and hugged him. Then she helped him with his tie.

Later that day, Willa stood in the kitchen ladling chicken fricassee into pastry shells. Lord Edward and Cynthia were visiting with Rodney in the living room, and the children were out on the front porch. The back door was open and a cool damp breeze wafted through the screen door.

To Willa's surprise, Cynthia walked in. She took a deep whiff, moaning in delight. "May I help?" she asked. Willa noted Cynthia's smooth ivory hands and enameled fingernails, her royal blue silk traveling suit with stand-up collar and fitted sleeves. She considered having her slice the pineapple upside down cake and put it on the Fostoria dessert plates. But she didn't have another apron. "No thanks, but sit down if you will. I need to talk to you," she said.

Looking puzzled, Cynthia did as she was asked.

"Emelye would really like to stay here for the rest of the summer," Willa said. "Suppose I bring her to meet you in New York City, before you sail? And if Elizabeth wants to stay with us, we'd enjoy having her, too."

Cynthia was frowning, nodding her head, as if she had half-expected something like this. "Coming here is all Emelye has talked about," she said quietly. "Poor dear, I don't think she got much out of our sightseeing in San Francisco and Denver." She grimaced. "But I hate to impose on you—"

"I wouldn't mind at all," said Willa. "You know, Emelye is like one of our own children, and we've missed her so much since she moved away." Again she thought of Emelye's pleas across the kitchen table this morning and, to her consternation, tears stood in her eyes. She blinked them back.

Thoughtfully Cynthia said, "Then, I don't see why she couldn't stay, but at least let Edward and I pay for your trip."

It would be tempting to accept the offer. But Rodney was proud. When he made a commitment, it was better not to interfere. "It's kind of you, but we'd like to do it," she said.

During lunch Willa announced the plans, then turned to Elizabeth. By now she felt guilty for her unkind thoughts, and was determined to make her feel welcome. "Would you like to stay with us, too? We'll go down to Galveston, and spend some time at our cottage on Lake Astoria."

Emelye cried, "Oh, please stay, Elizabeth! At Lake Astoria, we go swimming twice a—" she began, then abruptly halted, her mouth open. After a moment, she went on, "It's—it's fun to walk along the shore, and at night we have a camp fire and roast marshmallows. And sleep upstairs on a sleeping porch!"

Emelye's unfortunate slip of the tongue was mortifying for Elizabeth. Emelye knew that she did not, under any circumstances, go bathing, and obviously that was what they would be doing practically every day for the rest of the summer. She felt that the scar on her leg was suddenly exposed in all its repulsiveness. Out the corner of her eye she could see James's beautiful tilted eyes, watching her intently. Since coming here, she had felt awkward around him. It was as if her clumsiness at Geneva and Father's wedding nearly five years ago had only just occurred. Now, she could just imagine him asking, "Why don't you like to swim? Why do you wear black stockings all the time?" She looked down at her lap, searching for an excuse not to stay. There was the overbearing heat and humidity in Houston. By early afternoon she felt like a wilted flower, and dragged herself about for the rest of the day, with scarcely the energy to move. She just wanted to curl up with a book in one of the many nooks and crannies high up in the Younger house, pausing occasionally to look out the window at the treetops fluttering in the breeze. But she couldn't admit this, for it would injure the feelings of her hosts.

Finally the solution was obvious. Looking up, she said politely, "Thank you very much, but I believe I should like to see more of the States as long as I am here. Who knows if I shall ever return?"

James had paid no attention when Emelye burst in on the conversation. Once his mother invited Elizabeth to stay, he held his breath for her reply. Hearing her refusal, he did not know whether to be disappointed or relieved.

When he found out Elizabeth was coming to visit this summer, it was like a miracle. He had never really thought he would see her again after that first time, in England. All he could think about was how beautiful she was, how he loved the sound of her voice. He was determined to really get to know her while she was here. But then, Emelye soon wrote him a letter, with those silly hearts and butterflies all over the margins. "My sister is very smart, you know. She reads advanced books, the kind that grown-ups read. But don't worry. She's still real nice." Long ago he read *Treasure Island,* and a book of stories by Rudyard Kipling that belonged to his dad. But Hardy Boys mysteries, comic books, and the Boy Scout magazine were all he read anymore. If he read anything else, his friends would never let him live it down. But if Elizabeth found out what he read, he would die. He remembered, when first they met, feeling she was high above everyone else, way up in the clouds. Emelye's letter confirmed that he had been right. Even though he was two and a half years older, she was way ahead of him. He knew he would be tongue-tied around her.

And that wasn't all. Right after he got home from Tony and Gee's wedding, he drew a colored picture from memory of Gee walking down the aisle, as viewed through one of the chapel windows. He worked hard on getting the stones of the walls to look just right, and all the flowers and vines that covered it, and even the candles in the windows with flaming tips. It came out so well that his teacher entered it in an art contest for all the elementary schools in Houston, and it won first place. His mother asked his permission to mail the drawing to Gee. Weeks later Gee wrote him that she'd had the drawing framed and hung it in the front hall at Clearharbour. "I wouldn't be surprised if you grew up to be an artist!" she wrote. James used to like to imagine Elizabeth stopping to look at the picture as she came through the door, and maybe remembering how he helped her to her feet when she fell. His dad told him after the wedding that Elizabeth had been in an automobile accident—it was why she had a slight limp—and that she apparently lost her footing when she started down the aisle. James felt even more of a hero then, for helping her. He hoped she would think of him as her hero, while gazing up at his drawing.

But then a few days ago she arrived, and the first thing he knew, she was talking about how she liked to visit art museums. James thought with dread, *Oh no, she knows all about art, too!* He wished he'd never drawn that picture. Whenever Elizabeth passed by it, she probably laughed in scorn. He was glad he had stopped drawing pictures. He would never have been any good at it....

All through the morning and into the afternoon it rained. James hoped maybe the weather would keep them from going to the art museum because he would never stop wondering if Elizabeth were comparing his picture to the real ones there, and thinking how bad his was. But as luck would have it, after everyone had a serving of pineapple upside down cake, his father glanced at his watch and said, "We better get going if we want to stop by the museum." Soon they were all huddled under umbrellas again, hurrying to the car.

The Museum of Fine Arts was way out at South Main and Montrose, across from Hermann Park, and had a broad front lawn with spreading oak trees. Ornate columns spanned the long building front with two jutting wings, and there were winged bronze statues on either side of the entrance doors. Today rain splashed down relentlessly, and when they got out of the car, water was pooled at the curb. Everyone had to take a wide step across.

Elizabeth was wearing a pretty green straw hat and—under her rain slicker—a dress with a black background and bright flowers and leaves on it. And black stockings, which she always wore—James had no idea why, but he couldn't bring himself to ask her. Nor would he ask anyone else who knew her, because they might guess that he thought about her all the time, and that secret was sacred to him. Whatever she wore, she was beautiful, her arms and legs and body in perfect proportion. Unfortunately, his chest and arms were skinny, and his feet were too long. Serena called them freight cars. His dad said he'd soon grow into them, though that didn't help much. His profile was like the hall tree by the stairway in the entrance hall of their house.

James had visited the museum just once—on a school field trip one year. Today, when his dad bought their tickets inside the marble entrance, they were each given a guide book. Looking through it, James realized there was a lot more to see than he remembered. They strolled through galleries with dueling pistols from France and Morocco and Spain; furnishings from Spanish churches; Greek statues and jewelry ranging from the fourth to the first century B.C.; Egyptian and Oriental artifacts; Japanese wood carvings, Buddhas, and Chinese cloisonné vases. They briefly toured a room with a collection of laces from all over the world, and a library with antique books and manuscripts. Sometimes the group separated, then joined up in another gallery. James tried to keep Elizabeth within view, but he couldn't walk next to her because the others would notice. Besides, what if she struck up a conversation about some artifact she knew all about? He would feel like an idiot.

Finally, they entered Gallery A, a large rectangular room where many paintings hung along white walls, with a number of sculptures placed around the highly polished hardwood floor. Puncturing the high ceiling was a large skylight, and there were tall windows overlooking the rain-streaked front lawn. The oils and pastels were of varying sizes, and spaced wide apart. Elizabeth took a long look at each one, standing back for a while, then stepping closer as if to see how the paints were applied. Landscapes and seascapes; still lifes and portraits. James could hardly concentrate on the paintings for wondering what Elizabeth was thinking. She just stared at one after another, absorbed.

By the time they left, James's stomach was in knots and his mouth was dry with anxiety. In the car, his dad asked Elizabeth if she enjoyed the tour. "It was very nice," she said, "though I'm afraid I was unfamiliar with most of the painters. I did very much like Mr. Redfield's *Late Afternoon*."

"I liked it too," James quickly spoke up, but for the life of him he could not remember which painting that was. He hoped no one would ask him to talk about the details. All the way to Union Station he wanted to tell Elizabeth that he realized he was no artist and knew his drawing of the wedding was terrible. But he couldn't bring himself to say it, and besides, Emelye was sitting on his lap and Serena was between him and Elizabeth. Then his dad was pulling into a diagonal parking space in front of the station. Suddenly James realized he should have never doubted he wanted Elizabeth to stay, no matter what she thought of him.

James had been carrying one of the umbrellas each time they got out in the weather, but each time he thought he might shield Elizabeth, Emelye would grab his arm and Elizabeth would get under someone else's umbrella. This time he succeeded, and immediately he thought: *Oh no, what if I step on her feet?* As they walked along, she let her arms hang at her sides, instead of slipping one through his arm, which would have been nicer. Still, she was close enough that in spite of the rubbery smell of her slicker, he could breathe in the clean, soapy fragrance of her skin. *Please don't go!* he wanted to beg.

When it was time for the travelers to board the train, he found himself catching her hand from behind. She paused and looked around at him, surprised. With his voice all clogged up in his throat, he managed to ask, "Will you come back sometime?" As he spoke, the train whistle sounded. It was so loud, he wondered if she could hear him above the noise.

Elizabeth looked down. "Oh, I don't know. It's awfully hot!" Then she looked up and smiled. "Perhaps you'll come to England again someday," she said. They were calling her to board. She withdrew her hand from his. "Goodbye, James."

As she walked away the clouds parted; the sun burned through, and Elizabeth's beautiful green hat seemed to shimmer in the sudden bright light. It was as if she were a great oil painting just completed, and the brush strokes on her hat were the very last the painter had applied. His heart bursting, James thought, *I'll get over to England, somehow I will, if it's the last thing I do!*

CHAPTER 16

Over the next few weeks, Elizabeth traveled with her grandparents through Rhode Island, Connecticut and Massachusetts. The farther north they went, the more the landscape reminded her of home. There were many familiar trees—sycamores and maples and elms—rising from the gently rolling countryside. There were quaint villages with English-sounding names like Stockbridge and Chesterfield, and church steeples rising on the greens. Best of all, the climate was cooler and drier than in Texas.

Sometimes they hired a driver to take them to some out-of-the-way village with an intriguing name. One such place in Massachusetts was Orchard Hill, a Shaker village at the foot of the Berkshire Hills which, according to the driver, was named for its rather extensive apple orchard that produced an income for the sisters who lived there.

Elizabeth knew very little about the Shaker movement—only that it began in England and that Shakers didn't ever marry, and lived by very strict rules. She did not know what their rules were. As they drove down the long dusty road between broad green meadows leading to Orchard Hill, and the clean white buildings, three- and four-stories high came into view under a crisp blue sky, she felt she had never seen any place so lovely and serene.

The sisters wore thin white bonnets like delicate clouds of meringue, and large white collars shaped like bibs. Like Elizabeth, they wore dark stockings. As she and her grandparents walked round looking at the articles made for sale—apple butter and cider, maple candies and fresh herbs; embroidered linens, music boxes and even pieces of furniture, all produced by Shaker hands—they were welcomed with smiles and gentle manners. Elizabeth was drawn to the sisters. She sensed that as they lived and worked in this place, the serenity of the landscape pervaded their spirits. She and her grandparents selected gifts for the Youngers, and for their family at home. Grandfather asked her to choose something for herself. She would have liked a book about Shakers, but unfortunately there were none for sale. After much consideration she chose a Shaker doll. It was around six inches tall and was made almost entirely of silky, earth-colored corn husk—if you turned her upside down, you could see that she was all corn husk inside, and even her dress was made of corn husk. It had long, full sleeves and was nipped in at the waist, and over this she wore an apron that tied in back. The hair that peeked out of her corn husk bonnet was red like Geneva's, and made of yarn. Her eyes were two round black ink dots, spaced wide apart. How modest and endearing she was, compared to the dolls she and Emelye brought home from Normandy that wore fancy dresses and elaborate *bigouden* coiffes with high bonnets and wings of delicate lace trailing down each side. Her round black eyes seemed to express innocence, and trust in the goodness of the person looking back. Somehow she made Elizabeth think of the primitive cross left behind by the bearded Frenchman. She would place the doll next to the cross on top of her cupboard at home. Though she would have been at pains to explain it, even to Fr. Ogilvie, she felt the meaning of the two serendipitous events in her life—meeting the French stranger, and visiting Orchard Hill Shaker village—were somehow bound together.

Elizabeth imagined living in a little village like Orchard Hill, and as she envisioned this setting, she gradually saw herself sitting quietly at the end of the day, when her work was done, thinking of how pleasant it felt when James Younger unexpectedly clasped her hand.

CHAPTER 17

Serena persuaded her parents to let her go along on the trip to New York, to meet the Selbys and Elizabeth before the whole party sailed back to England. She was eager to see a performance of the Radio City Music Hall Rockettes, doing their famous high kicks. Serena idolized the grandmother for whom she was named, and whose picture hung in the living room. She hoped Serena Garret's unrealized dream would come true for her: being a dancer on the stage. Everyone said Serena was very talented, and James guessed it was true. He was forced to attend her recitals, and her solos always got a huge round of applause.

There was no question of James going along. It would have called for not only an extra train ticket, but a second hotel room. Besides, Coach Turner was holding try-outs for the Reagan track team at the same time. James had dropped out of Scouts in May. Now that he was going into high school, he felt he'd outgrown the organization. He was bored with the meetings and camp-outs, the rules and regulations, and how the leaders were always driving home the importance of being good citizens and helping others. He was capable of following his own conscience. Now he'd have plenty of time for extracurricular activities at Reagan, and he had high hopes of making the track team.

Apart from everything else, James savored the memory of Elizabeth standing on the platform at Union Station, urging him to come to England. Maybe next time they bid farewell, up there in New York, he'd say something wrong or stupid, and from then on he'd be tortured wondering exactly what Elizabeth thought of him.

He realized it would be a long time before he went overseas; he needed to save up enough money to pay his way. And that was just as well, too, because it would give him time to read important books, perhaps similar to the ones Elizabeth read. Then he wouldn't be afraid of making a fool of himself when he was around her.

In the autumn he got a part-time job with Mr. Dupuis at Yale Pharmacy, delivering prescriptions on his bicycle. By then he was checking out books regularly from the Heights library. His goal was to read at least fifty books by the time he saw Elizabeth again, including the ones he was assigned in literature class. First he read *The Great Gatsby*, by F. Scott Fitzgerald. Reading about Jay Gatsby's quest to win Daisy, the only love of his life, he could not help seeing himself when it came to Elizabeth. Naturally he kept hoping Jay would succeed. The end of the book put a lump in his throat, not because Jay failed to win Daisy, but because she proved unworthy of his adoration. Next he read *The Turn of the Screw*—the creepiest story he had ever read, even creepier than the stories on the Sherlock Holmes mystery series that came on KXYZ on Sunday nights. Since Henry James lived the last half of his life in England, according to the book jacket, he figured Elizabeth might have read that story. Ever since she left, he had been trying to get up the nerve to write to her. But what could he say that would interest her? Now he thought of writing to see if she had read *The Turn of the Screw*, and asking what she thought of it. Did she believe the governess was just imagining the ghosts haunting Miles and Flora? Or were Quint and Miss Jessel really there, transmitting their evil to the children? Still, maybe he was supposed to figure that out for himself, and Elizabeth would think he was dumb for not being able to. Anyway, what did the story really mean? His English teachers were always harping on understanding the theme of a story. He bet Elizabeth could figure it out a lot easier than he could. He did not write to her.

Once he started his part-time job, school assignments and tests seemed to multiply; and there were track meets practically every week. James didn't have time for outside reading anymore. He was always returning books to the library, feeling guilty because he hadn't read them and hoping Miss Hicks the librarian wouldn't stop him and say, "How did you enjoy the book, James?" He vowed to do better when school was out.

By the next summer he was working full days at Yale Pharmacy, part of the time behind the soda fountain, and part of the time making deliveries. His dad had bought him an old jalopy—a '29 Chevy Six Roadster. Having a car was a good way for a young man to develop a sense of responsibility, he said. Besides, Mother had begun working at the real estate office, helping out after Dad's long-time secretary and office assistant moved away. The real estate market was so slow, Dad didn't want to hire anyone until things picked up. And Mother had worked with him long ago, before they got married, so she knew how to run the office while he was out showing properties. Dad was fond of saying, "Times are hard right now, and everyone has to pitch in and help." Among James's duties was taking Serena to her dancing lessons way out on Milam, three times a week—a luxury his mother insisted on continuing. She wouldn't let her ride the bus by herself, and with good reason. Not yet fourteen, Serena was as glamourous and shapely as any eighteen-year-old girl. After she was chosen Queen of the May at Hamilton Junior High and her picture was in the *Leader* with the King and their court, high school boys started calling up and asking her out. She was forbidden to date until she turned sixteen, and had already been grounded twice, for sneaking out. With his mother away at the office, James was expected to keep an eye on her. Sometimes he'd be out in the driveway with the Chevy hood up—there was always something that needed fixing; oil and transmission fluid leaks occurred regularly—and a car full of boys would cruise by, all of them waving, calling to his sister. He'd look up and there she would be, sitting on the porch steps, looking like a movie star in a sweater and skirt and oxfords, smiling and waving back. James considered Serena a pain in the neck, and the feeling was mutual. He never seemed to get around to working on his goal of reading fifty books.

One day he ran across the slip of paper where he'd copied out parts of the Edgar Lee Masters poem long ago. The memory of his first meeting with Elizabeth shimmered before his eyes, how he'd wanted to share that poem with her, but was too much in awe of her. He reread the stanzas now, then refolded the paper and put it away. Somehow it reminded him of his failure.

Gradually the Houston real estate market recovered and Dad started closing more deals, often on houses that had sat on the market for as long as two or three years. If things kept up, he could hire a new assistant and Mother could begin staying home again—something they both wanted because they felt it was unfair for James to be stuck looking after Serena all the time.

One night in May of 1938, he got home from work around seven—later than usual because it was his night to clean up the griddle, scrub down the counter, wash and dry all the dishes for tomorrow, and refill the sugar bowls and salt and pepper shakers. His mother was waiting in the kitchen, warming up spaghetti and meatballs for his supper. She was still dressed in the brown suit and high-heeled shoes and stockings she'd worn to work. This made James a little sad somehow. He liked it better when she didn't have to work. He went to the icebox and filled a tall glass with cold milk.

She filled his plate, adding some steamed yellow squash and a piece of hot garlic bread, the scent of which filled the entire kitchen. She sat down across from him. "A letter came from Geneva," she said. "She's invited us for a visit this summer."

James had just plunged his fork into the mound of spaghetti. He rested it on the side of his plate and looked up, his mouth dry. The first thing that came into his mind was that he only had a little more than twenty dollars saved up. Then it dawned on him that if they accepted, his parents would pay the way. But how could they afford that? His mother was saying, "Your dad is too busy, and I won't be able to go either. He wants to wait till the first of the year to hire someone to take my place. But we thought you and Serena might like to go—I haven't asked your sister yet, wanted to talk to you first." She paused before saying tenderly, "I'm sure it would mean a lot to Emelye. You know how she misses you both."

The remark made James feel guilty. At the moment there were four letters from Emelye stacked on his dresser unanswered. It was obvious she had a crush on him, and he didn't have the heart to tell her she'd never be more than a sister to him. He kept hoping she'd figure it out for herself. "But how can we afford a trip like that?" he asked his mother now.

She grimaced suddenly, complaining, "These shoes are killing my corns," and leaned down to take them off and massage her feet. "Your dad and I have decided we can get by for another year without buying a new car," she said.

So they must have discussed all this at length. James wondered how long ago Gee had written that letter. He was touched that his parents would sacrifice to give him and Serena this trip. Reality finally soaking in, he thought with wonder: In just a few weeks from now, he was going to see Elizabeth. Yet, what about all those books he was going to read, so he could carry on a decent conversation with her? On the other hand, how could he afford to pass up this chance to see her? In another two years Elizabeth would be old enough to go out with boys; that is, if Gee and Tony had the same rules as his parents. What if she fell in love with an English boy? Ready or not, he had better go and make the most of it.

"You know, of course, you'll have to keep an eye on Serena," his mother reminded him, "especially aboard ship. But I really do think this will be a broadening experience for her. And maybe when she gets back she'll see there's something else in the world besides boys."

James grinned. "*Suuure*, Mom."

His mother laughed, then her eyes filled. She laid her fingers on his wrist. "You and your sister have never been that far away from home before. I'm going to miss you!" She sniffed. "You're a good son, James, better than I deserve."

"I know it, a real prince," he said, and winked.

She smiled, but then she looked serious again. "James, I've often wondered why you don't go out much with girls, even when you do have time—I know how busy you are. But surely you meet lots of girls at Reagan."

He wondered what she was getting at. "I—I just haven't met anyone interesting," he said, which, as far as the girls at Reagan went, was true.

"Well don't think I'm rushing you, Sweetie. I just want you to enjoy yourself, that's all. You've got years to find the right girl."

I found her when I was ten years old, he thought.

By the time they left for England on June 15th, James had read *A Room with a View* by E. M. Forster—he was determined to read British authors—which he loved because of how things turned out for Lucy and George in the end, true love winning out in spite of all the obstacles. From the ship's library he borrowed *Middlemarch* by George Eliot. He read just a quarter of the way through it, because there were so many activities on board and his only reading time was at night before going to sleep. Besides, every night he would have to double back and reread some, because he kept getting lost in the story. He was thankful they had plodded through *A Tale of Two Cities* in English Literature class last year. He didn't like it much, but at least he could say he had read it and—thanks to the papers he wrote about it—he understood its meaning reasonably well.

The closer they came to port, the more he found himself starting conversations with Elizabeth in his head. They all began with his asking her if she had read a certain book. He imagined the talk flowing endlessly from there, like the foam in the wake of the ship....

Since her trip to the States two years ago, Elizabeth had often thought of James, and wondered if he ever thought of her. It would be nice if they were friends. She would have written to him, but then that would seem rather forward, and besides, Emelye was always talking about how much she cared for James. And if he wrote her a letter she would positively glow, holding it to her breast as she went off alone to read it. Emelye never offered to let Elizabeth read James's letters, so she imagined he must like Emelye very much, and write very personal things. *Why would he care about writing to me?* she would ask herself.

For weeks before James and Serena arrived, Emelye spoke of nothing but their upcoming visit. Father promised to teach James to drive the Rover so that they would have transportation. Emelye began planning their days. They would drive to Hawke's Confectionary for ice cream. They would have a picnic on Beacon Hill south of Bodmin, where there rose a towering granite obelisk erected in memory of some distinguished commander in the Indian campaigns. On clear days one could see the obelisk from home. They would go to the pictures at the Bodmin Palace. They would drive to Brookhurst to see their grandparents. When James felt confident enough behind the wheel, they would go all the way to Ready Money Cove in Fowey, for a day of bathing. Knowing how Emelye missed her friends, how she longed to move back to where they lived, Elizabeth hoped that this visit would leave her with happy memories, and console her until she was grown and could move back to Houston. How she dreaded the thought of Emelye moving away! There would be no one to share her attic bedroom and talk to at nights after the lights were out. Perhaps by then she, too, would leave home, entering university. Yet the thought of being in a new place, meeting strangers, was daunting.

Once Serena and James arrived and Elizabeth observed the three of them together, she was completely in awe of how handsome they had all grown to be. They had such vitality, their presence filled the house and made her feel small and plain and rather out of place. Therefore she often found excuses not to go with them on their outings. Now and then she sensed James was disappointed, but then, it was probably her imagination. She tried to avoid showing that she noticed him, and most of the time Emelye and Serena were around so it was easy enough to do so.

Then came the long-awaited day trip to Ready Money Cove. Sometime ago, Father had encouraged her to take up the study of a musical instrument to take the place of the study of ballet, which she could no longer pursue. She had finally chosen piano, and soon an upright model was procured and placed in the corner of the sitting room. She had lessons with Mrs. Hearn in Bodmin twice a week. Elizabeth was not an inspired pianist. Mrs. Hearn did not consider her a worthy pupil, and—but for fear of reprisal from Geneva—would have registered her disapproval with an occasional rap on her knuckles. Still, Elizabeth was dutiful about practicing.

That morning as she went about it, the children were particularly noisy. Andy was tearing round the house, waving a toy sword above his dark blond curls, shouting in full voice, Kilty his Scottish terrier pup, barking at his heels. All of which sent poor little Chris crying to his mummy—Andy made sport of terrorizing his little brother. And Chris cried about the least thing, and ran to bury his face in Geneva's skirts, or Mrs. Greaves's apron, if she happened to be nearer. Elvira was on the stairs, demanding of Emelye that she, too, be allowed to go to the beach. Elvira's voice continued to carry with amazing force, and now, at the age of six—they celebrated her birthday on the night James and Serena arrived—she was so theatrical in her gestures that Father had already promised her a small role in *Pip 'N Pocket* this coming Christmas season.

"No, and that's final," said Emelye. Elvira burst into tears and fled.

Elizabeth played four bars, then she heard Father's voice on the stairs. "What was all that about," he asked irritably. Elizabeth suspected the confusion that reigned in the Clearharbour household quite got on Father's nerves at times, for when he was home he would often retreat, staying either out in his studio, or upstairs in his office. "Elvira wants to go with us, but she can't. She's too much trouble," Emelye complained.

"Ah—I had better go out and dry her tears then. Where's your mother?"

"In the garden. You won't say she can go, Daddy, will you?" Emelye pleaded.

"No, Emelye, I shan't…."

James was outside loading the rafts and the picnic hamper in the Rover boot—no doubt grateful to escape the noise. Happily Guy had come to join them for the day trip, and he was assisting James. Now out the corner of the window Elizabeth caught a glimpse of her husky cousin's dark head and his broad back, his bare arms, muscular as a boxer's, flexing as he smacked the boot shut. Then, quite unexpectedly, as she attempted to resume practicing, James appeared at the door of the sitting room and called her name.

She lifted her fingers from the keys and looked round to see his figure, clad in swim trunks, a bright yellow jersey top, and plimsolls on his feet. James was…well…his chest and shoulders were rather more filled out than she had realized.

"Emelye says you're not going with us today," he said, rather contrarily.

"I really don't care for bathing parties," she told him, conscious at once of her black-stockinged legs. "Besides, I must practice. My lesson's tomorrow."

His eyes blazing, he persisted,"You can practice when we get back. And if you don't want to swim, you can take a book along to read on the beach. And maybe we can…" he hesitated, "…talk."

So then she had been right. James did wish for her to be a part of the group. And he wanted to talk to her—pray, what about? Suddenly she was overtaken by shyness. Besides, she thought of the perfect figures of Serena and Emelye, and she herself in black stockings—"No, I—"

Another great war whoop from Andy, who was invading Norway at the moment. *I shall go mad if I stay.* "Alright," she said abruptly. James grinned. As she rose and closed the piano lid, she felt all the blood drain down to her feet.

Elizabeth loved the shingle beach at Ready Money Cove. When she was little, Father used to bring her here and hold her up on his shoulders so that she could look far beyond the slate boulders at the beautiful green, turbulent sea. From there her eyes would sweep up to the left, and high above the beach behind a stand of trees, was a great gray stone house. She always wondered who lived there, and were they happy? She decided they must be, and she liked to pretend that she lived there too. When it was warm enough, she and Father went bathing. That was before the auto crash. Now, occasionally on a Saturday during the colder months, when few others were apt to be about, she would come here by bus, and stay for several hours. If it wasn't awfully cold, and she found herself alone, she might remove her shoes and stockings, raise her skirt hem and wade out a bit.

Today she sat in a an old wooden rorky chair under a beach umbrella. There were not a great many bathers abroad, even on this sunny July day, and as she looked up now and then from the volume of poetry she'd brought, she could easily spot her companions at the water's edge. Serena stood out remarkably from the rest. She wore a bright yellow, two-piece bathing suit, which certainly enhanced her perfect figure and long shapely legs. And she had been flirting shamelessly with Guy since they all piled into the Rover to drive down, his face turning red as a telephone box. Elizabeth did not particularly like Serena. There was something off-putting about her absorption in herself, and a falsity in her gestures—how she would raise an eyebrow and cut her beautiful eyes at one. Still, one could not help admiring her in a way, for, like Emelye, she knew exactly what she wanted to do when she grew up. She had written to Emelye of her intention to audition for the Rockettes upon graduation from high school. Elizabeth had no doubt she would be accepted, and probably her high kicks would outdo everyone else's in the chorus line.

And Emelye.... *There, just look at her, so natural and pretty in her bathing suit of emerald green—teasing James, pushing his shoulder, laughing, running to catch the beach ball, her pony tail flying. Does she know—do any of them know—how fortunate they are, to be able to lose their awareness of themselves, and be free? I shall never be able to do so....*

But I shall be happy enough, as long as I am surrounded by books—

Elizabeth started from her thoughts. James had approached without her realizing it. He was toweling himself off. She felt dreadfully awkward, having him so close, his sun-bronzed chest and arms exposed. The force of energy radiating from him made her feel breathless, as if she had suddenly bumped up against him, and her body was at this moment in direct contact with his. Beads of water splayed over the book open on her lap. She brushed off the water and closed the volume.

James dropped to his knees and squinted up at her, his wet brown hair poking out in all directions. "Sorry about that."

"No harm done."

"What'cha reading?"

She liked his Texas drawl, broad and wide-open as the sky. She sensed that he thought with such openness as well. "Oh, just a little book of Edmund Spenser's poetry."

James seemed a bit disconcerted. "Is he your favorite poet?" he asked.

"One of them. His poems are..." her voice dropped off. She would like to say they were romantic. "...nice...they make one feel...encouraged."

James paused, absorbing this—if he had trouble grasping the themes of novels, poems were ten times more difficult. Except for *The Hill*. Maybe—No. He would say exactly what he had come to say, what had given him courage, finally, to come up here where she was sitting: "You know what you made me think of just now, as I looked up here and saw you, huddled under your umbrella?"

Elizabeth laughed. "I can't imagine! Something ridiculous, probably."

He shook his head. His eyes were serious. "Promise not to laugh."

She knew then that he was taking a risk. "Alright. I promise."

"You made me think of a pearl, hiding inside an oyster shell."

Elizabeth went tingly all over. She was smiling. "Why, James! That's—well—it's very poetic."

James felt he could float right off the beach. "You really think so?"

"Yes, I do."

He gazed out on the water, wondering if he should go on talking. But then maybe it would be smart to keep his mouth shut until he could think of something equally imaginative to say. "Guess I better get back." He reached for his towel.

Elizabeth watched James's suntanned figure, his slender back and narrow hips and long legs, retreating. When she opened her book, the water had made little blister marks on the page. Gently she traced her fingertip round them, then closed the book again, and sat thinking of James's words....

Halfway back to the water James paused in his steps, feeling like a coward. For a week he'd been trying to find a way to talk to Elizabeth in private, but someone was always around. Even at night he couldn't invite her to go outside and talk because Gee and Tony were always sitting out, having a drink and talking. Now there were only two days left in Cornwall, then the whole family would be going to London to spend what time was left before he and Serena went home. He gathered they would be very busy going to shows and other things. This may be the only opportunity he would have to talk to Elizabeth alone. Not knowing exactly what he would say, he nonetheless walked back to where she sat, the book of poetry still closed in her lap. Had she been thinking of him? He knelt beside her chair.

"Say, Elizabeth—ya know, I haven't read much poetry, but I like it when someone reads it aloud. I used to have a teacher who did that."

"How lovely. I believe poetry is meant to be read aloud, or recited...."

"You do? Have you ever heard of a poem called, *The Hill*?" She was shaking her head. "It's about all these townspeople who died, and are buried up on a hill," he said boldly.

"Can you recite it for me?" she asked.

His heart stopped. Reluctantly, he told her he remembered the refrain, and he thought he could recite one stanza anyway. He began slowly, with a pause between each name, just the way Miss Thompson did it, "*Where are Ella, Kate, Mag, Lizzie, and Edith...? The tender heart, the simple soul, the—*" he stopped abruptly, the next few words floating away. Desperate—he was aware of Elizabeth's frozen look—he finally picked up the end of the stanza—"*the happy one.*" He took in a breath. "*All, all are sleeping, sleeping, sleeping on the hill.*

"That's all. Sorry I ruined it," he said, wishing he were dead.

Elizabeth dropped her eyes. "No, not at all," she said, her voice tight. Her mind had hit a snag on the name 'Lizzie,' after which she was aware only of the sound of James's voice. Then came a long silence, in which she feared everything she wished to hide shone in her face. She barely heard him say, *the happy one.* "But it's rather morose, isn't it?"she quickly said, aware of a thrumming in her ears.

James could only guess at the meaning of the word, 'morose.' "Well, if only I could remember the whole poem, it really wouldn't be...like that. It's real long. There are old people up on the hill, too, and bad people." He shrugged. "I think it just means we are all connected—the living and the dead," he told her.

Then he hastened to add, "I—I read other things, too. I read all the time." And now he had lied. But at least he enjoyed reading.

Elizabeth was smiling.

"I was just wondering. After I go back home, I'd like to write to you. Would you write me back if I did? We could discuss books and things in our letters. Maybe even poetry. Might be interesting...."

"Why yes, James, I would," she said warmly.

He grinned. "Great!" he said. He doubled back to the water, this time for good.

Again Elizabeth sat watching James's retreating figure, but now her heart was beating hard and fast. He wanted to write to her. They were going to be friends. Emelye wouldn't mind, surely.

She saw herself presenting James with the Spenser volume, as a parting gift. And on the flyleaf she would write: "*To James—from your friend Elizabeth.*" But he must never know the dreadful secret of Lizzie, that 'happy one' who was dead now, sleeping on the hill. Elizabeth murdered her.

CHAPTER 18

❀

The evening was rather warm for the end of March. The sitting room windows were open and a soft breeze stirred the air as Elizabeth sat with her father, Geneva and Emelye, listening to the news on the wireless. Bertrand, Elizabeth's cat of questionable ancestry, was perched upon the cushion on the window seat, his head drawn down into his black, white, and golden fur as if it were a cape.

As the eight o'clock broadcast concluded, Father switched off the wireless and observed to all in a somber tone, "Poland is a time bomb…with the fuse lit."

Imagining German soldiers swarming through Bodmin with their guns, shooting people and taking prisoners, was terrifying to Elizabeth. *"You there, the crippled one, let's see if you can climb into the truck a little faster if I fire a few shots at your feet!"* Why couldn't people simply respect one another and live in peace? Instead, the strong waged war and prevailed over the weak; then, humbled and despairing—if not impoverished as Germany had been since the Great War—the weak would grow in strength and begin plotting their revenge. And inevitably another war would come. Yet whenever the subject came up in a discussion of political affairs at Harleigh grammar school, where she and Emelye were enrolled, her views were frowned on. She did not care. Besides, there were far wiser heads than hers who opposed the war: Bertrand Russell, for instance. *"Dear Miss Selby, how good of you to write. Those of us who disavow the popular view must be willing to pay the price, I'm afraid. As you may know, I was imprisoned for my views during the Great War and have never regretted taking a stand…."* It was shortly after receiving this letter that Elizabeth rescued a cat from a group of horrid little boys who would have drowned him in the fountain at Mt. Folly Square. Thus, in honor of the great philosopher, she named him Bertrand.

Now Father was saying to Geneva, "I suppose you had better write to Willa straightaway."

Remembering Emelye's secret plans for the upcoming summer, Elizabeth gave her a furtive glance, which she failed to notice. Emelye was sitting on a hassock in a white blouse and yellow sweater, a brown plaid pleated skirt draped round her knees like an open fan. Her face looked rather blank, as if she was taken completely off-guard. "Why? What for?" she burst out in perplexity.

Which brought a frown to Father's face. Then, apparently considering how much Emelye had looked forward to the trip to the World's Fair, he said, not unkindly, "Naturally, we'll have to cancel our plans. We all knew from the start that it might come to this."

"But you said we would go, unless there was a war. We're not at war!" Emelye argued. Her brown eyes darted desperately from one to the other of her parents, as if one of them surely would reverse the decision.

"Not yet, darling, but it's doubtful anything will stop Hitler from invading Poland, and you've just heard with your own ears our promise to stand behind Poland in that event," said Father patiently.

"But we don't have to cancel *now*, do we? Can't we wait, and if we're still not at war by the time we sail—"

"No we can't, because Britain and France might very well declare war on Germany while we're away," Father said, his color heightening. "I don't think you appreciate the seriousness of the situation, Emelye."

"And we could be stranded overseas for weeks—months," said Geneva.

"But who cares if we get stranded?"

Father and Geneva looked at each other blankly.

"I can't believe you're doing this to me!" Emelye cried, and flung herself out of the room and up the stairs.

"Poor Emelye, I'll go and talk to her," Geneva said resignedly, rising from her chair.

As she walked out, Elizabeth's eyes met her father's. She quickly looked down and traced her finger along the lace doily on the arm of her chair.

Geneva found Emelye sprawled across her bed, sobbing into the pillow. She sat down beside her and patted her shoulder. "I know you're disappointed, Honey. I am too. Look how many years it's been since I saw Willa and Rodney. But when all this is over, we'll go to America, I promise."

Emelye jerked up, her face pinched and red, her eyes blazing. "Mom, I don't want to just go for a visit, I want to *stay*. Willa wants me to live with them!"

Geneva felt as if she had been slapped hard across the face. Surely Willa would not have given Emelye any such notion without first discussing it with her and Tony. "What are you talking about? Did she tell you this?"

Emelye lowered her eyes. "Not exactly. But when I was there two years ago, I could tell she wanted me to. She asked me to stay longer than the others, you know, even though it meant she had to take a train all the way to New York."

"Well now that's quite a different thing than saying she wanted you to live with them, isn't it?" said Geneva, feeling somewhat relieved about Willa.

Emelye looked up. "Yes, but Serena told Willa how much she wants me to come back and live with them. And Willa said she'd like that, too."

Willa could hardly say anything else, when pushed into a corner, Geneva reasoned. And now that she knew Serena was involved, she suspected there was a plan being drawn up behind her back. After giving the matter some consideration, she said, "So you and Serena planned to talk us into letting you stay, once we got over there?"

Emelye lifted her chin impudently. Geneva could see a scaly patch where a tear had dried on her cheek. "Why would you and Daddy care, if Willa wants me to?"

"Because you're too young to move away from home, that's why," Geneva said firmly.

"No I'm not!" Emelye protested. "Listen, Mom, if I was there, I'd be able to go to Reagan with Serena. You ought to see how beautiful Reagan is. Harleigh School is nothing but a big old creepy house! And I wouldn't have to wear those dumb uniforms—" she paused, "—though they're nice for Elizabeth of course, with the dark stockings and all.

"Anyway, I know a lot of the other kids at Reagan, too, kids I knew at Harvard Elementary. So I'd fit in—see? I just stick out over here. No one likes me."

Geneva was encouraged that Emelye could give a thought to Elizabeth's welfare, when she was otherwise so thoroughly absorbed in herself. The fact that she failed to see that being accepted worked both ways was certainly a sign of immaturity, however.

Yet now Geneva remembered something she had overlooked, no doubt from her shock at Emelye's tirade. "Darling, your father and I have talked about your returning to the States one day—"

Emelye's face lit up. "You have? Then why don't you let me go now?"

"Just hear me out, Sweetie. We would have mentioned it, but we were afraid something might interfere—" she said, then added with a sour look, "—a war, for instance."

"But see, that's exactly what will happen if I don't hurry," Emelye said desperately, laying a hand on her mother's chest.

Geneva removed the hand, kissed it, wrapped her hands around it. "Now listen. In two years, when you're about ready for college, the world situation could be a lot better. If so, we could send you to college in Texas. How about that?"

"*College?* I could never get into college!" Emelye cried as if astonished at her parents' failure to grasp reality. She wrenched her hand away.

Here was the opportunity Geneva had dreamed of. "Yes you can," she said brightly, "if you'll spend the next two years bringing up your grades—"

"But what if I can't?" Emelye pleaded. "School is much harder over here than in America, Mom. I know that from Serena's letters. Look, if I went to Reagan, I really could bring my grades up, I know I could. I need to go *now*, Mom, don't you see how important it is?"

Geneva summoned patience. She knew as well as anyone how difficult it was to be at the age when you were no more a child but not yet an adult. Over the last year Emelye had grown nearly as tall as she was. She had developed small breasts; her waist had narrowed and her hips had become rounded. Before long she would begin the monthly menses. Geneva remembered the particular sense of loss she experienced at being cheated of her mother just as she was in these early stages of becoming a young woman. She had always considered it one of her most sacred obligations to help her daughters through this tender stage. "Listen, Honey, I was about your age when I lost my mother, and I needed her so much—you can't imagine! Now, you're beginning to grow up, just like I was then, and pretty soon you'll get your period—"

"Hah, some chance!"

"Just be patient. I can assure you, it will happen when your body is ready. Then all kinds of questions about being a young woman will begin to occur to you. And soon you'll start going out with boys, and having to make decisions about—about what is right and wrong," Geneva said. Emelye made no reply, and as Geneva puzzled over whether she had understood what she meant when it came to boys, she became aware that Emelye's face had emptied of all expression, as if she had swept all thoughts into some far corner where her mother could not discover them. She knew then there was something about all this that Emelye was hiding even yet. "What is it?" she asked.

"Nothing," she said vaguely, then after a pause, she went on, "I was just…just thinking that if you knew the boys I go to school with, you wouldn't want me to go out with any of them. They are rude, Mom, and they have dirty minds. They are not like—like the boys at home."

Home…. Geneva had no reason to be struck by her daughter's lapse in wording. Yet somehow it was more revealing than anything else that Emelye had remained stubbornly rooted in the Heights. She took in a breath. "Well, that's pretty typical of adolescent boys everywhere, I'm afraid. But one day you will meet someone who is more mature, and—Just trust me. In the next few years you will need your mother as never before," she said, then fell silent. How ludicrous she sounded, as if she were trying to sell Emelye on her value as a mother.

"But Mom, Willa's like—" Emelye began, then started over: "Willa can help me. She understands…things," she said, and shrugged.

So already she had begun thinking of Willa as her mother. What had gone on behind her back when the two of them spent all those weeks together? Geneva wondered, suddenly distrustful of Willa again. Well, she wasn't going to be drawn into this anymore. Quietly she said, "I'm sorry, Emelye, but I can't let you go now. Maybe in two years, but not now." She rose from the bed.

"In two years my life will already be ruined," Emelye said ruefully.

Geneva did not answer. When she walked out and closed the door she was trembling all over. That she had prevailed left her no less bruised by the confrontation.

When Geneva returned to the sitting room, Elizabeth was saying to Tony, "How can the Church refuse to take a stand against the use of force? If all the Christians in Europe refused to take up arms, there would be a lot fewer wars—"

Geneva interrupted, "I need to speak to your father alone, please."

Elizabeth looked around, her eyes bright with conviction. Her discourse with Tony right now was typical of those following the evening news these days. After a pause, she blinked and said, "Oh yes, I was about to go up anyway." Then, her eyes veering away from Geneva's, she added delicately, "Is…is Emelye feeling better?"

Geneva realized now that Elizabeth probably knew all about Emelye's plans. She started to ask her, but then, what difference did it make? "Emelye needs to come to terms with some things," Geneva said, already imagining the conversation about to take place on two pink floral bedspreads.

"I see. Well, goodnight, Geneva. Goodnight, Father," Elizabeth said. She scooped Bertrand up from the window seat and hugged him close as she carried him up to bed, thinking suddenly of Kilty, sleeping at the end of Andy's bed, and Father's Yorkshire terrier, The Baron, in London—a Christmas gift from his children last year. She wondered with dread what would happen to all the poor animals if the Germans invaded England.

Geneva sat down next to Tony and recounted all that Emelye had said. As she talked, his countenance darkened. She could only imagine what he was feeling. He had already lost out on the first seven years of Emelye's life. Her wish to live on the opposite side of the Atlantic for the remainder of it must be hurtful indeed.

Finally she told him how close Emelye came to saying Willa was like a mother to her, her eyes filling as she did so. Tony took her hand in his. "Now, Darling, she was only trying to show you that you needn't worry about her. You know how young people are—they assume adults are beyond having their feelings injured."

Geneva expected Tony to say they would simply forbid Emelye to move away. Yet he rose from the sofa and began to pace back and forth before the fireplace, deep in thought, his arms crossed, his fingers stroking the patches on his sweater sleeves. Geneva continued absorbing the shock of what they were facing. She would have never dreamed any child of hers would want to leave home before it was time. Children were driven from home when their parents treated them cruelly, or neglected them. No matter what they endured, those who were loved like Emelye had a natural desire to remain within the circle of that love—

"I think perhaps we ought at least to check with the Youngers. We haven't heard Rodney's side, you know. He may not be all that keen on having another teenager under his roof. And even if they do say 'yes,' as Emelye believes they will, the whole thing may just blow over."

"Blow over?" Geneva echoed, bewildered.

"Quite. You see, what makes Emelye so determined to have her way is that she knows we forbid it. If we tell her we shan't stand in her way, however, she may do some sober thinking about how far away from us she will be, and unable to come home. Perhaps two years will not seem such a long wait after all."

Geneva wasn't so sure. Emelye's argument about bringing up her grades before college was pretty astute when you got right down to it.

Tony returned to the sofa and took her hands in his. "Look here, Emelye has reached the age when just telling her 'no' won't do the job anymore. If we don't meet her halfway, she'll grow to resent us more and more, perhaps at some point rebel—that could be pretty nasty, you know."

No, Geneva didn't know. At age fifteen she was struggling to survive real tragedy. Emelye just didn't know how lucky she was. Still, she imagined Emelye packing her things and vanishing one night, maybe with some boy who seemed sympathetic to her cause; getting in trouble, or getting hurt, or worse. "I suppose you've got a point," she allowed.

The next morning Geneva dutifully sat down to write to Willa and Rodney. It was all she could do to keep from accusing Willa of betraying her by putting the idea of moving away into Emelye's head. Yet if she accused her wrongly, it would be the end of their friendship. No, Willa would not have done that to her, she just knew it….

Eager for a truce, when the letter was written she handed it to Emelye to read. Emelye quickly scanned the pages, then said, "Oh Mom, that's the best thing you and Daddy have ever done for me."

Geneva was crushed. What about all the love and devotion they'd lavished on her over the years? Did it count for nothing?

By June, Hitler had repeated his earlier demand that Poland restore Danzig to Germany; Germany and Italy had signed a pact. Though Britain and Poland had yet to sign a formal alliance, government rules and regulations on preparedness for war were already spreading like tentacles through towns and villages. Committees were being formed to oversee the placement of women and children in the event of a mass evacuation from London. Civil defense posters urging people to plant kitchen gardens and conserve water and coal were beginning to appear. Clifton had measured all the windows so that Mrs. Greaves, who let out the children's uniform hems every year and repaired their clothing on her sewing machine, could turn her energies toward making blackout curtains for Clearharbour. Clifton was Mrs. Greaves's only child. She was very worried he would enlist. Geneva often noticed the poor thing dabbing her eyes as she went about her duties.

Twice a day, Emelye hurried to the foot of the drive to collect the post, flipping through the letters for a Houston postmark, then, finding none, dumping the post on the kitchen table and trudging away in disappointment. *If war has to come, may it start soon,* Geneva thought, *then all this will have to wait until it's over.* Yet her memories of all the soldiers killed and wounded during the Great War, plus the dreaded Spanish Influenza that took Madame Linsky and

Gerry West and countless others, all over the world, forced her to hope that, against all odds, war could be prevented. She dreaded turning on the wireless, and she wished Tony hadn't subscribed to *The Times* here as well as in London. The daily headlines about the situation were like silent screams.

One morning Geneva was working in her garden. While generally this was the best way to relieve the burden of worry, since the night Emelye begged to move away, Geneva's guilt for failing to make her happy preoccupied her thoughts no matter what she was doing. This morning as she knelt above larkspurs, pansies, bluebells, snapdragons, hollyhocks, geraniums, pinks, and foxgloves running riot in the stone border, pinching off the dead matter to encourage the plants to continue blooming, her thoughts returned to her gardening days in the Heights. Emelye would skip around in her sandals with the breeze blowing her blond hair, sometimes pausing with her toy spade to dig a little hole for her mommy to plant a flower in, sometimes watering the plants with her small yellow sprinkling can. And Geneva could not resist stopping her work from time to time just for the pleasure of catching her daughter in a hug and breathing in her fresh little-girl scent, her small body prickly warm from the sun. But then they moved to England and before Geneva knew it she was dealing with Elvira's demands to be the center of attention, Andy's mischief-making, and Chris's crying jags. Had Emelye ever complained that she wasn't getting her share of attention, things might have been different. But she had not, and Geneva failed to intuit that she was gradually withdrawing. How often nowadays did she stop what she was doing and catch her daughter in a hug? Not nearly often enough—

"Mom!"

Geneva swivelled around on her heels, and there stood Emelye, the sunlight glinting off her hair. She thrust a letter in front of her. When Geneva rose to her feet, her heart went in reverse. She took the letter, covered with U.S. postage stamps, Willa's return in the corner. "*Dear Geneva, how we would love to have Emelye live with us, yet as things are—*" Thank goodness Tony was due home tonight. "Your father and I will read this together when he gets here," she said.

Emelye's face screwed up. "But *Mom!*"

"It is addressed to me," she reminded her, amazed at the shrillness of her voice.

"You're just being mean!" Emelye cried. Then, after a pause she tilted her chin and demanded, "How do I know you and Daddy won't pretend it says I can't come, just to keep me from going?"

Geneva was flabbergasted. "I'm not being mean. But you certainly are, saying we might lie to you, when we never have," she retorted.

Emelye stomped away. Geneva's heart contracted as if she were watching her walk down the gangway of a ship bound for America. "Wait a minute, Dear," she said tenderly.

Emelye turned on her heel, her face bright with hope. Geneva held out her arms. "Who knows what might happen, huh? Meantime, how about a hug?"

Emelye's expression darkened. "I don't want a hug. I've been miserable for eight years, and you don't even care," she said scornfully, and turned back toward the house.

Geneva stood there trembling. Tony was wrong. Emelye was not on the verge of rebellion. She was fully engaged in it. And the rejection of her hug—that most simple and basic act of love between a mother and child—was the cruelest blow Geneva had ever suffered from another human being.

That night when Tony arrived, Geneva took him into the sitting room and closed the door. "This came today," she said, pulling the letter from her pocket.

Their eyes met and held for a long moment. Tony opened the envelope and unfolded the letter. Geneva held on to his elbow and they read together:

"Waiting so long to reply to your letter doesn't mean that Rodney and I had to think twice about wanting Emelye to come. It's just that we realize how hard it will be for you to let her go. Then I had to figure out the right way to put all this. But it seems that every girl deserves some blissful years of high school, of football games and prom gowns and corsages, before life gets too serious. Reagan is a terrific school—James loved it so much that I think he viewed his graduation in May with mixed emotions. And Serena is thriving there. She has been chosen as a yell leader for next year. I just know Emelye will find her place at Reagan...."

"Life is apt to become deadly serious over here, in a very short time," Tony said quietly as they concluded their reading.

Geneva sank down in a chair and closed an arm around her abdomen. "I think Emelye's upstairs," she said.

CHAPTER 19

On the morning the family gathered to see Emelye off to America, Geneva was short of breath and giddy from the many cups of strong black coffee she had consumed in order to get her exhausted body on the move, and perhaps, too, from her empty stomach. She ought to have followed Tony's lead and eaten on the train, but her emotions were so raw, her nerves so frazzled, the very thought of taking a bite of the currant scone on the tray all but nauseated her, and the acid in the fresh orange juice would have set her stomach afire.

Last night as the *William & Mary* curtain rose for the first time on the grimy, cluttered newsroom and tough-talking characters of *The Front Page*, she'd sat mute in a swirl of copper-colored silk taffeta, the reality that just hours from now she would bid farewell to her daughter holding her mind hostage until a round of applause burst through at the interval and Tony patted her arm and smiled, reminding her to applaud. *Here I am in London, on Emelye's last night at home,* she despaired, and the fact that she must be *here* for Tony on the very night she ought to be *there* for Emelye seemed to epitomize the many painful decisions she'd faced since she and Tony married, over how to divide her time.

Her night was long and sleepless, an endless stream of intercessory prayers cresting on waves of weeping.

Upon arriving in Southampton this morning and being taxied into the hulking shadow of the *SS Olympia*, Tony and Geneva clasped hands and hastened forth among the swelling crowd, searching for the rest of the family. Geneva's head was covered in a white straw hat with a broad brim, and her swollen, red-rimmed eyes were hidden behind dark glasses. "There they are," said Tony at last, gesturing to the right. All Geneva could see from this distance were the heads of Cynthia and Edward. To her gratitude, Cynthia had offered to accompany Emelye to the States, saving Tony the trip, though he admitted his feelings were torn—hard as it would be for him to get away the day after an opening, he could think of no more meaningful way to express his love for Emelye than to accompany her safely back to the place from whence she had come at his urging. Geneva only hoped and prayed Cynthia would return safely before war broke out.

Now as they drew near, Geneva spotted Emelye standing between her grandparents. *My baby…*she thought tenderly. Emelye had never looked so young and vulnerable, in spite of—or perhaps on account of?—the grown-up white linen suit with a flounce over the hip line that she had purchased to wear today, and her first-ever pair of shoes with one-and-a-half inch heels. She wore a golden guardian angel pendant around her neck—Cynthia's perennial token of good luck. *God, protect my daughter at sea….* How hot it was, so hot that Geneva felt dizzy, as though the sun had singled her out as its victim and driven its thumb between her shoulder blades.

They stepped up to Emelye now, gave her a quick preliminary, "We're here" hug. "We were afraid you wouldn't make it in time," she said fretfully.

Time was growing short and Emelye was eager to board the ship because even now she could not quite believe she was really going, that something would not happen to prevent her. There were butterflies in her stomach. She would have traveled alone if need be, but she was relieved all the same that she would not have to, now that the day had come and the ship looked so huge and forbidding. She leaned down to hug her two brothers in turn. She doubted she would miss them much, never having been close to them in spite of the fact that they lived under the same roof. First she closed her arms around Andy, who was the spitting image of their father at the same age—she'd seen pictures at Brookhurst. To her surprise, Andy reached in his pocket and handed her a lump of hard candy. "This is to eat on the ship," he said gravely, as if he were giving her seasick tablets.

Her heart twisted into a knot: Andy loved his sweets and usually guarded them with his life.

When she reached for Chris, tears rolled from his eyes. "Don't go, Sis. Chris will be a good boy!" he pleaded.

She lifted him in her arms and hugged him close. "You're always a good boy, but I must go anyway," she said tenderly, putting him back on his feet. Maybe she would miss her brothers just a little….

Now Elvira grabbed Emelye and hugged her fiercely. "May I come and see you in America?"

"I guess so."

"When I come, will you take me to New York, to see a play? Grandmother says the plays there are jolly good."

"I guess."

"Oh Em, dear, I do wish so dreadfully that you wouldn't go away!"

Emelye felt sad leaving her impish little sister with auburn waves and freckles, and big brown eyes. Even though Elvira was a pest, she managed to get under your skin. "I'll miss you, but I must go," Emelye said.

Tony's composure was threadbare, after the weeks of being strong for Geneva, all the while a hollow sense of failure increasing inside him. When Emelye hugged his sister Nell, he very nearly broke down. He was grateful for the affection that had grown up between them—no one could have counted on this, Nell being the shy person she was, plus all that had happened before she and Emelye met. He could not hear what they were saying above the noise of the crowd, but presently Nell pinned a red camellia on Emelye's shoulder. Swiftly, Tony chucked the box with the orchid corsage that he'd brought for his daughter into the nearest trash receptacle.

Watching him, Geneva thought how very generous he was. He had taken great care in choosing the white orchid with royal purple throat for Emelye today. They'd gone to a florist in Knightsbridge. She was reminded then of the day after the disaster at St. Michael's, when a dozen white roses arrived for Emelye from London. "*Remember, PRACTI C E makes perfect. Heaps of love, Daddy,*" said the card. Tony could not have known anymore than she did how futile it was to try and repair the damage done by Miss Sloane. Geneva felt a surge of tenderness for him now, which was quickly engulfed by dizziness. It was so stifling here, and there were so many people crowding close. She touched her clammy forehead, then pressed a finger to her hammering heart.

Guy caught Emelye in a hug and lifted her off her feet. A mass of muscle from head to toe, and nearly six feet tall, he was nonetheless the soul of gentleness. She adored him. "Take care of yourself, you!" he warned.

"*Me?* What about *you?*" she said. Guy had joined the British Armed Forces and would report for duty in two weeks. She was frightened for him, going off to war. She pressed his big chest and looked sternly into his light blue eyes. "Listen, don't let anything happen to you!"

"Ah, those Jerries don't scare me. I'll take on two at a time, before breakfast."

Tears flooded Emelye's eyes. *What if you don't come back?* "Oh, I love you, Guy! You're the only nice boy in England. We'll write to each other."

Nell stood back with Morey, watching, remembering the child she had taken under her wing, and how easily she had come to love her. She would have given anything if Guy were going with Emelye today, instead of racing headlong into the perils of the battlefield. *How can he even think of risking his life, when we've already lost a son?* She had often asked herself. He had been set to go into training as a police officer, *"So I can help people, Mum."* And now all she heard was, *"It's only right that I go and do my part."* Though Nell had not dwelt on it for years, since Guy joined up, the memory of losing Gerry had returned again and again, and dreams of holding his small fevered body were so vivid they woke her up at nights, and she lay there, eyes wide open, catching her breath. *Dear God, if I lose Guy*—No, she mustn't think about it today. This was Emelye's day. She dabbed her eyes with her handkerchief and thought of Emelye and Guy tumbling down the hill at Camellia Cottage, laughing and gay. Which only redoubled her tears.

Now Morey was slipping an arm round her shoulders, no doubt intuiting the fearful thoughts she was determined to chase from her mind. *Dear God, don't let Morey lose another son....*

Geneva gazed wistfully upon the group gathered to bid Emelye farewell: *Here they all were, the family she was most anxious for Emelye to be a part of when they came to England, and who had exceeded all expectations, showering love on her like stars on the brightest of nights. Yet it was not enough....*

Feeling a little more unsteady all the time, she held on to Tony's arm. Memories flooded her mind, most of them good, though a few of them painful, like several days ago when Emelye said as if it would make everything alright, *"Mom, you don't need me anymore. You have plenty of other children now."* Perhaps for Emelye the bond between them that was formed nearly nine months before that treacherous, icy night when she was born, and strengthened by the years when they had only each other, was severed on the day they set sail for England. Thank God, she was returning to Willa. From one loving womb to another. She hated Willa for saying yes, loved her for not saying no, wondered, what if the Youngers had not been there to catch Emelye in flight?

Emelye and Elizabeth hugged tightly, then stood apart, clasping hands, their eyes held in a long soulful exchange. There was little left for them to say, after nights and nights of lying in the dark bedroom, talking. How Elizabeth admired her sister! *All her dreams will come true now, because she has the cour-*

age to seek them out. I shall never have that kind of courage. "Be happy, dear Emelye, Godspeed."

"Oh Elizabeth, I think I'll miss you more than anyone. I'm sorry I never could—well—never really belonged here. I tried."

"I know," Elizabeth whispered, her eyes filling.

The ship's whistle blew. The decks of the *SS Olympia* were already teeming with passengers, and others were jostling along the gangway, to board.

Emelye threw her arms around her father's neck. "I love you, Daddy!"

"I love you too, Darling." Feeling her body against him, his thoughts returned to the first time he held her, how tiny she was in his arms, how fragile she seemed. He had vowed to move heaven and earth, to bring her and her mother to live with him. Yet, only to say goodbye so soon—where had the years gone? At least she was bound for a place far safer than this one would soon become. This belief alone had got him through the last few weeks.

When Emelye and Geneva finally embraced, Geneva had labored so hard, for so long, to be prepared for this moment, all her emotions went numb. Emelye felt a twinge of remorse—her parents still did not know that part of her reason for moving to the Youngers' was her love for James. One day, when she and James were happily married, she would tell them, and they would understand. "I love you, Mom! And don't worry about me. I'm going to be so happy, just wait!"

Geneva dared not speak, or she would begin to sob so hard that she would be unable to see Emelye through her tears, and she wanted to take her in, detail by detail, imprinting her face and figure on her mind. *I will not see my daughter blossom into a young woman, but remember her as she looked when she was just on the brink.* She managed a nod. Suddenly, Emelye felt guilty for hurting her mother, and for the fact that she doubted she would miss her very much. "I'll write," she promised. She sniffed, and reached for her new alligator leather travel case, a gift from her parents.

Cynthia was at Geneva's elbow. They looked at each other. "Don't worry, my dear, she's going to be fine," said Cynthia.

Thank God for Cynthia's strength. "Thank you for everything," said Geneva, hugging her. Cynthia kissed both her cheeks. "Look after Edward," she whispered. Edward was seventy-five years old, and though from all signs he was in good health, he had not felt equal to making the trip and Cynthia was anxious about leaving him.

Watching Edward and Cynthia embrace, Geneva saw Cynthia shut her eyes tightly, as if to ward off tears. Their figures, joined together, seemed to swoon before her eyes, outlined in sharp, animated light. Geneva blinked, struggled to catch her breath. The sun's rays bore down relentlessly. Just a few more minutes....

Then Cynthia and Emelye were walking along the gangway, soon becoming lost among the crowd. As Geneva watched the moving tangle of figures, they seemed to lose solidity and become liquid, shapeless shards of color. Tony patted her arm, tears in his eyes, his voice tight as he said, "Alright, Darling?"

"I think so."

"She'll be fine. We did the right thing."

"Yes."

Opera glasses from the *William & Mary* were handed around. With the certainty that was characteristic of her, Elvira declared she had spotted Cynthia and Emelye high up on a deck. "Look, there they are! Can you see? Standing below the third lifeboat on the right. Everyone, wave! Hurry!" Geneva looked up dizzily through the opera glasses at the sea of waving hands, the sun burning her face, its light dancing in her eyes, her heart beating so fast and hard she felt it would burst. She lifted a hand to wave. *God, take care of my little girl, wherever she may be, and grant that she will return to us one—*

And from a stab of light she was falling....

Tony felt the heavy tug of Geneva's arm on his elbow as her body swayed for a moment and then went limp. The opera glasses spilled from her hand and struck the pavement.

CHAPTER 20

As Dr. Ashmore completed his examination, the sun swept through the high window of his surgery, criss-crossed with war-time tape, and threw a shimmering lattice shadow over the room. It was the first Monday in October, two months after Emelye sailed to America.

"Bit of a wrench, when children leave home, isn't it? Sometimes there seems to be a kind of primeval urge to fill the empty place," the doctor said to Geneva from the end of the table. The white drape between her upraised knees hid their faces from each other, concealing her blush. Confirming her pregnancy just minutes before, he had remarked with some delicacy on her age—"*Perhaps you might have a preventive stitch taken, directly afterward.*" She would be forty-one years old when this baby was born. All through those weeks of heartache pending Emelye's departure, Tony came home more frequently than usual, and their long late-night talks invariably left them tied up in emotional knots, desperate for the comfort of sexual intimacy. Now the term, 'primeval urge' made her feel as if she and Tony had been guilty of conduct unseemly for people their age.

While Dr. Ashmore did not believe Geneva's fainting spell was "a danger signal," she had a feeling that something was not right. Or was she simply uneasy because Tony was not at liberty to come home? A month ago, the Sunday that England and France declared war on Germany, she sat on the bed near his open suitcase, disconsolate as he placed his dancing shoes inside. It would be a long time before she watched him unpack those well-worn shoes, with their scuffed heels, and creases over the tops. Leisure travel was now restricted. Nor would Geneva be going to London for the birth of their child, for it was predicted that London would receive the brunt of attacks by the German Luftwaffe. Tony had telephoned Dr. Rand, her specialist there, for a referral. "Harold Ashmore in Truro. He's a first-rate O.B. man," said Dr. Rand. Dr. Ashmore was seasoned, too, Geneva observed now. His medical school diploma, posted within view of the examining table, was dated 1910. The skin sagged around his jaws, there were wrinkles around his gray eyes, and his full head of sandy colored hair was sprinkled with gray.

He offered her his hand and she sat upright. "Dizzy?"

"No."

"Good."

"Do I need to stay in bed?" she asked, even though with her last three pregnancies this had not been necessary.

"No reason that I can see at this point. Just avoid—"

"I know. The stairs." They smiled at each other. "And be careful not to overexert," the doctor added. "I assume you have help with your little ones?"

She told him yes, though it was a bit of an exaggeration given the fact that Mrs. Greaves had her hands full keeping house, and Elizabeth was busy with her studies—chemistry was proving the first academic subject she could not master easily. Ordinarily Geneva relied on Cynthia and Edward to help out during her pregnancies, but as soon as war was declared, thousands of children were evacuated from London and assigned to live with families in the country. Cynthia and Edward had taken in sixteen evacuees.

"Come and see me in a month, and call me if you have any problems," said Dr. Ashmore, and Geneva felt encouraged by his "everything will be fine" smile.

In the afternoon Clifton brought the double bed and chest of drawers out of storage and arranged them in the buttery. During her earlier pregnancies she and Tony had enjoyed the coziness of this small rectangular room, with its slanted ceiling and exposed beams. But now it seemed stifling. The heavy blackout curtains overpowered the large window behind the bed—a grim reminder of Tony's forced absence. Geneva asked Elizabeth to retrieve Madame Linsky's crucifix from the wall above Emelye's bed. She was disappointed Emelye left it behind, apparently feeling no attachment to it though it had been a fixture above her bed from the time she came into the world. As soon as she cradled the cross in her hand—for the first time in a very long while—she felt the unexpected thrill of tenderness she had experienced the day she found it rudely discarded after Linsky's death, and rescued it for her own. Feeling especially grateful to have it back, she mounted it on the wall opposite her bed.

In the ensuing weeks, every night when darkness fell, the fear that bombs were being dropped on London engulfed Geneva: Tomorrow a telegram or a trunk call would come, reporting that Tony had been maimed or killed; the *William & Mary* was burned to the ground; the house on Norfolk Square was reduced to a rubble. She would light a candle to see by—electric power must be conserved—and focus on the crucifix for so long and hard that when she doused the candle and closed her eyes, its outline was emblazoned inside her eyelids. She would literally pray herself to sleep. Every morning she would part the blackout curtains and gaze outside. From here she could see the corner of Nell's burgeoning camellia bush outside the conservatory, and the sweeping meadows beyond. The peaceful scene made her feel that surely all was well in London, and she would imagine Tony riding to work in the tube, wearing his business suit, reading the latest theatre reviews in the *Times Literary Supplement*. Day after day, she offered a prayer of thanksgiving for being proven correct.

By the early part of November, when the weather turned cold and rainy, Geneva was chronically fatigued and spending more and more time in bed. Fortunately, the evacuees living with Cynthia and Edward had been returned to their families along with most others, for the dreaded air raids on London had failed to materialize. *Perhaps they never will,* Geneva thought hopefully. Elizabeth walked back and forth to school each day, for Harleigh School was nearby and she seemed able to manage the uphill climb alright. Yet Elvira and Andy had to be driven to Bodmin Primary, all the way up in Robartes Road. So Merton came over early in the morning to drive them to school, then doubled back in the afternoons to collect them. On Fridays he took Elvira and Andy to spend the weekend at Brookhurst, where Elvira decorated the blackout curtains with silver stars, and put on plays in the library, coercing her brother Andy into participating. At age four, Chris was too much a mama's boy to leave Geneva at weekends. He was happiest when snuggled up with her in bed, looking at picture books, or quietly playing with his toys. He seemed to thrive on her undivided attention, and seldom had any reason to cry.

Geneva felt apologetic for this pregnancy, which inconvenienced her loved ones and, because of her age, may not be fair to the child in her womb. If she sat idle for too long during the day, she would begin to fret: *What if this baby is sickly…or abnormal?* The word, *defective,* would insinuate itself on her mind. How she abhorred that word, suggesting an object, rather than a person, one not useful to society and therefore to be dispensed with at the earliest possible convenience. Often her thoughts seized anxiously on her earlier pregnancies.

Had she felt this particular kind of dread? Granted, she had worried a good deal as she carried Emelye, but her worry was rational, since she had suffered a miscarriage at age sixteen—the unfortunate result of her affair with Victor Calais. And she was concerned that she might die in childbirth—also rational, since her child would be solely dependent upon her. Yet she could not remember ever fearing Emelye may not be a healthy child. And with Elvira and Andy and Chris, she was completely confident all would be well. Of course, Tony was there—not always by her side in the early part, but at least accessible should she need him, and toward the end he was with her night and day, his face a beacon of encouragement, his arms strong and assuring when they held her at night. Oh, this was crazy! Nights of worry about Tony. Days of worry about her child. She felt imprisoned by worry.

To help keep Geneva's mind occupied, Elizabeth checked out books for her at the Passmore Edwards Library. Virginia Woolf, D. H. Lawrence, Rebecca West and Elizabeth Bowen—she read them all with great absorption and a sense of gratitude for the escape from worry they provided. She had not read much during her years of living in England. Until now, with her growing family, she hardly had time for it. She had always made time to read the play scripts that Tony was considering for the *William & Mary*, however, and given him a few brief comments, either in person or over the telephone. Now when he sent her scripts, she read them two or three times, and sent him long critiques.

Otherwise there were letters to answer. From the time Emelye moved to the Youngers, she had written brief missives with a frequency that suggested Willa was holding her feet to the fire. Obviously, she was happy, and her life was as busy as that of any other teenager. She was working on *The Pennant*—Reagan's yearbook—selling ads for next year's edition. Not surprisingly, a half-page ad for Younger Real Estate was her first sale. Yet Willa said she was surprisingly forward about contacting business proprietors up and down West 19th in the Heights, and she took the bus to downtown Houston one Saturday, returning with four sales, including one from Wilson's Stationery. She'd joined the Glee Club, and the Girl Reserves—a service club that made up baskets for poor families at Christmas. And so far, true to her word, she was bringing home good grades.

In mid-November, she wrote: "Mom, guess what! I got my period! Don't worry. Thanks to Midol, I'm fine. Gotta go. Love, Emelye." From the tone, she had no desire for a long reply in lieu of the mother-daughter talk Geneva had always envisioned them having at this juncture. She could not help feeling cheated, though she was careful to keep it from showing when she wrote back.

Emelye's next letter reported that a classmate named Larry Cateau liked her. "He's good-looking, mom, with dark hair and DREAMY eyes, but he's only about an inch taller than me, and his cuticles always have grease around them because he works after school for an auto mechanic."

Willa wrote more: "Larry came over one evening to work with Emelye on a geography project, and he and Rodney chatted. A well-mannered, industrious boy, Larry works to help with expenses at home—his mother is divorced. She is a seamstress, and does monogramming for Kaplan's. Rodney was very impressed with Larry." Emelye's first boy friend, when she was a few months' shy of dating age? Again, Geneva felt shut out.

Painful as it had been to let Emelye go, Geneva had to admit that maybe she really would be better off in the long-run. Yet Willa's letter brought a sudden, excruciating sense of loss and a guilty longing to return to those days when she and Emelye lived together in the Heights. Had she really appreciated how precious that time was, while they were living in it? Was it ever possible to fully appreciate the present until it became the past? Kaplan's…. How well she remembered the two of them strolling hand in hand into that store, where everything from pillow slips to petticoats was for sale—this was when it was still pretty small, before Mr. Kaplan's two sons Bennett and Herman grew up and came into the business, adding the whimsical 'Ben Hur' to the name and many more products to the shelves. Willa sent her a *Leader* clipping sometime ago, about the expansion. Well, you couldn't go back and recapture the past, she told herself practically. Even Kaplan's had not remained the same….

On Christmas Eve around four o'clock, Cynthia and Edward arrived. The celebration was to be held here rather than at Brookhurst, in deference to Geneva. She watched as Merton carried in a stately eight-foot Douglas fir from the Brookhurst estate, still redolent with the fragrance of damp evergreen and freshly cut timber. Soon everyone was in the sitting room trimming the tree. Geneva retreated to her bed, to rest until Tony arrived. He had not been home since the war began nearly four months ago. He was driving the Rolls-Royce, which he intended to store in the garage for the duration. Pet dogs were not allowed in London now, so he was bringing along his Yorkshire terrier. Happily, The Baron had spent enough time here that they were reasonably sure all the pets would get along. Geneva worried about Tony driving such a long distance when road lights all over England had been extinguished and drivers were allowed to burn only one head lamp, most of it masked off. Well it was lucky at least there was neither snow nor icy rain coming down to make road conditions even more treacherous.

Just after the clock in the hallway struck the hour of eight, Kilty began barking. Geneva put out the lamp and raised the corner of the blackout curtain. She rubbed a clear space in the misty window glass, and peered outside. The Rolls-Royce moved stealthily across her line of vision, its tiny slit of light beaming no brighter than a small torch. Geneva could not fathom Tony keeping the Rolls-Royce all these years. Driving in London was impractical, so most of the time it stayed in a rented garage space; and he usually rode the train back and forth to Bodmin so that he could catch up on work during the journey. Tonight the luxurious auto seemed grossly out of proportion to their driveway.

She released the curtain and switched on the lamp, and lay against the pillows, a smile curling at the edges of her mouth. Tony was home! Oh, how she had missed him. She waited for the cacophony of happy voices and barking dogs to play out. Then the buttery door swung open and there stood Tony wearing a moss green sweater under his wool jacket, and a plaid tie in muted tones of maroon and green. He had never looked more handsome. Or desirable. Geneva's lethargy was no more; the blood in her veins quickened. "Welcome home!" she said, and held out her arms.

Tony gazed across at his wife. She had always been rosy-cheeked and radiant during pregnancy. All the way home tonight, he had envisioned finding her just that way, the memory of her peculiar sexiness when she was with child, beating in his loins: not the kind of sexiness of other times, when the sight of her naked body made his heart leap, but a soft womb-like curling-round sensuality, drawing him into its warmth. The closer to home that he came, the harder he pressed the accelerator. And now he was quite startled to find his wife pale and gaunt, with dark patches beneath her eyes. He felt frightened; his thoughts spun in confusion. "Hullo, Darling!" he managed to say, cheerfully enough, shutting the door behind him. He came to the bed and cradled her in his arms, trying to conceal his alarm. She burrowed her head in his warm, hard-muscled chest, squeezing him, inhaling deeply the familiar, combined scents of spicy cologne and wool and leather. "Oh, how I've missed you!" she cried. They kissed and they kissed, until they heard Edward's patient voice on the other side of the door: "Come along, Chrissy, there's a good lad. Sister is going to play Christmas carols on the piano, and we'll all sing!"

Tony and Geneva gave each other a wicked look. Tony rose to lock the door.

Later, after everyone had gone to bed, Geneva and Tony lay naked far into the night, talking, basking in the pleasure of having nothing to separate them, not even the thin fabric of nightclothes. At length Geneva admitted to Tony Dr. Ashmore's advice about taking a preventive measure. "In a way I know he's probably right. Still, now that you're here, I feel young again! Maybe we should wait until afterward to decide…."

They had always wanted a houseful of children, and Tony had felt rather smug, knowing they had the means to provide for as many as they brought into the world. But now he saw what a strain this was putting on Geneva. He wished to scoop her up in his arms and take her back to London. He felt somehow that in caring for her he could restore the color to her cheeks, and her vitality. Yet, how ridiculous! London, ever-ready for attack, was no place for an expectant mother. Besides, owing to the decimated staff at the *William & Mary,* he was working especially long hours. He would be so glad when this child was delivered. Thank God Dr. Ashmore was more progressive than most physicians hereabouts, and delivered babies in hospital rather than at home. *What if Geneva does not survive the birth of this child?* The mere thought brought cold terror to his heart. Losing Geneva was the one blow in life that Tony would not survive. He doubted he could love a child whose birth had destroyed his wife.

Before Tony slept, he prayed to God that Geneva would survive. He knew they must not risk future pregnancies. He also sensed her feelings were delicate at the moment, however, and decided to let the matter drop for now.

On the morning of his return to London—on Boxing Day—it was deadly cold outside and the wind was howling. Snowfall was predicted by nighttime. They lay in each other's arms upon the pillows, both feeling cheated. It seemed that Tony had only just arrived. He looked down the length of Geneva's body. How thin her limbs had become. Tenderly he laid a hand on the hard round lump of her belly, rising from the valley of her groin. An unspeakable dread surged through him. *There's something wrong.* He did not want to leave her, knew he would not have a moment's peace in London. "Darling, I don't want to risk another pregnancy. I want you to take Dr. Ashmore's advice. *Promise me.*"

"But we can wait and discuss it when you get here," she argued.

He kissed her forehead tenderly. "Dear heart, I may not be able to come home when the baby is born," he said.

"But that isn't considered 'leisure travel,' is it? Going home to be with your wife in childbirth?" she asked, perplexed.

"I shall certainly try to get here, but it will depend entirely on how matters stand in London. One must be prepared for the worst. *Please,* just do as I ask."

Finally, with great reluctance, she agreed. Immediately, she felt uneasy. "But I sure hope you can come home when the baby is born," she added quietly.

CHAPTER 21

On a cold gray morning in March, Geneva sent Mrs. Greaves to the local civil defense bureau to request an infant gas mask for the baby. The rest of the family had acquired their gas masks at the onset of the war, and dutifully practiced wearing them for a few minutes each day, looking like a family of grasshoppers lounging in the sitting room with a pair of mice their guests—those for Andy and Chris were designed to look like Mickey Mouse. Elvira would not hear of having a Mickey Mouse. She wished to be able to impersonate whomever or whatever she chose.

As Mrs. Greaves was leaving, Nell arrived to have tea with Geneva and discuss plans for the garden, which she had offered to look after beginning this spring and until Geneva was able to care for it herself. Nell was always eager for an opportunity to demonstrate her loyalty to Geneva, and besides, having finished pruning and mulching her many camellia bushes, she desperately needed a diversion. She was obsessed with concern for Guy, who was now a member of the 7th Armoured Division, stationed in Egypt. If her son must meet the enemy, Nell was grateful at least that he would do so in the relative safety of an armoured vehicle. Yet, the word *relative* was always lurking, to rob one's mind of peace. Of course, Geneva's garden was hardly Nell's only project at hand—there were ongoing food drives and clothing drives for the Women's Voluntary Services, for instance, and she had planted a small victory garden at Camellia Cottage, with runner beans and turnips, onions and carrots and potatoes. The problem was that all her activities these days were war-related, and therefore constant reminders that her son was in danger. She could not even gaze out her sitting room windows and savor memories of Guy as a young lad, scampering up the ladder on the trunk of the sweet chestnut and vanishing into its tree house. For now, directly below the rung where he would have taken his first step up, an Anderson shelter—inevitable for country houses—displaced ten square feet of ground, and one's focus was immediately drawn to the mound of earth covering its corrugated iron roof.

Poor Geneva apparently felt cooped-up in the buttery, for she had insisted Mrs. Greaves bring the tea tray into the sitting room this morning. Now Geneva lumbered in, wearing a shapeless dress and one of Tony's old sweaters with sleeve patches, the palms of her hands reaching round to support her back. Nell had not seen Geneva since Christmas Day, when she and Morey motored over with roast beef and Yorkshire pudding for the holiday meal. She was heartened to notice that she looked more rested than she had then, though she was still rather pale from being shut up inside all the time. Obviously she hadn't been to the hairdresser in some while, and her red waves, parted down the center, had grown to shoulder length. She sank down in a wingback chair by the fireplace, the great lump of her belly rising between the two chair arms. Chris followed close behind his mum, in sweater and overalls, and after greeting his Auntie Nell with a hug, he sat down at his mother's feet, reached for a toy truck nearby, and began to pull it by its string within a small radius of his mother's chair. Nell wondered how Chris would cope with having to share his mother with a newborn. Secretly she believed that Geneva babied Chris a bit too much.

They had just decided on hollyhocks for the south side of the stone plinth—or, border as Geneva referred to it—when the dogs began to make a fuss in the hallway. Soon Mrs. Greaves came in bearing a cube-shaped cardboard box. She handed the box to Geneva and offered to freshen their tea. "Wot'll be rationed next, after butter and sugar? I ask meself. Tea won' be far down the list, so's best to enjoy it whilst we can if you know wot I think."

When Mrs. Greaves was gone, Geneva took in a deep breath. Summoning all her reserved energies, she opened the box and unfolded a long olive-green canvas drapery to which was attached a large, globe-shaped helmet with a clear face mask—resembling what deep sea divers wear. Altogether it was pretty gruesome-looking, especially for a baby, Geneva thought. Chris was at her knee at once, his dark eyes wide, "Where is baby's Ickey Mouse?"

"Baby will be too little for a Mickey Mouse until he—or she—grows a little bigger," she said. There was a hand pump on the side of the helmet, which apparently operated like a bellows for administering oxygen. "Here, let's find out how we regulate the amount of oxygen going in," Geneva said, handing the instruction sheet to Nell. She noticed a frown of concentration on Chris's face.

She had long since concluded that, of all her children, Chris was probably the brightest and most observant, and this accounted for the fact that he was so sensitive. She went on holding up the odd-looking garment, examining it, while Nell fetched her eyeglasses from her handbag and put them on.

Just as Nell began to read aloud, Chris cried out, "Don't put baby in there!" He burst into tears and buried his face in Geneva's lap.

Laying the gas mask aside, Geneva put her arms around his shoulders. "What is it, Darling? Are you afraid of the gas mask?"

"Ye-e-es!" he wailed.

Nell knelt down and gently stroked his soft dark hair. "Christiaan, listen to Auntie Nell. The gas mask won't hurt baby. Let me show you how it will work, and then you'll see for yourself—"

"No, no, don't put baby in there!" he sobbed.

Nell sat back on her heels. "Chris is a bit of a—he takes things rather hard, doesn't he," said Nell.

Geneva realized that Nell was on the verge of labeling Chris a cry-baby. Nell did not understand what a sensitive child Chris was, for she was not all that sensitive herself, she thought defensively. She kissed the top of Chris's head and stroked his back. "Now, Chris, tell Mummy exactly what frightens you."

Soon it became clear that Chris was afraid the baby would be swallowed up inside the large helmet, and no one would be able to hear its cries for help. He had never seen a newborn baby, only Elvira's baby dolls, which were a good deal smaller in size and probably would have easily fit inside the helmet. No wonder he was frightened.

Obviously not convinced when she assured him that the helmet would cover only the baby's head, he cried yet again, "Don't put baby in there!"

Finally Geneva gave up. He would just have to wait and see for himself. "Why don't we ask Auntie Nell to take the gas mask away?" she suggested.

"Yes, take away," Chris said, and pushed out his lip.

Geneva asked Nell to put the box in the closet under the stairs, where such things as her marketing bags, and various mackintoshes and rain gear were stored, and where the children's presents were hidden prior to birthdays and Christmas. She pulled out her handkerchief and dried Chris's eyes.

When Nell opened the closet door and pulled the light string, she was suddenly flooded with fear for Guy. It often happened just when she thought she was coping admirably well. Some new reminder of the war would set her off. Her heart would begin palpitating, her forehead would grow clammy, and nausea would overtake her. She placed the box upon a shelf, turned off the light, and shut the door behind her. She leaned against the door jamb for a few moments, until she regained her composure.

Returning to the sitting room, she admitted to Geneva, "All these war contraptions…they're a bit scary to me, also."

Geneva made a mental note to retrieve the box and read the instructions one day when Chris was napping. Yet the threat of a ground invasion seemed to become more and more remote as time passed. Surely there was no need to rush.

CHAPTER 22

Cynthia Louise Selby was born at East Cornwall Hospital, at 2 o'clock on the afternoon of April 12, 1940. As the nurse held her near Geneva's chest for her to see, she anxiously took in every detail, from the shape of her head to her tiny fingers and toes. She was so perfectly beautiful, Geneva could not imagine why she had been so tormented with worry all through her pregnancy. After they had washed the infant and handed her into Geneva's arms, she noted her crown of red hair and fringe of red eyelashes. *At last, a baby who looks like me!* she thought with a rush of pride. As mother and daughter exchanged a long, silent gaze during their short journey to a private room, Geneva had a mystical feeling of oneness, as if she herself had been born again into this world. *Thank God for the gift of this child*, she prayed, hugging her daughter close.

If Cynthia Louise's first cry was more of a whimper—it dawned on Geneva now, as they were wheeled along the corridor—rather than the lusty cry she had come to expect of her newborns, Dr. Ashmore had not remarked on it, so surely there was no cause for concern. And if her color was a little more dusky than that of her other newborns, it was nothing to worry about, either. That every child was unique, was a miracle in itself. And in a few minutes, when the two laid up on the pillows in their room and Geneva opened her robe to offer her breast, that Cynthia Louise showed little interest in the thin stream that preceded her rich mother's milk was probably the sign of a quiet, sensitive nature. Andy and Elvira were like hungry tiger cubs from the start, but Chris—she seized on the memory—Chris was several hours old before he showed signs of hunger.

Nurse Tinsley stood by in a white ruffled cap and a long dark dress with a shirt collar and tie, her chin drawn back on her neck as she peered at mother and child. If there was a kink of concern between her eyes, it vanished soon enough. "Well, perhaps she just needs a little time, eh? Mummy can rest a bit for now, and we'll try again later." Before leaving, she took the baby from Geneva's arms and laid her on her stomach in the portable crib beside the bed. Soon her eyelids fluttered and she dozed off. Geneva kissed her fingers, then reached down and pressed them tenderly on her daughter's cheek. *How contented she is,* she thought, yet immediately a feeling of doubt lodged in her heart: *But what if she isn't alright?*

As she lay back on the pillows, she noticed a large vase of red roses on the sunny window ledge. Gingerly she rose from the bed and crossed the room to breathe in the fragrance of the roses, then read the card: *"I love you, Darling, and I'm on my way. Tony."* Thank God. Geneva could not have explained why the card brought tears to her eyes, why she felt Tony's presence would be vital, if something was wrong with their daughter. Who would have believed that after seven and a half months of war, England remained safe from enemy fire? Buildings in London—the *William & Mary* among them—were banked with sandbags; people on staff were trained to spot fires from the roofs; air raid shelters were established. Yet, night after night passed uneventfully. And Tony was coming home.

Geneva made her way back to bed. As she dozed off, she imagined Cynthia Louise lying between the two of them, absorbing the warmth and strength of their bodies to help overcome whatever was wrong…if anything was wrong….

She was sleeping lightly when the arrival of Cynthia and Edward awoke her. She sat up to greet them. "Meet your namesake and mine, Cynthia Louise Selby," she told her mother-in-law proudly. As Cynthia peered into the crib, a slight frown crossed her face, then vanished. Geneva looked down upon her daughter, who lay quietly, her eyes open. Then she glanced at the bedside clock: 5:05. Why had she not cried out to be fed by now? What had gone through Cynthia's mind in that unguarded moment when first she laid eyes upon her?

"Look what a little angel, Edward!" Cynthia crooned, reaching down to lift up her tiny namesake. Edward stood by, his hands locked behind him. "I daresay, before long, this one will be giving the lads a run for their money!" he said, peering over Cynthia's shoulder, his brow lifted, his mouth opened in a smile. By now Geneva was used to Edward's reticence around newborns. He always waited until his grandchildren were several weeks old, then he would sit down and have them placed in the cradle of his arms. She was heartened to note that his expression seemed free of concern.

Soon the baby began to whimper in Cynthia's arms. She felt of her diaper. "Her nappie's dry," she reported.

"She hasn't eaten yet," Geneva admitted.

Again, that disquieting frown on Cynthia's face. *There's something wrong,* that's what she's thinking, Geneva realized. But then Cynthia said brightly, "Looks like she's hungry now." She kissed her granddaughter's cheek then tenderly placed her in Geneva's arms.

Edward turned away discreetly and headed for the door.

"Have you any idea when Tony will get here?" Geneva asked.

He paused. "I'm afraid not. When we rang up his office round noon, he said he would leave the theatre straightaway. Of course, with all the troop movements nowadays, trains are not running on schedule.

"Shall I put a call through to Mrs. Fairfax, see if she has heard anything?"

"Yes, please. It has been—what—five hours?"

When Edward was gone, Geneva opened her robe and brought Cynthia Louise to her breast. "Hungry now, Sweetie?" she asked, stroking her silky red hair. Her lips parted and formed a little O, then quickly brushed by Geneva's nipple and closed. Well, maybe she would get the hang of it in time.

Cynthia stood watching closely. Occasionally the baby's mouth would open. Geneva would touch her nipple to her mouth and she would begin to suckle. Yet she would soon appear to have lost interest, and close her mouth. "Perhaps if I leave, she'll be more relaxed," Cynthia said softly, stepping back.

"I don't think so," Geneva told her, for suddenly she felt frightened and wanted Cynthia to stay. While continuing to urge her daughter to suckle, she said in a hushed voice to Cynthia, "I just can't understand why she isn't hungry yet. And why she's so—" she searched for the right word, "—so lethargic."

Cynthia nodded, her brow furrowed. "Perhaps we ought to have Dr. Ashmore take a look," she said. "I can ask the nurse to contact him."

No sooner had she made the suggestion than Geneva noticed with alarm that her baby's breathing had become rapid; her eyelids were fluttering continuously, as if in surprise, or fear—Geneva looked up at Cynthia. "See how she's breathing?"

When Cynthia came closer and looked at the baby, her face drained of all color. Without a word, she flew out the door.

Geneva gazed down at her daughter again. Her focus seemed sharper, as if a veil had been lifted from her eyes. *Something is wrong.* Her strong instinct all through her pregnancy had been correct; there was no fooling herself anymore. In a way, she was relieved, for now the problem would be identified and corrected. Cynthia Louise went on breathing hard and fast, her mouth in a lit-tle O, her eyelids fluttering. Her eyes remained fixed on her mother's face, as though she sought reassurance. "Don't worry, Sweetie, it's going to be fine," Geneva said, hugging her close, yet feeling utterly powerless. "Dr. Ashmore will know just what to do," she assured her.

In minutes Dr. Ashmore hurried in, wearing a suit and tie. Nurse Tinsley and Cynthia were close on his heels. "Let's have a look," he said, taking the baby from Geneva. He placed a hand on her diaphragm, frowning in concen-tration. Soon he and Nurse Tinsley exchanged a look, as if they were acknowl-edging some secret between them. "Down the hall, post-haste!" he said.

Abruptly they were hurrying through the door, Cynthia Louise's pink blan-ket trailing down Dr. Ashmore's shirt front. Geneva felt as if a huge hand had reached down and yanked out her insides, leaving an empty shell.

Cynthia sat on the edge of the bed and took Geneva's hands. "Isn't it lucky? He had just gotten back to the hospital, coming to check on you." *Why, was he already worried? And what could be so urgently wrong that he did not even stop to tell me what it was?* Geneva wondered. She recalled Dr. Ashmore's words about the primitive urge to fill the empty place when a child leaves. *Dear God, you sent Cynthia Louise to fill our empty place. Please, make her well....*

Cynthia had seen enough newborns to have a general idea of what was the matter. It was something wrong with the oxygen supply. The child was not going to make it. She had suspected the worst as soon as she laid eyes on that dark, wizened little creature; then, when she wouldn't eat—She would not pre-empt Dr. Ashmore by saying anything to Geneva, however. Her mind was reel-ing. At the first possible moment, she must summon the vicar. And where was Tony? He ought to be here.

They waited. Around half past six, a young nurse with fair hair and freckles brought a tray of steaming broth and crackers for Geneva. She put the tray down and checked Geneva's vital signs. When she had removed the thermom-eter from her mouth and screwed up her eyes to read the measurement, Geneva said, "Do you know anything about my daughter?"

The nurse smiled blankly and shook her head. *They never tell you anything in a hospital; you might as well be invisible,* Geneva thought bitterly.

Before leaving, the nurse turned on the bedside lamp and pulled the black-out curtain over the window. It screeched across the rod, like fingernails scratching the inside of a cook pot. Geneva resented the war and all its manip-ulations. Not a bomb had been dropped on London, yet her husband could not get here just when she and their baby needed him most. But it would do no good to agonize over it. She reminded herself of the heroic efforts going on in her daughter's behalf, Dr. Ashmore bringing all his years of experience to bear on her condition, deciding on the best alternative to make her well, setting the treatment in motion. Everything would be fine, regardless of when Tony arrived. She must remain positive....

Edward walked in.

"They've taken the baby to examine her," Cynthia said. "Something wrong with her breathing."

A troubled expression crossed Edward's face. "Ah..." he said.

"Did you find out anything about Tony?" Geneva asked.

"Mrs. Fairfax says he telephoned at half past three, still waiting to board the two-fifteen at Paddington, apparently." He went to a chair in the corner and sat down heavily, then stared ahead, his finger tapping his chin.

Geneva envisioned Tony sitting on a bench at the station, checking his watch as the hours passed, rising, pacing up and down, his patience at the breaking point. She gazed across at the red roses. Now, with the opaque black curtain as a backdrop, the roses looked stiff and dead, as if the closing of the curtain had sucked the life right out of them.

Still they waited. Thirty minutes. Forty-five. An hour. Edward drummed his fingers on the metal chair arm, shifted in the chair, crossed one leg over the other. Cynthia paced back and forth, her mouth set in a grim line, her arms folded. She wore a two-piece suit of fawn and brown checks with a box-pleated skirt and a single-breasted jacket reaching to her hips; and a smart brown hat with a tall flat peak, slightly angled. Geneva imagined her carefully choosing the ensemble she would wear to come here today, anticipating the joy of seeing her new grandchild, only to find—

Why were they taking so long? Geneva began imagining her daughter, forced into the harsh light of the examining room, strangers probing her, their faces grave, their voices abrupt as they spoke to one another of her condition. She must be terrified that she would never see her mother again, Geneva realized, and suddenly she thought of Emelye, forced in the back of a truck in Soho, bound and gagged, terrified her mother would not be able to rescue her. She could not bear it. She must go to Cynthia Louise. As she threw back the covers and swung her feet to the floor, Cynthia cried, "What on earth—?"

Abruptly the door opened and Dr. Ashmore came in, wearing a pair of black-rimmed eyeglasses that were like a high gate closing off his usual look of optimism. Geneva laid down again. The doctor sat on the edge of the bed, removed his glasses and put them in his pocket. His voice heavy with sadness, he said, "Mrs. Selby, I'm afraid your daughter has developed a very serious problem, what we call, 'severe respiratory distress.'"

Geneva tried to square this daunting term with what she had seen for herself. "You mean, she has trouble getting enough air?"

"That's right. It happens sometimes, in newborn babies. It can be for a variety of reasons—a problem with the lungs, for instance, or perhaps a congenital heart defect."

Defect. The word sent a chill up Geneva's spine.

Dr. Ashmore was saying, "Just now, we're giving her oxygen through a little mask, in hopes she will begin to respond."

Geneva was suddenly encouraged. Her thoughts leapt to the iron lung she had read about, developed at Harvard University. "Do they have iron lungs in England?" she asked anxiously, thinking—in case they didn't—of having Rodney arrange to ship one over here, to charter a plane if necessary, never mind the expense; she was suddenly grateful there was a great deal of money at their disposal. If it took every penny they had—

"Yes, we do have them. Unfortunately, though, they can't be used for infants, for their lungs are not sufficiently developed, and there is no way to successfully regulate the volume of air."

How ironic, Geneva thought, mothers of newborns all over England were learning from a sheet of instructions to administer oxygen to their babies through a primitive hand pump attached to a helmet.

"So you'll just keep giving her oxygen until she responds," she said.

"That's right." He grimaced, as though a sharp pain had suddenly overtaken him. "But I must tell you honestly, Mrs. Selby, we don't hold out much hope." He smiled consolingly, pressed her arm, and rose from the bed.

His words sent a frisson of fear through Geneva. But no. She wouldn't let his lack of hope sink hers. "You'll stay with her, won't you? I mean, you're not just going to leave her in someone else's hands—" *who doesn't even know her,* she almost added, then realized that no one except for herself, not even Dr. Ashmore, really knew this child she had carried beneath her heart for nine months.

"I shall be here," he promised, "and I'll keep you informed of any change." He paused for a moment, as though weighing the possibility of saying more. Then, with a respectful nod toward Cynthia and Edward, he left.

Cynthia came to the bed and took Geneva's hands in hers. She must convince Geneva to have the little girl baptized as soon as possible. Before she could speak, however, Geneva read the resignation in her face. She wouldn't have it. Gathering all her resolve, she said, "Now listen, we're not giving up. My daughter's life is in God's hands, and God can give her *his* strength to breathe, until her body is strong enough to take over."

Cynthia opened her mouth, but Geneva cut her off.

"I'm going to start praying right now, and I won't stop for anything. I want you both to do the same."

From the corner came Edward's husky voice: "Chins up, that's the way!"

Geneva knew that even with Edward's bravado, neither of her in-laws held any more hope than Dr. Ashmore. She didn't want them here. She wanted to be left alone to pray without distraction. "Perhaps you might check on Tony again," she said, looking from one to the other.

"Good idea," Cynthia lied. She hoped to God the vicar was at home.

Edward rose. "You're sure you'll be alright?" he asked worriedly.

"I'll be fine," she said. "Thank you."

Yet, after they left, Geneva felt terribly naked and vulnerable. She began to pray, her shoulders back and her chin uplifted. Her mind returned to the miscarriage she suffered years ago, when she felt there was a void where God was supposed to be. But she knew better now. God was the creator of miracles; nothing was beyond him. *God, you alone can save my little girl. I love her so much already, that I can't bear the thought of losing her—*

Inevitably, the door swung open. The night nurse came in to check Geneva's vital signs again. *How ridiculous! I'm not the one you should be worrying about!* As she pumped air into the blood pressure contraption, Geneva felt the familiar strangling sensation in her arm and wondered, *Is this how it feels to my daughter as she struggles to breathe? God, please breathe your breath into her tiny lungs....*

Afterward the nurse eyed Geneva's untouched supper tray. "You had best get something into your system, Madam. I can warm up the broth, if you like."

You mean, to fortify myself for my daughter's death, Geneva thought darkly. "No thank you. I'll eat when my daughter is better," she said. She closed her eyes and resumed praying.

Sometime later, Dr. Ashmore returned, with Cynthia and Edward behind him. The fact that they accompanied him told Geneva all she needed to know, even before she read defeat in his solemn face. He sat down on the end of the bed and looked across at her. "Mrs. Selby, I'm afraid your daughter has not responded at all," he said gravely.

"But she's still alive—" she cried, leaning forward anxiously.

"Yes, she is," he began slowly, "but my experience in these cases is that, within another twenty-four hours at the very most—perhaps a lot sooner—"

"Then bring her to me, please," she interrupted stridently, reasoning that they had tried the only paltry method known to medical science. But healing was still the business of God, and God needed nothing more than a strong faith and an unwillingness to give up, which obviously the experts did not appreciate.

"I would have suggested that, of course," he said with feeling. "But if you will permit me...I've been practicing medicine for a very long time—since before the last war—and one thing I have learnt: God, in his infinite wisdom—" (this with the palms of his hands open, as if to encompass the entire universe) "—has a way of working things out. What seems impossible to accept today, very often turns out to have been a blessing in the end.

"Please, do consider this," he begged.

"Yes, yes," she lied, desperately. "But please, my daughter needs me. Bring her to me now."

When he was gone, Cynthia stood looking at Geneva, her hands folded together as if she had a question to ask. But then, apparently thinking better of it, or perhaps just sensing Geneva would like to be alone with her daughter, she walked out. Edward quickly followed.

CHAPTER 23

When the nurse returned Cynthia Louise to Geneva's arms, she held her closely and steeled herself against the legion of tears threatening. All she wanted was to go on holding her daughter until the end of time. If she said *I love you* in these early moments, it would prove her undoing, and there was much ahead that they must do together. Silently she gazed into her daughter's eyes, willing her to survive, convinced that in the gaze she returned lay profound under-standing. Geneva had never felt more surely that this precious infant's body was an extension of her own, the mystical umbilical cord unsevered. If they could just be left alone—

But no. Cynthia came in to say the vicar was waiting in the hall with Edward, having come to "receive Cynthia Louise as a member of the Body of Christ." The vicar's language of diplomacy, no doubt.

Geneva was startled by the news. It took her reasoning a few moments to catch up. Then she said, "My daughter is going to survive, and besides, if you think that an innocent child would be shut out of heaven, just because of some—some *technicality*—"

Cynthia had dark patches beneath her eyes. Her blue-violet gaze had a dull cast, and her hair was slightly windblown as if she'd stood outside the stone facade of the hospital, anxiously awaiting the vicar. She wagged her head, and made a steeple of her hands. "I hope and pray she'll survive, but in case—it's just—this would be so meaningful for all of us, as a family," she stammered, letting her hands fall.

Geneva remembered her other children born in England, how tiny they looked when presented at the St. Petroc's baptismal font, its splendid wooden baldachino, ornately carved, arched high above like an umbrella. She wanted that for Cynthia Louise, the heirloom Selby christening gown and bonnet brought out of storage, cleaned and pressed and readied for the occasion. Yet, if her life were to be saved, Geneva may have to defer to Cynthia to be free of her interference. "Alright, only let's wait for Tony," she said.

Cynthia sighed forbearingly. "Tony could be tomorrow getting here, the way things are. I know he would not want us to wait for him," she argued, her voice weary.

"Very well, then, at least have Elizabeth brought here. It will mean a great deal to her, I'm sure. She would feel slighted if we left her out."

When will this nightmare end? Cynthia agonized. It had been five hours since the shock of seeing the newborn, even then just barely alive. And from that moment her mind had begun leaping ahead, to all the arrangements that must be made. She was fatigued beyond words now, barely able to retain her composure. One thing she knew: Elizabeth must be spared the sight of the poor, darkening creature, exhausted from the struggle to breathe, her mouth making a circle with every labored breath, like a fish mouth. How could Geneva believe she would survive? "Unfortunately, Mrs. Greaves has already left for the day, and Elizabeth is looking after the others," she lied. In fact, Mrs. Greaves had insisted on staying the night. *"Oh, wot a terrible thing to happen to a sweet parson like Mrs. Selby, and Mr. Selby too. I love them as though they were me own, I do."*

Aware of the minutes ticking by, Geneva reluctantly agreed to hold the ceremony. With a look of profound relief, Cynthia went out, shortly returning with Edward and the vicar. Fr. John Key had dark hair, clear skin and a boyish face, the kind that would always look young, no matter his age. He came to the bed, gently laid his hand on Cynthia Louise's blanket and peered at her for a few moments, as though trying to assess her chances of survival. Then he took Geneva's hand in his and looked across at her silently, as if no words were adequate to express his sorrow. Apparently even the vicar had no faith in miracles, but at least he wasn't rushing her. For this she was thankful. "Good evening, Fr. Key, thank you for coming," she said evenly.

"I was only too glad," he said with tenderness. "Now, there are two versions of the Rite of Holy Baptism. The one we use when in the church is longer than the other, but the shorter form contains all the necessary elements."

No doubt the shorter version was reserved for emergencies, she thought, and he was wise enough to leave the choice to her. As eager as she was to be alone with her daughter, it made no sense to choose the longer version. But now that the vicar stood waiting calmly, in his white starched clerical collar and solemn black shirt, his smooth hand tucked around hers, she felt the weight of this ancient sacrament upon her. It would be her daughter's only baptism, no matter how long she lived, and therefore it should not be rushed. "I prefer the longer version, please," she said.

He patted her hand, smiled and said, "As you wish."

As he laid out the tiny font of baptismal water and the vial of anointing oil on the table over Geneva's bed, she thought—though she was not certain—that her daughter's breathing had slowed down ever so little, and that it was not quite as labored as before. Her heart swelled with hope. *Oh God, please give this child your breath, and help her not to give up....*

The vicar looped the priestly stole around his neck, then took the baby in his arms, peering into her face and smiling. "You are a beautiful child, Cynthia Louise, in our eyes and in the sight of God," he said warmly.

It proved Cynthia's undoing. Tears flushed from her eyes and rolled down her cheeks. Edward gave her his handkerchief and closed an arm around her shoulders. She could feel his fingers trembling. Poor Edward! So awkward around babies, as if they were made of spun glass. She wondered how he had continued bearing up through this crisis. *Bearing up.* Suddenly it was as if she were hearing this British phrase, so concise and profound, for the very first time. *Bearing up.* How odd, but she felt now that in pausing to examine it...appreciate it...she had unleashed its power to strengthen her as well.

With his free hand, Father Key opened his Book of Common Prayer. Its thin gilt-framed leaves were curled at the corners from many years of being handled. He turned them carefully, using the tips of his thumb and index finger. Soon he stopped at the correct page and began to read aloud. As the lyrical words flowed from his mouth, they seemed to Geneva to expand in the air and linger above them, a heavenly baldachino. It was as if the world did not exist beyond this small peaceful space where they were all enveloped in God's embrace. And she could have sworn her baby was caught up in the beauty, responding to the soothing rhythms and sounds, growing in strength....

At length, Father Key instructed, "Name this child."

Geneva took in a breath. She wanted her name to ring out, to reach the highest peak of the heavens in praise to God. "Cynthia Louise Selby!" she proclaimed, her voice shaking with the effort.

"Cynthia Louise, I baptize thee in the name of the Father, and of the Son, and of the Holy Ghost...." As the baptismal water ran in tiny rivulets down her forehead and cheeks, Geneva braced herself. When Chris was blessed with baptismal water, the sound of his desperate cries echoed in the huge sanctuary of St. Petroc's Church. But Cynthia Louise made no sound. Her eyelids fluttered.

When it was over, the vicar offered to stay for a while. Geneva knew he believed the end was near. She had never been more convinced that it was not. "No, but thank you so much for all you've done. You can't imagine how much it means to me, and…to my daughter," she said, her voice breaking.

"I shall be at the vicarage if you need me," he said quietly, and squeezed her hand. Cynthia and Edward walked out with him. Geneva noticed as they passed that Cynthia's eyes were red. She could not remember ever before having seen her moved to tears.

Geneva looked after them for a little, caught up in the numen of the ceremony even yet, bolstered by it. Then her eyes fell on Cynthia Louise, and she urged her, "You must keep trying for your mother, for she loves you more than anything, and can't bear for you to give up." Cynthia Louise's eyes locked on hers, and from that moment, mother and daughter wheeled and wheeled, farther and farther into a world of their own, apart from all else. Whether or not her child's breathing was improving, Geneva shut out of her thinking. Her mind and spirit, and—she believed with all her heart—her daughter's as well, were lifted up far beyond all physical limitations, by faith. In between Geneva's prayers, she whispered encouragements, to keep trying, to never give up.

After a while, hoping her daughter might be persuaded to suckle—proof positive that her faith was not misplaced—Geneva opened her robe. From the corner, Edward cleared his throat. She had not even realized he was there. He rose from his chair, his eyes averted, a bright blush on his cheeks. Suddenly she realized how much her father-in-law must love her and her child, to have kept vigil over these long hours when he could have easily pleaded the fatigue he must have felt and had Merton come to drive him home. She felt a rush of tenderness for him, as if he were her own father. Never before had she felt this. "Please stay with us, I want you to be here," she said.

Edward inclined his head a little toward her. "I—I thought you might like for me to bring Cynthia. I believe she is checking on Tony just now." In truth Cynthia had admitted to Edward that she could not bear to stay in this room and watch helplessly as Geneva clung to the futile hope that her child would live. He left her pacing up and down the corridor, hoping to head off Tony when he arrived so that she could explain the situation in case he had not received the telegram they sent to Exeter.

Geneva did not want Cynthia. "No, I'd rather you stay," she said.

Edward nodded and turned toward the window as Geneva resumed her attempt to feed her daughter. But the window, shrouded in black, turned his mind in on itself and cut off escape from certain uneasy memories. *"But it just isn't done,"* he had said to Cynthia, when she wished to nurse Tony. In the black void before him, he saw the look of deep regret on her face. Not for years had he thought of this, and now he wondered why it was considered improper in his class of society for a mother to nurse her child, and why he had deferred to custom rather than to his wife's desperate wish. By the time Nell was born, they had disagreed on virtually every issue of child rearing, and he was weary of arguing. Besides, whereas with the firstborn son and heir, one had to abide by the strictest guidelines—or so he thought then—with a daughter it was not so important. Edward left many things regarding Nell to Cynthia's discretion, among them breast-feeding. He did not consider this menial, wet-nurse business suitable for a husband to witness, however. He never was present when she breast-fed Nell. How could he have been so indifferent?

Yet somehow, with his American daughter-in-law and her children, breast-feeding had always seemed the most natural of processes. It struck him now that Geneva had opened up his thinking—not to say he didn't feel frightfully awkward in this moment, for he did. Still, might he somehow tell her this? Discreetly, he glanced her way. The baby was cradled on her shoulder again, Geneva's eyes downcast from still another failure to have this process completed by her child. Edward had a tight place in his throat, for he felt not only Geneva's sorrow, but the sorrow of knowing that the gift his wife wished to give their son all those years ago, he would have eagerly accepted. *I am justly punished,* he thought.

"I say, Geneva" he began, then paused, finding he was quite at a loss for words. Yet her sad eyes were lifted to his. He cleared his throat. "These years since you married my son...all of us together as a family...they have been the best years of my life, by Jove! I count my blessings, yes, count my blessings for a fact!" he said, not precisely what he meant to say, but probably close enough.

"Oh yes, mine too," Geneva said with kindness. *Dear God, don't let Edward lose this grandchild....*

Edward turned toward the black-shrouded window again. "Awful things, these curtains," he said dejectedly, fingering the edge. Then suddenly he wheeled around, his eyes luminous. "But d'you know what, Geneva? I have discovered these past few months that if one walks out in the night and gazes up at the sky, it seems far more beautiful, more filled with bright stars, than ever it seemed in peacetime." He paused, turned away again, latched his fingers together behind his waist. "Strengthens one, somehow," he murmured to himself.

"I never thought of that; I suppose I ought to try looking," said Geneva. She glanced again at Tony's roses, seemingly so devoid of life there before the blackout curtain, you would have sworn they'd never been alive at all.

"Come on, Sweetie, be strong, keep trying," she coaxed her daughter now. As she watched her little mouth forming an O with every breath, she found herself imagining Cynthia Louise—several years hence—blowing soap bubbles through a wand, following her mother around the garden in her sun dress and sandals, her red curls tossed by the wind. *Please God, save my little girl....* With the contour of the child's body melded into her, some part of her was already seeking to imprint on her mind how it felt to have her there, in order to always remember. Yet no, God did not waste people. Cynthia Louise had come into the world for a reason. Again and again, she begged her not to give up. What did it matter if they had to lie here for weeks just this way, until her tiny lungs grew strong?

Then, abruptly, her baby ceased breathing. The world stood still. "Please, Sweetie!" Geneva begged. And miraculously, the child recovered her breath, then took another breath, and another. *Oh, thank God! Just look how much she loves me!* she thought with unspeakable pride. But then, as Cynthia Louise continued laboring to breathe, her pride whip-lashed. Was it possible a baby could cling to life in order to spare her mother the heartache of losing her?

In that moment Geneva felt she had dropped into a fathomless pit, her soul severed entirely from her creator. She looked into her struggling daughter's face. *God, what have I done?* She kissed her, held her close, weeping, "I love you I love you I love you, and it's alright if you're tired and can't try anymore, it's alright, I love you so much for trying so hard just for me." At length, and with great effort she was able to urge her child, "Rest now, sweet little one...rest...."

Still, on and on Cynthia Louise struggled, breath after breath after breath, quick little puffs on her mother's neck, and yet she was not getting better, only struggling harder and harder, her breathing more and more rapid and desperate as if she were incapable of stopping what her selfish mother had put in motion.

It was a long while before Geneva found the courage to plead: *Dear God, forgive me, and release this child from suffering.*

They lay there together, Geneva rocking her child, murmuring, "I love you," over and over and over as her daughter's breathing gradually became less and less audible, barely discernible wisps of air against her mother's neck. How long they lay there, rocking, Geneva could not have said; it may have been minutes, or hours. Time was suspended in a silent lullaby, the most intimate of love songs ever written. And then with the sudden ease of one nodding off to sleep, Cynthia Louise was set free. Geneva ceased rocking and closed her eyes, and for a few moments she remained very still, feeling a faint pressure on her eyelids as a pair of gossamer wings, lighter than air, expanded, fluttered away.

When she opened her eyes the spell was broken. She felt disoriented, as if she were dancing on the stage and her mind suddenly went blank about the next step. "Edward, I don't think she's—I think—"

He was there at once. He drew near, laid a hand on his granddaughter's back, and listened. "Yes, let me take her now," he said gently. With the utmost tenderness and ease, he took the child from Geneva's arms and cradled her in his own, kissing her forehead, a tear rolling down his cheek. He carried her out.

Geneva stared fixedly at the empty crib beside her, its bedclothes but lightly stirred.

CHAPTER 24

From the time he learned Geneva was in labor, at noon, Tony had been distracted with worry, the memory of her unhealthy look at Christmastime haunting him more with every hour that passed. But then he spoke to Mrs. Fairfax at half past four o'clock, shortly before his train finally departed from Paddington Station. Her happy report that Geneva was fine, and they had a healthy baby girl, restored his peace of mind, not to mention his patience, during the interminable train ride: lurching to a halt, people pouring on; starting up, halting again—just at dusk—while a track was being hastily repaired; starting up, halting again for still more people to board, and so on and so on, mile after mile. All the way to Exeter, the ratio of passengers boarding, to those getting off, was easily ten to one. The carriages were so packed, so hazy with cigarette smoke, one could scarcely breathe. But Geneva and baby were fine, that was the important thing. He could hardly wait to see for himself. Then, awaiting him at the Exeter station, the shocking telegram from his mother, that they were giving his daughter oxygen. It forced him to revise the rosy picture in his mind of Geneva with their child at her breast. *Cynthia Louise will have responded to the treatment by the time I arrive, and be on her way to recovery,* he told himself, again and again, in the last two hours of the journey to Bodmin.

As soon as he approached his mother, standing alone in the corridor outside Geneva's room, and saw her somber face and red-rimmed eyes, he knew that his daughter was dead. She had only to confirm it. She took his arm. "It happened just a few minutes ago," she said consolingly.

Tony could barely absorb the reality that had lain in wait for him at the end of his long journey, his shifting expectations. "And Geneva—?"

"I think she's in a daze. She didn't seem to understand the inevitability of it," Cynthia told him.

He must go to his wife. She needed him. Yet when he started toward the door of her room, his mother restrained him. "Tony, first—if you want to see Cynthia Louise—they've already called the undertaker. He could be here any moment now. She's in a room at the other end of the hall."

He hesitated, not at all sure that he could bear to look upon the dead infant. Yet, how could he refuse? His mother, his father, Geneva—all of whom had lived through what must have been agonizing hours of watching her die—would not understand. And so, in somewhat of a daze himself, he yielded.

"Shall I go with you?" Cynthia asked discreetly.

Without even thinking, he told her no. He had an instinct to guard this one and only private moment he would ever have with his daughter.

A nurse opened the door of the small examining room and turned on the harsh ceiling light. There lay a small form on the table in the center of the room, a blanket draped over it from head to toe. The nurse went ahead of Tony and folded the blanket down, exposing the baby's head and shoulders. Then she turned and left, closing the door behind her.

Immediately he noticed Cynthia Louise's shock of red hair, his eyes blurred and he felt dizzy. He took in a few hasty breaths, then forced himself to pick up his feet and walk to the side of the table. How peaceful she was, lying on her stomach as if she were sleeping. For a long while, he just stood staring, his mind feeling blank, emptied out. Then he remembered thinking once, if Geneva lost her life because of this pregnancy, he probably could not love the infant who survived her. Now, peering down at this poor, defenseless creature, at the fringe of red lashes on her closed eyelids, at her little fingers curled tight, he felt weighed down with remorse.

At last, he reached out a shaky hand and lightly touched her hair. How soft it was, like her mother's hair. "I love you, Cynthia Louise, and I'm sorry," he whispered. He leaned down and kissed her goodbye. His eyes flooded.

When he opened the door of Geneva's room, she slowly turned to face him. She did not speak. Her eyes were empty, as if she did not recognize him. When he sank down on the bed and gathered her in his arms, he felt the distance in her limp embrace. He was crushed. Had he lost her, too?

The next morning Elizabeth held the door open as Geneva walked unsteadily through the small conservatory entrance at Clearharbour, leaning on Tony's arm. She wore a brightly printed robe with wide lapels and gathered sleeves. Elizabeth gave each of her parents a consoling hug. She had been crying off and on through the night. It seemed to her that, assuming her mother had told the truth long ago about Father and Geneva's scheming, then surely the loss of their child was all the recompense that could be asked of them. She felt small and mean-spirited for the times when she had distrusted them; felt guilty for withholding her forgiveness. *I have forgiven them now,* she must write to Fr. Ogilvie.

The younger children waited in the hall. Having no idea how to react to the situation, Elvira and Andy stood stiff and silent, their eyes wide, waiting on their parents to say something to make everything alright, to restart the engine of their lives. Mrs. Greaves stood holding Chris's hand. "Welcome 'ome, Madam," she said to Geneva, her voice nasal and her round eyes puffy behind her glasses, from frequent crying spells.

Abruptly, Chris broke free and ran to hug Geneva's knees. He threw his head back and looked up at her, bewildered. "Baby won't come?"

Geneva's knees began to shake; her forehead was clammy. She sank down on the telephone bench nearby. Tony scooped Chris into his arms and hugged him close. "Your sister has—has gone to live in heaven, with Jesus," he assured him, his voice husky. "She is going to be very happy there."

He could not tell from Chris's face if his words were any help at all. But they were the best he could do for now. He hugged him again, then put him on his feet next to Elizabeth and gave her a pleading look. Perhaps she could be more helpful. He turned to Geneva. "Come, Darling, I shall carry you upstairs. Mrs. Greaves has got the room all ready."

"But I don't need to be carried," she said coolly. Nor did she want him to linger up there with her. She wanted to be alone with her thoughts.

She doesn't want me to touch her, Tony thought, injured. "Dr. Ashmore insists," he said, and so she shrugged and put an arm round his neck.

When Tony carried her inside their bedroom, she expected to find the baby's crib and small wicker chest that Clifton was instructed to bring up some weeks ago. They were not there. "Where are my daughter's things?" she demanded.

My daughter. Tony laid her on the bed and plumped the pillows behind her. "Mrs. Greaves felt it might be easier—" he began, at a loss.

To Geneva, it seemed an effort to deny the child had ever existed. She didn't say anything then. She wanted to be left alone so that she could recall the way it felt when Cynthia Louise was cradled on her shoulder. She wanted to concentrate on her face, so that it would be imprinted on her mind forever. "It's a pity we have no picture of her," she said.

Tony lowered his eyes. "Yes," he said, though in truth, he found Geneva's notion worrisome. Hard as it was, they must get over this and carry on. He sat on the edge of the bed and looked longingly into her face. He kissed her forehead and smoothed the wide lapels of her robe. "Pretty robe. I don't believe I've seen it before."

"Willa sent it," she said. A sleeping gown was included in the gift box, of clinging black silk chiffon, with filmy sleeves that unfolded like the butterfly wings of the *Chimaera* costume from their vaudeville days. "*Something to wear home after the baby is born…and something sexy for a little later,*" said the card. Geneva felt no desire for Tony's touch upon her body. She did not tell him of the gown.

Now, noting the dark places beneath his eyes, his unshaven face, and his rumpled clothes, she felt a pang of guilt. He had spent the night in the chair beside her bed.

"Will you be alright for a few minutes while I get cleaned up? Later, I'm going over to see the vicar about…" he hesitated, "…arrangements."

Would she be alright? What could possibly befall her that was worse than what already had? "I'll be fine," she said dully.

He kissed her forehead again, as if she were his child in sickbed. "I love you," he said tenderly.

"I love you, too," she managed to say. He sensed the lack of feeling behind the words, just as he had sensed the lack of warmth in her greeting when he entered the hospital room last night, and in all the exchanges between them that followed before they finally fell into silence and he dozed off. Was this what losing a newborn child did to a mother? All night his thoughts had wandered through a maze, looking for an answer to this question. Perhaps the vicar could give him some insight, show him the end. He felt unspeakably lonely.

When he left the room, Geneva closed her eyes, crossed her arm over her chest and immediately called back the memory of Cynthia Louise, lying on her shoulder. *Yes, my daughter is here,* she realized, feeling the warmth of the tiny body against her, the downy hair and the nape of the baby's neck in the cradle of her fingers. As soon as she heard the shower running in the bath, she dozed off.

When she awoke, the air was filled with the clean scent of shower soap. Tony and Mrs. Greaves were talking in hushed tones. She did not open her eyes.

"Yes, by all means, do go home at once—you must be exhausted. Thank you so much, for everything" he said. "You've been an absolute brick."

"The next few weeks'll be 'ard, sir," Mrs. Greaves said in a quavering voice.

"Yes, I expect you're right."

"Takin' out the baby's furniture was the right thing, I 'ope?"

"Yes, quite. We've got to start somewhere."

"Well, enjoy your tea, and I made one of me fish pies for your supper. Miss Elizabeth will put it in th'oven, and take it out when's done."

"Fish pie, my favorite! Thanks ever so much. See you tomorrow."

Geneva heard the door softly close, and in moments the rocker across from her bed creaked with Tony's weight. She still did not open her eyes. She hoped he would soon leave to see the vicar. She heard him rocking slowly, back and forth, back and forth. Then, the rapid intake of his breath, followed by a series of sniffs. She realized he was weeping. She felt nothing for Tony, not love, not pity—nothing, as if he were someone she had known long ago and not very well. The only feeling alive in her was her love for Cynthia Louise, and the even greater love her daughter returned. She had never known such love existed. She went on pretending to be asleep.

CHAPTER 25

For the rest of Saturday and all of Sunday and Monday Geneva rested in bed, sometimes sleeping, other times gazing out the window, recalling the feel of her daughter cuddled at her breast, the tiny bones of her back and neck against her hand. Tony arranged for the burial to take place on Tuesday. As he described the funeral spray he'd ordered, then sought her help as to certain other details—which of the little gowns in her layette should she wear, which shoes, and should she wear a bonnet?—Geneva felt woozy and her heart began to palpitate. She informed him she did not feel up to attending the service. He looked somewhat taken aback, but fortunately he nodded in compliance. She asked him to make all the decisions, then added, more bitingly than she intended, "You'll have to inquire where Mrs. Greaves put all my daughter's belongings." She laid back on the pillows and turned her head towards the window. Presently she heard the door close.

Later Tony came in to tell her Nell had telephoned and offered to stay with her during the service.

But it should have seemed obvious that she wanted to be alone, or else she would have asked for someone to stay. And it would not have been Nell, who, with all good intentions, would say, *I know just how you feel*, when she did not. Nell's tragic loss of her two-year old child was entirely different from that of Geneva, for whom there were no comforting memories of her child being healthy and whole; no photographs to spare her looking up one day and realizing she had forgotten her face; and—most of all—no way to repay the sacrifice that she made by struggling to take one breath after another, until Geneva finally said, *It's alright*, and prayed to God for her release.

"Tell her thanks, but she needn't do that, I'll be fine," said Geneva.

After some hesitation, Tony said, "Well alright."

She considered the matter settled, and assumed Tony had conveyed her apologies to Nell. Then on Tuesday morning he sat down on the edge of the bed to lace up his shiny black dress shoes. His immaculate white shirt was stiffly starched, his dark blue silk tie knotted perfectly at his throat. She could smell the rich scent of his cologne. As he finished lacing his shoes and turned to Geneva, she noticed a tiny red dot on his chin. She felt a twinge of pity. He'd cut himself shaving this morning, for he was rushing, having overslept from exhaustion. Cynthia and Edward, Nell and Morey were already waiting downstairs with the children, to go to the cemetery. He took her hands in his and implored, "I should feel ever so much better if Nell was with you. I don't want you to be alone." His eyes were circled in dark shadows.

But it's what I want, she thought, annoyed. Yet she felt guilty for three days and nights of averting his attempts to comfort her, and be comforted; for the number of times she had pretended to be asleep when he came into the room. Surely she owed him a little peace of mind. "Alright," she said reluctantly.

Tony gripped her hands tightly and kissed her cheek. "Good." He rose from the bed, reached for his suit jacket and put it on. As she watched him walk to the door, she noticed how loosely the dark suit hung on his shoulders. He had lost weight since the last time he wore it. She wondered why, then abruptly she remembered what her own ordeal had completely driven from her awareness: London was preparing for attack by the German Luftwaffe; everyone was pitching in to fortify the city, working very long hours, worrying at night when they went to sleep that they might be dead before morning. How fragile life was, just one breath after another.... She must ask Nell how Guy was getting along over in—where? She could not recall where he was stationed. How awful to have forgotten.

At the door, Tony turned back, his face a study in fatigue and heartache. "Pray for us, will you?"

Somehow she had not expected this entreaty, and for the first time she felt unsure of her instinctive desire not to have the memory of Cynthia Louise's burial superimposed on the memory of her valiant life. "I will," she promised.

One could never be sure of oneself with Geneva, Nell thought, approaching the bedroom door. Up to now, she had felt certain she was doing the right thing, staying up very late for the past two nights, memorizing those sacred, comforting lines, the Book of Common Prayer lying open on the bedside table as Morey lay with his back turned from the light, snoring. She did not fault

Geneva for her decision not to attend the service, not in the least. Yet, one of the hardest things about losing a loved one was stitching up the deep wound that was left open, and carrying on. The real purpose of the burial service was to take the first stitch. Nell had realized this long after she stood above Gerry's tiny grave, her father holding her on one side, and Tony holding her on the other, her deepest wish to sink down in the hole with her son, and die there.

Now, she would give Geneva the means of taking that first stitch. Or, so she had thought, before this morning when she dressed in her black silk dress suit, just in case Geneva refused to have her stay—Tony had never actually given her an answer; before her hands grew clammy and her breath, short. Oh, she never could seem to give enough to Geneva; she often dreamt she was walking towards her, bearing a priceless gift that would make up, finally, for the wrong she had done. It was her own private hell, of which she was deserving. *'I am the resurrection and the life….'* She hoped her voice would not tremble awfully.

She knocked lightly on the door. Geneva's dispirited, "Come in," sounded more like, *"Go away."* Nell squared her shoulders and walked inside.

Geneva had been struggling with the question of whether she had actually failed her daughter by refusing to go to the service. Perhaps it was wrong for her not to be there, when she was the most important person to Cynthia Louise, the one for whom she had sacrificed. Geneva would do more than Tony asked. She would pray all the way through the service, without ceasing. But how? What would she pray? What was needed by each person standing there? She understood no one's relationship to her daughter except her own. Glancing at the clock on the chimneypiece, which she and Tony always referred to as their "wedding clock," she was panicked to note it had run down.

Nell was pulling the rocker close to the bed. Swish-swish went the taffeta lining of her skirt. Geneva could smell the heavy floral scent of her perfume. She wished she would not sit so close. "What time is it? Apparently Mrs. Greaves hasn't wound the clock, and I don't know where she keeps the key." Mrs. Greaves had gone with the family to the cemetery.

Nell settled her heavy, corseted figure in the rocker, then checked her watch. "Nearly twenty past," she said, then, realizing that she was quite unprepared to carry on a conversation with Geneva over the next ten minutes, she added, "There is a stack of cards downstairs, and a cable from Houston. Shall I bring them up?"

Geneva shook her head. She did not want to be distracted from keeping track of the time. How relentless time was. In the last hours of Cynthia Louise's life, the two of them had floated somewhere beyond the limits of time, as though they tiptoed at the edge of heaven. Perhaps they had. Only, Cynthia Louise stepped inside, while Geneva was forced to come back, always to remember. She laid against the pillows and gazed through the window. The sunlight felt warm, like a kiss, and the April morning breeze rippled through the thin net curtains. *Cynthia Louise was skipping through the garden, her red waves tossed by the wind.* The image was so real, Geneva could feel the breeze on her daughter's face, the warmth of the sun on her head. *Is all of this just a bad dream? Will I wake up and find myself downstairs in the buttery, still pregnant?*

She looked across at Nell, who had not said, *I know just how you feel,* but was staring out the window also. "Nell, I'm so sorry to ask again, but—"

Nell checked her watch. "Twenty-seven past." After a pause, she said with gravity, "The burial will begin soon now."

A frisson of fear went through Geneva. "Do you think I'm terrible, for not going?" *Have I let my daughter down?*

Nell shook her head. "Not at all," she said with real compassion.

Twenty-seven past. They would have stepped out of the car by now, and would be walking from the main drive that dissected the Old Cemetery like a spinal cord, down the narrow lane leading off to the right, that led to the Selby family plot. Geneva imagined the small casket poised above the grave, the spray of pink roses and peonies from Miss Pennett's Florist, friends who had seen the notice in the papers or heard the announcement during Sunday worship gathering around the family beneath the great overhanging trees. "Tony asked me to pray for everyone," Geneva said.

"Did he?" Nell said, encouraged.

"But I'm not sure I know how to do that for them."

Nell nodded in understanding. *Thank God, I shall give her the words.* Again she looked at her watch. She sighed. Her eyes met Geneva's. "It's half past the hour," she said tenderly, her eyes crimped at the edges.

Geneva felt her spirit being rent asunder. Her heart pounded with dread and she was breathless. She had an urge to gather herself into the fetal position. *Heavenly father—please, please—.* She wrung her hands, looked out the window at the leafy treetops, shivering in the breeze.

Nell unlocked Geneva's hands and took them firmly in her own. "Now, close your eyes and be still," she commanded. Geneva glanced at her, bewildered, then obeyed. Nell allowed a period of silence, while she composed herself. Then she began, "'I am the resurrection and the life, saith the Lord; he that believeth in me, though he were dead, yet shall he live: and whosoever liveth and believeth in me, shall never die...."

As Nell continued in a clear, unfaltering voice, the words, "shall never die" echoed in Geneva's mind. Cynthia Louise would die only if her mother let her die in her heart, and this she would never, ever do....

"'Jesus called them unto him and said, Suffer the little children to come unto me, and forbid them not; for of such is the kingdom of God....'"

Cynthia Louise was blowing soap bubbles from a wand, her tiny mouth a circle. Up and up the bubbles floated, wheeling, wheeling toward a blue sky with twirling white clouds....

After this passage Nell paused, and it seemed to Geneva that her instinct for pacing and rhythm were as remarkable as her brother's. "'The Lord is my shepherd...'" she began then, the words of the Twenty-Third Psalm rising from her voice with a quiet forcefulness, as if their meaning was embedded deeply in her consciousness. *These words comforted Nell after the loss of her son,* Geneva realized, only then understanding Nell's true purpose in coming to be with her, and the depth of her generosity. As Nell continued reading the psalm, Geneva began to rock back and forth on her hips, back and forth, to the beautiful rhythm.

At the end of the well-loved, ancient psalm, Nell's voice fell silent for a few prolonged moments. Then, her eyes closed, she began humbly, "Our Father, who art in heaven..." Geneva joined in, her voice barely audible through all the appeals, one after another, not so much hearing the words as feeling their timeless rhythm flow through her. Upon saying "Amen," the two women gazed at each other, their eyes luminous. It was as though they were beholding each other for the first time. Suddenly Geneva broke into sobs. Nell leaned near and cradled her in her arms.

I have given her the gift I have been carrying in my dreams, Nell realized. At last, she felt cleansed of her sin against Geneva.

CHAPTER 26

Late that night clouds gathered and heavy rains came, pouring down for days and days, soaking the ground and the trees, flooding like rivers through down spouts, washing out low places in roads. Mrs. Greaves recalled with foreboding the flood of several years ago, when the leat that ran beneath Bodmin like a cave was clogged with rubbish and the streets wouldn't drain, and goods were washed right out of the shops. Tony advised her to stay home until the weather cleared, but she would not. Her only concession was that, instead of walking to work as she usually did, she had Clifton drive her.

Tony needed to get back to London. In June, a psychological thriller by Helmut Aydes entitled *The Chess Player*—for which he'd gone to bat with the Lord Chamberlain's office over the use of suggestive language, and won, with minor compromises—would open at the *William & Mary*. Bill Rutgers was swamped with trying to handle both his workload and Tony's, and they were three short in the technical staff owing to employees having enlisted in the armed services. What was worse, shortly before Tony left, Bill announced he had decided to join up. A bachelor with no one depending upon him for support, he felt it was his duty. With his tall, lean frame and spectacles, Bill looked to be in his twenties. Yet he was thirty-five years old, just past the age of compulsory service. Admittedly, Tony had hoped this would preclude his going off to war. "I shall certainly wait until after the new baby arrives, so that you can spend some time at home with Mrs. Selby," he said. Just how long Bill would be willing to wait, Tony didn't know, but he felt he shouldn't detain him any longer than necessary.

Still, despite all that was hanging fire in London, he was determined to remain at Clearharbour until he and Geneva could visit their daughter's grave together. Thus did he watch the weather as anxiously as he watched his wife.

"Just give her time," the vicar had counseled—adequate advice when all he had to go on was Tony's vague admission that Geneva had become "rather withdrawn" since the loss of their child. He could not tell the vicar that she treated him like a stranger; could not say that he was frightened that something in her had changed irrevocably and nothing would ever be the same for them again; and above all, he could not say, *It's as though she has fallen in love with someone else. If I did not know better I would swear she was having an affair.* One simply could not say such things to the vicar.

At nights, he longed to hold Geneva in his arms, but she retreated to her side of the bed, as near the edge as she could get. If he asked her to tell him about their daughter's brief lifetime—something he had every right to know, and which she obviously experienced very differently from the terse way his mother described it—she would shrug and say, "some other time, I'm too tired now." So eagerly did she toss down the sleeping tablets Dr. Ashmore prescribed, Tony suspected she was using them as a shield to hide behind, for afterward she would sleep for twelve to fourteen hours, her body so still that Tony would often feel compelled to be sure she was breathing, fearful she may have used the pills to take her life. He was not sure Geneva had been wise to avoid attending the burial service, and there was no way to be certain that seeing the tiny grave now would give her a sense that her daughter was at peace and that life must go on. However, he hoped that as they stood together in the quiet, his arm about her shoulders, she might at least begin to realize that it was their loss, and not just her own, and be moved to open up to him about what she was feeling. Certainly that would seem a good place to start.

Finally, one morning after he'd driven Elizabeth, Elvira and Andy to school, when Chris was napping and he and Geneva were having their tea in the bedroom, the clouds parted and sunshine flooded the room. Never in his life had he been so thankful for the simple gift of sunshine. He went to the large window and peered out into the distance at the wet rooftops of Bodmin surmounted by the towering steeple of St. Petroc's Church, each plane and angle shiny as glass in the bright light, like an enchanted city in a fairy tale. Close in, beneath the bedroom window and directly across a narrow gravel walk from the bay window in the dining room, stood a rowan tree that would be laden with red berries a few months hence, a wooden bench with a curved back beneath it and rose beds on either side. The roses were beginning to push their heavy heads up on stems that were bowed from saturation.

Tony looked across at Geneva, who lay in her sun-drenched bed listlessly, her tea cup in her lap. "I need to get back to London pretty soon, Darling, and I should like for us to visit Cynthia Louise's grave together, before I go," he said, trying not to reveal his apprehensiveness.

Geneva did not know what to say. She was relieved that he needed to return to London. She had feared he would wait until Dr. Ashmore released her and they could resume making love, as Tony surely wanted to do. She did not know why she felt such an aversion to his touching her. However, she could not fake feelings that she did not have, and she dreaded the moment when the truth must emerge, for what would happen then?

On the other hand, the last thing she wanted was to visit her daughter's grave. So it seemed now she must submit to one or the other. After some deliberation, she realized that she dreaded Tony's lingering even more than she dreaded visiting the grave. If she could get through it, just once, then Tony would go away. "We'd better go this morning so you can catch a train before noon. The trip to London takes such a long time these days," she said, the memory of waiting and waiting in vain for him to come following Cynthia Louise's birth suddenly opening in her mind like a lock will open in the moment all the pins are aligned. She put her tea cup aside.

Tony was startled by her haste. "I didn't mean to rush you," he said. "I just meant, let's go sometime in the next couple of days." He looked for some sign in her expression that she was relieved not to have to say goodbye so soon.

Averting her eyes, she threw the covers back. "It's alright, there's no need for you to delay; I know you must be awfully behind at work. Just give me time for a shower." She rose too quickly to her feet, stood still for a few moments to overcome a sense of dizziness—it was from the sleeping pills, she was sure, but they were her only means of escaping Tony's solicitude, and they put her so far under that she did not even dream; it was as if she were dead—then took a wobbly step towards the bathroom. Immediately Tony's arm closed around her shoulder. She felt panicked. She did not want him to go in the bath with her, did not want him to see her naked. She pulled free more abruptly than she meant to; then, too late, she smiled up at him. "I'm alright, thanks."

When she closed the door she could feel his eyes staring at her back.

As hot needles of water pricked at the surface of her skin, her heart pounded with dread. Since Nell held her hands and recited the words from the Book of Common Prayer, assuring her that her daughter was in the loving presence of the holy father—and, unfortunately, perhaps because that memory was now superimposed on the memory of her daughter's valiant life—whenever she summoned the feeling of the warm imprint of the child on her shoulder, it eluded her. How long before she would be unable to remember Cynthia Louise's beautiful gaze, locked on her own? How long before she would be unable to remember her face? *That's what Tony really wants, for me to forget her and think of him instead,* she thought bitterly, then was seized with guilt.

When she emerged from the bath, wrapped in her robe, Tony was not in the bedroom. Good. She dressed carelessly in a loose-fitting cotton dress with puffed sleeves and a princess waist, and a pair of walking shoes. When she looked in the mirror she was amazed to find her hair was so long, but then she had not had it trimmed since—when? Since shortly before Emelye left. It seemed a lifetime ago. She brushed through it, pulled it back and tied it with a scarf.

Downstairs the sitting room door was ajar. She caught a glimpse of Tony inside, behind his newspaper. She went into the closet under the stairs and rummaged inside the box where ribbons for gift-wrapping were stored, and found a length of white satin. She picked up her flower basket and clippers, and started out the door. Finding that the weather was chilly, she doubled back for her old cardigan sweater, hanging on a peg in the hall.

Outside she took a deep breath. The pungent smell of damp earth and drenched flowers flooded her nostrils. She surveyed her garden. Masses of hollyhocks, petunias, pansies, marigolds, snapdragons, busy lizzies and periwinkles shimmered in the stone border: Nell's generous handiwork. And now, after a long succession of rainy days, followed by warm sunshine, the flowers reared their heads proudly. As Geneva made her way along the border, clipping some of each variety, she tried to imagine Cynthia Louise skipping along behind her in sandaled feet. Yet she could not make the image come. *And now I must visit her grave, where death's power of separation is undeniable.* Geneva paused, feeling woozy; no matter how long Tony stayed, she could not do this. But he had pulled the Rover around and now he was standing beside it on the drive, in his tan-colored jacket and brown brogans, waiting for her. How many nights before he would be lying in bed, waiting to kiss her? She wrapped the ribbon around the flowers and went to the car.

The Old Cemetery was located high up on the northern rim of Bodmin, a considerable drive from Clearharbour. During the journey Geneva's every muscle was taut with resistance. She clutched her bouquet so tightly that her fingertips dug into her palm. Again and again she told herself, *She isn't there;*

just go this once and then Tony will leave, and you can go back to bed and lie there and concentrate until she comes back to you. If you keep trying, she will come; you know she will. Then they were inside the cemetery and Tony was parking the Rover near the Selby plot. He looked across at Geneva, his eyes anxious as if he doubted she was equal to this visit.

As he stepped out of the car and approached to open the door on her side, she avoided facing the grave, peering out on the ancient rolling grounds where towering trees stood in silence, and tall pointed cedar shrubs poked up here and there—all a shimmering, sun-soaked green, achingly *alive. In my heart she is alive.*

Tony opened her door and held out his hand. How shrunken and pale Geneva looked, wrapped up in her green wool cardigan. It made his heart ache with guilt for urging her to come. "We really don't have to do this today," he said, "I'm afraid the ground is still rather wet."

She was clutching her garden flowers. Her lap was wet where they had pressed down. "No, I'm ready."

When she stepped from the car, Tony was overcome with tenderness. He pulled her close. "I love you," he said longingly, searching her eyes.

"You too," she said vaguely, studying the ground, wishing he would release her but remembering with remorse her abruptness when she shrugged him off in the bedroom. When he released her she took in a breath, then bravely pivoted around to face the grave, several yards away. All she could see from here was a mound of funeral flowers, surrounded by the rain-darkened granite tablets of the Selby plot. The flowers were sad things, rain-pelted, wilting. They seemed to say, *It's over; time to forget.* She brought her fresh bouquet up against her breast and held it there.

Walking toward the grave, Geneva weaved on Tony's arm. Her eyes blurred. *I cannot do this.* Tony gripped her tightly. "Let's not—" he began.

"No, I'll be fine," she said. *Just get through it, this once.*

Yet, when they finally stood before the grave, Geneva felt a strange tingle of awareness that she had entered into the realm of her daughter's love. Her mind reeled. Could it be, when the spirit departed the body it did not flee at once, but only began to pull away gradually, so that for a while it was still present? And what was Cynthia Louise's spirit composed of, except pure, uncorrupted love? Cynthia Louise was waiting for her mother to come here and find her.

Geneva lifted her chin against the chilly breeze, yet her whole body felt feverish. For as long as Cynthia Louise was here, so would her mother be. Breathless with gratitude, she sank down on her knees in the wet earth, pushed the dead, sodden flowers away from the center of her daughter's grave, and placed her fresh flowers there. *I am here now, and I love you.*

Tony knelt down and closed his arm around her. The memory of touching his daughter's red hair formed a lump in his throat. After some hesitation, he said tenderly, "How sweet it must have been, those hours she was with you."

He felt Geneva stiffen within his embrace. He sighed. They were not here together at all. She was alone. "We must order a pretty marker," he said.

"Look what a little angel, Edward!" "Yes, with an angel on top, for your mother," Geneva said, and looked at him, her green eyes bright with tears.

Tony patted her hand, grateful at least that she had shared this much with him. Surely it was a positive sign. "What a lovely idea, Darling. We can make arrangements before I leave," he said. They continued kneeling there, each of them lost in private thoughts. Geneva had not felt this close to her daughter since she held her in her arms in the hospital. She closed her eyes, cupped a hand around the soft nape of her baby's neck. She could feel her little chin in the cleft of her shoulder.

Tony saw Geneva's eyes close, and her hand rise up slowly across her breast, then caress her shoulder, her chin resting there, the ghost of a smile curling on her lips. As if she were holding her baby. As if she had not absorbed the fact that she was dead. It shocked him so, he felt sick inside. He should not have brought her here; it was the worst mistake he had ever made. "Shall we go? You don't want to overdo," he said hoarsely.

Emerging from her reverie, Geneva realized she had forgotten Tony was there. Ready to go on with life, to forget. She was not ready to go on, and she would never be so callous as to forget. As soon as Tony left for London, she would return, alone. *I will be back soon. I won't forget you, I promise. I love you, sweet, brave, Cynthia Louise.*

She touched her fingers to her mouth, then pressed them to the grave.

CHAPTER 27

As they exited through the high cemetery gates, Geneva glanced at her watch. "It's only a little after ten," she reported. "Isn't there a train at eleven-fifteen? That is, if it's on schedule."

Tony was more than ever reluctant to return to London. He hardly knew what to make of Geneva behaving as if she thought her child were still alive. And now, her eagerness for him to leave immediately seemed to confirm his fear that she wished to have him out of her sight. Yet, why? He had done nothing to turn her against him. Did she not realize the Germans could start bombing London at any time, in which case he might very well lose his life? With a spasm of longing he remembered driving his children to school through the rain this morning. As they said goodbye, they were counting on his greeting them this afternoon. The thought of their innocent faces very nearly brought him to tears. "I've no intention of leaving for London this morning, so just forget it," he said shortly.

"I see. I thought you were feeling pressured to return," she said coolly.

"I am, but d'you think I'd leave without even saying goodbye to my children?" he said, his voice cracking.

"Oh, I hadn't thought about that," she admitted.

And no surprise, Tony thought bitterly. She who used to bend near to embrace her children all day long, who seemed nurtured by the very touching of their bodies against hers, had neither reached out her arms to them, nor tried to reassure them, since they lost their baby sister more than two weeks ago. In fact, she hardly seemed aware they were about. This wounded Tony even more deeply than her indifference to him. Elvira and Andy, and especially Chris, were bewildered, and moreover stifled by the gloominess in the household. *"Mummy is not herself just now,"* he would say, but what would happen when he was gone? Fortunately Elizabeth treated her siblings with patience and love. She was already taking Geneva's place helping Andy and Elvira with their studies—both of them seemed to regard school as rather an inconvenience. But Elizabeth had only so much time, and Chris, who would not begin school until Michaelmas term, would be home alone with his mother for many hours of the day—hours when he used to receive her undivided attention. *"He needs me more than the others,"* she used to say, and not without pleasure.

Feeling desperate at the thought of going away and leaving poor little Chris behind, he said, "You know, Darling, you've just got to accept the fact that you can't bring Cynthia Louise back."

He was about to point out that she was hurting her other children, when she demanded, "What do you mean by that?" He glanced her way. Her lips were trembling and she was looking at him suspiciously.

Delicately, he said, "Back there, at the grave, it was as if you imagined her…in your arms. Perhaps you weren't aware that it showed." Now he felt guilty of invading her privacy, yet somehow they must get this out in the open.

Geneva's eyes blazed; she took several shallow breaths, then implored, "What's wrong with just wanting to remember how it felt when she was in my arms? It's all I have now, you know."

Tony sighed. *No, you have a husband and five other children, three of whom need you desperately,* he wanted to remind her. But just then his heart was filled with pity for her. "Darling, no one wants to take that from you. As long as you realize it's just that…a memory. One can't live in the past."

"Who said I was?" she cried. "You know, I'd be a lot better off if you'd just let me get over this my own way." She was crying now.

He felt dreadful. "Oh please—I'm sorry! I didn't mean to upset you." He reached for his handkerchief and handed it to her. "It's just, you seem to be in your own little world, shutting everyone out."

"Because everyone just wants to forget the most beautiful, courageous child who ever lived," she said stridently. "You have no idea what it was like, what she went through—" her voice broke off. She took in a shuddering breath.

"No, I don't, so why don't you tell me about it?" he implored.

But how could she tell him of the love of Cynthia Louise, that it was far greater than Tony's love for her, or hers for him; that to say it was the love of Christ on the cross was the only way to express its deep humility and sacrifice. It would wound him terribly to know that, and convince him, no doubt, that she had lost her mind. "You wouldn't understand. You had to be there," she finally said.

"God knows, I wanted to be there," he said hurtfully.

"But you weren't," she said, and her quavering voice made him think of a poor injured animal who has withdrawn into a dark secret place to lick its wounds.

For the rest of the trip home they were silent, and when they arrived Geneva fled into the house and up to her room, closing the door behind her.

Tony decided to leave her alone for a while. When he went up later, she was lying diagonally across the bed, in a dead sleep. Her bottle of sleeping tablets was on the night stand. He wanted to shake her shoulders, to force her out of the state she was in; he wanted to scoop her into his arms as if she were his child, and hold her tenderly until she was herself again. He sank down in the rocking chair, hung his head, and wept softly. It occurred to him that this was exactly like the day they came home from the hospital. And they were neither of them any better off now than they were then.

Next morning broke under sunny skies. As Elizabeth left home to walk to school, she hugged Tony fiercely. "Take care, Father, I shall be praying for your safety," she said. *Deep down, she is still my Lizzie!* Tony thought desperately. It was the first time since the auto crash that he felt she truly cared for him. He only nodded, for his throat was too thick to speak.

Shortly he drove Andy and Elvira up to Bodmin Primary, giving each one an especially prolonged goodbye hug, which left his chest tight and his eyes moist as he watched them walk into the school house.

Later when it was time to walk to the station, Geneva and Chris accompanied him outside. Geneva had assured him she was up to driving the children to school now, but he was not so sure, given her continued dependence on sleeping tablets. "If there's a problem driving the children to school, perhaps Clifton could help until you're...you're better," he said. Yet even as he made the suggestion he felt doubtful. With so many Bodmin men away at war, Clifton was in constant demand for odd jobs. "Or Merton, better still," he added, though Brookhurst was short-staffed. Well damn and blast, where else could she turn?

"There won't be," she assured him. She did not confess that she intended to go directly to the cemetery afterward. Whereas she used to stop by St. Petroc's and pray, she had felt no inclination to do so since losing her daughter. God seemed as remote now as when she had suffered a miscarriage at age sixteen.

"The sooner you can get off those sleeping tablets, the better you'll feel," he encouraged.

"I only have around six left anyway," she said.

"Good. And, do be sure to write thanking people for all the flowers and letters," he said.

"Yes, I will," she said wearily.

When he hugged her goodbye and kissed her cheek, she did not return his kiss. "Take care," she said in the detached tone he had come to expect of late.

He gathered Chris in his arms and hugged him closely. "When will you come back?" Chris asked, touching Tony's face, his big brown eyes anxious.

"Just as soon as I can, I promise. I shall miss you so much!" He hugged him once more, then put him on his feet, sniffed, and picked up his suitcase.

As he started down the long drive, he paused and looked back. Chris was gazing up at his mother, his hand raised for her to hold. Geneva's arms were folded. She seemed to be studying something far away in the meadow. Abruptly, as if she were unaware that Chris was nearby, she turned and walked toward the house. He half-skipped, half-walked, a few steps behind, his head bowed. Tony resumed his path, a knot in his throat.

Nor was he encouraged when he passed by the Clearharbour sign at the stone entrance. With what confidence he and Geneva had installed the sign nearly a decade ago, that their home would be a place of happy retreat. He made a mental note: the sign wanted repainting. Its deep blue lettering was faded.

CHAPTER 28

Back in London, Tony telephoned Geneva every evening at five, as he had always done. Yet, unfortunately in war-time it was not always possible to get through, with so many parties all over England using the long distance lines. Often when he managed, she was far from the telephone and had to be fetched, reminding him with a pang of regret how she used to be waiting nearby every evening, eager for the sound of his voice. Well, perhaps since the connections were spotty nowadays she saw no reason to wait. And indeed, when they talked she seemed eager to know of the conditions in London, and how things were going at the *William & Mary,* though her concentration wasn't quite up to par and often he had to stop and repeat himself. Overall, he felt there was reason to hope she really was becoming less absorbed in her grief. Finally one evening she told him she had resumed her gardening. This seemed the most positive sign of all.

Sometimes Tony would have his young children come to the telephone, but he had difficulty cutting the conversations short—poor Elvira was especially chatty—so he made up for it by writing them frequent letters about life in London, keeping the tone cheerful and reassuring.

Tony slept on a narrow cot made up in the butler's pantry in the basement, with a floor lamp, and a writing table crowded with books, an ever-changing pile of scripts, and pictures of his family. He felt fortunate for the basement. All over London in the parks and squares, shelters were being established below ground for people who had no other safe place to sleep in case of an air raid. Platforms in tube stations were being utilized for the same purpose. People brought their mattresses from home.

Mrs. Briscoe was Tony's only live-in servant these days. Her small basement office doubled as her sleeping quarters during the week. She spent weekends in the country with her daughter, and it was just as well for there was little house-keeping to be done at Norfolk Square. The furnishings and light fixtures on the main floors were covered with dust sheets. All fragile articles—mirrors, pic-tures, china, glassware, and so forth—were stored in the basement. Tony dined out most of the time. It provided some relief from the boredom of being alone, and also from the boredom of food rationing.

The nights continued without event. Tony would wake up each morning as the sunlight burned a bright rectangle in the high basement window, and hear the birds singing in the cherry tree nearby. He would marvel at how thankful one could be, just for passing a peaceful night.

Then Bill Rutgers was informed that he was to report for duty the fifth of July—three weeks hence. Tony wanted to give him a nice send-off party. Shortly after, *The Cherry Orchard* would go into rehearsal. Hopefully Chek-hov's classic would go over better than *The Chess Player*, which, in spite of its critical success, had not caught on with audiences. Perhaps in times of uncer-tainty they preferred the old familiar, and he was planning accordingly for the foreseeable future, though he'd have to suspend the annual staging of *Pip 'N Pocket*, for one could not count on children being in London to attend.

There would never be a better time to get away for a couple of weeks. By now Geneva was free to resume sexual intimacy and he was hopeful that she would be as eager as he was. He could remember a time before the war when he felt cheated if two or three weeks went by that he was deprived of making love to his wife. He didn't know how lucky he was then! It seemed like an eter-nity since they last made love. At nights when he lay alone on his cot, he imag-ined turning to Geneva, and her slipping happily into his arms. If he closed his eyes, he could smell her scent.

Apart from this, he had obtained some important information from Dr. Rand, which he'd kept to himself until he could share it with Geneva in person.

He wrote her a note to expect him on Friday next.

As he stepped up to the Clearharbour entrance off Castle Canyke, vines along the fence were covered with ripening berries, and up ahead, along the drive, he spotted the bright green bracken growing in thick spiky masses at the base of the sycamore trees. Ah, summertime in the country! The air smelt grassy and clean. He began to whistle a tune. Which must have alerted Elvira, Andy and Chris, for at once they were rushing down the drive into his arms. He felt so blessed he nearly broke down in tears. Each seemed to have grown taller in his absence, which reminded him how quickly children grew up, and made him feel cheated for having to spend so much time away from them. They walked him over to the Anderson shelter that Clifton had installed under the double sycamore tree. "Now we've got our own basement, just like yours! And I shall guard the door from the Germans," Andy said gravely. Tony sensed that he was trying to fill his absent father's shoes. Poor lad. He was only six years old.

"Thanks, Andy. And a fine shelter it is!" Tony said, though in truth, the humped structure was a crude reminder that nowhere in England was one really safe. Just now he wanted nothing more than to stay at home and protect his family.

"Where is Mummy?"

"At the cemetery, of course," Elvira said.

"*Of course.*" "I see…." said Tony, a chill coming over his heart.

Inside, he put his suitcase down beside the stairs and walked into the sitting room. It was cluttered with toys and magazines, and someone's half-filled tea cup and saucer were on the chimneypiece. It was not like Mrs. Greaves to let things go like this, especially when he was due home. Then he noticed the pile of letters and florist cards on a table at the end of the sofa. He walked over to sort through them. In addition to the many expressions of sympathy Geneva was supposed to have acknowledged, there were two unopened letters from Willa, and one from Emelye. Emelye had decorated her envelope with hearts and flowers and butterflies. It brought a rush of love to his heart. And her mother had not even unsealed it.

"Welcome 'ome, sir," said Mrs. Greaves behind him.

He glanced around. "Yes, thanks. Eh—has my wife responded to any of these?"

Mrs. Greaves shook her head dolefully. Her eyebrows were crimped together. "All she dos is sleep, work in the garden and carry flowers to cemetery. Everyday, usually on foot, 'n stays for a couple of hours." Her hands flew up in dismay. "I'm worried, Mr. Selby. She's not lookin' at all well, either. Pale and thin she is, 'ardly eats a bite."

"Why wasn't I informed of all this?" he asked.

"Lady Cynthia positively forbade it—wot could you do, but worry, far away in Loandon? She says. Comes over at least once a week, tries talkin' sense to Madam, and sometimes Lord Edward comes too. But as she pots it, hit's as if she's tied to the poor little dead thing and can' get loose. I told meself you'd be 'ome soon enough, 'n see for yourself."

Now Tony was truly alarmed. Again he thought of what Dr. Rand said. Perhaps it was just the thing Geneva needed to hear, to snap her out of it. Or so he hoped. "Where's Elizabeth?"

"At 'er music lesson, sir. Sir, I realize the house is not op to scratch. It's hard keepin' it, and watchin' the children at same time."

Tony took a long look at the wrinkled face framed in frizzy gray hair, the round eyes behind thick spectacles. Poor old Mrs. Greaves. "Don't worry about it. I'll just drive up and fetch Geneva."

"Aye, sir, that'll be best thing I'm sure."

The *Phantom II* had not been driven since Tony brought it home last December. Though Clifton stopped by occasionally to start it up and let the motor run, nothing was better for the engine than a good drive out in the open air. He ought to have sold the thing years ago—he had few occasions to drive it, especially with the war on. Yet, every time he thought of selling it, he was reminded of that glorious honeymoon drive with Geneva, down to Lyme-Regis. He could not bear to part with it. Perhaps they would drive up to Beacon Hill today, and have a long talk about Dr. Rand's report.

Later, cruising down the main thoroughfare of the cemetery, he spotted Geneva's solitary figure in the distance, clad in a red dress. His heart swelled. She was the love of his life. As he pulled to a stop where the lane turned off to the Selby plot, he had a much better view. Mrs. Greaves was not exaggerating. Geneva was positively skin and bones, her dress hanging loosely on her. Her hair had grown down past her shoulders. She looked very odd, like a character miscast in a play.

Geneva did not hear a motor running until just before it was switched off. Having forgotten Tony was due home today, she turned around, curious. There was the Rolls-Royce, in all its pretentiousness, the sun glinting off its silver radiator. *The lord of the manor arrives,* she thought with contempt. As Tony stepped out of the car and walked towards her, she turned back to the grave. It was covered with grass now, and the marker had been set in place. She'd filled the vase at the top with her daily offering of garden flowers, and banked the base with flowers too. The marker was of rose granite, and the vase was engraved with an angel with beautiful imbricated wings. Below were the words: *In Loving Memory of Cynthia Louise Selby–April 12, 1940.* Tony had composed the simple epitaph. Not until Geneva saw the marker had she realized how inadequate it was, for it gave no hint of her daughter's true nature. Since then, she had written out several alternatives on note paper, and stuffed them in the cubby holes of her desk. Someday she would have the marker changed—

"Darling—" said Tony. Then he was putting his arms around her. She felt guilty for forgetting he was to arrive. She managed to pat his back lightly.

He released her and turned to the grave. It was the first time he had seen the marker, and he stood looking at it for a while. A fine piece of work, fulfilling all his expectations, though the sight of it brought the heavy weight of his daughter's death down on him all over again: a lifetime of a single day. As to the prodigious offering of fresh flowers—well, unfortunately he suspected this explained Geneva's renewed interest in her garden. There were a half dozen bouquets, each bound with a colored ribbon. It was as if the grave were a shrine, Geneva its single pilgrim. He reached for her hand. It was cold as ice. "Let's go home, Darling, alright?"

"Alright," she said indifferently. Pulling her hand free, she knelt down, pressed her fingers to her mouth, then pressed them lingeringly on the grave, her eyes closed as though in prayer. She rose to her feet, picked up her woven bag nearby, stuffed with yesterday's flowers, and started towards the car as if she'd forgotten he was there.

Tony caught up with her. "I say, how about a drive up to Beacon Hill? I should like—"

"But it's become an observation post," she reminded him. "I don't think we're allowed up there."

"Oh, I had forgotten about that," he said with regret.

He'd have to wait until they were home to talk with Geneva about Dr. Rand's findings. He couldn't stomach any more time at the cemetery.

As they drove along, Geneva tried in vain to remember if Tony's note said how long he planned to stay. Not long, she hoped. She was much better off when he was in London, occupied with the theatre and not prying into her business all the time. Still, he'd come all this way and she hadn't even welcomed him. "Welcome home," she said, with an effort to bring warmth into her voice.

"Thanks. It's good to be here," he said sweetly. He caught her hand and kissed it as though he were encouraged by her words. "Cold," he said of her hand, and gave her a tender, expectant look.

Cold hands…warm heart—the trite words were begging—but it wasn't for him her heart was warm. Which reminded her suddenly that he would expect to make love with her tonight. Or maybe even as soon as they got home. She felt panicked. Quickly she asked, "And how are things going with *Three Sisters?*"

Puzzled, he released her hand. "We're not doing *Three Sisters.*"

"Yes you are," she said defensively. "I distinctly remember from your note that you are going into rehearsals in July. After Bill leaves."

"We are. But for *The Cherry Orchard.*"

"Oh. I'm sorry," she said dejectedly. "Well, I knew it was Chekhov, anyway," she said, with an attempt at lightness. In truth, it frightened her sometimes how forgetful she had become, how mixed-up. She realized now that she had forgotten to write the notes thanking people, as she promised to do. She had not even read the messages of sympathy, in fact. Or, had she?

A few minutes later they were home. Tony parked the car by the conservatory and switched off the engine. The children were not about. This was as good a place to talk as any. Yet when he turned to face Geneva, she said, "I'm a bit tired. Think I'll go up and rest." Her hand was on the door handle.

"Wait just a moment. There's something I need to tell you," he said. She turned to him. "I rang up Dr. Rand not long ago and laid it all out for him. I wanted to be sure that our daughter received the same quality of care she would have received in London."

The thought that Cynthia Louise may have been saved had she received better care was terrifying to Geneva. "Yes—what did he say?"

"In fact, Dr. Ashmore had already written him, explaining the circumstances in detail. Dr. Rand was confident that nothing more could have been done." He looked out towards the peaceful meadow, the bright green grass furrowed with deep green hedgerows. "He also said—" he began, and his voice faltered momentarily as he remembered his daughter's red hair and fringe of red eye lashes; he had not realized this was going to be difficult. "—that, had Cynthia Louise somehow pulled through, she most certainly would have had severe brain damage." Again, he faced Geneva. "So, you see, it really was for the best. She would not have had a good life."

Brain damage. *Cynthia Louise was skipping along the garden border, her red hair tossed by the wind....* Perhaps that was the most she would have been capable of. Geneva would have loved her just as much, perhaps even more, would have taken care of her for the rest of her life—. Her thoughts broke off as she remembered the Elizabeth Barclay Home. Her blood froze. "Tony, if Cynthia Louise had lived, and been—" she took in a hasty breath—"what would have...have been done with her?"

He had not expected the question, and for a prolonged moment he just stared at her anxious face. Then, thoughtfully he said, "I'm only so thankful not to have to deal with that."

Deal with that. She saw an auto hurrying away, her daughter in the rear seat, not knowing where she was being taken. "But, would you have...have forced me to place her somewhere—institutionalize her? I want the truth. You owe me the truth," she demanded, her voice raspy.

To her surprise, tears stood in Tony's eyes. "I should hope that we could—Geneva, I have the most ghastly feeling that you've come to regard me as—as your *enemy*."

She shook her head, opened her mouth to speak—

"No, don't argue, please. Whenever you look at me, it's as though you don't trust me, don't want me in any part of your life."

She looked ahead, stung by the truth in his words.

"Geneva, do you think I do not care, do not hurt as you do?"

No, it wasn't the same. But how could you explain that to a man never connected to a child by an umbilical cord? Perhaps she ought to tell him that Cynthia Louise had clung to life only for her, and that was what drove her to keep remembering. Yet she now held that to be the most sacred knowledge in her heart. She didn't want to share it with him. "I'm sorry. I didn't mean to hurt you," she said, sincerely. She got out of the car and hurried inside.

That night when they went to bed, Geneva was determined to somehow get through making love without injuring Tony's feelings. She returned his tender smile at the beginning, her lips feeling wooden. He kissed her mouth. He kissed her neck and throat, slipping the strap of her gown off her shoulder. She held her breath. Her arms were stiff; her fingers clutched the bed linens. When his lips brushed her nipple tenderly—a gesture that used to send an arrow of desire from there all the way down her body—the memory of opening her robe to Cynthia Louise swept over her. She felt that Tony was violating her. She flinched.

He looked up. "Still tender?"

She didn't think fast enough to lie. "No—no, I'm just not ready. I'm sorry. Truly I am." She gave him a pleading look.

Tony lay back stiffly on the pillows, his blood racing, his loins aching with deflected desire. Fighting down resentment, he reasoned that forcing the issue might drive Geneva further away. He would be home for two weeks. There would be other nights. He took a gulp of air. "It's alright," he said hoarsely. "Come, let me just hold you." Perhaps that would be a start.

She moved close to his chest, filled with both relief, and terror at what she could not help. It was the first time in their marriage that she had rejected him. What was worse, she could not imagine her feelings ever changing.

CHAPTER 29

"Please, give me another child," she begged.

"Yes, yes," he said, his breath coming in gasps as he gathered her hips in his hands. There was no warm secret cleft in her body that his tongue had not entered and tasted, no curve untraced by his hands. His heart was thrumming wildly against the breast that he had suckled. He had never felt so completely loved—

When he awoke he had her arms pinned down; his legs had forced hers apart; his face was buried in her shoulder, and there was no stopping himself. He spilled a torrent of semen into her.

Afterward, she felt rigid beneath him. He raised up, heaving with exhaustion, and pulled himself free. He'd left a sticky trail on her thighs. He lay back on his pillow. He felt a kind of self-loathing that he had not experienced since he was an adolescent, having had a wet dream between the sheets. Thanks to the blackout curtain, the room was utterly dark. He could not see the expression on her face, was almost afraid of what it might hold. "I was dreaming. I—I'm s—"

He could not quite force the word out, not being sure that *sorry* was the right word. He had been at home for a week, and every night when he touched Geneva, his hopes had been dashed against the wall of *I'm just not ready.*

"It's alright," Geneva said quietly, telling herself that it didn't change anything, was just an act of nature that could not be helped, that was all. At first, Tony's feverish acting out of his dream had set in motion a dream of her own: Cynthia Louise at her breast, eagerly taking the nourishment awaiting her.

Geneva felt sick with revulsion. She began to shiver.

Tony groped along the night stand top till he found the torch. Switching it on, he started toward the bath, to wash himself, then remembered her sticky thighs. "Would you like to go first—"

"No," she said with an intake of breath.

While he was washing, he remembered her words in his dream, *"Please, give me another child."* Did Geneva's wish emerge as he slept because he had been denying its possibility while awake? Was she angry that—because of his insistence—she had reluctantly submitted to the irrevocable step of preventing another pregnancy, and now there would be no replacing the child that she lost? When he opened the door, he heard Geneva weeping softly. *How she must hate me,* he thought miserably. He left the bath light on for her. Christ, how he hated those blackout drapes; how he hated conserving electricity; how he hated the bloody war! He wished to God they'd get it over with.

He lay down beside her and closed his hand around hers. He didn't dare try to hold her. He wasn't even sure that he wanted to. He heard her take in a shuddering breath, and realized she was weeping. "Please, don't cry Geneva," he begged.

She let out her breath and sniffed, then pulled her hand from his and touched her damp hairline. She felt as if she were sinking into a pit of quicksand from which she would never emerge. The integrity of her marriage was destroyed. It occurred to her that the only hope of recovering it may well lie in forsaking Cynthia Louise. But then she thought of her daughter, looking into her eyes adoringly as she struggled to breathe, and was filled with remorse. How could she? Why should she? What sort of basis for a marriage could that be, when the very child she must forsake had been the fruit of Tony's seed?

"I think I know why you…you feel as you do…towards me," Tony said haltingly. "You feel I've cheated you, by insisting there be no more children."

"No, that isn't it at all," she said reasonably. "The fact that Cynthia Louise was…" she bit her lip, "…so frail…proves you were right."

Being wrong about her feelings, yet again, infuriated him. "Then what is it? Why are you shutting me out?" he demanded.

"I just need time, I guess."

It crossed Tony's mind that he could forbid Geneva to return to the cemetery, and all their problems would be solved. Or, could he? First of all, he wouldn't be around to assure that she obeyed his command, nor would he sink so low as to have someone spy on her and report to him. And even if he could stop her from going, would it help her overcome her loss, or only drive it deeper?

At length, he rose from the bed and reached for the torch again. "I'm going down to sleep in the buttery," he said dully. "I shall go back to London tomorrow, and I believe it will be better if I stay there for—for a while."

CHAPTER 30

It was five o'clock on a Saturday evening. Tony had tried without success to get a call through to Clearharbour, and he was about to walk through the door and head for the *William & Mary* when the deep, mournful wail of the air-raid siren sent him diving under the dining room table a few feet away, his heart pounding in fright; and within seconds there was the shriek of descending bombs, then the townhouse was reverberating with the thunderous impact of explosions. It wasn't as though anyone had a right to be surprised that the German Luftwaffe was finally launching an air attack on London. Two weeks ago the RAF gave Berlin a good scrubbing; it was only a matter of time before the Germans retaliated. Still, Tony was breathless with shock and horror. And it was only by the grace of God that he was not outdoors at this moment.

Soon the two tall dining room windows blew in, and—tape and black crape notwithstanding—sent shards of glass within inches of where he lay. Chunks of plaster struck the table above his head and pummeled the wood floor all around. Dust flew into his nostrils and throat. One could only guess at the specific areas being targeted. The way the earth shook beneath him he would have sworn Norfolk Square was taking a series of direct hits. He wondered if the *William & Mary* was in the line of fire. The technical crew and cast of *The Cherry Orchard* should have arrived at the theatre by now, preparing for the seven-thirty performance. At the sound of the siren they would have headed for the nearest cover. He prayed to God no one was out on the street en route.

At last the barrage ceased and there was only an eerie silence during which Tony held his breath, wondering when the next round would come. He lay there for what seemed an eternity, until he heard the all-clear signal. Blowing out his breath in relief, he drove one violently shaking hand down into his coat pocket, withdrew his torch, fumbled until he'd managed to switch it on, then groped his way down the stairs to the basement to spend the remainder of the night. It proved a peaceful few hours.

The next morning there was a layer of white dust over every inch of the main floors of the townhouse. The windows on the upper floors had been boarded up previously, but every single one on the ground floor had blown in. He'd have to board them up before leaving this morning, and contact the local council about replacing the glass. While the electric lights worked, he soon found there'd be no using the lift—the carriage was jammed at the basement level. Just as well to let it remain there till the war was over. He'd hate like hell to be caught between floors when a bomb hit.

When he walked outside just after seven o'clock, a blue sky above and the pleasant feel of warm sunshine on his face choked him with emotion. He found many of his neighbors about. Mr. Sherwood, from two houses over, told him there was a direct hit in Edgware Road a few blocks away—he had already checked it out. Someone else had heard a report on the wireless: While there were strikes all over London, the East End, with its heavy concentration of industry and dock works, was hardest hit. Suddenly it occurred to Tony that the Bledsoe family may have come to harm; he certainly hoped not. Such kind people, Stella and Joe, who discovered Emelye bound and gagged in the back of a truck, where Benjamin Calais finally abandoned her. Every year he mailed their family premium tickets for *Pip 'N Pocket*. Mrs. Bledsoe always sent him one of those thank-you cards with pale pastel flowers on the front that one purchased from a shop, and said they enjoyed the show. He made a mental note to check on the Bledsoes. Yet they were working-class folk, and he doubted they could afford telephone service.

Except for windows blown in, a good bit of debris lying about, and white dust covering everything—the trees in the square, beneath which his children had so often played, looked as if they'd been sprinkled with talcum powder—Norfolk Square was blessedly untouched.

Yet, what would tonight bring? And tomorrow night?

Tony went back inside to telephone the *William & Mary*. He was somewhat relieved when he heard a steady ring on the line. Yet to his chagrin, no one answered it. He wasn't sure what to make of this. As soon as he boarded up the broken windows, he must get down there, be sure everything was alright. He would then close down the facility until he could commiserate with other theatre owners about whether to risk reopening, or remain closed till the end of the war. Somehow just now, closing down the *William & Mary* struck him as an extraordinary measure, even though he'd known it was likely to come to this eventually.

He telephoned Clearharbour. To his amazement, on the first ring Geneva answered. In spite of everything, he was so grateful to hear her voice that hot tears welled up in his eyes and his hand began to tremble round the receiver. "It's—it's Tony here," he said, his voice quavering.

"Thank God, you're safe!" Geneva cried. He could hardly believe the tide of emotion carried on her voice. She said that Cynthia rang up a few minutes ago, having heard the news of last night's attack on the wireless. But when Geneva in turn attempted to contact him, she could not get through. Now at her urging he told her all about it, and she was obviously relieved when he said he was shutting down the theatre for the time being. "Don't go out at night anymore unless you absolutely have to, promise!" she urged him. Not for months had she expressed herself with such passion, except if she spoke of Cynthia Louise. Perhaps last night's episode had shaken some sense into her.

"Are the children about?" he asked. Suddenly he would give anything to hear the sound of their voices.

"They're still in bed. I was about to get them up for church. Shall I bring them to the phone?"

"It's alright. I really need to get busy now. Just give them my love. I shall ring again later."

When they said goodbye, neither added *I love you.*

Afterward Geneva sank down on the telephone bench to catch her breath. She thought of the tinny, uneven sound of Tony's voice, and his remark: "*Within moments, I would have been out on the street.*" In the year since Britain went to war with Germany she had become complacent about the possibility of aerial attacks on London, for gradually it seemed they would never materialize. For all her thankfulness that Tony was far away and prevented from returning, she had never once imagined him coming to harm. What had begun last night was bound to be repeated, over and over again. Tony could very well lose his life. She was thoroughly shaken.

Attendance was higher than usual at St. Petroc's Sunday worship that morning, and for the first time in many Sundays Geneva felt that she was truly present, body and soul, eyes and ears alert to the messages conveyed in prayer and scripture. At the time appointed for the sermon, Father Key removed his reading glasses, dispensed with his notes, then looked down with great tenderness upon the congregation below, as if they were his beloved children. He preached with compassion on the topic uppermost in everyone's mind. In referring to the increasingly troubled state of the world, he made no judgments, but said with conviction, "Through these times, make no mistake, God is speaking to all nations and to all people, and we must each of us pray and search our hearts to hear what it is he is saying to us...."

For Geneva the words were a dose of strong medicine. Could it be that God was speaking to her through Tony's narrow escape from harm? Giving her a second chance to love him as he deserved? But no—she could not create passion that she no longer felt, and surely God could not be telling her to pretend. Was it her fault if the loss of her daughter had built a wall between her and those she loved? Truly, she felt as separate from all her loved ones as she felt from Tony. It was just that they made fewer demands on her emotions. Oh, sexual performance was the true revealer, she despaired; the marital test from which there was no escape.

Stubbornly she thought of her precious daughter, taking one breath after another, only for her. Holding on to the misery that was life, only for her. The whole Christian religion was propelled by multitudes honoring the supreme sacrifice of one life, so why was it wrong for her to honor her daughter's ultimate sacrifice, when she was the single beneficiary? A visit to her grave once a day; an offering of flowers. How little it was to give in return! Geneva found herself thinking of the first time she visited there, how surprised she was to discover that her daughter's spirit lingered.

Yet now came the inevitable question: in continuing to visit the cemetery, day after day, was she holding her daughter's spirit hostage just as she had held her life hostage when they lay together in the hospital bed?

CHAPTER 31

On Monday morning she telephoned Miss Pennett's Florist. She asked that they remove the flowers she'd left there on Saturday, and starting that very day, fill the vase on her daughter's marker with fresh flowers once a week, until further notice. Then she walked to St. Petroc's, resuming her custom of kneeling each weekday morning in silent prayer. Humbly she asked forgiveness for any harm she had done. She prayed that God would rekindle her feelings for those she loved, and especially Tony. She prayed for Tony's safety.

Every morning along her route, the war seemed to press in on every side. A command supply depot had been erected on the vacant tract of land adjoining Clearharbour. It supplied the troops with food, cigarettes, and sweet rations. There was a constant rumble of army vehicles trundling back and forth through the gates, and the air was hazy with shell dust. Down Castle Canyke Road just before it turned into St. Nicholas was the home of the Duke of Cornwall's Light Infantry, with its high stone barracks and hospital—now a teeming military post for soldiers from all over England. Soldiers were billeted in various public buildings, and in church fellowship halls—they swelled the congregations on Sunday mornings. The streets of Bodmin were crowded with soldiers, and a military band played zippy songs on Mt. Folly Square, the tuba's *oom-pah, oom-pah!* giving the town a false carnival atmosphere. Members of Women's Voluntary Services in their green tweed suits, red pullovers and felt hats, rolled carts down the streets filled with used aluminum pans—"*Did ye know, Mrs. Selby, hit takes 2,000 aluminum pans to make one aeroplane? Do ye think we could give op this auld sauce pan?*" said Mrs. Greaves, Geneva's kitchen becoming part of the war machine. When the wind was blowing from the north, she could hear the sharp report of rifles from the practice range on Bodmin Moor.

Hard to imagine that, during the days when she walked back and forth to the cemetery, she had been virtually oblivious of all that surrounded her. Now it served as a grim reminder of the dangers Tony faced in London.

The raids continued nightly, not only there, but all over Britain in centers of commerce and industry. Because of its bowl shape, Bodmin was not clearly visible from the air and therefore—thankfully—not so vulnerable to air attacks. But at nighttime you could hear German planes passing over, headed for Plymouth, which was not so fortunate. If the newspapers were to be believed, the British anti-aircraft guns were effective in combating the German Luftwaffe; damages were minimal, the work crews were efficient in cleaning up and the population just went right on with their daily activities as if everything were normal. Still, every time the telephone rang, her heart quickened and would not slow down until she was sure that there was no bad news waiting.

Whenever she spoke with Tony, her voice was genuinely warm with encouragement, yet she would not tell him she was praying for a transformation within herself. It would be cruel to build up false hopes, and especially now. He anticipated coming home on Christmas Eve, for the family gathering at Brookhurst, and remaining through the weekend. She imagined herself packing the alluring black sleeping gown from Willa to take along. It had not been out of the gift box since she received it, whereupon she'd held it up in front of her pregnant body, wondering if her stomach would ever again be taut enough to fit inside its narrow proportion.

Every day she spent away from the grave, she grew a little stronger in her resolve. She believed that God would give her back desire for her husband, but only if she remained faithful to her decision. Yet as the days passed she was disconcerted to find she was forgetting small details about Cynthia Louise, such as the exact shape of her mouth and nose and ears, whether her hairline went straight across her forehead, or came to a point in the center—she pondered her hairline long and hard, yet could reach no conclusion—and exactly the shape of the eyes that peered into hers. Only the milky blue irises and tiny ebony pupils were still vivid. She wished that she had gone back to the cemetery one last time, to say farewell and leave the imprint of her kiss upon her daughter's grave. Why had she not done that, instead of just abandoning her? She tried not to dwell on this, for it froze her with guilt.

Geneva enrolled Chris for Michaelmas term in Bodmin Primary School, beginning at the end of September. He seemed eager to start, and did not cry when she left him on the first day of class, as she'd feared he might. She thought with satisfaction how much he had grown up since she stopped babying him. By now all of her children were spending weekends at Brookhurst, where Cynthia and Edward were housing a dozen or so children—there had been another mass evacuation from London after the initial bombing, this time voluntary. Geneva knew that Elizabeth tutored those children having trouble adjusting to school in Bodmin—where they had been thrust in the middle of the term—and that with Cynthia and Edward she took them on field trips into Bodmin, to the picture show and the library. Just how Elvira and Andy and Chris helped out, Geneva did not know. All she knew was that they seemed eager to go when Merton arrived to pick them up on Friday afternoons. The little ones would give their mother an absent goodbye kiss, as if some adult had told them it was their duty. Then she would watch them troup out the door. Even the pets went along, Kilty and The Baron wagging their tails as if they were as glad to be away as the children, and Bertrand contentedly tucked in Elizabeth's arms, his tail curled around her elbow. After Merton tipped his hat and she closed the door, she would go upstairs and rest. She still felt exhausted most of the time.

Geneva was now afraid to be left alone with only Mrs. Greaves's puttering around, breaking the silence in the house, and on Sundays not even this. While alone she could not help longing for Cynthia Louise, trying to recall the details that were slipping away from her memory; and she was often tempted to go to the cemetery, to see if it would help her recall. *I have no picture of her to remind me*, she would think defensively. But no, she must hold on to her resolve.

One chilly Saturday near the end of October, when curly leaves of red and orange and golden were fluttering down from the trees, lining the top of the Anderson shelter and banking along the garden border, she felt particularly tempted to return to the cemetery. She decided to create a diversion by having her hair cut and styled. Perhaps if she could make herself attractive, she would feel more confident about meeting Tony's needs. As she sat in the high chair at Cape's Hairdresser, snippets of her hair falling to the floor like autumn leaves, she was encouraged to remember many years ago, the first time she had her nearly waist-length hair bobbed. It was just before Tony came back to the States, and the cutting of her hair was a ritual marking a new era in her life. Yet as she studied herself in the mirror now, there was no denying that her hair was neither quite as deep red nor as wavy as it was then. She had known she was accruing a few gray strands, but now she realized there were quite a number of them. Still, when she left the shop with her cropped hair, the waves seemed a little springier than before.

At home she put a little make-up on her face. She had not bothered with make-up since the death of her daughter. Sitting back from the mirror, assessing her new look, she thought, *I am getting better, I will be alright.* Yet for some reason she could not fathom, she started to weep, tears seeping between the fingers she held before her eyes. Afterward she felt exhausted, and lay down for a while. When she woke up several hours later, her throat was raw and her nose was congested, and she felt feverish.

After taking two aspirin she dragged herself downstairs. Mrs. Greaves was putting on her hat, ready to leave at the end of the day. Seeing Geneva, she frowned. "You're lookin' a bit piqued, if ya don't mind me sayin' so."

"Yes, a cold coming on I think. I need a good strong cup of tea. Do we have any?" One never knew, now that the purchase of tea must be accompanied by coupons, and Mrs. Greaves did most of the shopping.

"Aye. You go back op to bed. I'll bring it. It's no surprise, the way you neglect yourself. Ye'll roon yer health, 'fore long." She was already removing her hat pins.

Geneva was tired of Mrs. Greaves's steady stream of advice. She'd gotten so she talked to her more like an errant daughter than an employer. "Never mind. I'll get my own tea. I want to sit downstairs anyway."

"I left a pot of me vegetable soup on stove. Mrs. West brought over a sack of runner beans and squash and potatoes and leeks from her garden yest'day."

And stopped long enough to lecture her on the virtues of being involved in the WVS. Geneva was tired of being lectured.

As soon as Mrs. Greaves was out the door Geneva put the soup in the icebox. She wasn't hungry. After a cup of tea, she went back to bed.

All through November she could not seem to get well from one cold before the onset of another. Finally in early December she made an appointment with a general physician whose name she found in the Bodmin directory. How odd to be seeking a doctor. This was the first time she'd been ill since she moved to England. After a blood test, he announced she was seriously anaemic. He prescribed iron tablets to be taken twice a day and a diet including yellow and green leafy vegetables, and animal liver—if she could obtain any. The thought of eating liver turned Geneva's stomach. Her father used to like it floured and fried with onions, and when her mother cooked it, you could smell it all over the downstairs rooms and up the stairwell. The doctor told her to come back in a month, and they'd see if there was any improvement in her blood.

Shortly after that Elvira asked if there would be Christmas presents this year. "Well of course," Geneva said, though in truth she had not given the matter any thought. The next day she began acquiring gifts for her family and stowing them in the customary place, in the closet under the stairs. There was not much available for sale in Bodmin, but she managed to find something for everyone on her list, including a pair of deep wine-colored silk pajamas for Tony. According to the clerk at Marshall's, the fabric was made before the war, when standards of quality were much higher than now. The price tag was proportionately high. The ensemble seemed a fitting counterpart to Geneva's sexy black gown, even though the thought of going to bed with Tony continued to make her so anxious that she chased it from her thoughts. *I will be ready when the time comes,* she told herself.

In spite of the fact she had gotten over her spell of colds, and she was taking the iron pills faithfully, she was still worn out all the time, and after returning home from these outings she would feel compelled to go up to her room and rest for a couple of hours.

Almost at once Elvira began asking when she would wrap the presents. What an overwhelming project it seemed: getting everything out of the closet, bringing it to the dining room table, then standing on her feet until the job was done. She kept putting it off. On the last school day before the holiday began, she decided she had better get busy and wrap all the gifts while the children were not around. But she soon discovered there was very little wrapping paper left, and—much to her guilt—almost no ribbon at all, for she had used it to bind the bouquets for Cynthia Louise. She took her woven bag and walked into town to buy the needed supplies, but unfortunately, there were none left. Perhaps she would have more luck in Truro, but it was too late to drive there today and get back in time to pick up the children from school.

Elvira may not have trusted her mother to come through, for that afternoon when Geneva admitted the gifts were still unwrapped, she said, "Never mind. I shall take paste and make stickers for all the presents with what little wrapping paper we have."

"That's nice of you, dear, but you don't know who is to receive which gift, so I'll have to do it."

Elvira frowned. "Not a bit of it! Just put a little gift card on each box."

But there were no gift cards, either. Embarrassed, Geneva said, "I'll write the name on each box, but just be careful not to cover up the names when you decorate them. And Elvira, you must promise not to open yours and peek."

"Upon my honor," said she, touching her heart. "In fact, I shan't open any of them, that way Andy can't badger me to tell him what he's getting." So Elvira went to work, and by bedtime all the boxes were decorated and waiting in the closet beneath the stairs.

CHAPTER 32

The holiday began badly, with Tony's train arriving three hours late, the family hastening to leave Clearharbour for Brookhurst before dark, and Tony in a cross mood because the car still had to be packed. Already light snow was falling, making the streets slushy, and more was predicted overnight. The closer they came to Brookhurst, the thicker it would be; it always was, out in the country. "But how could we have known which car to pack?" Geneva retorted, thinking, *what a way to begin the holiday.*

While Elizabeth and Elvira helped Tony load the Rover boot with gift packages, Geneva stuffed two woven shopping bags with tins of Christmas cookies that Mrs. Greaves had made. Andy and Chris were already at Brookhurst, which would at least save the proverbial need to double back at least once, for some article one of them had forgotten. As Tony cautiously maneuvered the Rover down the long drive between the trees, he was guided by the slit of dim light from one masked headlamp. The house, with its black-draped windows, looked stark and lonely, and strangely anonymous to Geneva, as though no one lived there. It made her feel sad and, somehow, hopeless. Hours from now, the light would go out in a Brookhurst bedroom and Tony would turn to her. *I am not ready I must be ready I must....*

The celebration was held in the Brookhurst library—the drawing room, where it was usually held, had been closed off in order to conserve electricity. There were hundreds of candles lit on the high Christmas tree standing between the casement windows, and the pleasant aromas of hot wassail and an assortment of holiday refreshments spiced the air—everyone had been saving sugar and butter coupons for holiday baking.

Now that they were here, the holiday spirit seemed contagious even for Tony, Geneva noticed. In spite of her efforts to get into the spirit, however, she felt apart from it all, and observed the scene as if it were inside one of those paperweights with a glass globe that one upturned to make snow come down on a beautiful winter scene. Cynthia wore a stunning white satin blouse and deep green velveteen skirt; a small Christmas wreath collar pin studded with diamonds, rubies and emeralds, sparkled at the top of her lace jabot. Obviously grateful to have the whole family under her roof, she wore a radiant smile.

Morey's Santa Claus suit was procured when he was younger and more slender. The red flannel coat barely accommodated his beefy mid-section, and the sleeves strained around his shoulders like pulled taffy. Abraham and Sarah circled and barked, their tails wagging. When Chris sat down in a library chair, Abraham pinned him with his giant front paws and licked his face, which sent Chris into gales of laughter. *He doesn't laugh very much at home,* thought Geneva guiltily. In fact, none of the children did, now that she thought about it. Even Elvira, usually the clown, was solemn as she went about her gift-wrapping chore.

Everyone was commenting on how nicely Chris was adjusting to school. Like Elizabeth, he was proving exceptionally bright, and therefore the teachers adored him. Though he was small for his age, others did not bully him because they knew they would have to contend with Andy and Elvira. Andy wasn't too keen on protecting Chris, but he would do whatever Elvira told him, and Elvira feared no one and nothing. Presently Cynthia said to Tony, as if talking across Geneva, "There you see, I knew Chris would be alright." So apparently Tony had been concerned about Chris just as Geneva had, but had shared this view with Cynthia and perhaps others, rather than with her. She felt a little hurt. She imagined all kinds of concerns being discussed among the family, excluding her.

Everyone was a bit awkward with Geneva, as if they didn't know quite what to say to her. Yet Edward, dressed in his traditional dark green vest and red plaid tie, clutched her hand and smiled encouragingly. The bond established between them on the night of Cynthia Louise's death remained strong. He never lectured her about getting on with her life. He alone probably came closest to understanding her loss, and yet she would never try to talk with him about it for she understood—though she'd never been told—that while in crisis the shield of his reserve came down, other times it was left intact. Perhaps this explained his deep reservoir of strength, at the ready when needed by those he loved.

Soon Morey handed the gifts around, with Andy's assistance. Tony had managed to find some traditional Christmas crackers for sale in London—left over from last year. Colorful paper tubes came apart with a bang, and paper toys spilled out, the children giggling in delight. Apparently they had been warned not to expect any this year. As they paraded around wearing their paper hats and blowing party whistles, Tony slipped a tiny box from his pocket and closed Geneva's fingers around it. "It's a happy 9th wedding anniversary—rather belated I'm afraid—and Christmas present, in one," he said.

She opened the box and beheld a silver heart-shaped brooch. "It's beautiful," she said, smiling up at him. Until now, their anniversary on October 17th had not even crossed her mind. The personal nature of Tony's gift made the pajamas she had purchased for him seem impersonal if not thoughtless, and she felt a sense of guilt, edged in tenderness for him. She handed him the brooch and he pinned it to her blouse lapel. He looked into her eyes. "You look lovely tonight. I must say I like your new hairdo!" Geneva smiled with pleasure. Just for a few moments, she felt younger, more free.

She's going to be alright, Tony thought, his heart leaping. He felt that if he could return to London when the holiday was over, knowing that things were back to normal between them, he could manage to get through whatever he must. At least he would have one less thing to worry about, night after night, as he lay in a somnambulant state. Bombs were being dropped over the whole of London now, with all bets off as to how much devastation they would bring before it was over. No one got any sleep there. One rose each morning feeling he had been beaten about the head for hours and hours, and walked outdoors with trepidation. Two weeks ago, one corner of Norfolk Square was shaved off by a bomb. The estate agent's office, the grocer, and newsstand were destroyed, though luckily no one was harmed. Broken water mains flooded streets; debris was everywhere. Maintenance crews worked round the clock repairing damages; firemen extinguished fires from incendiary bombs which were used to light the way for the Luftwaffe bombers. Though the *William & Mary*—which he reopened late in October—had escaped damage thus far, other theatres had been less fortunate. The *Queen's* had taken a direct hit, which destroyed the entire facade and the back portion of the stalls. Many years ago, Tony had a job doing exposition tango tea dancing there. Seeing the *Queen's* ravaged, he felt sick at heart, as though a very old friend had been mortally wounded. He felt an increasing dread that the *William & Mary* would be destroyed. St. James's

Church of Paddington, where they worshiped when Geneva came to London, took a disastrous hit in October. More than fifty feet of the spire was swiped off, and many windows were destroyed, including the one above the baptismal font. Tony wanted very much to tell Geneva about it and suggest that, when the war was over and the church could be restored, they might perhaps contribute a new baptismal window, in memory of Cynthia Louise. Except that one could never feel free to say anything about the child, for fear of how Geneva might react.

When he got this far away from London, he could scarcely believe the abominable conditions one managed to put up with there. God, how he dreaded returning....

The time had arrived to cut the string and open two brown cardboard boxes from Houston. A note on each warned: "Do not open till Christmas!" Poor Willa and Rodney; they were not feeling very cheerful this holiday. Tony had been corresponding with Willa regularly since he replied to her two letters Geneva ignored, one of which reported that, much to the despair of his parents, James planned to drop out of engineering school in January, join the U.S. Army Air Force and apply to flight school. Having taken extra college courses during this past summer and the one before, he would have two years towards his degree by January—a prerequisite for becoming an air force pilot, along with excellent grades. There seemed a very good chance he would one day wind up risking his life among the Allied Forces.

To everyone's amazement, the gaily-wrapped gift boxes were tightly padded with packets of sugar and flour, coffee and tea—part of the holiday surprise. After the second of the boxes had been opened, Morey picked up still one more large cardboard box, with gay stickers on it. After examining it on all sides, he said, "I don't see a name on it." At which point Andy—in great high spirits by now—rushed by him and grabbed the box. "What's in this one? Who's it from?" he sang. Being top-heavy, the box flipped out of Andy's grasp. The lid fell open and the infant gas mask dropped to the floor, its hand pump poking upward, its trailing olive-green gown settling in a heap.

Seeing it, Geneva's stomach pitched. She clamped a hand over her mouth and fled from the room and up the stairs.

CHAPTER 33

When Tony came up to their room a few minutes later, Geneva was lying in bed in her skirt and slip, having dragged herself there from the bath, where she had vomited up the contents of her stomach in one violent rush, soiling the front of her blouse, the image of the infant gas mask assailing her like a ghost in sickening green raiments. She felt overwhelmed with sadness, guilty for trying to forget Cynthia Louise, for paying someone to pick up the last flowers she placed on the grave and never even returning to say farewell. This would have been her first Christmas, and Geneva had been so intent on forgetting her life that she never even thought of this until the lid came open and out spilled the tiny infant who struggled to breathe.

She did not trouble to explain to Tony why she had removed her blouse, and only when he sat down on the bed did she remember the brooch he gave her was still pinned to it.

Tony kissed Geneva's damp forehead, a hollow feeling at the pit of his stomach. "Dreadful luck, having that thing appear. Elvira solved the mystery of how it got mixed up with the Christmas presents. Then Chris said something that showed remarkable insight for his age, I thought: 'Baby doesn't have to wear that in heaven,' he said."

Geneva's chest knotted up. "It would have been her first Christmas."

"Yes," he said pensively, and took her hand in his. They remained silent for a few moments, Tony stroking his wife's hand, feeling a twinge of sadness himself, and a little guilt, for he had not thought of this until she brought it up. Their lives were so haunted by Cynthia Louise, in fact, that it hardly seemed she was not actually with them. "Darling, I want to ask you a huge favor," he entreated. "Could you rejoin the party in a little while? The children from London are having their own celebration down in the servants' dining hall—a couple of them have their parents here, thanks to Mother and Father paying their way—and they intend to bring them all upstairs to join us in singing carols. I've got Christmas crackers for us to give them. I'd like for you to be there," he said. He did not say that everyone in the family was feeling gloomy because of Geneva's hasty flight from the party, or that life was growing unbearable altogether because of her continuing state of upset, and if they could redeem this evening, for the sake of the children, he would be ever so grateful—

"I'll try," she said, not promisingly.

Tony let out a breath. "Thanks," he said quietly. He kissed her forehead again, rose from the bed and left the room.

Geneva knew she would not make it through the first verse of *Silent Night* without losing all composure, that Tony was wrong to believe that her return would accomplish anything except to ruin the party for everyone.

She knew, also, that when he finally came to bed, she would not be able to make love with him, for there had been no answered prayers, no transformation; and she couldn't fake her way through making love, no, she just couldn't. The shocking sight of the infant gas mask had made her realize how raw her feelings were even yet, how unresolved she had left things: not so much as a goodbye.

After an hour or so, Tony returned to the room and began to undress. Though Geneva stared at the ceiling, she was excruciatingly aware of each article of clothing being discarded, from his blazer and shirt to his trousers. As he slipped into bed, both her hands clenched up into fists as if to ward off a blow. "I'm sorry," she apologized. She could not force another word past her throat.

Oh, how he hoped she was talking about not having returned to the party. "Not to worry; actually it went pretty well. As soon as our guests came in, Elvira and Andy and Elizabeth took things in hand, making them feel less awkward. Quite a distance between the Brookhurst library and London's East End! But you have some very remarkable children indeed." *Do you realize how lucky you are?*

"Yes," said Geneva softly. Tony turned to her and pulled her close. "Come home to me, Geneva, I miss you so," he said longingly. He kissed her mouth and pressed his forehead against her cheek.

She lay there stiffly as he went on kissing her, her thoughts traveling to the black gown folded carefully inside the suitcase in the corner. No.

Tony kept trying for a little while longer, then, finally, the rejection so eloquently expressed in Geneva's unyielding body snapped the thin thread that remained of his patience. What a fool he had been tonight when he gave her the heart-shaped brooch and she looked up at him so tenderly, to think surely she would not turn away from him again. Even when the sight of the gas mask upset her, he told himself it did not portend another disaster in bed; that she loved him too much for that to happen: look how she worried when he was in London. Resentment roiling in him, he stood up and looked down at her. "I won't go through this anymore, or put our children through it," he said, his voice growing strident. "I shall return to London tomorrow, and henceforth I shall arrange to visit my children at Brookhurst.

"And...and...when the war is over—whenever *that* may be—we shall figure out what to do, how to—how to live...once and for all...apart." His voice broke on the last word.

As he crossed the room and picked up his suitcase, Geneva stared at the ceiling. Presently she heard the door open and close. She let out a breath. It was almost a relief, not having to try anymore.

When the family returned to Clearharbour the next day, the weather was warming, though an icy wind blew hard. The snow which had fallen overnight was already melting, and patches of dead grass poked up here and there, as if to remind everyone who cared to look that this was the season of death, and snow was only a pleasant facade. The bleak landscape matched the mood in the Rover as Tony drove up the long Clearharbour drive under the skeletal branches of sycamore trees. All the children were present, but not even Elvira was talkative.

Tony stopped the car by the conservatory, and everyone helped to unload the gifts and luggage. Inside the house, the dogs were barking cheerfully. How pitifully innocent they were, always hoping for the best, Tony thought.

"I shan't be coming in," he told Geneva, putting his suitcase aside. He looked more fatigued than when he arrived, she thought guiltily. He hadn't slept last night, and now he was going back to London, where he wouldn't sleep tonight, or any other night, either.

Elvira could no longer suppress her need for assurance. She did not know what was the matter between her parents. She only had the most awful dread that they no longer wanted to be married. And if they stopped being married, what would become of her, and Andy, and Chris? Would they be forced to move away to America? "But I thought you were staying through the whole weekend," she said to her father, rather fiercely, in hopes that his doing so would somehow bring about a reversal of the situation.

Elizabeth, who had arrived at the same conclusion as Elvira, put an arm around her shoulder. "He has to go back to work. Boxing Day isn't a holiday this year, you know."

Elvira looked up at her sister. "But, he *said*—" she protested through clenched teeth.

"Sh. Don't worry Father now," Elizabeth said softly, and smoothed Elvira's unruly waves.

Andy grabbed the handle of Tony's suitcase. "I can carry this to the station for you, Father. I'm big enough now." The suitcase probably weighed more than he did.

It was all Tony could manage to hold back his tears, at still one more sign that Andy was maturing. He imagined all the tomorrows, all the sudden, unlooked-for changes in his children, that he would not be around to see. He ruffled Andy's hair. "There's a good lad, but I believe I can manage. Suppose you help out, after I've gone, taking all the gifts inside?"

When the farewells were over and Tony had parked the Rover inside the garage, he picked up his suitcase and started to walk down the drive. The children began taking things inside. Geneva stood watching Tony's sad retreating figure, in a dark bowler and overcoat, framed by the arbor of bare trees, with the bleak sky overhead and snow slush beneath his feet.

I'm so tired of feeling guilty, she thought. Remnants of a quote from scripture flitted through her mind, something about a person not being able to serve two masters. She went inside.

CHAPTER 34

When Joe Bledsoe presented himself to the woman at the bureau desk, his mind was made up. She wouldn't send his Jenny to no stranger's house again, not when she had lost her mother, and her three brave brothers off fighting for England. Lit'tul 'uns was treated like swine in some of them grand houses out in the country; Jenny was given nought to eat but table scraps, and a hard cot to sleep on out in the stables; well he wasn't having any of that. Every year until this one, Mr. Selby sent his family tickets to see *Pip 'N Pocket*—good seats, too, down close to the stage, they were. He always wished them a happy Christmas and said where he and the missus and the children would be spending the holiday—sometimes in London; other times at the family home near Bodmin, Cornwall. And so Joe had used his landlord's telephone and rang up Mr. Selby at his theatre, day before Christmas it were, to ask if Jenny could stay with his family until he found another place for them to live. A man there said he had gone to Cornwall for the holiday, but th'office was closed till Monday after Christmas and he didn't know Mr. Selby's telephone number down there.

A hundred and fifty people were killed when that bomb destroyed their tenement house, during the Christmas party. Bomb sheared off one side of the building and left th'other, walls of some rooms collapsed in a heap, and others left with furniture standing and pictures hanging, open to the moon. All the while Joe was safe at work, on the night shift, and now Jenny was left without her mum, and he without his Stella. Jenny was in shock, her eyes wide with fear, sitting out there on the bench right now, quiet as a mouse, waiting. He wasn't taking no chances sending her somewhere, where they might mistreat her. And Joe Bledsoe didn't mind giving some uppity bureau official what-for, if it come to that.

All of this emerged in a rather garbled fashion as Mr. Bledsoe, tall and thin as a fence post, his eyes bulging, stood before Hilary Locke's busy desk, telephones jangling all over the office, people in need of assistance lining the walls. The only Selby she could find on her list was a Lord Edward and Lady Cynthia Selby of Brookhurst, near Bodmin. They might not even be related to the Selbys Mr. Bledsoe knew, or even if they were, might be just the sort of people he wanted to avoid. One could never tell about relatives. Noticing the firm set of Mr. Bledsoe's jaw, however, and the length of the queue behind him, Hilary Locke decided just this once to waive bureau regulations. "I suppose we can ring them up."

When Hilary Locke telephoned on the Friday morning after Christmas, Cynthia hardly listened as the woman began her explanation, for she was already framing her diplomatic but firm refusal.

She would never forget watching the trainload of children from London being herded into the Bodmin Public Rooms, Lowestoft labels around their necks, gas masks dangling from their arms by the straps. Their faces bore the marks of confusion and fatigue; most were obviously very poor—their shoes were scuffed and run down at the heels; their clothing was old and faded, if not tattered. This was during the first major evacuation of London, last year. Some of the hosts looked the children over as if they were offered for sale as slave labor. They elbowed themselves to the front and whisked away the most desirable-looking ones. The sight of those left behind, looking as forlorn as though they'd just been orphaned, broke Cynthia's heart, and Edward's too. Children suffering from need were nothing new to Edward, not after all the years of operating a tin mining business. That was one reason they wound up with sixteen, when their quota was ten, the other reason being their refusal to separate one sibling from another, as some hosts were only too willing to do.

To their relief—regardless of first impressions—the children they took in proved to be well-mannered and clean. Caring for them was largely a matter of organizing activities to keep them from getting bored, and once Michaelmas term began, establishing them in Bodmin schools and helping with their studies. Edward discovered that one ten-year-old boy with poor reading skills had a serious vision problem. He took him to Bodmin and had him fitted with eyeglasses. The frames were left over from pre-war stock, and were a little too large in proportion to his face, so that the other children took to calling him, "Headmaster;" nonetheless, his reading skills improved.

Within two months, all of these children were returned to their families in London because the expected aerial attacks had not begun. That was the end of compulsory evacuations.

When the bombings finally did begin, there were plenty of parents anxious to get their children out of London, and even though most of their servants had now moved elsewhere to do warwork, or joined the armed services, Edward and Cynthia took in another dozen refugees. Unfortunately, many of these were obviously victims of neglect. Their language was abominable, and they had not been taught about personal hygiene. On the first night, one boy urinated all around the wall of the room where he slept. Another had head lice, which spread to all the others before it could be contained. One girl, large for her age, sneaked into the main rooms to steal small articles—a golden clock; two silver candle stands; a pair of alabaster doves that belonged to Edward's grandmother—the sum total of which fell out of the child's pillow slip on the first wash day.

A week before Christmas, the children were told that anyone who broke a rule within the next week would not be invited to the holiday celebration. As a result they were all on good behavior, and thankfully the party came off well.

The Selby family celebration was a different story.

By the time Geneva and Tony and the children left Brookhurst on Christmas Day, Cynthia had a throbbing headache from strain and worry. It was obvious her son's marriage was in deep trouble. She had not seen such disillusionment in Tony's face since he was married to Jane. Their children were frightened, it was easy to see. She must do something. But, what on earth could she do, with a houseful of other people's children to care for?

She would not take in any more evacuees, and that was final.

"…and I realize you may not be related to the Selby family of Mr. Bledsoe's acquaintance; still, he insisted I try…."

Cynthia became alert. "He knows us? What did you say his name was?"

"Joe Bledsoe. And his daughter is Jenny, eleven years old. She was one of the few survivors when her mother was killed."

"From Spitalfields? The Bledsoes who rescued my granddaughter Emelye?"

"Hold a moment, please," she said.

Soon Cynthia heard Joe Bledsoe say to Hilary Locke, "Yes, locked up in the back of a truck, bound and gagged she were."

"Oh my God!" cried Cynthia, rising from her chair. "Yes, for heaven's sake, send the child to us. Can you put Mr. Bledsoe on the line, please? Oh—Mr. Bledsoe? I'm so dreadfully sorry to hear about Mrs. Bledsoe…."

Jenny Bledsoe arrived at Brookhurst late on Friday night. From what Cynthia could remember of Stella Bledsoe, the child resembled her, with smoky blond hair—she wore it in braids, with straight bangs in front—fair skin, freckles, and round blue eyes. She was given the room usually reserved for Elvira, and Mrs. Ivey unpacked her small suitcase and put her few things in a dresser drawer.

Though Jenny must have been exhausted, she refused to go to bed. She would not even remove her coat. She seemed in a daze. She sat trembling on the blue velveteen bench at the dressing table, her back straight, her feet together, her hands crossed in her lap, clenched tight. She did not say a word except to answer all inquiries in a whispery voice, "Yes, m'um," or, "No, m'um." She left untouched the bowl of soup and biscuits Mrs. Ivey brought up from the kitchen.

Cynthia's heart ached for the child. She tried everything she could think of to coax her to relax so they could both get some rest. She offered to lie down beside her until she fell asleep, but she declined; likewise, she declined Cynthia's offer to read her a story from one of Elvira's numerous books. Finally she threw open the cupboard and pulled out a few of Elvira's many costumes that she used when putting on her plays, laying them out on the Empire-style bed. "Let's see, oh guess what! This pair of plus fours and vest were worn in *Pip 'N Pocket*. Have you liked seeing the play every year?"

"Yes, m'um."

"I'm sure Mr. Selby will put it on again as soon as the war is over. Oh yes, and this little yellow satin gown with diamonds—well, paste diamonds—on the skirt was for Tinkerbell, from *Peter Pan*. Do you know that story?"

"Yes, m'um."

"Do you ever like to play act, like my granddaughter?"

"No, m'um."

"I wish Elvira were here. I think you'd really like her. She's about your age."

"Yes, m'um."

As a matter of fact, she really ought to take her to meet Geneva, for surely after what the Bledsoes did for her, she would be moved to reach out to Jenny, try to help. Or, would she? One never knew what to expect from Geneva these days. She may treat the child with the same aloofness she treated her family. And hearing of Stella Bledsoe's death, added to her own heartache, may wind up increasing her melancholy. (She envisioned Geneva clamping a hand over her face and fleeing upstairs, just as she did after the infant gas mask came tumbling out of the box.) On the other hand, Jenny's loss may help place her own in perspective, make her see how selfish she had become, ignoring her duties to her family. Cynthia loved Geneva as though she were her own, but the truth of the matter was that she was as worn out as Tony, dealing with her.

She was still puzzling over what to do when she noticed the hands on the bedside clock were pointing at two a.m. No wonder her mind was fuzzy. Her eyes felt gravelly behind their lids. "I'm going along to bed if you think you'll be alright," she told Jenny.

"Yes, m'um."

She returned the heap of costumes to the cupboard, removed the row of Elvira's dolls from the bed pillows, and turned down the covers. How strange to be doing all this for a child, rather than calling in a servant. It gave her a warm, motherly feeling inside. She pulled out dresser drawers until she found Jenny's things: a tortoise shell hair brush, felt house slippers, and a flannel sleeping gown. It was a pretty little gown, she noticed while unfolding it, with pink smocking on the bodice. It was brand new, too, the flannel still downy soft. A mother's gift to her daughter—but no. The Bledsoe flat and all its contents were destroyed in the bombing. The thought of Joe Bledsoe presenting his money and coupons at some sleep wear counter for little girls caught Cynthia off-guard and brought her close to tears. She laid out the gown on the bed and put Jenny's house slippers nearby.

At the door she turned. "Unless you'd like to sleep in my room. There's a cozy lounge chair near my bed, and a thick comforter; I often fall asleep there."

For the first time Jenny looked as if she might cry, the rims of her eyes turning red, her nostrils flaring. But she shook her head. *Poor child. She's afraid to fall asleep anywhere, for fear of nightmares.* Had she slept at all since her mother's death? "Well, my room is to the right, far down at the end of the hallway. The door is recessed—back in a little alcove. If you change your mind, just knock on the door."

"Yes, m'um."

When Cynthia finally laid her head on the pillow, she could not stop her mind from going round and round. She thought back on her days as a vaudeville scout and manager—it seemed an eternity since then. How sharp her instincts were, how reliable in making decisions! She knew real potential when she saw it in a performer, and her reputation for being right made all the difference in negotiating contracts. Those were the days when both she and the business were at their peak. Yet she knew when the first feature film appeared on the bill in a vaudeville house that it was time to give up and make her exit with dignity…

…knew when it was time to return to Edward….

But she was sixty-two years old now, and her brain was not as nimble as it used to be. Taking charge on that anguished night at East Cornwall Hospital—knowing Cynthia Louise would not survive, yet dealing with Geneva's inability to face facts, arranging the baptism with her reluctant consent, pacing up and down the corridor, praying to God that Tony would get there in time to see his infant daughter before the undertaker arrived—put Cynthia to bed for the entire day after. All she wanted to do now was relax, let someone else work things out. Yet Geneva and Tony—what if they wound up separating? Divorcing? She could hardly bear the thought. All those years of waiting until they could be together as a family, and now, three children later—well, four if you counted Cynthia Louise—and this is what it came to. Well, she would make up her mind in the morning about whether to take Jenny to visit Geneva; at least then she would be fresh.

On Saturday afternoon, Elizabeth took her young siblings into Bodmin, to spend their Christmas money. Geneva stayed upstairs in her room. Since Tony left, she had spent most of her time there, thinking, growing more and more angry. Contrary to Mr. Selby's point of view, marriage was not a fairy tale in which bride and groom lived happily after. Events happened that changed people, and they adjusted and went on together. It was part of the commitment. And yes, you settled sometimes for less than you wanted, but that was life; and sex wasn't everything. Well, so be it. She must look to her future now, and that future was going to be very different from what she once believed. If Tony refused to set foot in this house again, fine. She would have all his things packed up and sent to Brookhurst, though she would wait until the children had returned to school in order not to upset them further over the holiday. Not that he cared as much as he claimed about their feelings, or he would not be so cold as to insist they meet him there instead of coming home. And when the war was over, well, she would decide whether to stay in England or take her children and move back to Houston. Just let Tony try and stop her. She paused in thought: How would Emelye feel about living with her mother again? Well frankly Geneva did not care where Emelye lived. In fact, she hardly felt Emelye was her daughter anymore. After all, it was her choice to break away. Even now it hurt deeply to remember Emelye refusing her hug in the garden that day when Willa's letter arrived. She would never, ever forget standing there, her fingers clutching the letter, her arms open, watching Emelye stomp away....

Suddenly she longed for Willa, in the way she used to when first she moved to England. Willa had always understood her better than anyone else. She thought for a moment. Hadn't Willa written her a couple of times lately? But where had the letters gone? She searched through the drawers of her small writing desk, but they were not there. She could not remember their contents at all, nor could she remember having answered them.

She sat down at her desk and pulled out a sheet of her personal stationery. Her fountain pen, she discovered, had dried out from lack of use. She flushed it out with water in the bathroom sink, then refilled it with blue ink. "Dear Willa, Tony and I are separating. Things have not been good between us since I lost my daughter." Here she paused to reread the sentence. My daughter. *Tony was sitting in the rocking chair, weeping....* She chased away the pity nagging at the edges of her anger. She continued, trying to be fair: "And as I look back over the past few months, I cannot help but feel that our troubles stemmed in large part from the fact that the war has created a false sense of urgency in people; somewhere in the exhaustive list of war-time regulations, it must be stated that grief is to be dispensed with immediately as the war machine rolls relentlessly forward. I—"

There was a knock at the door. "Lady Cynthia is 'ere to see you," said Mrs. Greaves.

Geneva took in a breath. She had been wondering when Cynthia would step in to try and fix her son's marriage—no doubt he had filled her in on all the details by now. "I'll be down in a minute," she said, and returned to her letter, trying to complete her thought. "—I seem to remember there used to be a period set aside for mourning that—" Mrs. Greaves knocked again. Geneva threw down her pen. "Alright!" She looked down at the page she was writing. The pen had slung blue ink all over it. She could not remember ever having done that before.

Cynthia stood at the foot of the stairs. She had told Jenny just enough so she'd understand how her mother and father helped Emelye get back to her parents on that night long ago, leaving out the frightening details of Benjamin Calais holding Emelye against her will for hours on end, her family sitting by helplessly, as the London Police conducted their search. "Hello my dear," she said tenderly, enclosing Geneva in a hug. She felt her body stiffen.

"Cynthia, I—"

"I've brought someone to meet you. A young girl who came to us last night. Her mother was killed in a blast a few days before Christmas. I think she's still in shock because she hardly speaks. Her name is Jenny."

Geneva did not have time to respond before Cynthia turned and walked into the sitting room. She followed, feeling at a loss. She was ashamed of herself for suspecting her mother-in-law's motives. Cynthia had the biggest heart in Cornwall, and apparently had overextended herself by taking in one too many unfortunate children to care for. Still, she could not even solve her own problems, much less, look after some poor child who lost her mother.

Inside the girl stood very straight, her feet together, looking out the sunny window. Two blond braided hair loops hung down her back. Her coat was light blue but faded, giving it an orchid hue. Its shoulders were a little too broad; its sleeves a bit too long—a hand-me-down, perhaps? Her socks were clean and white; her brown and white oxfords, polished. *Her mother loved her,* Geneva thought, unexpectedly moved.

Cynthia went to the girl and coaxed her around to face Geneva. "Geneva, may I introduce Jenny…the daughter of Joe and Stella Bledsoe. Jenny, this is Mrs. Selby, Emelye's mother."

CHAPTER 35

At the name Stella Bledsoe, the events of that night broke inside Geneva's memory like a dam: the doors on the back of the truck thrown open at last and Emelye emerging from the dark, frightened, confused; the warm, loving woman in her head scarf standing there, plain and soft as fresh bread dough rising in a bowl; her arms opening to hold Emelye and comfort her and dry her tears as she promised they'd find her mother; the woman on whose shoulder Geneva later released her tears of relief and gratitude, inside the stage door at the *Palladium*. *"It's alright, I know just how it is,"* said Mrs. Bledsoe. That gentle mother, with her generous heart, killed by an indiscriminate bomb; by the madness of the world. Geneva was not even aware of having crossed the room until she'd gone down on one knee and wrapped her arms around Jenny. "Oh, Honey, I'm so terribly sorry! Your mother was one of the—the—*dearest* people I've ever known." Jenny stood immobile, her blue eyes staring at Geneva.

God, she is lost, Geneva thought with alarm, *help me to help her.*

"Let's sit down," she said, leading Jenny to the sofa. Cynthia sat down across from them. Geneva tried to summon words of comfort for the child, but there seemed nothing adequate to say about the wasteful, senseless death of Mrs. Bledsoe. Finally she asked, "Would you like to tell me about it?"

Jenny's eyes grew fearful.

"Never mind, it's alright," Geneva told her, instinctively closing a hand over hers and stroking it.

Jenny stared down at Mrs. Selby's warm hand, stroking her hand like her mum used to do. *Mum was standing in the small kitchen of Mrs. Bromley's flat, helping out, putting buns on a tray. And would Jenny go into the sitting room and see how the punch was holding out, said Mrs. Bromley. So Jenny walked down the*

hall past Mrs. Bromley's bedroom, looking in to see the bed with the yellow flow-
ered spread and iron rails, and the lamp with a shade with strings of purple beads
all around the edges so that light shone through them and made them sparkle.
When she heard the siren, she leapt through the bedroom door and scooted under
the bed, as she had been taught to do; and closed her arms about her head. When
the bomb hit, the floor rumbled beneath her and she struck her nose against it.
Her eyes blurred. She heard the sound of glass breaking and things knocking
about. Then all was silent, and she kept her head tucked in her arms.

When the all-clear signal sounded, Jenny got up to look for her mum. There
was still a wall between Mrs. Bromley's bedroom and her kitchen, but there was
no kitchen, only the black sky and the moon shining down. She started to cry.
"Where's me mum...?"

Jenny went on staring at Mrs. Selby's hand. It was smaller than her
mother's, and the inside felt smoother. If she were Emelye, this is what it would
feel like when her mother stroked her hand. Presently, without looking up, she
asked, "Is Emelye here?"

Cynthia was cheering inside. It was the first real sentence she'd spoken.

"No, my dear, I'm afraid not," said Geneva.

"What does she look like?"

"Well, she's blond, like you, but her eyes are brown—wait! I have a picture
of her. Would you like to see it?"

"Yes, m'um."

As Geneva removed the small black and white photograph from the chimneypiece, she glanced at the images captured in it: Emelye and Serena, with
James between them; three all-American smiles on suntanned faces, their eyes
squinting from the sun's glare. The girls had their hands resting on James's
muscular shoulders. Emelye had chosen the pretty silver frame for the picture,
and sent it to Tony and her as a present Christmas before last. She could not
remember feeling touched by her thoughtfulness, or any inclination to place
the picture at her bedside in the buttery. She realized now she had hardly
thought of Emelye since the death of Cynthia Louise. Until today, and
then—she thought reproachfully—with bitterness she had not even realized
she felt. There was a letter, she recalled now, with flowers and butterflies drawn
around the edges of the envelope. Had she answered it? She did not know. She
could hardly believe how many blanks there were in her memory over the
past—what? She counted up. Eight months. Had it really been that long? Yet
suddenly it seemed forever.

She handed the picture to Jenny, pointing out Emelye. "Emelye lives in America now, and these are the friends she lives with, James and Serena."

Geneva expected her to ask why Emelye didn't live with her mum and dad, but she did not. She studied the picture at some length, then handed it back and looked up at Geneva. "Me dad says that Mum lives up in heaven now, with Jesus."

Tony was holding Chris in his arms. *"Your sister has gone to live in heaven, with Jesus...."* Again Geneva's heart stirred unexpectedly, but by which image of father and child, she had no time to distinguish. "Oh yes, Honey, I'm sure that he is right," she said to Jenny. She glanced at Cynthia, who was leaning forward in anticipation.

Jenny said, "I don't like Jesus anymore. He took me mum away from me."

Geneva was taken aback. "Oh no, Jenny, that—that isn't what your dad meant, I'm sure. Jesus didn't take your mother away from you. He—he took away her suffering...and pain. And she won't ever hurt again, or be afraid."

Cynthia was looking intently at Geneva, wondering when she would realize the same was true of Cynthia Louise. She rose from her chair, encouraged that Jenny had taken a step toward recovery, if not Geneva. "Well Jenny, suppose we go back to Brookhurst and have our tea?"

At the conservatory door, wrapped up in her coat with its huge fur collar, Cynthia turned to Geneva, a look of pleading in her eyes that Geneva did not understand. At last, Cynthia caught her in a quick, tight hug, then took Jenny's hand and walked out.

Geneva went back into the sitting room. She returned the picture to its place. She stood there for a long time, gazing upon Emelye's smiling face. *You could not help your unhappiness any more than I can help mine,* she realized. Then, before she knew it, she was kissing her fingers and pressing them lingeringly against the image of her daughter. "I love you, and it's alright," she whispered.

CHAPTER 36

By the time Geneva climbed the stairs a few minutes later, her spirits were lifting with every step. How tall these stairs had loomed over the past eight months—climbing them often left her breathless. No longer. It was somewhat like the time she contracted the Spanish influenza during the Great War: her body ravaged by pain, her fever so high that behind her closed eyelids her mind escaped into delusions. Then one day the fever broke. She opened her eyes and knew with the clarity of light surrounding her that while she was not yet completely well, she had reached the threshold of becoming so.

She crossed her bedroom floor and stood beside her writing desk, gazing down at her letter to Willa, splashed with ink: her anger spilt out. Then, feeling apologetic, she gently replaced the cover on her fountain pen and returned it to its cradle in the lap drawer. She folded the page and tossed it in the dust bin.

There was no denying she had reached a major juncture in her life, and there was much she needed to think about, but it seemed her mind had been locked in a struggle forever, and she wished, just for a few minutes, to sweep it clean and experience the present. She sank down in the familiar comfort of her rocking chair and began to rock slowly, listening to the patient ticking of the clock on the chimneypiece. At length she recalled that the clock had not been running that day of Cynthia Louise's burial. How very odd, but only now did she notice it had resumed ticking. What an encouraging sound to hear as she continued rocking, like a strong, steady heartbeat. Yet eventually the jaws and wheels inside the clock paused with a click, and the chime sounded five times. She became very still. In spite of the fact Tony had not called her since he left on Wednesday, the many years when he did so without fail at this time of day prompted her to listen for the ringing of the telephone. It did not come. She resumed rocking, but from then on all she could think of was the minutes ticking by. Of course, sometimes Tony didn't call right at five. Sometimes it was before, sometimes after. Five after five, ten after, a quarter past. *He isn't going to call tonight,* she acknowledged at last, with a sting of loss that she had not felt last night or the night before, when the hour of five passed into history. She wanted him back suddenly, would give anything for him to walk through the bedroom door right now and take her in his arms.

Presently she heard the dogs barking downstairs. The children had returned from their shopping. She leaned forward in her chair, her spine tingling with anticipation. Abruptly she realized, but for the holiday coming mid-week and changing the schedule, they would have gone to Brookhurst last night. How glad she was they had not. And yet, she had ruined their holiday; it was her fault their father returned to London early when he should have been here with them. When she heard the door close she hurried downstairs and into the hall, where they were hanging coats and mufflers and caps on the pegs. How much taller they seemed, as if each one had a growth spurt during an afternoon of shopping. *My children.* It occurred to her that any one of them might have come into the world with the frailties of Cynthia Louise, and who was to say they would not have struggled just as hard to live, knowing how profoundly she desired it? "Welcome home!" she cried.

Either because they were surprised to see her or because her voice had more life in it than usual, they all turned at once. Three pairs of eyes stared at her. No one said a word. "May I have a kiss?"

She knelt down and they all three pecked her cheek quickly, then grabbed their parcels and headed for the stairs. She did not want them to go. "Wait a minute. Show me what you've bought?" She begged.

Dutifully they showed her the fruits of their shopping excursion. Elvira had a long string of amber glass beads, several bracelets, and a length of deep blue velveteen, for her costume collection. Andy had a model ship building kit, but the side of the box had been torn and taped up, Geneva noticed, which made her suspicious that parts of it were missing; and this—unexpectedly—brought her to the verge of tears. Why had Elizabeth failed to notice, and warn him against buying it? But then, why was it left to Elizabeth to take her children shopping? And also, whose fault was it that, even if all the parts were there, Andy's father wasn't here to help him navigate through the lengthy instructions and build it? She reached for Andy to tuck in his shirt tail—it was invariably out long before this time of day—but she was too late. He was already halfway up to the first landing of the stairs.

Chris had a book of Bible stories, quite large, with colored illustrations. The front cover was a bit faded, probably from having been displayed in Spear's shop window over a long period of time. But never mind. He showed her the centerfold picture of Noah and the ark with all the pairs of animals trouping inside. "Shall I read you this story later?" she offered.

"No thank you. I can read it myself," he said.

"Of course," she said. Last month Chris turned five years old. She was in bed with a bad cold, but—thankfully—there was a celebration at Brookhurst. Yet now she realized she had completely overlooked Elvira's birthday in July, and could only hope it, too, was celebrated. Surely Elvira would not have permitted her birthday to go by unremarked.

Soon all three children had hurried up to their rooms, taking their purchases with them. *They don't want to be with me anymore; they have moved on and left me behind,* she thought. Stella Bledsoe would never have done anything to cause her children to become indifferent toward her.

Elizabeth had slipped into the kitchen and returned with a bit of cheese for the dogs—their treat for the day. As they lapped it from her hands, tails wagging, Geneva looked at her becoming profile, noticing the curve of her hips beneath her pleated wool skirt, and her small breasts filling out her sweater. She had not realized how the child's figure was maturing. She would be seventeen in May. What had they done for her sixteenth birthday, that special coming-of-age? Geneva could not remember doing anything for it. Even more than for her younger children, she hoped they had celebrated Elizabeth's sixteenth birthday at Brookhurst.

A feeling of gratitude surged through her, for all Elizabeth had done to make up for her many failures as a mother. She caught her in a tight hug. "Thanks for everything."

Elizabeth stared at her quizzically at first, then gradually her eyes narrowed and a sanguine look spread over her face. In that moment Geneva saw her strong resemblance to Tony, which was not readily apparent except on occasions when her head was tilted at a certain angle. The sweep of her jaw and the peaks of her high cheekbones, and the cast of her forehead above her eyes—oh yes, she was very like Tony. Again, a sharp sense of loss overtook Geneva. Tony wasn't coming home. He would see his children at Brookhurst.

That night as Mrs. Greaves put on her coat and hat, she peeked into the dining room where Geneva and the children were having their supper. *Well God be thanked, all that chatter, hit sounds like old times, and didn't I always know things would come right again someday!* Were she not so tired, she would stay and listen to them awhile, for her little flat up top town was lonely now, with Clifton gone off to war since the first of October, and after leaving the Selby home every night until this one, her weary feet taking her up the steep incline of her street, she could only think, *Well, where I'm goin' to is no sadder than where I've come from, and that's a fact.*

"See you Monday mornin'," she said brightly, and left amidst a cheery flutter of waving hands and goodbyes.

Seldom lately had Geneva sat down at the supper table with her children, and even then she'd let their conversations swirl around her without listening. Tonight she was determined to involve herself in their lives, to make them see that she cared about them. "What were the children boarding at Brookhurst like?" she asked. This led to a long and mixed review by everyone at the table, to which Geneva listened intently, asking additional questions as they went along. Gradually she could see the looks of awareness dawn in the faces of her younger children, as she had seen in Elizabeth's face, and as they went right on talking she could only think what a blessing it was that her children were so resilient, willing to give her a second chance without even demanding an explanation. What happened to that resilience in the world of adults, where there were always lines being drawn in the sand? Conditions to be met? Joyful as the mood was around the table, Tony's vow to separate from Geneva was a cold undercurrent always tugging at her heart. What would happen if she said, *"Your father is leaving me. I'm moving back to Houston."*? No doubt the admission would be met with stunned silence. Her children would quickly remember what they had been generous enough to forget. Naturally Elizabeth would not go, because the fact she was not of Geneva's flesh and blood would suddenly be an important issue, after years of effort—at least on her part and Tony's—to ignore it. And Elvira? Well, no doubt she would be vocal about her wish to remain with Tony, whom she adored, and who obviously could help her far better than Geneva to realize her dream of a future in the theatre. As to Andy? The firstborn son and heir to the Selby estate, he would be expected to stay and Tony would fight tooth and nail to keep him, Geneva was sure. Tenderly she thought: maybe just Chris would come along with his mum to America. But even he may be reluctant; after all, she'd left him no choice but to learn to get along without her. *I do not want to go to America all alone,* she thought desperately. How ironic it was to remember the 'condition' she set for marrying Tony and moving over here with Emelye: that there must be peace and harmony among the family, and full acceptance of her and her daughter. She would never have dreamed she'd wind up being the cause of disruption and discord.

After supper Geneva volunteered to do the washing-up alone because she needed to do some thinking. The possibility that Tony might be willing to give her another chance had begun flickering in her mind almost as soon as she realized she wanted one, yet it was not that simple. She had wounded him deeply, and he was not by nature quick to forgive. Even if he could find it in his heart to forgive her, what if he now felt utterly detached from her, as she had felt, for months, from him? *There is positively nothing you can do about that.* The notion was so alarming that she stopped her chore abruptly, her hands dangling in the soapy water. It took but a few hours of one night in her life for her to change completely toward Tony. And he had endured months of her rejection, just at a time when he must have needed her more than ever.

On the other hand...suppose Tony was both willing and able to give her another try. Could she reward his expectations? All she knew was that, since five o'clock passed and he failed to call, there had not been a single moment when her heart was not aching for his presence. In spite of all her prayers over the past few months, for a transformation within herself, she had never felt this. Until tonight.

Almost before she realized she had turned off the water and dried her hands, she was climbing the stairs, heading for Tony's office where she could talk on the telephone in private.

CHAPTER 37

Tony would soon leave for the theatre. Eugene O'Neill's *Desire Under the Elms* was to open on January 2nd, and rehearsals had been under way since mid-November. The play did not fall in the category of 'old familiars,' but O'Neill's other works were certainly well-known. Besides, the cast was small, and the major character was an aging man—real advantages with the war-time attrition of stage actors. All was going well until yesterday, when Richard Foxworth, who was to play Ephraim Cabot, suffered a heart attack. At age 73, Foxworth was among the most accomplished actors on the British stage, having played every monumental role in Shakespeare, to critical acclaim. Special rehearsals got under way today, with his understudy taking over, and the director asked Tony to step in tonight and have a look at a couple of scenes. After that he had a rather intriguing appointment scheduled for half-past eight in Chelsea. A new top-secret government bureau had been formed as a liaison in obtaining the safe passage for certain parties out of occupied countries. Apparently many people prominent in the arts community were being recruited, and he had been contacted back in July when the thing first got rolling, after the fall of France. But he told them quite plainly that his wife was unstable since the loss of their child, his family was under a dreadful strain, and he could not commit until she was improved. That was when he still lived in hope that she would improve. Upon returning to London on Christmas Day, feeling more despondent than ever in his life, he got himself together and made a telephone call, and the next thing he knew he was being summoned to tonight's recruitment meeting. Well, he had no idea how he could be of service to the Special Operations Executive, as it was called—he could hardly imagine a bunch of creative artists coordinating espionage activities. Still, one must do one's part and it would certainly be good for him to be extra busy, keep his mind off the disastrous state of his family. And this would be as good a night as any to be out late. Things had been quiet since Christmas, with little bombing activity, the periods following all-clear signals lasting longer and longer.

Since learning from his mother of the death of Mrs. Bledsoe, his heart had gone out to Jenny and her father. And this had made him miss his own children terribly, for he, too, could very well lose his life and if he did, they'd be left with a mother who had lost her capacity to think of anyone except herself. He decided to try and get a call through to Clearharbour before leaving, and say *I love you* to each of them.

When he placed his hand on the receiver, the telephone rang. It gave him a spooky feeling, as if it had come alive in his hand. He lifted the receiver. "Yes, hullo?"

"Tony? Is it you? Oh!" That was as much as Geneva could get out before all composure deserted her. She started to sob.

"What has happened? Are the children alright?" Tony asked sharply, thinking some crisis had erupted owing to her neglect.

"Oh yes, everyone is—" she sobbed some more. "Oh Tony, I need—"

She heaved her breath, trying to regain her composure. "I need to—to talk—to—to *see* you. Oh, wait!" She blew her nose into her handkerchief. Momentarily she started again, her voice nasal. "I'll come there—"

It's my Geneva, come back from the grave! Tony thought, his heart soaring. Tears sprang to his eyes. "No, no, better you stay put and I'll come home. Listen, I've got to get to the theatre, and after that I've got a meeting. I may be rather late, I'm afraid. Into the wee hours, probably."

"I don't care what time it is, I'll be waiting for you," she swore. She tried to say *I love you*, but she could not get it out without breaking down again.

He started to say *I love you*, but wouldn't risk it, not until she said it first.

When Tony rang off, he warned himself to get a grip on his optimism. It was likely that, when it finally dawned on Geneva their family was about to break up, she became distraught. But that didn't mean her feelings toward him had changed. Perhaps she only wanted him to agree to put up a front, for the sake of the children. Well, he'd put up a front for eight years of marriage to Jane, and he bloody well wasn't about to do that again, ever. Still, judging by her emotional state just now, he could swear—

He checked his watch. Dash it, he needed to pack a bag, for one never knew where one might get stuck in transit. But there wasn't time. He'd have to nip in later, on the way back from the meeting. Hopefully this *truce*—for want of a better word—on the part of the Luftwaffe would last through the night.

As it happened, it was nearly nine o'clock when Tony got away from the *William & Mary*—major problems in the first scene of Act Two, the director feeling uncomfortable with the understudy and no surprise. Poor fellow was twenty years younger than Foxworth and hadn't a tenth of his experience. Tony stayed until they got things smoothed out. By then he'd rung up the chap in Chelsea and asked to be rescheduled for one week hence.

He stopped by the house and hurriedly packed a bag, thinking, on the other hand perhaps he still ought to make that meeting. He might hire a taxi. If he hurried he wouldn't miss all that much, and Geneva was prepared for him to be late. But no, he was too eager to get home and see, had she really come back, or was he in for another disappointment?

He headed through the darkness for Paddington Station, his small torch making a dim glow on the pavement as he stepped off his porch and down his front walk. How long ago it seemed that people were cautioned to never go out without carrying a gas mask, for a ground invasion could come at any time. Tony didn't even know where his gas mask was anymore. Since leaving the theatre, he had been aware of the disheartening sounds of anti-aircraft fire in the distance, followed by the whistling down of bombs, then far-away explosions—one was "street-wise" by now, as it were, and could gauge pretty well how far away the bombs were dropping. If far enough away, one simply kept going and "held one's breath" until the all-clear. It was amazing how one learned to adapt to the most abhorrent conditions!

It wasn't the best of circumstances to leave in, he thought a little nervously as he groped his way very slowly up one side, then down the next, of the pitch black square. The dark shapes of house fronts and trees and hedges were barely discernible. Probably the worst danger was that of stumbling over his feet, he chided himself. He started to whistle a cheerful tune, but it sounded rather eerie somehow in the darkness, so he stopped. He was just two houses from the corner now and in a few moments he would be—

The piercing shriek grew so quickly in intensity that Tony barely had time to drop to the pavement, his arms covering his head, his heart pounding in terror. Every choice he had made tonight that brought him to this particular place, at this particular moment, flashed through his mind in an instant, for he knew in his very bones exactly where this bomb was headed. His last thought was to regret that he had not said *I love you* to Geneva, or to his children, over the telephone. The last words he uttered were a prayer.

PART III

1942–1944

CHAPTER 38

❀

For the first eight months James was in England, he made no attempt to see Elizabeth. For all the years he had lived in the hope that someday she would love him as much as he loved her and want nothing more than to be right next to him for the rest of her life, it was hard to believe that now, when he was no further away than a train ride of a few hours, he wouldn't take the opportunity. But that's how it was.

By the time he sat down to write her that he intended to join the service, he had thought long and hard about the decision. His parents were completely against it—it was hard to convince them that the Army recruiters haunting the University of Houston campus had not brainwashed him. Naturally they were scared for him, and they also disapproved of his dropping out of college. But he figured that when he came back one day, he'd finish school. He had the rest of his life to be an engineer, and he could already tell there wasn't much excitement in it. He told his parents this was a once-in-a-lifetime opportunity to do something really important, and that was the truth though not all of it. He didn't tell them that he couldn't just continue sitting on his thumbs while Elizabeth's country was at war.

As he composed his letter to Elizabeth, the weight of all the changes about to occur in his life bore down on every word. He knew from her letters that she was opposed to war on principle. So was he. But to his mind, defending against an enemy out to destroy you was something else entirely. He assumed she felt the same. He wanted to pour out his heart, to tell her that he had been in love with her for years, and he was determined to do all he could to protect her. He was sure she would admire him, and be grateful.

In the end he settled for leaving out the part about being in love with her. He wanted to wait and tell her when they were face to face, so he could see if love for him was reflected in her eyes as she listened. Besides, she had given no indication that she was ready to speak of love. For the first time, he replaced the usual closing—"Your friend,"—with, "Always yours, James." It seemed so much more intimate, the perfect way of giving her an opening, yet without coming on too strongly. Yes. Just those three words said it all.

At three full pages, this was the longest letter he had ever written to Elizabeth, and after he read through it numerous times, there were grooves in the tissue-thin stationery where his fingers had gripped it.

His letter barely had time to reach her before the Germans launched their long-expected aerial attacks on London. Now he knew more than ever that he was doing the right thing. He was itching to get over there and fight back.

To his astonishment, she replied, "Oh, James, I thought you understood how I felt. Please do not do this! I could not bear to have it on my conscience that you risked your life for me, and that in so doing you were perpetuating the evil that is war. I could not bear for you to come to harm. Your friend—."

He felt bruised, there was no getting around it. That she accused him of "perpetuating the evil that is war" hurt particularly. Wasn't that the same as saying he was evil? Surely not, or the next sentence would have been different. Still, it wounded him. He waited a long time before writing her again. Finally, consoling himself with that last sentence, if not with the closing, he wrote that she was certainly entitled to her opinion, but that he disagreed, and he had to be true to his own convictions. By then he had been accepted in pre-flight school. If everything went right, he would spend the next year in one training school after another, and emerge as a commissioned air force pilot. Admittedly he took some satisfaction in telling her this.

James was in Harding, Louisiana, nearing the end of his last stateside training—finishing school for combat—when Pearl Harbor was attacked. He was as outraged as anyone, but now he feared it would be just his luck to be sent to the Pacific. The whole focus of the war had changed. It seemed like everybody he knew was being sent over there. He thought about it night and day. They weren't about to send him to England now. For the first time, he realized the sheer magnitude of the war machine, and its power to manipulate the plans people built their lives around, not to mention the hopes.

When he received orders that he'd be shipping out to England right after the first of January, he stared at the words in disbelief, then he read them again, to be sure. He gave a yelp for joy. It seemed like a miracle.

Stationed at Grafton Underwood—around 250 miles from Bodmin—James's squadron was soon getting organized and trained to carry out the first U.S. Eighth Air Force missions of the war, escorting the 97th Bomb Group into France and the Netherlands. They spent considerable time in classes, and on practice missions, and in general working out ways to help the RAF—not as easy at it appeared. Though they spoke a common language, the differences in nomenclature and rank designations brought a lot of confusion. But the main difference between them was in their strategy. The Americans could not fathom the RAF policy of dispatching heavy bombers into combat individually in the dark of night, relying on radar to stay on course; it made more sense to send out well-armed bomb groups in tight formations, in broad daylight. In addition, the B-17s were not suitable for nighttime flying because their turbos would glow red underneath. The British liked to joke that the Yanks had to fly during the day, because that was the only time they could see. In fact, they had a good time ragging them in general. But it was obvious that behind all the jibes, they knew they were damned lucky the Eighth had shown up, for they weren't doing all that well by themselves. And of course the Americans were not shy about reminding them of the fact.

The two occasions when James was given sufficient time off to travel all the way to Bodmin and back, allowing for the unreliable train schedules, he struggled in indecision for a while, then his resentment got the better of him and he let the opportunity pass. From where he stood the Allied effort to crush Hitler's Germany was the most noble cause in the history of mankind. Like all the servicemen around him, he put on that cause every morning along with his flight suit and cap, and his every waking hour was focused on one goal: destroying the enemy from the air. He was proud of his contribution. He always thought of the fighter pilots as being like drones, escorting the queen bee who was heavy and cumbersome, vulnerable to attack by predators, as she transported her eggs. He could not help wondering what Elizabeth would think of this analogy—would she consider it poetic?—but all he could imagine was her face closing up with reproach when she heard it. *"The evil that is war…."*

Since it was obvious there was little about his daily life as a pilot that Elizabeth would want to hear of, he wrote her fewer letters than he used to. Meantime, he went out with British girls. There were plenty of opportunities to meet them, even on base, where they had dances on weekends. They would bus in from the neighboring towns, most of them taking a break from warwork themselves. Fresh-faced, in high heels and flared skirts that came to a little below the knee, their hair rolled up like long sausages in back, they slow-waltzed and boogied with servicemen to the music of an ensemble made up of saxophones and trumpets, clarinets and trombones, guitar and piano. Apart from being out for a good time, every couple on the dance floor had at least one thing in common between them: they were lonely, and just a little fright-ened. British girls were warm and tender toward American boys—fascinated, or at least pretending to be so, by the Yanks' accents. Nights with them were long and sweet. Often it was easy for James to put his feelings for Elizabeth aside while in the arms of someone who was little more than a stranger, espe-cially when she made him feel he was the most important guy in the world. But he always wound up thinking of Elizabeth after a while, and wishing it were her body lying next to his.

How many times had he told himself he was crazy to be obsessed with someone as different from him as she was, and so remote he'd probably never reach her, letter after letter closing, *"Your friend"*? But it didn't change things now any more than it changed things when he was in high school or at the University of Houston. There was only one Elizabeth.

Finally, in August of 1942, the first Eighth Air Force mission was launched. Early in the morning they met in the briefing room, dimly-lit like a theatre. At the front, lights flooded a huge wall map with jagged lines showing the course they would fly, and the location of the targets; weather conditions in the target areas, and what to expect in the way of opposition; where the fighters would cover and where they wouldn't, and where they'd pick up again. At the end of the briefing, they synchronized their watches.

Afterward they were served a breakfast of bacon and eggs, which James could hardly taste for the anxiety building up in him about all the things that could go wrong, the possibility that he may not make it back alive—a prospect he'd never thought about while he was still over in the States, his mind fixed on the glory of battle. Then they had a chance to relax for a while—as if anyone really could. James owed his folks a letter, but when he tried to write, he couldn't concentrate. Finally they went down to the crew room to put on their gear, and a crew bus took them out to the flights. James checked out his air-plane—everything from the tires and wheels to the controls and the radio, guns and parachute—just to be sure. Then it was "start engine" time. The thunderous roar of all those engines starting together gave James a thrill of anticipation that went all the way to his head, made him feel like nothing could stop them. This was what they were born to do. They began taxiing off in the assigned order, and pretty soon he was locking the tail wheel into position and pushing the throttle forward.

They were lucky—they encountered no difficulties on that mission. Within a few hours the B-17s had dropped eighteen tons of bombs on the railway marshaling yard in Rouen, France, and they were all on their way back to base. There was a big group of USAAF and RAF personnel cheering for them when they landed. They all felt pretty invincible, and full of themselves. They were going to win this war, by golly, one mission at a time.

In the next few days the weather was good, and there were several more sorties, all of them coming off as planned. The streamlined formation of fighter planes and bombers was pretty audacious, roaring through the air, and the Germans be damned, they wouldn't sneak around under the cloak of night like the British.

Then one day a group of a dozen bombers, en route to Rotterdam, were late for rendezvous with their escorts. Short of fuel, the escorts were forced to leave them halfway to their target. Soon the bombers were surrounded by enemy fire. They put up one hell of a battle—destroying two German fighters and damaging another five. But one American bomber barely escaped. One of its crew members was seriously wounded. Chalmers—the short, affable tail gunner, nicknamed "the Don Juan of the dance floor" because of his failed attempts to pick up girls—was killed. James didn't know the guy very well, but he was still a lot more than just a name and a face. Watching Chalmers' buddies pack up his gear that night turned James's heart inside out. Somewhere back in the States, his family still believed he was safe, and coming home to them when the war was over. They would be none the wiser until the telegram arrived informing them he was KIA. James found himself wondering: as long as Chalmers' family had no knowledge of his death, was it not yet fully real? Like something that happened light years away on another planet wasn't real for the people on earth? What was reality, anyway? Did it exist outside of knowledge? If, say, Chalmers' father happened to die of a heart attack before he received the news, would it mean he died without ever having lost his son? It was the kind of question that would be interesting to talk over with Elizabeth. Unfortunately, the lead-in would keep James from ever doing it. He wished somehow that Chalmers' family could go right on believing he was alive, though.

Everyone was pretty shaken up now. The limited fuel capacity of the fighter planes was frustrating to James; he hated being helpless when someone was depending on him. The experience brought home how vulnerable they all were, how quickly a mission that was going well could turn around and go bad. The next time out, it could be American fighter planes that went down under German fire, and his might be one of them. Then it would be his family who, just for a little while, lived with the illusion that he continued to be safe.

Later he lay on his cot, too wound up to sleep. In the far distance, plunging through the silence, was the whistling down and low rumble of bombs exploding. Somewhere, someone was being killed. Maybe, in the universal scheme of things, Elizabeth's argument was valid after all. Not that it was any help right now. Still, he found himself missing her in a way that you miss someone you love after a quarrel, and even though you know you were right, you feel so cut-off and alone, you are compelled to abandon your pride and patch up things. That was exactly what he would do, he decided, because the two of them may never have anything more than what was here and now.

Yet…a question occurred to him that he hadn't thought of before—maybe because he was just too angry: would Elizabeth feel reluctant to go out with an air force pilot? Suddenly he thought of all those less-than-intimate closings at the end of her letters. Whereas he had always taken them as a sign of her reserve, what if they had come to mean something different when she found out he had joined the service? "Always yours, James," he wrote, and it didn't even seem to register with her. It seemed so plausible—maybe even likely—that she had drawn a line, he felt almost sick with apprehensiveness. Well, he had enough to be apprehensive about, twenty-four hours of every day. He'd be damned if he was going to take this worry up there with him, mission after mission. The next time he got a pass, he was going to Bodmin, to find out where she stood.

CHAPTER 39

Shortly after that, during a run of bad weather when all missions were scrubbed, James was given a three-day pass. Well, not quite three days; it was after eleven o'clock on Friday night when his C.O. signed off on it, too late to call Elizabeth and say he was coming. He went out for a few beers with his buddies, then collapsed on his cot and slept till seven the next morning.

Geneva answered the telephone at Clearharbour. "Hey, Gee, I'm coming down, if it's alright." For some reason, he felt silly just then, calling Geneva by the nickname he had adopted in childhood because he couldn't articulate her whole name. Yet, to call her 'Geneva' might make it seem to her that he no longer appreciated what she meant to him in the days when she was like a second mother. He would always love Gee.

"Well it's about time!" she said cheerfully. Soon after he was posted at Grafton Underwood she had written to assure him he had an open invitation to Clearharbour. Now he felt guilty for having waited so long.

"By the way, is Elizabeth around?" he asked.

"No, she just left on a day trip to Ready Money Cove, to get some studying done. Said she'd be home before dark."

Elizabeth graduated from Harleigh School at the top of her class last spring, and she hoped to be accepted at Newnham College—one of two women's colleges at Cambridge University—to 'read' Philosophy. But she didn't feel quite ready to go away to school, and she had decided to spend this year brushing up on her Latin and doing some reading on her own, before taking her entrance exam. James was glad because she was probably a lot safer in Bodmin than she would be in Cambridge.

He looked at his watch. Unfortunately, he probably wouldn't get much time with Elizabeth. Of course, depending on how things went, he may not need much time. "If I'm real lucky, I may be there by one," he told Geneva.

To his surprise, when Gee came to the door that afternoon she was dabbing her eyes with a handkerchief. Cynthia had called a few minutes earlier with the sad news that Lord Edward had suffered a stroke. Gee could hardly talk about it for crying. James didn't know Lord Edward very well, but he seemed to be a gentleman of great dignity, and he was always kind to James and his family. He felt awkward now, having walked into this crisis. Maybe he should turn around and go back to base. Yet, he felt sorry for Gee, especially after all she'd been through. How many times had she dried his tears when he was little? He put his arms around her and held her close, saying he hoped everything would be alright. He could tell by the way she leaned against him and cried harder that she really needed someone to comfort her. On the wall beyond her shoulder, he could see his colored drawing of Gee walking down the aisle at her wedding. How it used to shame him, knowing it wasn't any good compared to a real work of art. But not anymore. What was wrong with a child having his dreams? As soon as you grew up, you had to put them all away, and you were never quite as happy again. That was life.

Gee was smiling, pulling away. "Thanks, Hon, I needed that," she said, patting his cheeks. She looked him up and down. "Four years! My, my, James, you're all grown up," she said wistfully. "And so strong and handsome! Not that I'm surprised." She dabbed her eyes again, and smiled. For the first time, James really looked at Gee. She hadn't changed much since he last saw her, yet the gray strands in her hair reminded him that she was getting older, just like his parents. She was a little thinner, too. Thanks to the war, no doubt. It hit him suddenly how unfair it was that his parents' generation were living through their second major war, and all its worries and privations. With that, he thought guiltily of all the anguish he was putting his folks through right now.

Before he knew it, Gee was handing him the key to the Rover. "I think there's enough petrol in it to get you to Fowey and back. I'll wait for the children—they've gone to the pictures. When you and Elizabeth get here, we'll all go to Brookhurst," she said. "Oh, James, pray for Edward, please! Oh—and be prepared: Elizabeth will take this hard. She's crazy about her grandfather." He was nodding. She sniffed, gave him a coupon for petrol in case he needed it, kissed his cheek, then hurried him out the door. James knew that, whatever stood between him and Elizabeth, it would have to wait. He felt almost relieved.

A little more than an hour later, James drove into the car park at Ready Money Cove under an overcast sky through which thin sunlight bled: a kind of watered-down sunny sky. As he recalled, it was quite a distance from here to the beach. He hurried along the meandering footpath, spiked with thick bracken at the edges and overhung with branches of big old trees that were so leafy, they shut out all view of the sea. He thought of the summer day when he walked down this path with Serena and Emelye, Morey and Elizabeth, carrying Elizabeth's beach chair. That day was the first time they ever really got to talk, though at age sixteen he was almost too shy for his own good, at least around her. Then at the end of the summer she gave him the book of Spenserian verse. What would she think if she knew that volume was now his good-luck piece, that he never went on a mission without it?

Now the leafy path made a hairpin turn, then took a plunge toward the beach. As James made his way down, he looked around. No sign of anyone there. The place appeared just as he remembered: waves slamming against those hulking boulders on either side, sending sprays of water high enough to wash the entire city of Galveston, Texas off the map, but of no apparent conse-quence to the gulls that perched just about anywhere they liked along the rock strata. The murkiness of the water rippling into the cove. The multitude of limpet shells clinging to the rocks, and the many clumps of slimy seaweed.

Yet now, tall iron bars formed a fence all the way across, as a barricade against enemy landing-craft. There was no getting around the fact that it ruined the view, and maybe Elizabeth thought so too, because apparently she had already left. Just to be sure, he walked a little farther, looking. Finally he spotted her figure on the other side of the bars. She had her hair in a braid, trailing down her back. She was wading slowly out into the water, her full skirt lifted high above her knees and looped over one arm. *So she does like the water; she just likes it when she's by herself.* He remembered shortly after that day they came here together, he overheard Serena ask Emelye why Elizabeth wore black stockings, even to the beach. He listened carefully as Emelye told Serena there was a scar on her sister's leg, and she was obsessed with keeping it hidden. *"And don't say anything to her about it. She'll consider it an invasion of her privacy."*

Even though Elizabeth wasn't more than a few yards out, the wind was blowing hard. James would have to be pretty close behind her before she could hear him calling. He stepped between two prison-like iron bars and walked toward her. When he reached the water's edge, he saw the portion of the long purplish scar that was above the water. *It isn't as bad as she believes,* he thought, though he realized it may look worse if you were closer. Not that it mattered to him. He cupped his hands around his mouth and called her name two or three times. Finally, she swivelled around, pushing the hair back that had come loose and blown in her face. "James!" she cried, apparently pleased to see him. Then abruptly her mouth dropped open and her face went blank, as though he had turned into a monster before her very eyes.

She dropped her skirt hem in the water, and stood there frozen.

Now James was astonished. He felt somehow that he ought to apologize, but then he remembered his errand. He went closer. "Your grandfather has had a stroke—I'm…sorry. Gee sent me in her car, to bring you home."

Elizabeth uttered a small cry. Her hands flew to her mouth. Then she was hurrying toward the shore, pushing the hair from her face, her skirt floating on the surface of the water like a jellyfish.

Standing on the beach, wringing out her skirt, she said, "Please will you get my book satchel and take it to the car? I'll be right behind you." He didn't understand why she wanted him to go ahead—what would that accomplish? Then it dawned on him she wanted to put on her stockings and shoes in privacy.

"Alright," he said. Her satchel was so heavy he wondered how she could carry it; it felt like she'd put a chunk of slate boulder inside. He walked toward the car park slowly, to give her time to catch up. Once she did, and they were walking side by side, she averted her eyes. Her figure was more slight than he remembered. She was smaller than Serena or Emelye. He was aware of the difficulty she had walking fast, with her limp. He didn't know what to say, so he kept quiet. When they reached the Rover, she rushed ahead and opened the passenger door, climbed in, then shut the door. He noticed part of her skirt hem hanging out, so he opened the door again, and swept it inside. "Oh yes, dear me, thank you," she said, looking down, her voice quavering.

When James slipped behind the wheel he was met by a blast of moist, blossom-laden air that reminded him of how the bathroom would smell right after Serena or Emelye washed their hair, the steam making the scent all the more potent. He imagined Elizabeth standing in the shower early this morning, her wet dark hair glistening against her ivory white shoulders and neck. *She was coming toward him, tossing off her bathrobe, apologizing for her wet hair—though he didn't mind—and slipping into bed beside him.* Somehow he felt they were finally, and for the first time, occupying the same space. Yet unfortunately there may be more distance between them than ever. He started the engine and they sped away.

As they drove along, Elizabeth pressed James for details about Lord Edward's condition. After he told her what little he knew, she took in a shuddering breath then turned and gazed silently out the window, one hand on the door latch as though she wanted to be ready to leap out as soon as they got home. He noticed her wet skirt hem dripping on the floor. Somehow this brought home the fact that she was not so high up there after all, just human like anyone else, and it touched him so deeply that he was tempted to pull over and stop, take her in his arms and kiss her. *Take it easy,* he told himself.

After a while he said quietly, "Gee says you're very fond of your grandfather. But I could tell that from your letters."

She started to weep, as though he had just thrown a jolt into what little composure she held on to. He gave her his handkerchief, and she held it to her face. He liked the intimacy of her pouring her tears into his handkerchief. He had a sudden wish to preserve it forever, like a small boy keeps such trophies. After regaining her composure, she worked the wet handkerchief through her fingers. She had small hands and slender fingers, and her nails were clipped very short, which made her seem all the more serious-minded, mature; she would never use that bright pink nail enamel Serena and Emelye were always painting on their fingernails and toenails. She reflected quietly, "When I was a little girl I often stayed at Brookhurst for weeks at a time. My parents, well—it was difficult," she said.

Did she mean they were too busy in London to look after her, or that her parents didn't get along? She'd never mentioned this in her letters. It occurred to him now that in all their correspondence she had given him few concrete details about her past. "What do you mean, 'difficult'?"

Ignoring the question, she went on, "And during all those weeks when I was recovering after the auto crash, Grandfather would sit and talk to me, or read me stories. When I was well enough, he would carry me downstairs and we'd sit out on the terrace and have our tea. Sweet old Angus and Kenegy—they're dead now—would sit out with us.

"Please, James, can you not drive a little faster?"

James hadn't realized she was impatient with his driving, and it hurt his pride. He was doing his best, having had little experience driving the English way. Every time they came to a roundabout—there must have been a hundred between Fowey and Bodmin—his nerves froze up until he had safely managed to enter the circling traffic. At least now, with petrol rationing, there wasn't as much traffic as there had been the last time he drove to Ready Money Cove.

Still, he would swear that flying a P-47 was easier than driving in England. And now she wanted him to speed up.

But after all, she was upset, he thought forgivingly. In spite of his reluctance, he sped up just a little.

At Brookhurst, Elizabeth and Gee hastened into Lord Edward's room and stayed there, with Lady Cynthia. Someone—a servant, he gathered—was calling Camellia Cottage repeatedly, getting no answer. James didn't know what to do with himself. He went and stood out on the terrace overlooking the garden. It was certainly neat and well-tended, but he seemed to remember that it was a lot more colorful when he visited here before. The war probably changed that. Pretty soon Gee's young children gathered around him. They must have felt at loose ends just like he did. Chris suggested they set up the wickets and play croquet, but Elvira said she had a better idea. "We're not putting on a dumb play," said Andy, pushing out his bottom lip. Elvira said no, they were going to wash Abraham and Sarah.

Those dogs were enormous. James's look of amazement was met with a toss of her auburn curls. "Not to worry, they like to be washed. Since they live in the house my grandparents don't want them to be stinky, you see," she explained, pinching her nose with her fingers and crossing her big brown eyes. "So they're used to it, don't you know, and Mr. Malone hasn't time now, with most of his helpers gone to war." James assumed Mr. Malone was the gardener.

Elvira led him to the garden shed where there was a big wooden tub mounted on wheels, with a mound of soap and brushes and towels stowed inside. He rolled it outdoors while Elvira uncoiled a garden hose. As Elvira filled the tub with water, James thought there was probably some war-time restriction against wasting water on bathing family pets.

Sarah looked like a great snowy mountain in the middle of the tub. Every few minutes she shimmied soapy water all over the four of them, making them all leap back, which sent the children into gales of laughter. Everyone was having fun. Then, as they were rinsing off Abraham, Andy suddenly turned the hose down Chris's back. At the time Chris was toweling off Sarah. Chris started shrieking, his arms flailing. Elvira grabbed the water hose and aimed it at Andy in retaliation. Abraham took a dive for the ground, spattering water all over James, and ran off soaking wet, Sarah quick behind him. James, who was finding it hard not to break down laughing, shouted above the mayhem to the children, "Come on now, y'all behave!" He packed them off to change clothes, then emptied the tub, thinking it would be hard to overlook the similarity between the breaking out of a fight among three children, and the war raging all around them which continued drawing nations into it on one side or the other.

Fortunately, by the time the rest of the family arrived that evening, Lord Edward was showing real signs of improvement. The doctor felt it was likely he would recover completely. A servant went around closing the black crape curtains.

James wondered if it would be alright now to have a talk with Elizabeth. If they didn't talk tonight, there was a good chance he'd wind up going back to base tomorrow, knowing no more about her feelings than he knew when he stepped off the train at Bodmin station. It occurred to him she probably didn't even realize he had come all this way just to see her.

He was still mulling this over when Elizabeth invited him to join her out on the terrace. So maybe she realized, after all. And if so, this was surely a bad sign. *"James, I'm terribly sorry, but under the circumstances I don't believe we ought to see each other...."*

They sat at a little iron table, under a slice of moon and a host of bright stars: the perfect setting for speaking of love. It was too bad the time for that had not arrived. Would it ever? He waited, a tight feeling in his diaphragm.

Elizabeth looked away, made a peak of her hands. "James, tell me, when I was out in the water, and...and you were calling to me, did you see...my legs?" She asked, swallowing her words at the end.

It was the last thing he expected. He pitied her because she could barely utter the question, couldn't look at him when she did, and more than anything, because she could not bring herself to be more specific. It was as if she were asking if he had caught a glimpse of her naked body. He was afraid if he admitted the truth, she'd never speak to him again. "No."

A pause. "You're positive?"

"Yes."

Elizabeth nudged back in her chair, and gazed up at the stars. James didn't hear her sigh of relief, but he felt it as surely as if it had swept through him. He was seized with guilt for lying, but he knew he would never betray the trust on the breath of that sigh.

There would never be a better time than this. "Elizabeth, there's something I need to ask you," he began.

"Yes, James?"

"I—I'd like to come down and see you again."

"Well of course, James, I should like that too," she said warmly.

James felt like he'd swallowed one of those stars up above. Emboldened, he persisted, "And you wouldn't mind being seen with me?"

Another pause. "Dear James, why should I?" she asked, real perplexity in her voice.

"Well, if people see you with a fellow wearing a uniform, they might think you're not all that sincere about your convictions," he said. He hadn't meant for the injury to come through in his voice, but he was pretty sure it did. He thought of all the girls at the dances on base; of a face smiling up at him to waltz time.

Elizabeth looked down at her hands for a few moments, then said quietly, "I must admit I never thought about that. But no. I don't think it's anyone's business whom I see, or when. Besides, one can't let such things get in the way of friendship. The war can't last forever, after all."

Friendship. It was right on the tip of his tongue to swear, "*I want much more than friendship from you!*" But no, now that they'd gotten this behind them, he'd show her. He imagined all the times he would come down here, to do just that; regretted all the time he'd wasted; hoped to God he wouldn't get transferred far away any time soon. The blood was thrumming in his ears. *Take it easy.*

Abruptly Elizabeth rose, a hand on her forehead. "James I'm awfully tired and you must be too," she said. Let's get some rest, eh?"

So they went into the house.

On Sunday morning the family had breakfast in the small dining room. There were real eggs from the Brookhurst farms, fried sunnyside up, and back bacon, thick and juicy—the kind of food you were served on the morning of a mission, instead of the regular powdered eggs and spam. Happily, there was plenty of it. James ate as if it were his last meal. Everyone was much relieved that Lord Edward was resting peacefully upstairs. A nurse had come on duty at six o'clock. Geneva was to drive James to the station at St. Tudy, then return. Everyone else would stay behind. As they were out front getting ready to leave, Andy, Elvira and Chris walked out with Elizabeth to tell James goodbye. Three heads thrown back, looking up at him. They begged him to come see them again. He promised he would. Then Merton came out and said that his lordship had asked to see his young grandchildren. As they bolted inside, he thought, wouldn't it be wonderful someday to have a couple of kids with Elizabeth.

When Geneva got in the car, Elizabeth stood there with him. He had a sudden feeling of vertigo, just knowing they'd have a minute to say goodbye with-

out anyone else around. *Please do come back as soon as you can. I shall miss you!*
"Thanks ever so much for all you've done," she said.

"I didn't do much. I'm just glad Lord Edward is improving."

Her eyes grew moist. "Yes, our prayers have been answered."

James realized he had not remembered to pray for Lord Edward, as Gee asked him. James hadn't really prayed since he became old enough to realize it didn't make much difference one way or the other. The chaplain always offered a short prayer just before they left on a mission, and he would think: the only thing keeping the whole crew from getting blown to smithereens was timing. Winding up in the wrong place at the wrong time meant you were done for, prayers or not.

Elizabeth smiled now. "May your next visit be less eventful!"

James returned her smile. "I'll just be glad when I can see you again." He threw his duffel bag into the Rover and climbed in. As Geneva drove them away, he waved at Elizabeth from the window. When she waved back, he thought he perceived a blush on her cheeks.

CHAPTER 40

Back on base that night, James wrote Elizabeth to say he would let her know when he could come visit again, and hopefully he'd have more time. Meanwhile, he hoped Lord Edward would continue to recover. "Please keep me posted. Always yours, James."

After the first week, he was looking for a reply. He lived for daily mail call, and every time he came back from a mission all he could think about was whether a letter might be waiting. Nothing. Finally one Friday, he called. Mrs. Greaves answered. "Miss Elizabeth and her mum 'ave gone to Exeter. They'll be back on Sunday."

"I see," James said, wondering what they were doing in Exeter. People didn't take pleasure trips these days.

"Shall I have 'er ring you op?"

"No, I'm hard to reach. Just say that I called. I'll try again later."

In the middle of the next week, a letter finally arrived. "Dear James, Mrs. Greaves said you telephoned. I'm sorry to have missed you. I've been meaning to write, but since you were here I received a letter from the Dean's office at Newnham College, listing a dozen works 'it would be most advantageous' if I could read in preparation for enrolling. I daresay, I brought this on myself, having written to the Dean to say that I should appreciate some guidelines. I've been able to engage a Latin tutor at Exeter University beginning next week. I shall be going there at weekends, from now probably until I take my entrance exam next spring. And in between I shall be wading through readings and commentaries, &c., on Hegel and Nietzsche and Kant—happily I shall be able to make use of the university library. How I wish my dear old friend Fr. Ogilvie were here, to help me through. Oh James, I do feel so 'out of my depth.' My stomach churns with fear I will not be accepted. While I regret I shall have very little time for anything other than study over this next year, I must not allow myself to become diverted. After all, as I'm sure you will understand, my future hangs in the balance. Of course, demands on my schedule should not keep you from coming down. Geneva adores you, as you well know, and E., A., and C. talk about you constantly. And we all hope you will get a pass at Christmas, for I shall certainly be home and eager for a break. Grandfather is gaining strength daily, and should be quite well by then. Keep in touch—. Ever your dear friend, Elizabeth."

The letter was a severe letdown for James. After encouraging him to visit her, Elizabeth now seemed to be shutting the door in his face. "*...I must not allow myself to become diverted.*"

He found himself thinking soberly of her fears for her future. He had always envisioned her future as being with him, and naturally that meant they would marry and he would provide a living, and—Suddenly he thought of Emelye. She had never gotten over her crush on him, despite his efforts to discourage her. At times it proved downright embarrassing—there was that night of her senior prom, for instance, when she stood up her date to go with him. All Emelye wanted out of life was to be a wife—preferably James's, she'd made that clear—and a mother. She excelled in sewing and home economics courses. Why had he never given any thought to the possibility that Elizabeth did not want that kind of life? In fact, maybe she feared that was all he was willing to offer, and this made her reluctant to ever be more than just his friend. If he didn't give her the space she needed, and she failed that exam, it would be at least partly his fault. He'd never forgive himself, and it would ruin his chances with her for good.

James did not get the hoped-for Christmas pass, and whenever he did get away to Clearharbour for a couple of days, he spent most of his time with the kids. He took them down the street to play bowls, and to the pictures, and went to Andy's cricket games. If Elizabeth happened to be there, he was careful to keep his mouth shut and not interfere with her studies. Usually she was in Exeter when he arrived, and didn't return till he was on his way back to base. He wondered if he'd ever have any time with her again. Grafton Underwood was around twenty miles from Cambridge—the perfect set-up if she was accepted there. But James could be moved from there at any time, and sent just about anywhere.

At least he was thankful to get caught up on his sleep. Gee had a double bed brought in and made up in the buttery for him. The buttery was the most functional room in the house, she said; in the years they had lived there it had been at various times a bedroom, a playroom for rainy days, Elvira's theatre, and a storage room. James slept more peacefully at Clearharbour than ever he did on base. There you could never tell when they were going to wake you up in the wee hours and tell you to get dressed and hurry to the briefing room. They'd ply you with black coffee so you could stay awake during the mission. Then half the time the weather would change and the mission would be scrubbed. You'd go back to bed high on caffeine, and lie awake the rest of the night.

About the time Elizabeth took her entrance exam, James was reassigned to the 91st bomber group at Bassingbourn. It was one of the nicer bases, having been established before the war, with paved roads and ivy-covered buildings housing all the necessary quarters, plus amenities such as a barber shop, a canteen, a library and a cinema, and a spacious crew room in the hangar. Best of all, Bassingbourn was around the same distance from Cambridge as Grafton Underwood. James waited anxiously to hear the results of Elizabeth's entrance exam. Shortly, she wrote that she had been accepted at Newnham College for the fall. "As you can imagine, I am positively ecstatic, and at the same time, humbled by the opportunity to be in a place where ideas have always been valued above all else. Oh James, I feel my life is just beginning—"

James was grinning. Now Elizabeth was coming to him. His life was just beginning, too.

CHAPTER 41

Elizabeth had barely settled in at Clough Hall—the term had not even begun—and already she felt she did not fit in with the other residents. First of all, there was her appearance. The other women were all so pretty, and they were more sophisticated in dress and manner than she was. It was a pity they did not wear academic gowns, as they would if they were full members of the university, for then—at least the majority of time—everyone would look as if they belonged. Of course, a gown wouldn't be long enough to hide the scar on Elizabeth's leg. She felt rather like the ugly duckling, limping about in her black stockings which had been darned repeatedly since the war began.

Apart from this, judging by the conversations at the round of teas hosted by various college societies, and the spur-of-the-moment cocoa parties held in the residents' rooms, everyone was preoccupied with the latest film at the cinema, or the latest news of the war—the morality of which no one else seemed to question as she did.

The Clough dining-hall was a stately room of ornately-carved woodwork, high arched windows, and paintings of college dignitaries along the walls. On the evening it was Elizabeth's turn to be among the guests at High Table, she conversed with the faculty more intelligently than any of the other young women. At length she was emboldened to express her views on the war to the distinguished Miss Chrystal, Tutor and Vice Principal, and ask how they were likely to be received here at Cambridge. One had to speak very loudly, for the noise level in Hall, with everyone at the long tables talking at once, and chairs scraping against the wood floor, was positively staggering. To her relief, Miss Chrystal, her eyes kind in a long brooding face, raised her voice and assured her that her views would most certainly be respected. With a sage look, however, she went on to express her doubt that Elizabeth would find many who shared them. She reminded her that she would be expected to do some sort of warwork regardless of her convictions. Elizabeth told her she understood. Her name was already on the rotating schedule to help with the washing-up after luncheon, beginning next week. Apart from this, she had not yet been advised what war-time task would be assigned her, only that there would be one.

Miss Chrystal nodded in satisfaction, then, gazing rather despairingly at a bowl of thin soup sitting before her, she lowered her silver spoon into it. After taking a rather loud sip, she looked up abruptly. "And how old are you?"

"Nineteen."

"Too young to be called up, probably," said she.

Elizabeth had her National Registration Identity Card, with the "Removed To" section dutifully filled in with Newnham College, Cambridge, and stamped by the authorities. She kept her card tucked inside her handbag, and often checked to be sure it was there, for one may be demanded to present it to a police officer or some other official at any time. The warning on the card was clear and chilling: if one failed to report a lost or stolen card, the penalty was a fine or imprisonment, or both. One felt the government was following one about all the time, spying on one. How she dreaded being called up, being forced not only to leave Cambridge, but to devote her entire workday to a cause she abhorred. Fortunately at present there weren't many women being called up from university, but if the war continued much longer, that may very well change.

Being out of step did not dampen Elizabeth's enthusiasm for Newnham College. After all, fitting in socially was hardly her purpose for enrolling here; and besides, she found many reasons to be thankful. According to Geneva, American college coeds shared their rooms with at least one, and sometimes two or three, other women. Not so in England. Elizabeth lived in a corner room on the second floor, with a splendid golden maple tree outside the window, its leaves fluttering in the chilly late September breeze. A bed heaped with warm coverlets and pillows, a wicker armchair, a desk, a study lamp, and two bookcases—already filled to capacity with books she brought from home—completed the furnishings. Unlike some of her fellow residents, she did not have a wireless set, for she wanted no diversion from her studies. She had already been warned that attending too many lectures—there were lectures given on every conceivable subject, all over the university!—could seriously cut into one's reading time. There was a coal-burning fireplace for which one was provided half a scuttle of coal per day, according to war-time regulations. Not as much as she would like, of course, but sufficient if one conserved. Here, surrounded by her books, and with pictures of her family lining the chimneypiece and shelves, plus her beloved Shaker doll and Frenchman's cross, Elizabeth felt more at home than ever she had felt anywhere, even at Brookhurst. Naturally, knowing that she must use the community bath had kept her awake nights as the time drew near for her to pack her belongings and move here. She feared her loss of privacy so dreadfully that she wondered if she ought not to have applied to study here after all. Yet, somehow she simply must overcome this if she was to carry on with her life. Happily, so far she had managed by wearing her ankle-length bathrobe to and from the bath, tightly bound about her, then taking care to position herself while showering so that only the fronts of her legs were ever exposed beneath the tail of the shower curtain. Admittedly, she was never completely confident with this situation. If possible she showered when the bath was empty, and in any case, her showers were always as brief as possible.

Elizabeth was inspired by the feeling that a vast accumulation of knowledge had become distilled in the very walls of Newnham College, as if every woman who had ever studied here since it opened in 1871, left behind the essence of ideas developed in her mind; like leaves, dropped from a forest tree in autumn, would gradually break down and become a part of the earth surrounding the tree, nurturing, enriching it. Since that day in France long ago, when she retrieved the stranger's unfinished cross, she had known the purpose of her life would be revealed to her. Now she believed with all her heart that her purpose awaited here. After completing her studies and earning her degree—which, unfortunately, must be conferred by some other university—she might stay on first as a Research Fellow, and eventually a College Tutor; and even become the College Principal one day. Oh, the very idea made her spine tingle with anticipation. Of course, meantime she must strive to succeed one term at a time, and ultimately be prepared when at last she sat her Tripos.

One evening after coming downstairs for the six-thirty sitting of the evening meal, Elizabeth took time to check her mail. In the background, she could hear music played upon a piano in the common room. There were lots of young women about, talking in groups as if they had known one another for years. Feeling awkward, she nodded politely as she threaded her way across the floor.

Drawing near the rows of mail slots, she noticed a letter in hers. She felt somewhat gratified knowing that when she retraced her steps among the knots of women, she could appear to be very absorbed in reading it. As she reached for the letter, however, she heard a crisp, intelligent voice at her shoulder. "Millicent Flake here. How d'you do?" She turned round to find a rather stout young woman with light brown hair, wearing eyeglasses with round wire rims.

"Elizabeth Selby, nice to know you," she said.

"Fresher?"

"Oh, but I was afraid it was all too obvious!" Elizabeth laughed.

"Really! So am I. Just arrived this afternoon. What's your field?"

"I shall read Philosophy," she said, with pleasure. It seemed natural to broaden the study she had found so engaging with Father Ogilvie as her mentor once upon a time, and in so doing, honor his long life. Father Ogilvie read Philosophy at Oxford before and after his conversion to Christianity. He considered no question or subject of discussion taboo, for he believed that God waited at the end of every sincere journey of the mind, as well as the spirit. She had come to believe that struggling with his faith as a young man made him especially compassionate towards others. After all, he had assured her of God's forgiveness for her sin of treachery in Dartmoor Forest, even if she could not forgive herself. Father Ogilvie died peacefully in his sleep during the harsh winter of 1942. Elizabeth was among several hundred people who attended his funeral at St. Paul's Knightsbridge on a bleak afternoon, then, muffled against the frigid wind, witnessed his burial in the church yard. Not a day passed but she thought of him, and many of the books in her room upstairs were those he had given her. "And yours?" she asked Millicent.

"Classics."

"Jolly good! That was my second choice. We shall have lots to talk about," said Elizabeth. "I say, what floor is your room on?"

"Two. I've been told I've got the only room left in Clough Hall with Morris wallpaper. Quite overpowering it is, too, a yellow background with blue cornflowers. Makes one go cross-sided. And you?"

"I'm on two also," said Elizabeth, delighted. She did not tell her that Morris wallpapers hung on a great many walls at Brookhurst.

"Splendid! Any mail in your slot?"

"Eh—yes. Probably from my father in London," Elizabeth said truthfully, so that Millicent would not expect her to have a letter from a young man, which would of course make her look foolish when it turned out this wasn't the case.

Again she started to reach for her letter, but Millicent asked, "What's he doing in London?"

Elizabeth paused. "He owns a theatre," she said. In fact Father was also deeply involved in some sort of warwork, but this was strictly confidential. As his spouse, Geneva had been informed of its nature, but not even she was privy to the details.

"Fancy that. A theatre. West End?"

"The *William & Mary*."

"You don't say! I used to see *Pip 'N Pocket* there every Christmas."

"Fancy!" Elizabeth said. Then she told her that her father was seriously injured in a blast several years ago, and nearly lost his life. At Millicent's urging, she briefly outlined the story of his injuries and recovery. In fact, the details were quite immediate for her just now. Geneva had stayed a couple of days to help her get settled into her room at Clough Hall, before going on to London to see Father—things were relatively peaceful there at this point, though how long it would last, no one knew. Perhaps because the two of them had never really talked about the incident at length, they found themselves doing so.

It happened near the beginning of a long night of destruction, the worst night since the attacks by the German Luftwaffe had begun. Before the night was over, the City of London was on fire. The roof of St. Paul's Cathedral was severely damaged by incendiaries, and many public buildings were left in ruins. As a consequence, millions of priceless documents and books were destroyed.

Father was hurled fifty feet down one side of Norfolk Square, and landed with his right leg embedded in a small crater left from a previous bombard-ment. Apart from the injury to his leg—mostly his knee—he suffered a mild concussion, a few broken ribs; and a good bit of shrapnel had to be dug out of his backside. *"Tell Elizabeth, she and I now have something in common!"* he would quip later to Geneva. *"Just opposite legs."* The townhouse that he was passing by when he heard the bomb zeroing in was now nothing more than a gaping hole between its neighbors, utterly destroyed.

Geneva did not learn what had befallen her husband until the following morning, after having waited up all night expecting him to arrive. Around six o'clock, the telephone rang downstairs. With a sense of foreboding, she threw off the bed covers and rushed down to answer. Mrs. Fairfax was on the line. She relayed the bad news, and said that Kenneth Owsley had gone to be with Father at St. Mary's Hospital casualty. Shortly, Father was to be "put in line among other injured persons," for surgery.

All of this Elizabeth discovered soon after she came downstairs and found Geneva sitting on the telephone bench, wearing a sheer black sleeping gown with rather elaborate sleeves that she had never seen before. She was shivering. Her feet were bare. For some reason it struck Elizabeth as extraordinary that her toe nails were varnished red. She removed an overcoat from the peg and wrapped it about Geneva's shoulders.

As Geneva conveyed the news, she was sobbing so hard that it was a struggle to understand her. "I've got to get to London as soon as I can, and I don't know when I'll be back. Will you help look after the children?"

Elizabeth hastened Geneva on her way. Over the next few days she prayed constantly for Father, until Geneva telephoned to report that the surgery had been performed successfully and that he was on the mend. Geneva stayed in London for six weeks, until she was able to bring him home to Clearharbour, to finish convalescing. Elizabeth, Andy, Elvira and Chris all waited anxiously for their arrival at Bodmin Station. To everyone's relief, as soon as the couple emerged from the train carriage, Father relying on a pair of crutches, his face pale but rested, it was clear they were as warm and loving towards each other as they used to be, before Cynthia Louise's death.

Even after all this time, fluid would occasionally collect on Father's right knee, and have to be drained. And sometimes he went through periods when he suffered a lot of pain, and would be forced to use a cane for assistance in walking. He claimed he was not at all bitter, only thankful to be alive.

Now Elizabeth retrieved the letter in her mail slot. She was amazed to find 'First Lt. Sidney James Younger, Bassingbourn RAF Base,' on the return. The last time James wrote, he was awaiting new orders. It hardly seemed possible he would once again be despatched to a base nearby Cambridge. And yet…Bassingbourn. They were about to be thrown together: the thing Elizabeth had often found herself dreaming of; yet the thing she most feared and had tried desperately to avoid. She had no right to wish to be thrown together with James.

Millicent was peering at the envelope. "Oh, from a flying officer!"

"Just a friend, really," Elizabeth stammered. "An American. Eh—my sister is—well, he's a family friend," she faltered, then at once she felt guilty for revising her sentence, as if to erase all Emelye's hopes that James was in love with her. "*Dear Emelye…. I can scarcely tell you how helpful it was for the whole family to have James nearby when Grandfather suffered stroke. He drove us all to Brookhurst, then entertained the children during the long day. He anticipates visiting us at Clearharbour in the future, and the children are delighted….*"

"Well, I suppose I'd better go upstairs and see what it says," Elizabeth told her, yet acutely aware that one need not retreat to the privacy of one's room to read a letter from a family friend, not when the dining-hall was beginning to fill.

Having grown up stout and bookish and unpopular, Millicent regarded most of the women in Clough Hall as dreadful snobs. Convinced romance was in the air, she could not resist turning round and announcing to the chattering females, "Look here, ladies, Michaelmas term has not even begun, and already Elizabeth's got her first love letter. From a flying officer."

The room fell silent as all the women slowly turned to stare. Elizabeth's cheeks were flaming. It seemed to her that a hundred pairs of inquiring eyes were upon her.

CHAPTER 42

At five minutes before six on a Friday evening in October, Elizabeth's neighbor from across the hall knocked on her door. "You've a visitor downstairs. He says you're expecting him."

But not for five more minutes, Elizabeth thought with racing heart. The word, *expecting*, hardly described the turmoil she had endured since receiving James's letter saying he'd got a weekend pass, and would like to spend it with her at Cambridge. Night after night she had agonized over what to wear. Her college wardrobe, the majority of which was acquired before the war, consisted of two solid-colored straight skirts, and one plaid drindl—her favorite; a worsted blazer, two sweater sets and three blouses. As she lay awake on her pillow, her mind was a kaleidoscope, with various color combinations flashing across it. Unfortunately not one of them would make her look as attractive as James, whose athletic figure, with muscular chest and limbs, was positively dashing in a stiff-starched khaki uniform and cap.

Now Elizabeth stood before the mirror for one last look, despairing of the bright splotches on her cheeks: an irrefutable sign of nervousness. Her long hair was swept up in curls piled high atop her head. Millicent had styled it for her, and while she had liked it at first, now she could only think: *Oh dear, I look ten years older!* She was tempted to remove the pins and brush it out, but it had been in place for two hours, and it might look even worse, all creased in the wrong places like a paper sack that's been crumpled, then smoothed out again. She smoothed down the straight black skirt she'd finally chosen to wear—it was more compatible with black stockings than the others—and slipped into her blazer. After pausing at the door to take several deep breaths, she hurried downstairs.

James's look of uncertainty when he said, "Good evening, Elizabeth," was not lost on her. Her fussy hairdo no doubt made her seem desperate to please him and therefore quite foolish. In an effort to appear a little more detached, she began, "Good evening, James, welcome to Cambridge." Oh dear, now she sounded like a tour guide. Oh well.... He took her arm and she smiled up at him.

"Shall we go?" he said.

By now she was so scattered, she almost forgot the necessity of signing out for the evening—an omission that would result in a fine.

Within a few minutes they were in Silver Street, wending their way past shop fronts through the crowd of pedestrians and bicyclists wheeling round. James remarked that he had seen more bicycles since he got off the train at Cambridge Station than in his entire life up to that point. The town was swarming with them. Small talk was about all he could manage as they walked; and Elizabeth's mouth was so dry she could hardly speak. As she limped alongside James, she was painfully aware of his continuing efforts to relax his pace so as not to get ahead of her.

They went to a small restaurant near the Corn Exchange. Arriving a little earlier than the dinner crowd, they were shown to a table in a quiet corner, by a window. After ordering fish and chips, a beer for James and a pot of tea for Elizabeth, they gazed out the window, each utterly at a loss. Never before had they been at such pains to make conversation, thought Elizabeth. *Of course, how many conversations have we had?* Tonight it seemed they were little more than strangers. Her chest felt as if it were coiled up in a knot.

Soon a young woman bicycled past, wearing an evening gown and cape, with a corsage on her shoulder and a ribbon in her hair. James watched, fascinated, as she expertly negotiated her way through the crowd, pedaling with silver-slippered feet, the long tail of her skirt draped over the handle bars. It reminded him of Elizabeth wading into the water with her skirt draped over her arm. It gave him an opening. "Lord Edward must be real proud of you, studying here," he said.

Elizabeth beamed. "Oh yes, though he does give me a bit of a hard time—all in fun, of course—for choosing Cambridge rather than his and Father's alma mater." James was relieved that she seemed more like herself now, in spite of the sophisticated hairdo. He'd been worried that a few weeks at Cambridge had turned her into an intellectual snob. He was about to ask her how she liked it here, when she said, "And I'm sure your family is proud of you, too."

But you're not, James thought with a sting. Since that night when he and Elizabeth finally spoke frankly about their views on the war, he had been telling himself that her opposition didn't bother him anymore. But now she had pushed him up against a wall. He shrugged. "I was always taught to help out a neighbor who's in trouble. That's what I'm doing over here now, what we're all doing over here," he said.

So, on top of everything else, she had managed to offend James. She wanted to tell him that he was braver than her, that since coming here she had passed up numerous chances for debate on the subject of the war because confronting her peers made her knees shake violently and her heart pound with dread. What she had finally faced up to was that her aversion to the violence of war came not only from her studies, as most people—including James—surely assumed, but from having lived in a household filled with bitterness and strife, for the first six years of her life. That if not for Fr. Ogilvie counseling her to forgive her mother as Christ had forgiven those who persecuted him, she would undoubtedly have grown up as violent as her mother because a part of her had always wanted to strike back. Yet all these admissions might lead James to ask questions that she was not prepared to answer.

The waitress arrived with their beverages—a welcome interruption, Elizabeth thought, in a conversation that could only wind up at a dead end. She busily stirred her scalding tea, the prospect of the next couple of days with James stretching out before her like an eternity. What ever would they say to each other now? Perhaps she ought to remark on Emelye's bravery in joining the Women Airforce Service Pilots, following the lead of the adventurous Serena, who months earlier left the ranks of the Rockettes to join up. In a letter arriving only yesterday from Avenger Field, where she was in training, Emelye asked for Elizabeth's prayers, lamenting, "Suppose I crash a plane and kill myself, or someone else, or both? But I've gotta do something to make James think of me when he's about to climb in that Thunderbolt and risk his life, something that will make him want to write me more often…."

Yet Elizabeth really didn't want to bring Emelye into the conversation, even though it made her feel guilty not to want to. She thought again of her ill-chosen hairdo. It served her right that her attempt to look attractive had backfired. She touched the bare nape of her neck, feeling quite naked suddenly. "I say, you must wonder just what I'm getting on, with this hairdo," she blurted out. Whereupon she felt completely idiotic.

James was so surprised at the outburst, not to mention, that she'd apparently seen right through him, his mouth broke into a sheepish grin. He looked down, then up again. "No, it's nice. But it's just…well…different from what I'm used to seeing when I…" he paused; they were looking deeply into each other's eyes now, "…when I look at you, Elizabeth. I'll get used to it, though."

"Oh no, you needn't do that," she quickly swore, shaking her head, "this hairdo is far too much bother to be done with any regularity." She lowered her eyes, realizing he might think she was taking for granted that after this weekend he would want to go on seeing her. She looked up at him helplessly. Could he guess this was the first time she had ever been out on a date? "What a relief to get all these hair pins out tonight!" she declared, smiling.

Only now did James realize her new hairdo was just for him. The thought filled him with such tenderness, it was all he could do to keep from reaching across for her hands and saying *I love you.* But he sensed this was not the right time, and it certainly was not the right place. Somehow, before the weekend was over—

The fish and chips arrived. James soon ate all of his dinner and most of Elizabeth's, for her excitement at being with him had quite robbed her of appetite, as she'd known it would, despite the fact she'd been hungry since she entered Newnham College where the food was barely sufficient; and she kept encouraging him to help himself to her plate as they went on talking. In between bites he asked, "How do you like it here, so far?"

"Quite well," she said warmly. "Better than any place I've ever been. I shouldn't mind staying here forever, in fact."

James had not expected her to feel quite so strongly attached to Cambridge, especially at this early date. What if it proved an obstacle when he asked her to marry him, and move all the way to Texas? He was getting ahead of himself, though. The war was far from over. "Where shall we go tomorrow?" he asked.

"Oh, there is so much to see," she said, grateful this was true, for it would help to pass the time. "Not that I know my way about very well as yet," she added. "Perhaps there are places in particular that you would like to visit—some of the buildings are quite beautiful, for instance, King's College Chapel, Clare, and Magdalene. Of course, there are guidebooks we can use. Unfortunately, many of the best paintings at the Fitzwilliam, and early books and manuscripts in the university library, have been moved elsewhere for safe-keeping until—. I know—perhaps we could take in a play at the *Arts.* I've heard there is quite a good production of *MacBeth* just now." There she went again, sounding like a tour guide.

James took a swallow of beer. Elizabeth watched his Adam's apple bob up and down. She noticed a small grease stain on his shirt cuff. How awkward it was, dining alone with a member of the opposite sex. One noticed the most remarkable things. Yet James did not seem to feel the least bit awkward.

"You know where I'd really like for you to take me—for starters?" he said.

"Where?"

"To your favorite spot—the place that makes you feel deep down that you're really at Cambridge University. If that makes sense."

"Oh yes, you want to see the place where one can feel the heartbeat," Elizabeth surmised, only at that moment she wasn't quite sure just where that would be, for she had never really thought of it in terms of a specific place.

"Right," he said. That she had grasped his meaning and taken him seriously encouraged him more than anything she had said tonight. "I want to know what it would feel like to be in that place with you," he said, looking into her eyes.

The intimacy of the remark brought a blush to Elizabeth's cheeks. She imagined James remaining in England when the war was over, entering Cambridge, so that together they could embark on a lifetime of study. Then she thought of Emelye: all her hopes and dreams pinned on James coming home to her.

CHAPTER 43

The great halls of Newnham College were imposing red brick structures in the Queen Anne style. With graceful arches softening their roof lines and scores of shining mullioned windows, trimmed in white, they peered down upon the gardens and all who crossed them in a benevolent way that made Elizabeth think of a chorus of unassailable, doting spinster aunts.

Arranged here and there among ancient broad-trunked trees and flowering plants and hedges were small wooden tables and chairs. It was to one of these that Elizabeth led James on Saturday morning.

She could hardly have hoped for a more splendid showcase for the place she had chosen: a sky of clear azure blue, streaked with soft, feathery cirrus clouds; and a crisp autumn chill in the air. As they sat down, she felt the deliciously warm kiss of the sun upon her face. Soon she was explaining, "It seems to me, as the true purpose in entering university is to explore ideas, then a place that's quiet and peaceful, inspiring one to formulate thoughts unhurriedly, then freely exchange them with others, must surely be at the heart of the university." Fearing she had sounded a bit speechy and high-minded, she added simply, "Anyway, this is my favorite spot, and that's what I realized as I thought it over last night."

Had thoughts of him kept her awake last night? James wondered hopefully. For a long time he had lain awake on his narrow cot, until he determined exactly the way he would tell her that he was in love with her. And this morning, with her hair swept straight back and caught with a ribbon at the nape of her neck, she looked just like he had always imagined she would look when the time finally arrived to say those words. For now he looked around him, eager to enlarge on her idea, to show he understood. "What's great is that it never wears out its potential. I mean, these chairs are always waiting to be occupied by somebody with a new idea, or a new slant on things, and others who are willing to listen."

Elizabeth was delighted that James's thoughts were in tune with hers. "Yes, and it isn't like in the rooms where we have tutorials, where the discussion must be restricted to a specific topic. Though I considered such rooms, I dismissed them almost as quickly as the university lecture halls." She paused, and, smiling to herself, opened her arms wide and gazed at the sky. "Here, one is free to examine and express one's thoughts on any subject."

It was all James could do to keep from preempting his own strategy, asking right here and now, "Is it okay for me to say I've been in love with you since I was ten years old, and you've gotta marry me, because if you don't it will kill me as sure if my plane goes down in flames?" His heart thumping in his chest, he resumed looking around. He was struck by the contrasts: the warm rosy red of the brick buildings against the blue of the sky, and the veil of gray shadows slanting down on green grass; the multitude of colors in leafy trees and vines growing up the building walls—"I'd like to do a drawing of this place, a colored drawing," he said impulsively, amazed at the passion he felt.

"Well then by all means, you must do so!" Elizabeth cried.

James quickly said, "I doubt I could do it justice, though. You know, it's funny, but I remember as a kid, how excited I got over a brand new box of crayons. First thing, I'd open it up and bring it to my face, to breathe in that waxy smell. Then I'd look over all those colors in paper wraps, those clean, sharp points just waiting to be put to use. I'd imagine all the pictures I would draw...."

"All that potential...so evident in your drawing of Father and Geneva's wedding," Elizabeth remarked sagely.

He looked at her. A smile played at the corner of his mouth. No matter that he'd forgiven himself a long time ago for that drawing, he was still glad to know she had always admired it. "Yeah. But I stopped drawing for fun a long time ago," he admitted.

"Why?"

James hesitated. All his life, the importance of growing up to be a 'responsible citizen' and a 'good provider' had been drilled into him by his father—the principles needed no reinforcement by the Boy Scouts, which his father encouraged him to join. Though he could not remember being told in so many words, he knew that to fail in these areas would be to disappoint his father deeply. It occurred to him now that even as a child he had never entertained the idea of growing up and working at something he loved to do. It gave him a frozen feeling in his stomach, the kind you get when you see the train you were supposed to catch barreling down the tracks without you. He shrugged it off. "You can't make a living as an artist," he said.

Elizabeth sensed that James was not as happy with the prospect of being an engineer as she had been given to believe from his letters. Father had often said he should never have been happy as an engineer, regardless of his degree from Oxford, that only his work in the performing arts made him feel truly alive. "I think you ought to be drawing, if that's what makes you happy, James, even if you're struggling and poor for all your life," she said grandly.

He gave her a long measuring look. The only material sacrifices Elizabeth had ever known were those imposed by the war. He found himself asking, "Would you be happy, married to someone who was struggling and poor?"

The color drained from Elizabeth's face. Quickly he said, "Not that—personally—I'd dream of marrying a girl unless I could provide for her. I'm just arguing an idea, one that every man, worth his salt, thinks about seriously." He winked. "That's what we're here for, right? Arguing ideas?"

"Ah yes," she said, smiling, feeling foolish for having leapt to conclusions. Just being fond of her did not mean he was thinking of marriage, and besides, it was all academic for she would never marry at all. "I—I am not altogether certain that my opinion on the matter is relevant, though, since I shall always work to support myself," she said.

James was aching to tell her he'd already given serious thought to her desire for a vocation, that it was part of his plan for their future. But a lot of things needed to be said between them before he talked about that. And the look on her face just now when he overstepped himself reminded him of it.

They spent the rest of that day and evening sightseeing, though James could hardly concentrate on what they saw. There must have been a hundred times when he came close to taking Elizabeth in his arms and kissing her. While lounging on the banks of the River Cam, for instance, with the shadow of Trinity Bridge reflected in the water below, her shoulder was no more than an inch from his. It would have been so easy, and natural, just to turn towards her—. But he was always afraid of rushing her, and besides, there were always other people around.

Late that evening when they stood in the moonlight at the Clough Memorial gates, he clasped Elizabeth's hand and said, "I don't have to be back on base till eight o'clock tomorrow night, so that gives us nearly all day tomorrow. Why don't we see if we can wrangle a couple of bicycles, and go on a picnic some-where out in the country?"

Luckily Elizabeth already owned a bicycle, and hiring one for James could be easily done. She knew a place in Devonshire Street. She sensed he'd like to go where there were not so many people about. And this gave her a thrill of anticipation, though it also made her feel terribly vulnerable. What would happen between them when they were alone? Inevitably she thought of Eme-lye, then immediately forced the thought away.

After some consideration, she suggested they go to Ely. She had taken a day trip there last spring, when she came up for her entrance exam. "It's a small vil-lage on the River Ouse, roughly sixteen miles from here," she said. "Ely Cathe-dral is there—and that's about the only thing of note," she went on, though this wasn't entirely true, at least, not for her. It was in the River Ouse, not so far away from there, that Virginia Woolf drowned herself, and her despair over the war largely contributed to her desperate act. She, too, was a pacifist, and her convictions, like her prose, were deep and complex. So then, one of Britain's most brilliant women of letters had become yet another casualty. Elizabeth was burning to tell James all this, but of course she could not. "I can't bicycle that far, but it's only about half an hour by train, and we can take our bicycles on board," she said.

James promised to scare up a picnic lunch.

He seemed reluctant to let go of her hand and for a few moments she thought with dread that he was going to kiss her. She had no idea how to respond to a young man's kiss, the mechanics of the thing, and she feared she was about to appear as foolish as she had done on Friday night with her fussy hairdo.

Yet at length James bid her goodnight and walked away. Relieved, she hur-ried through the porter's lodge to sign the book, then into Clough Hall and up the stairs to her room.

In the night a cold wind blew across the fens, and on Sunday the first taste of winter was in the air. Elizabeth cycled ahead of James in her drindl skirt of black, gray and violet plaid wool, and a warm sweater set. Pretty soon they spotted Ely Cathedral rising dramatically from the countryside, with its famous free-standing lantern surmounting towers and arches and parapets. All around were rolling green meadows with widely-spaced maples and elms, their abundance of amber and red and orange leaves standing out in vivid relief against their slate-colored trunks and the intense green of the grass below. The scene wanted a crayon drawing, Elizabeth thought with relish as she and James wheeled along a dirt path leading away from the river, farther and farther into the shadow of the cathedral. Then the sound of an engine pierced the peaceful air and a lone aircraft appeared on the horizon. Elizabeth glanced back at James. His head was up, his eyes on the alert as it passed over. "Brand new Lancaster," she heard him say, as if to himself. Then their eyes met and he looked as if he was afraid he may have offended her.

She smiled. "Made in Britain," she said, generously.

Presently she pointed off to the left, where there appeared a huge weeping willow tree with a gnarled trunk, and branches like great green feather plumes reaching to the ground. They parked their bicycles, spread their picnic lunch, leaned back against the willow tree and ate with robust appetites: cheese sandwiches on brown bread, plums and oranges, filberts and Brazil nuts, and a bottle of *Chardonnay*. "I think the hotel management took pity on me, since I've slept for two nights on a cot in the hallway," said James. The Bull Hotel was overrun by soldiers on passes.

Best of all, for dessert there were Cadbury chocolate bars—Elizabeth's favorite. "How did you manage? I haven't seen any sign of Cadbury chocolate since the war began."

"I have connections," James said slyly. He ate all but the last bite of his, then insisted she have the rest, for hers was long since devoured. "Oh, but I couldn't possibly deprive you of your chocolate!"

"Are you sure?" he coaxed, bringing it close to her mouth.

She closed her eyes and breathed in the dizzying sweet aroma. "Oh, alright," she laughed, opening her eyes. But when she reached for the stub of chocolate, James's long fingers drew it back. "Open your mouth," said he, which somehow seemed a very intimate suggestion. Reluctantly, she obeyed. He placed it on her tongue and she moaned with delight and let it melt in her mouth, all the while gazing at him wickedly. Elizabeth could hardly believe how she was behaving, how natural it had become to banter with James. It seemed a very long time since the awkwardness of Friday night.

James reached inside the hamper, pulled out a slim volume and held it up. "Remember this?"

Quickly she recognized the book of Spenserian verse that she had given him years ago. She felt pleased that he had saved it, and said so.

His face becoming somber, he said, "It's my good-luck piece. I always take it with me up in the plane. I was afraid you wouldn't like me doing that.

"Just say so, if you don't."

"Oh, James, I want you to have more than your share of good luck while up in an airplane," she said, the risk he was inevitably taking each time he did so having become increasingly real for her in the past thirty-six hours.

He grinned. "I promise to bring it down safely." They looked into each other's eyes for a long moment. "Here, put your head in my lap," he said at last.

Once again disconcerted by the intimacy in his gesture, she obeyed him nonetheless. How lovely it was here, under the willow tree. She gazed up at the drooping willow plumes. All round, they shivered in the breeze, brushing the ground ever-so-lightly, like a lacy veil.

James opened the volume. "This is going to be a test," he said, "to see if you can name the poem when I read it aloud."

She was certain she could do so. "Oh yes? And is there a prize?"

"A Cadbury."

"You have more, hidden away somewhere?" she asked in amazement.

He smiled down at her. "Just don't you worry about that. You may not pass. Then the Cadbury is mine."

"But you might share it."

"Maybe."

"Alright. You may begin."

"Ah! Here's my favorite," he said. He took a deep breath, then he began to read, and though his broad Texas drawl seemed incongruent with the ancient language of the poem, he read with clear understanding, as if he were reading a well-loved story:

"One day I wrote her name upon the strand,
But came the waves and washed it away:
Agayne I wrote it with a second hand,
But came the tyde, and made my paynes his pray."

James paused momentarily. Elizabeth had already recognized this as one of the Amoretti sonnets, which she had committed to memory long ago. Rather than to rise up and announce it, and break the spell, she pressed his arm lightly, closed her eyes, then recited the next few lines, if a bit haltingly:

"'Vayne man,' said she, 'that doest in vaine assay,
A mortall thing so to immortalize,
For I my selve shall lyke to this decay,
And eek my name bee wyped out lykewize...'"

Now Elizabeth remembered these love poems were written for a woman named Elizabeth, who eventually became Spenser's second wife. Such facts were noted in the volume, she was sure. Had James read them? She was speechless. She opened her eyes.

James continued:

"'Not so,' quod I, 'let baser things devize
To dy in dust, but you shall live by fame:"

Now he stopped reading, put the book aside, and, looking down at her, recited:

"My verse your vertues rare shall eternize,
And in the hevens wryte your glorious name."

He paused. "Can you finish with me?"

She knew what it would mean to him if she did. It would be the same as saying that she loved him. Did she love him? Did all that she felt for James amount to romantic love? She had a sense that she was teetering on the edge of some new discovery, and she could either step back, or take a risk and go forward. James's lips parted. He waited. She felt a shy smile working its way round the edge of her lips. She opened her mouth. Their voices rose:

"Where whenas death shall all the world subdew,
Our love shall live, and later life renew."

Their eyes held a moment longer, then James put his arms around Elizabeth and drew her up against him. He put his mouth on hers. It seemed to her that there was more tenderness in that one caress than in all the tender lines of poetry ever written.

CHAPTER 44

After James left that night, Elizabeth fled upstairs to her room, drew the black sateen curtains shut, lit a small bedside lamp, then sank to her knees beside her bed, James's parting words echoing in her mind along with the memory of his soft caresses on her cheeks and chin and eyelids as he spoke them: *"I'm coming back as soon as I can, even if it's just for a few hours."*

Her hands locked together, she earnestly prayed: *"Holy Father, protect James from all harm, wherever he may be, during every single moment of every day and night until the war is over. Return him safely to me. Amen."*

Afterward she remained kneeling with her eyes closed, reliving the moment James drew her near and kissed her for the first time, all her inhibitions melting away in the warm press of his mouth on hers. For a long while they had continued sitting beneath the willow tree, gazing far out over the tranquil meadow, James's arms locked about her shoulders from behind. How natural it seemed to feel his broad chest cradling her back. How amazing to hear him say that he had fallen in love with her at Father and Geneva's wedding, in what was surely the most awkward moment of her entire life! Could lasting love be born at so young an age? Surely not. And yet…conjuring his handsome boy's face, his tilted eyes looking down at her as he offered his hand, she thought, *Yes, oh yes, in a soul so deep and pure, anything was possible.*

When she declared her love for James today through the words of Edmund Spenser, she was speaking with the certainty that his love for her inspired in that moment. Yet, while he had been sure of his feelings for many years, she'd had no time to consider her own. Again, she asked herself if what she felt for James was truly love. Of this she had no doubt: from the moment he kissed her she'd felt a happiness unlike any she had known before, certainly since the auto crash in Dartmoor Forest, and even before that, yes, because happiness was always tempered when her mother was alive. When she rushed into her father's waiting arms at the theatre, or when she sat upon his shoulder high above the sea at Ready Money Cove, these were sacred and beautiful moments of happiness, yet always they were tinged by the dread of her mother's violent outbursts.

Was love untempered happiness, then? And yet—her spirits plunged—there was always the danger that James could be injured or even killed in the war, and this, she knew, would temper her happiness during every waking hour. *Please, God, protect him, for he has a gentle heart, not the heart of a warrior.*

Eager to find the word *love* analyzed by the philosophers she so admired in a way that would resonate in her heart like the pealing of a bell, she searched among her bookshelves. She was soon leafing through the pages of one volume after another, trying to recall who among the world's great thinkers had written the most eloquent essays on the subject of love. At first she passed over the works of Bertrand Russell, not being keen on him since he reversed his position on the war. He had suffered nobly for his pacifism during the Great War, being forced out of his lectureship here at Trinity College, and even being imprisoned for one of his published articles. Yet now, faced with Hitler's aggression, he had changed his views, which suggested they were lodged no deeper in his soul than a shallow-rooted tree was lodged in the ground it occupied.

After a few tries at the essays of Paul Valéry, and even those of Michel Montaigne and William James, she inevitably wound up with Dr. Russell once again, for among the essay collections on her shelves, he spoke more often than the others on the subject of love. As she thumbed through the index of one volume, she happened to glimpse the word *passion*. She had a tingling sensation beneath her ears: with James she had experienced at least the beginnings of passion. For the moment she diverted her search to this topic. Dr. Russell's essay entitled, *Cleopatra or Maggie Tulliver*, began with a provocative question: "What shall we do with our passions?" According to his reasoning, the intensity of a moment's passion was reinforced by thought of future occasions on which we would feel similar desires—a larger universe, if you would, inside which the initial passion existed—and to resist one's passions, one must have either a strong will or weak desires.

Elizabeth paused, recognizing a dilemma: How could she resist her passion for James? Yet if not, would she be diverted from her serious purpose at Cambridge? Or, could they both exist, one inspiring the other? Oh, she did hope so! She imagined them standing together high upon a hilltop, exploring ideas and theories, their words taking wing.

Reading further, she found, "A person who has resisted a great passion and prevented it from venting itself in action may come to regard with hatred all those who do not so resist." Would her failure to recite the closing lines of Spenser's sonnet with James have brought the possibility of romance to an end? Probably so, regardless of James's reaction at the time, for if she could not take a risk at that particularly auspicious moment, then it seemed unlikely she ever would. In which case, she would have gone through life wondering if she'd made a mistake, and then in a need to justify herself, she may have developed intolerance in others. Yes, of course! Oh, this was exactly the kind of transcendence beyond her own experience that she desperately needed, the very reason for her unending fascination with the writings of the great philosophers. Eagerly, she read to the end of the essay.

Unfortunately, Dr. Russell concluded that in order to be ethically good, the exercise of those passions must bring a "universal harmony," which meant that it must bring satisfaction not only to oneself, "but to everyone affected by it, to the extent possible."

She closed the book, her thoughts inevitably turning to Emelye, who would feel not only dissatisfied, but deeply betrayed, by her passion for James. Or, was there an escape in the four words, *to the extent possible*?

Whatever the answer, she had for the moment lost her desire to explore the definition of love, for it seemed inevitable that if one exchanged the word *love* for the word *passion*, one would be led to the same awkward conclusion.

As she lay in bed that night, the persistent drone of the nightingales roosting in the nearby golden maple tree could hardly be blamed for her inability to sleep. Again and again she indulged in reliving the events of the day. Yet there was no escaping the fact that, even if the war came to an end tomorrow, and James was never again in danger, her happiness at being loved by him would always be tempered by knowing she had betrayed her sister.

Shortly after that weekend James was chosen to be among the first pilots to train in the modified P-38 escort fighters that were beginning to arrive on base, with their ranges increased to 450 miles. Along with them came the B-17G bombers, equipped with nose turrets to combat head-on fighter attacks. A month ago in an attack on Stuttgart, Germany, the Eighth Air Force lost 45 bombers, again because the escort fighters hadn't the fuel capacity to go the full distance with them. It was a severe blow. Now, like everyone else, James felt confident these modified planes were just what they needed to turn things around.

Thankfully, as long as he was in training he would not be moved anywhere else. Now that he knew Elizabeth loved him—he had been wise to get around her shyness by using Spenser's words to draw out her feelings—the next step was to propose marriage. Yet, again, he didn't want to rush her unnecessarily. Hopefully they would see a lot of each other between now and Christmas, and he figured that by then he could pop the question. Hopefully she'd say yes. He was pretty sure he could get a pass for the holiday, and if so, they'd go home to Clearharbour together, and announce their engagement to the family. Just imagining it gave him gooseflesh.

Over the next few weeks James was not able to get up to Cambridge except for a few hours on an occasional Saturday or Sunday afternoon. In between visits he and Elizabeth exchanged letters. With his evenings free on base, he was able to try his hand at that drawing they'd talked about. He decided not to mention it to her until it was finished, because it might not turn out.

He soon found it was a far bigger challenge than even he anticipated. Choosing a standard size, roughly equivalent to an 8 X 10, he started by making a dozen studies in graphite. He was lucky to find a set of pastels gathering dust at a shop in Cambridge, but he had not worked with this medium since art class in high school, and his first few attempts were discouraging. The shadows on the grounds looked like pools of muddy water, and the green vines looked like seaweed clinging to the buildings. The building bricks were too orangy; the blue of the sky was too dark. Then there was the problem of the table and chairs failing to suggest the transitory theme, which was crucial. He tried adding a couple of figures, but he was way out of his league there. (He wondered how the Impressionists could put a few dabs of paint on a canvas and make them recognizable as human figures.) He toyed with the idea of a scrap of paper on the table, but clutter implied disrespect. Maybe a scarf, draped over the back of a chair—it might be nice, having a little color to offset the bleached wood. Still, an article left behind may imply nothing more than carelessness or distraction. In the end, he left the table and chairs empty, but turned one chair back at an angle in an effort to make it look inviting.

Finally when he felt the drawing was about as good as it would get—and it wasn't half bad, he thought—he had it mounted in a ready-made wood frame at a shop in Cambridge, with glass to protect the pastels from getting smudged. He picked it up on his way to Newnham College the first Saturday of November, and was relieved to find it still looked as good as he thought. But as he carried it down Sidgwick Avenue, wrapped in brown paper, he was already worried Elizabeth wouldn't like it. He was almost sorry he had told her he was bringing it today.

The sun was shining and the temperature was down in the low forties. In just a few weeks, all the deciduous trees had shed their leaves, and the verdant grass was fading to yellow. They sat out at the table featured in his drawing—a place they had come to think of as their own because they wound up gravitating here every time he came to visit. Elizabeth wore a deep purple sweater that brought out the violet cast in her eyes and drove him crazy to kiss her, but there were too many people criss-crossing the grounds. In the few seconds it took her to unwrap the drawing, James looked around him in despair. His drawing had failed to convey the personality of this place. It was one-dimensional; flat. And how had he overlooked the knobbiness of the tree trunks? Such a significant detail, and it would have been so easy to include! He had heard it said that love could make a fool of a person. He had been a fool to attempt—

"Oh James, I can't believe it!" Elizabeth cried, her face lit up in delight.

"You really like it?" he asked, pride swelling in him as it had the first time he actually got a plane off the ground and up in the air.

She looked across at him. "Well of course I do!" Narrowing her eyes, she took a long, careful survey. She praised the composition, the vivid colors and the variety of detail. At last she held the drawing at arm's length and remarked in a low voice, "It's very provocative."

But how much more provocative it would be, James reasoned, if only he'd added the colorful scarf. He could have kicked himself. Yet when he admitted this to Elizabeth, she declared, "No, it's perfect as it is. The chair, pulled back slightly, is just the right touch." She paused before declaring, "I shall hang it above my writing desk." Then she added with passion, "Oh James, you must promise me that you will never again give up drawing."

He wanted to tell her he'd promise on one condition: that she promised to marry him. Instead he said, "Well, at least as long as you're around to appreciate it," and winked.

Earnestly she said, "But I shan't go anywhere. It's you I worry about. Please don't let anything to happen to you!"

Whereupon James felt invincible.

On Monday he applied for a Christmas pass.

CHAPTER 45

To Elizabeth's delight, her growing passion for James did not divert her from her purpose; rather, it inspired her studies. She was increasingly outspoken in tutorials, and confident in the writing of papers. She wrote on the relativity of morals. She wrote on the question of whether any person or state had a genuine right to claim ownership of real property. She wrote on the question: If the effect can determine the cause, can the cause determine the effect? Vigorously she wrote both sides of an argument of whether evil was inherent in the act of bribery. The process gave her no end of pleasure as she wrote page after page, reference volumes heaped about her.

Sometimes she worked in the Newnham Library with its thunderous walls of books, its long tables and hard chairs, and narrow cat walks providing access to the higher shelves. Sometimes she worked at her writing desk, James's drawing above never failing to inspire, to make her feel he was watching her work, urging her to think creatively. After a while she would lean back and massage her tired neck muscles, glancing at the clock in surprise at the amount of time that had passed. Replacing the cap on her fountain pen, she would leave her desk and take a long walk, or if it was after dark, lay in bed staring at the coal fire, analyzing her words and conclusions carefully. Often, in a fever of enthusiasm, she would return to her desk and make brutal revisions.

Comments on the papers returned to her were most encouraging.

She even began writing a bit of poetry—something she'd always dreamed of doing but never would attempt because she knew her verse would be scorned by the poets she loved and admired. Her fledgling efforts resulted from Miss Welsford's urging her to join the Informal Club, where each member was encouraged to write a poem and present it to the group. Elizabeth owned a leather-bound address book, engraved with her name, which Auntie Nell and Uncle Morey had given her upon her graduation from Harleigh School. She had always felt it was rather too nice for the inevitable marking-through of outdated information, so she put off making entries in it. Now she took the liberty of writing her verse in its leaves, and soon discovered the inevitability of marking-through and changing the lines of her poems. She was never satisfied with them, and would be embarrassed for anyone else to see them. Luckily there were no deadlines imposed upon members of the Informal Club for presenting their work.

Naturally, most of her poems were inspired by thoughts of James, and through composing them she became more and more certain that she loved him. She did not show him her verse, however, for it might leave the impression that she hoped their love for each other would lead to the full physical communion of marriage. Of course it was possible he already understood this could never be. After all, he was aware of the extreme awkwardness she felt until she was satisfied he had not seen her legs that day at Ready Money Cove, and—more to the point—he had not caught a glimpse of her scar. Still, it seemed more likely he would not comprehend that she could love him with all her heart yet be unable to marry him. Oh, if only they could continue just as they were, indefinitely! Perhaps in time he would come to treasure so highly the richness and fruitfulness of their companionship that he would accept her physical limitations. What could be more dear than those sweet kisses followed by long tender looks into each other's eyes whenever they were together? Down through the ages there had been many such relationships between two lovers who were prohibited by circumstances to marry.

As the holidays approached, Elizabeth was looking forward to the long vacation, for she had not been home since she entered university. She intended to spend as much time as possible at Brookhurst, though with petrol rationing curtailed, transportation to and from the estate would present a problem. Perhaps one could hire a pony and cart in St. Tudy. Somehow, she must get there. Grandfather had contracted a severe bronchial infection some weeks ago and was only now beginning to recover. Since suffering the stroke, he was prone to infections of various sorts, which were complicated by his advancing age—he would soon be eighty. He would not live forever.

Then on November 30th she found a letter in her pigeon-hole from James, saying he had been given a three-day pass at Christmas. "I'd like for us to go down to Clearharbour together on Christmas Eve," he wrote.

So he must have assumed her willingness to remain at Clough Hall until he was free to accompany her home. Wasn't this rather presumptuous of him? she wondered defensively, then immediately felt guilty. A flying officer's life was at risk twenty-four hours a day, and this was no doubt why James was jealous of his time with her. Yet apart from the fact she had her reasons for leaving as soon as possible, the college was not equipped for women to occupy their rooms over the long holiday. She must vacate hers no later than the 12th of December and not return until after the first of the year. In addition, as of this morning, she would be free to leave earlier still, for her last two tutorials before the holiday had been canceled owing to a death in the tutor's family. That night she wrote her apologies to James, explaining that she would be leaving for Clearharbour on Tuesday the 7th, and the reason she was anxious to do so. She concluded, "I shall be looking forward ever so much to meeting your train at Bodmin station. Meantime, do please let me know that you've received this. Fondly, Elizabeth."

As of Sunday she had not heard from James. Could it be, her letter had injured his feelings? Oh, surely he was more understanding than that. There had been barely enough time for him to reply. Perhaps a letter would come tomorrow.

By noon the sky was heavy and bleak, pregnant with snow. The weather forecast for the next few days was dire, and Elizabeth feared she might be prevented from leaving after all. She often found herself peering anxiously out the window of her room, surveying the sky.

Around half-past three as she was darning a pair of stockings, Millicent knocked, then opened the door and peeked inside. "Your flying officer's here. He looks a bit down and out, if you ask me," she said, pulling a long face.

Elizabeth rushed downstairs to find James standing in the hall, wearing his bulky military overcoat, his cap in his hand. His cheeks were rubescent from the cold; his eyes were as bleak as the sky, and he looked fatigued, as though he hadn't been sleeping. "Is everything alright?" she asked anxiously.

"Can we go some place and talk?"

"Of course. I won't be a moment," she promised, then hurried upstairs to get her things.

They walked down Sidgwick Avenue under the high archway of bare tree limbs, huddled close together in silence, James's face immobile as a stone. Elizabeth wore a wool cap, gloves, and a heavy muffler wrapped around the high collar of her overcoat. Her nose and ears were aching regardless. It was almost too cold to open one's mouth to speak. Yet she could hardly bear the suspense.

Finally she said, "You've got new orders, haven't you? Your leave has been canceled?"

"No," he said laconically.

She was so relieved, it seemed the warmth of her spirit alone could have raised the temperature.

They stopped at a cozy little tea shop in St. Mary's Passage, and were shown to a window booth—the only one available, as the shop was quite busy. James hung their coats and hats upon a peg. In the background, barely audible above the clatter of plates and flatware, and the buzz of conversation, Elizabeth could hear Mozart's Piano Concerto No. 23 in A, *Adagio*. She had learnt to play the piece while studying with Mrs. Hearn. In spite of the fact that she found the music beautiful and haunting, she played it badly. Father, always one to encourage her enjoyment of fine music, gave her a recording by the London Symphony at Christmas that year. Perhaps he also hoped this would discourage her from desecrating the piece on the piano in the sitting room.

James leaned across the table and said, rather desperately, "Look, I can't keep going on like this—"

Elizabeth looked down at her hands. His impatience was precisely what she most feared. She was not prepared for this declaration, had hoped it would not come for some time yet, if at all. He added, "There's a good chance I won't be here very long, once my training's over."

She looked up, the fear they might never again see each other closing over her heart. "Where will you go?"

He shook his head. "I have no idea."

"Nothing can truly separate us, James, no matter how far apart we are," she said helplessly.

The waitress brought their tea and filled their cups. James sat back until she was gone and the tea cups sent clouds of steam rising between them. Leaning near again, he persisted, "That isn't good enough. I'm crazy about you, Elizabeth. You're all I ever think about."

Oh, what compelling words! They beckoned her as a light glowing in a door glass on a dark night. Yet she must put them in a context that she could manage, and pray he would accept it. "I feel the same about you, James. When I came here, I was content to believe that I should spend my life alone. But now I want to share everything with you. I often fancy us standing high on a hilltop, conversing for hours, inspiring each other—"

"Elizabeth, come down to earth!" he moaned. "I want you to love me with your whole body, not just your mind and your heart."

The image of the sickly purplish scar flashed down the center of her mind, forming a ragged dividing line between what she desired and what she must live with. She looked away, her heart thumping madly. "I don't believe that sort of life is—that is—that I am meant to have that sort of...intimate...relationship, James. You see—"

His voice low, he interrupted, "Do you like it when we kiss?"

Why must he pin her to the wall? When she looked at him again, her cheeks were burning. "Of course I do, you know that I do."

"I want to kiss you from the top of your head, all the way down to your toes. I want to kiss that scar—"

Instinctively, her leg drew up beneath the table in defense, and she felt as if she would faint. "No, no, you mustn't!" she cried, with such vehemence that people at nearby tables turned to stare, no doubt expecting a very entertaining scene to commence.

James realized the effect this was having on her. And there was no need. He took a risk. "I've seen your scar, Elizabeth. And it doesn't matter."

She was so shocked that her eyes blurred. She saw herself at Ready Money Cove, innocently wading out in the sea, her skirt hitched over her arm. Saw herself turning at the sound of his voice. "You lied to me!" she cried.

He sat back. "It didn't seem like the right moment to tell you that night when you asked. I'm sorry."

She was at the point of telling him that there was no excuse for lying. Then she remembered the many years that she had continued to hide the truth of her betrayal in Dartmoor Forest. She made a fist and buried her chin in it, looking down, her emotions caught up in a storm.

"Elizabeth, there isn't an inch of your body that I am not in love with. Look at me!"

Slowly she obeyed him.

"Haven't you figured it out? I want to *marry* you," he said.

Again, he had preempted her. How paltry all her rationalizing seemed in the powerful force of James's masculinity, his large chest and broad shoulders inches away, his eyes riveted on hers.

"Before you come back to Cambridge in January," he quickly added, thinking of the sorties into Germany. Though he didn't dare allow himself to dwell on it too much, he'd had a bad feeling about that since he first stepped into a modified P-38. "If I have another month before losing my life, or if I live another fifty or sixty years, I want to be with you."

Tears stung Elizabeth's eyes. "Oh James, that's the dearest thing anyone ever said to me. And I want to be with you as well. But in all fairness—even if I were—" she paused, bit her lower lip, for she had never uttered the words before—"*perfect*, physically—I am not the sort who would make one a good wife."

"Just listen. I want you to go right on with your studies, wherever we are. Teach, write, lecture—whatever you want. I wouldn't have you waste your gifts, not for anything. I'm not asking you to cook my meals and keep my house," he said. "And if you think children would interfere with your career, and would rather not have any—" he added tentatively, searching her eyes. Elizabeth was shaking her head, for the idea was terrifying. James was crushed; the tender memory of washing the dogs with Andy and Elvira and Chris flooded his mind. He only said, "—Maybe motherhood would be right for you someday, I don't know, but I would never insist. I promise."

Elizabeth was astonished at his unselfishness; she knew she was dreadfully unworthy of him.

He went on, "When you go home, will you think about this till I get there?"

She nodded in some confusion, knowing that she would hardly wait until she went home to begin thinking about it.

"I know it's all new for you, but I believe, as much as I have ever believed anything, that we were meant for each other," he said. Finally a smile broke on his face. "And not just talking."

Elizabeth blushed. James leaned back and glanced at his watch, grimacing. "I gotta go. I'll write you at Clearharbour." He looked both ways, then put his hands around her face and kissed her with such yearning that she was breathless. "*I've seen your scar…and it doesn't matter.*"

She wrapped her hands around his. "Be well, and keep safe, James. I do love you so awfully much!"

It was the first time she'd said she loved him in her own words. It was all he needed to hear. She was going to marry him; he knew it for certain now. He rose, and tossed some coins on the table. He reached into his breast pocket and pulled out a folded slip of paper, gave her a tentative look, then handed it to her. She noticed his fingers were trembling. She would not take her eyes off him to look at what was written on the paper. He removed his hat and overcoat from the nearby peg. Then without looking at her again, he made his way amongst the tables and through the door. The small bell tinkled above as if it wished him to be safe and well as much as she did.

Elizabeth rubbed a clear place through the frost on the window glass and watched James's retreating figure until it seemed the bleak sky had swallowed him up. She unfolded the paper and found a brief, untitled verse:

"*For Elizabeth—*
I can do the work of dull men,
Who draw their lines straight and
make their numbers match;
As long as I can look out and see the
Bright, Shining, Glory of you,
who defy all shape and exactitude."
James Younger, November, 1943

Was this the real meaning of love, then? A willingness to give up everything for the sake of another? A sudden, inexplicable feeling of sadness welled up in her.

When she looked up from James's verse, she became aware once again of the music of Mozart, wending its way softly through the air. She took a sip of tea. It had only just cooled off enough to drink. She looked across at James's cup, still full to the brim. And he'd gone back out in the cold, without his tea to warm him. Again she was gripped by sadness.

How amazing that in a few short minutes, one's whole perspective, perhaps one's whole future, could be altered. She felt as if she were an entirely different person from the one who walked into the tea room, and she was not at all sure who this new person was. She glanced out the window. The snow had begun to fall.

CHAPTER 46

While Geneva toiled away contentedly in the Clearharbour kitchen, Elizabeth sat at the table with a steaming cup of cocoa before her, Bertrand curled up in her lap. Since arriving for the holiday, she had often gravitated to the kitchen, for it was the coziest room in the house. Over the last few weeks of Michaelmas term, she seemed always to be freezing in her room at Clough Hall, her fingers like icicles round her pen as she worked. Like other residents, she had developed the knack of changing from her sleeping gown into her street clothes while under the shelter of the bedclothes—though the gyp came early each morning to lay her small fire, she delayed lighting it until retiring for the night, for once it had burnt down there would be no relighting it till the following day. Still, her reasons for sitting here with Geneva this afternoon were even more urgent than staying warm: she must seek her advice about the means of avoiding children. She had considered approaching Grandmother on this matter—her views had always seemed rather more progressive than Geneva's—yet since she arrived ten days ago, Brookhurst had lain under a thick mantle of snow, prohibiting a visit to the estate for any reason. Even ringing up to check on Grandfather had proved unsatisfactory, as the lines sputtered annoyingly, if they worked at all. Unless the weather improved dramatically by Christmas Day, how the family would gather at Brookhurst was a riddle to which only Grandmother knew the answer. "Just take the train to St. Tudy, and leave the rest to me," she had assured Geneva mysteriously.

Geneva's annual holiday baking was well under way this afternoon, with certain war-time concessions. Apart from a basket of brown eggs—happily, fresh eggs from the neighboring farms were always in supply—the counters were lined with containers of cocoa powder, syrup, corn starch, flour, almonds and hazelnuts, and a tin of pecans that had journeyed all the way from Willa's tree in Houston. Two mince pies with golden brown crusts stood cooling on a rack in the windowsill—Auntie Nell had taught Geneva how to put up her own mincemeat—and a bowl of yeast dough sat rising atop the ice box. Clove and cinnamon and ginger spiced the heated air rising from the oven. Geneva's ability to coordinate numerous baking projects at once quite amazed Elizabeth, who had avoided learning to cook by perennially volunteering to do the washing up.

Geneva was aging rather handsomely, Elizabeth observed, perhaps because she possessed everything she had ever wanted in life: a happy home with a loving husband and children. Her springy waves were swept back from her face and tied with a ribbon. Her complexion was youthful and radiant; her figure, clad in a pair of dark slacks and a white jersey top, was well-toned for a woman her age.

Of course, Elizabeth could not seek Geneva's advice about avoiding children unless she announced that James had proposed marriage, and she had put off making this announcement for one reason only: given Geneva's strong ties with James's family, established long before she and Emelye moved to England, it seemed reasonable that she expected Emelye and James eventually to marry, and therefore may resent what Elizabeth was about to confess. "I say, Geneva, I wonder if you'll mind terribly, but James has asked me to marry him," she began.

Geneva was just reaching up to check the dough rising on top of the ice box when Elizabeth's words plunged through her concentration and scattered the many details she was struggling to keep straight. She could never say no when she was asked to volunteer for holiday baking—her garden club open house, a reception at the vicarage school parties for her children, Elvira's choral club, plus several trays of cookies to be handed out at the command supply depot next door. Not to mention the family celebration at Brookhurst. Mrs. Greaves could always be counted on to help, but this year she had caught a very bad cold and only got as far as the Christmas pudding now in the pantry, and which—she only just remembered—was due for a spoonful of brandy.

Geneva turned to Elizabeth with a distracted frown.

"Is it so shocking?" she asked defensively.

Geneva sat down across from Elizabeth, expelled a fatigued breath, and smiled. "Why no, Dear, it's just a bit sudden, that's all."

Elizabeth lowered her eyes. "Yes, I know."

"I have noticed James seems to be fond of you," Geneva said helpfully. "I've often wondered how you felt about him."

"I love him dearly," she said with feeling, looking up again. "I haven't given him my answer, though. There are many things to consider. Emelye's feelings, for instance." *"Dear Elizabeth, I understand James asked you to show him around Cambridge one weekend. What a relief, he hasn't found a girlfriend in England to take up his spare time!"* Elizabeth paused, to give Geneva an opening. Geneva made no remark, so she continued, "Since we were children she has confided in me her dream of marrying James one day. She may never forgive me for betraying her. Oh, how I dread telling her!"

Geneva kept up with Emelye's behavior towards James through Willa's letters, and it had become a real sore spot. It now seemed evident that her main reason for moving back to the States had been a foolish obsession with James. And Geneva was downright ashamed of her daughter for the way she jilted that nice young man Larry Cateau—leaving him stranded at the last minute for the senior prom, because she found out James was coming home on leave. Larry had already ordered her flowers for the evening, and arranged to borrow the boss's fancy car.

Geneva was quick to correct Elizabeth: "James is not in love with Emelye, and never has given her any reason to believe he is, so don't think for a minute you've betrayed her." Her tone softening, she went on, "She may be angry at first, but one day she'll realize it's for the best. There could be nothing worse for any woman than to be married to a man who doesn't love her," she said.

Elizabeth's heart stopped. *"It drove me positively mad that your father didn't love me." The white-gloved hands on the steering wheel; the bright red lips parted....* "Yes, I suppose so," she said quietly, searching Geneva's face for a sign of awareness that her remark hit home in more than one way. There was none.

"Would you like for me to break the news to Emelye?" she asked now.

"Oh, no, if I'm to marry James, then I must tell her. Otherwise, she will consider me a coward, along with everything else." The clock in the hall struck three, reminding her that time was short. The children would soon be home from their last day of school, bursting through the door in high spirits. She took in a breath. "It isn't only Emelye that I'm worried about," she said. Then, feeling it necessary to qualify James's physical attraction to her, she said, "James is not put off by my...disability. My—" she shrugged.

This hardly surprised Geneva. James wasn't the type to worry about superficial things. Yet now she thought of Elizabeth's fetish about concealing her scar, and she was troubled. She was not sure how to state her fears delicately, but she knew that guiding Elizabeth in this one area may well be the most important thing she would ever do as her mother. "I hope you don't mean to conceal that scar from James, after you're married?"

It's much too late for that, thought Elizabeth. "Oh no," she said, though she dreaded having that part of herself exposed to James time and again, and doubted that she would ever grow accustomed to being kissed there. Often she had lain awake nights, wondering if he intended to kiss her only once there, or repeatedly throughout their married lives. "What I really mean is that James and I are quite attracted to each other—*physically.* And yet...well...the truth is, I'm afraid I shan't want any children."

Geneva paused to consider this. Though Elizabeth was kind and loving toward her younger siblings, and truly a godsend during the times when she needed her help, she did not appear to have a strong maternal instinct. However, from all evidence, James would be a natural as a father. "What about James?"

"He does want children, I think, but he's willing to forego them, at least until I'm ready. Perhaps one day I shall be; perhaps not. But the thing is, in the meantime, how can one be certain to avoid pregnancy? Of course, I know there are devices. But I have no idea which ones are reliable."

Geneva knitted her brow. "None of them, unfortunately,"she said. "The only sure way is to abstain at certain times of the month. But as long as your menstrual periods are pretty regular—that is, I assume they still are?"

"Reasonably so, I should think," Elizabeth said.

"That's good—then it will be easy to keep track," Geneva said.

"It doesn't sound too complicated," Elizabeth told her.

"Well, not in theory, but it isn't easy for two people in love to use the necessary restraint when they're together," she cautioned. "With your father away so much, in my childbearing years it was hard for us—" she began, then, noticing the color flaring in Elizabeth's cheeks, she fell silent. After a moment she said simply, "You might want to check the calendar before you choose a wedding date."

Yet their wedding date was practically locked in! Suddenly resenting the war for forcing people to rush when making the most vital of life's decisions, she stressed, "Remember, I've only promised to consider marrying James." Then she admitted, "Though if I accept, he wants to be married before I return to Cambridge for Lent term."

Geneva's eyes widened. "My goodness, that is soon. Your grandmother and Auntie Nell and I need to put our heads together, to organize a nice reception."

Why must you keep presuming my answer will be 'yes'? Elizabeth thought, annoyed. Until this moment, she had given no real consideration to the wedding celebration itself, and now she felt not only rushed, but overwhelmed.

When Tony came home late in the evening on the 22nd, it was the first time he had seen his family for nearly three months. The Germans had begun menacing England with their new far-ranging V-1 weapons, launched from strategic locations in France. These bombs struck without warning, and therefore were far more deadly than their predecessors. The Allies were frantically trying to identify the launching sites so that they could combat the missiles before they reached their destinations. Naturally, it was far too dangerous for Geneva to visit him in London these days, and between running the theatre and dealing with the increasing demands of the SOE, he had been unable to leave. Since he spoke French with reasonable fluency, he was now being called on quite a lot as a liaison for the French Resistance. The SOE had installed a special telephone line to Paris in his basement at Norfolk Square. He felt as if his home had been appropriated by the government.

Therefore, he was particularly glad to be at Clearharbour for this holiday, and he was anxious to be alone with Geneva—God, how he had missed her! Who would have guessed when first they met, that their lives were destined to be plagued by endless separations down the years? Yet, Elizabeth greeted him at the door with her big news, and so he asked her to remain downstairs in the sitting room for a fireside chat, after everyone else had gone up to bed.

Tony was not surprised that James and Elizabeth were in love. Last year, when the crisis of his father's stroke had hastened the family to Brookhurst, James along with them, Tony noticed that James seemed fascinated by his daughter. Just a few months ago, when she wrote from Cambridge that he was to visit her, it seemed likely that the lad was about to make a move—it certainly took him long enough! Tony knew he could not ask for a better husband for Elizabeth. Yet, he wished they would wait until after the war to make a decision. The poignant farewells and reunions of war-time romance led many a young man and woman to the altar before they were really sure about what they were doing. And with Elizabeth and James, there was an additional problem. As they stood together before the sitting room fire, he said, "I'm sure James will return to Houston, after the war. Are you willing to move there? I seem to remember you weren't particularly keen on it."

"The heat and humidity were taxing," she admitted. "But I must learn to endure it, I suppose; after all, James is offering to give up a great deal for me."

"Such as?" Tony inquired.

"A wife who will be a homemaker…" she began. A little embarrassed at the intimacy associated with the topic, she hesitated before adding, "and…and bear his children."

To Elizabeth's surprise, her father's countenance darkened. Somehow she hadn't thought this would matter to him in particular. "May I ask why you don't wish to have children?" he asked rather brusquely.

"I don't know exactly. I just don't seem to feel the desire, and besides, I'm not at all sure that I would make a decent mother."

Elizabeth was disturbed to see a most queer, haunted expression come into her father's eyes. "I hope you don't think that you'll be anything like your mother Jane," he said. "I can assure you, you have not inherited her—" his voice dropped—"her nature; not at all. There is no reason whatever for you to fear that you'll be like her."

It wasn't exactly what Elizabeth meant. And her father's reassurance perhaps would bear out her mother's claim that not being loved had changed her for the worse, kept her emotions tied in knots. "How can you be sure, when you don't know what made my mother the way that she was?" Elizabeth asked. "It's what you told me in Paris, long ago, remember?" To her chagrin, her heart was pounding violently. The fact she was merely reminding Father of his own words made it no easier to broach this subject with him. She felt she was entering a mine field.

"Yes of course I remember," Tony said abruptly. He turned from her and gazed into the fire. "It doesn't matter. The point is, you are nothing like her," he said with the inevitable finality in his voice.

Elizabeth was just at the point of saying boldly, *"She told me before she died that you had never loved her, that you only used her, for her money."* Then she considered her father's graying temples and the tired lines of his face, made more apparent by the shadows of the firelight playing upon them. And there was his cane, looped over the chair arm. Even if he needed the cane only on occasion, and was quite fit—as he claimed—he had endured much hardship over the past few years. Elizabeth had not the heart to bring the words forth now. Besides—and though this was not her first consideration, it followed soon enough, bringing its ever-ready companion of guilt—she was not prepared to deal with Father's questions bound to follow.

She quickly excused herself and went up to bed, then lay in the darkness mulling over his heated protest that she had not inherited her mother's nature. Almost as if he had been watching her for all her life, for fear she may have done. Was there some terribly virulent trait in the Tremont family line, apt to rear its head unexpectedly in succeeding generations?

Elizabeth was now more determined than ever not to have children.

CHAPTER 47

When James telephoned on Christmas Eve at four o'clock, Elizabeth expected him to report he was en route, calling from Exeter to say approximately what time she should meet his train. To her surprise, he had not even left Bassingbourn. "I'm running late," he said, his voice a bit strained. "It may be after midnight when I get to Bodmin, so I'll just see you at Clearharbour."

Elizabeth was relieved to be spared walking to the station, for it was cold and drizzly outside, and slushy underfoot due to the melting snow. She warned James that the jingle may not be running at that late hour. The jingle was Bodmin's solution to the absence of petrol: a horse-drawn open cart with sufficient bench space to carry four passengers, plus a limited number of suitcases, to and from the station. A rug was furnished to cover one's legs in the cold. "If not, I trust your torch has reliable batteries," she said.

"Brand new," he said, after which they fell into an uneasy silence. *He wants me to say, 'I'll marry you'* Elizabeth thought nervously. Yet she was still struggling with her answer. More and more she felt burdened by the words of the poem which he'd pressed into her hand just before hurrying from the tea shop on that frigid afternoon when he proposed. Was it fair to allow James to devote his life to ensuring her happiness? Yet, on the other hand, had she any right to make the choice for him? It seemed to her that it would be more sensible for them to talk things out carefully over the holiday, then come to an agreement, than for her to say simply, 'I shall,' or, 'I shan't.'

At length, James asked rather timidly, "Could you leave the door unlocked for me?"

His obviousness brought a smile to her face. "Of course, but never mind; I shall be waiting up for you no matter how late it is."

James could have left the base by noon, but instead he had lain on his cot in trousers and undershirt, thinking. Things were going fine until he learned Elizabeth would be going home early for the holidays. Nearly three weeks, lost! Still, he should not have panicked, and put her on the spot about marrying him. What if she refused him when he got to Bodmin?

There was a clerk in the base commander's office who did calligraphy for two pence a line. She had a pretty good business, printing cards for airmen to send home to their sweethearts. James had found a good thick piece of ivory parchment paper, and paid her to copy the Amoretti sonnet on it. She charged him extra because of the archaic spelling, but when he saw the finished product he knew it would have been worth twice what he paid. Inspired by the romance of the poem, she had added extra flourishes in green and gold to the bold black letters at the beginning of each verse. Before having it framed, James drew a small green willow tree in the bottom right-hand corner. Beneath it, he intended to write, "To *my* Elizabeth. With all my love, James. Christmas, 1943." But in turning it over in his mind, he decided to delete the qualifying word, *my.* He didn't like recalling the coincidence that Spenser's second wife was named Elizabeth. Elizabeth Selby would be his first and only wife. As he lay on the cot, he picked up the sonnet and read it to himself very softly, slowly, remembering his elation when Elizabeth recited the last few lines of the verse with him that day of their picnic, and how they sealed it with their first kiss. If she refused to marry him, he'd feel like the biggest fool in the world. And he would have no one but himself to blame.

When he finally got up the courage to call her at Clearharbour, he couldn't bring himself to say, "*Well, have you decided?*" He hoped that she would volunteer her answer. Then he could tell her that he had requested a pass for them to get married, on January 7th. He was disconcerted that he still didn't have her answer when they said goodbye and he hung up the receiver, but he told himself that if it was 'no,' she surely would have said so, or at least have sounded upset. He reflected on her tone of voice when she promised, "*I shall be waiting up for you....*" Pretty upbeat, he thought. Maybe she wanted to wait and say 'yes' in person. But on the other hand, could it be, she was still undecided? Well, if so, maybe just seeing him again would persuade her. If not, he'd have three days to do it. Unless he got called back early. He put on his shirt and tie and jacket, then stuffed the framed sonnet inside his duffel bag.

Long after everyone else had gone to sleep that night, Elizabeth lay in bed reading, or—more to the point—staring blankly at the words of William James, all the while thinking of her James. When she heard the dogs barking downstairs, her heart began to beat so hard and fast that she could scarcely recover her breath. *Do let's take our time and talk about all this....* She rushed from her room and down the dimly-lit stairway, pausing a few steps from the bottom to watch James emerge from the pitch-black conservatory. He was distracted by the barking dogs, petting their furry heads and speaking their names reassuringly, trying to shush them before they awoke the entire household. He did not see her standing there.

There was only one thought in Elizabeth's mind: *Thank God, he is here!* All she wanted was to be enveloped in James's arms, to feel the warmth of his body pressing against hers. She found herself imagining all the tomorrows when he would come through the door of the home they shared. Then she tried to imagine the absence of all those tomorrows. She knew then that without James, life would be unbearable. This was all that really mattered.

When he looked up and saw her on the stairs, their eyes met and held. Love for James flooded her entire being. She spoke not a word, but headed straight into his arms. He caught her up in a smothering hug, lifting her from the floor. Eagerly they kissed and hugged, and kissed again. Finally James held her away and searched her face. "How about getting married on January 7th?"

"Do, let's!" she cried.

CHAPTER 48

When Tony and his party boarded the train in Bodmin on Christmas morning, light snow was falling and the sky was milk-colored and opaque, presaging still more snow. Though all seats were soon taken and many passengers were left standing in the aisle, the volume of bodies clothed in wool did little to raise the frigid temperature inside the train carriage. The farther they traveled out into the countryside, the thicker the snow lay on the ground.

In less than an hour they pulled in at the tiny St. Tudy station, which, like all train stations throughout England, had its sign removed, making it appear anonymous. Tony thought with regret how the war-time absence of signs at train halts—particularly at small villages like St. Tudy—robbed the country of a unique part of its personality.

Upon lugging bundles of presents and baked goods and suitcases outside, they were met by a most romantic surprise. His mother had dispatched an ancient sleigh, with two roomy compartments, which had been gathering dust in the Brookhurst stable for over a quarter of a century. A matched pair of mottled gray horses with red ribbons and bells on their bridles stood ready, snorting loudly and tamping the frozen ground with their hooves.

Tony noticed that Merton looked none too pleased to have been appointed the driver. He wore an enormous greatcoat, probably dating from before the sleigh, and a wool hat with ear flaps. A plaid muffler was wrapped round his neck, peaking at the tip of his nose. To Tony he complained, "I says to Lady Cynthia, 'with all doo respect, Madam, not since the first war 'ave I driven one of these con-TRAP-tions. When the au-TO-mobile came on the scene, I 'oped those days was over and doan with.'"

Tony was beside himself with delight. As children, he and Nell had often ridden through the snowy countryside in this sleigh. He told Merton he hadn't realized it was still in existence, let alone in good enough shape to be put into service. "It weren't," Merton grumbled.

"Well, Happy Christmas, Merton!" Geneva said with enthusiasm.

"Yes, and a jolly good sport you are!" said Tony, laughing.

Soon they were all aboard the sleigh with heavy rugs warming their laps, gliding slowly away from the station. Up front, Chris and Andy sat on each side, with Tony and Geneva snuggling like young lovers between them. In back, Elizabeth and James happily shared a thick rug, holding hands underneath, their faces feeling bruised with cold. Elvira sat to the right of Elizabeth, fortunately too mesmerized by the vast white wonderland surrounding them to demand everyone's attention.

Elizabeth turned to gaze with longing at the retreating scene of snow-covered rooftops, with the tall steeple of the St. Tudy village church rising above. The peaceful, slumberous countryside seemed inviolable, as if it were in a world apart from the torn and aggrieved planet on which they lived. One could almost believe that the sleigh was carrying them deeper and deeper into its safe, snowy bosom, where they would be enfolded forever. She wished it could be so.

"I feel like we're riding across a Christmas card," James said pensively. Elizabeth smiled at him, struck yet again with delight at how closely their spirits were attuned. "I love you," she said. He answered her with a kiss, and a frozen nose rubbing which made her giggle.

After a while, Tony was inspired to lead them in Christmas carols. One after another, they sang the familiar hymns, their warm breaths forming clouds on the frozen air. Even through the dense weight of the air, Elvira's voice carried amazingly well, though it was by no means melodic. A member of Sidney Hearn's choristers, nonetheless, she knew by heart all the verses of every carol, having learned them for the recent Christmas concert in the Bodmin Public Rooms. If Tony chanced to begin any verse out of sequence, she was quick to rise to her feet, and insist that the mistake be corrected at once.

They were still singing when they entered the Brookhurst gates and saw the house nestling in the distance, smoke curling from the chimneys. Elizabeth grew morose. All her life, Brookhurst had been her center of gravity: the one constant in a series of upheavals. Now, standing in sharp relief above the snow, with snow lodged in the bare limbs of the great trees surrounding it, and caked on its granite window sills and in all the dormers and angles of the roof, it had never seemed more a safe refuge from life's vicissitudes. How could she bear to live thousands of miles away? she wondered, her eyes stinging. And—she realized all at once—depending upon the length of the war, this may well be her last Christmas here, for many years to come. It was a pity Auntie Nell and Uncle Morey and Guy would not be here. With Guy away at the war, Auntie Nell found holidays difficult. The happy memories associated with Brookhurst seemed to close in on her, she admitted. This year, she and Uncle Morey accepted an invitation to spend Christmas with his elder sister Margaret and her husband, in St. Agnes. Margaret was rather bossy, which quite annoyed Uncle Morey, so the two couples did not often get together. Auntie Nell told Geneva, "It will be a bit of a strain, I'm afraid; still, it's better than being in the doldrums and bringing the whole Selby family with me."

For now, Elizabeth wished to pause and absorb this image of Brookhurst so deeply into her consciousness that it would never be lost. Suddenly it occurred to her that James must draw a picture of Brookhurst in the snow. Only he must be sure to show all the front windows not dark as they were now, but brightly lit, so that the privations of the war would not be in evidence to spoil it.

She had no time to suggest it to him, for all too soon, the horses were drawing the sleigh round the circular drive. Though just how Merton discerned it in the broad white field stretching to the house, Elizabeth could not guess. From inside the house came the spirited yelping of the dogs—always a thrill to her heart. No sooner had Merton pulled on the reins and the horses shuffled to a halt, than Andy and Chris were begging to be helped out of the sleigh. James sprang down and helped each of them to the ground. At age eleven, Elvira was all gangling arms and legs. As she leapt from the sleigh—she needed no help from anyone, thank you very much—she managed to plant the heel of her boot in the middle of Elizabeth's foot.

Elizabeth moaned in pain, and Geneva and Father and James all glanced around in concern. Elvira was already clomping towards the house, leaving footprints in the snow, oblivious to what she'd done.

"It's alright," Elizabeth assured them through clenched teeth, trying to massage away the pain radiating through her foot. James held out his arms for her, smiling. She opened her arms and leaned down to him. Just then, in her mind's eye, James was reaching up to pull her down into bed. Her heart began to pound violently, and her mouth went dry. "...there isn't an inch of your body that I'm not in love with...." One would soon be putting words of romance into action, with nothing held back. It was both exciting and terrifying.

Inside, despite all the confusion of Abraham and Sarah circling and bark-ing, and everyone hastening to praise Grandmother for the ingenuity of the sleigh ride, Elizabeth noticed immediately the vast change in her grandfather. He had lost at least a stone of weight, perhaps more—it was hard to judge on a man of his size. His complexion was unnaturally pale, and more transparent than Elizabeth remembered, with tiny blue veins more visible, and the skin looser round his mouth and chin. "It's only that I haven't been able to spend any time outdoors lately," he assured Elizabeth in a husky voice. "And, well, liv-ing on beef broth and dry toast will take the weight off. Haven't had much of an appetite.

"But I'm much better now," he added cheerfully. Looking into her eyes, he held her face in his dry, satiny fingers. "And so very glad you're here, for I have missed you!"

"Oh, I've missed you too, ever so much!" Elizabeth cried. How could she bear to live thousands of miles from Grandfather?

Cynthia had been closely observing the look on James's face as he watched Elizabeth talking to her grandfather. It was a rather proprietary look, she noted, and a tingle of recognition went up her spine. "Alright, what's going on, you two?" she demanded now, looking from one to the other.

Elizabeth glanced at James. "I hope you won't mind, but there's no keeping a secret from Grandmother."

James grinned and took her hand. "We're gonna be married, on January 7th" he said proudly, his broad Texas drawl seeming more pronounced than ever inside these walls that were so very, very English.

"I knew it!" Cynthia cried, and gave each a congratulatory hug.

Edward was unprepared for the news, and felt at somewhat of a loss. "Oh dear, then will you be taking my granddaughter off to Texas?" he asked James.

"Yessir," said James firmly, though the old man's look of bewilderment made his heart skip a beat.

"But not until after the war," Elizabeth added consolingly. For the very first time, she had a guilty wish that the war would not be over very soon.

"We hope you and Lady Cynthia will come and visit us in the States," said James.

Before either could reply, Elvira turned up her impish face to James, "May I come, too?"

Elizabeth raised an eyebrow. "Yes, but pray do leave your boots at home!"

A frown of puzzlement so thoroughly engulfed Elvira's face that you could have seen it for a mile, and certainly from the back row of a theatre, Tony

observed. Every time there was any change in Elvira's emotional temperature—which was often—it was just that obvious in her face. He could hardly
wait until she could come to London and begin studying drama.

"But why?" she demanded of Elizabeth now. "I should think you would
never be without your boots, in Texas. Everyone wears them there."

Everyone laughed, which pleased Elvira supremely. "Oh never mind," said
Elizabeth, giving her sister a swift hug. Indeed, she was thankful for the diversion which saved Grandfather from responding to James's invitation. Though
he didn't realize, Grandfather was far too old and frail to make a long journey
overseas.

Andy and Elvira sped to the library to arrange the gifts they'd brought
among the others already beneath the tree, and chiefly to read each tag to see
where their names appeared following the word, "To:" During the war, gifts
were seldom all that one hoped for, and there were fewer of them. Still, the
anticipation always ran high. Chris remained with the adults, standing off to
himself, absorbing not only the remarks being made about Elizabeth and
James, but their general significance. Chris believed that grown-ups always
told the truth and did exactly what they said they would do.

Cynthia rang for Merton to bring a bottle of champagne from the cellar, to
toast the betrothed couple. Poor Merton, thought Elizabeth, he ought to be
warming his feet by the kitchen fire. Yet there were only a handful of servants
at Brookhurst these days.

In the meantime, everyone went in to light the tree and open gifts.

James and Elizabeth had already exchanged their gifts, following his arrival.
Feeling pleased with what she'd chosen, she insisted he open his first. In a small
shop in Silver Street, she'd found a framed quote from Aristotle: "The aim of
art is to represent not the outward appearance of things, but their inward significance." She enclosed a card on which, after many, many unsatisfactory
attempts, she had finally composed this message: "For James—May your
inward beauty continue shining through your art, forever. All my love—"

When she unwrapped the splendid copy of Spenser's sonnet with James's
tiny willow tree at the bottom, she was not only moved by his thoughtfulness
but humbled by his creative imagination. Her gift now seemed paltry by comparison, in spite of his obvious pleasure in receiving it.

Throughout the war, the Youngers and Selbys had upheld their tradition of
exchanging Christmas gifts, although since the United States entered the war
two years ago, and rationing of goods was established soon after, the Youngers
could no longer include packets of coffee and sugar and tea. All the gifts were

designated, "from the Youngers and Emelye." Therefore, James was surprised to be handed a separate cardboard box from Emelye, which had been mailed to him at Brookhurst, postmarked Avenger Field, Sweetwater, Texas.

Just before cutting the string with his pocket knife, he looked uncertainly at Elizabeth. She nodded and smiled. Last night in the wee hours, she had admitted to James that she felt she had betrayed her sister. James's reaction was very much like Geneva's. He swore he had never encouraged her; quite the opposite. "Let me write to Emelye for you," he offered. Yet that would seem even more cowardly than allowing Geneva to write to her. Elizabeth declined his offer.

Inside the box, wrapped in tissue paper, was a long, bright red knitted scarf. As James removed it from the box and unfolded it, all eyes were drawn to the article. A card fell to the floor. "I'll get it," Elizabeth offered, then picked it up and held it for him as he examined the scarf. At a glance she could see there was quite a lengthy message on the card, and inevitably her eyes swept down to the ending: "With all my love—" She quickly looked away, her cheeks burning with guilt for having read what was not intended for her eyes. Was she condemned to spend the rest of her life feeling guilty?

On each narrow end of the scarf, woven into the wool, was the Eighth Air Force insignia: against a circular background of royal blue, a golden eight with upraised wings; inside the bottom portion of the eight, the star with white points, and red center. To Elizabeth, the quality of the stitches seemed flawless. She assumed the scarf had been made by a professional.

James's eyes lingered on the scarf, as if he were mesmerized by it. From around the room, came exclamations: "How exquisite!" "Who is it from?" "Pass it around so we can see it!" "Was that in the box from Emelye?"

James looked up. "Yes, it's from Emelye," he said, his tone bordering on reverence.

"Well, I wonder where she got it?" asked Cynthia. "We might have something like that done up for Guy."

"See if this will explain," said Elizabeth, handing the note to James. He scanned it. Then, after a glance at her, he said in a tight voice, "Alright, here it is: 'Dear James, when I started this scarf almost a year ago (I won't say how many times I started over—I was just learning), you had said it was cold up in an airplane. Since then, I've learned that for myself—and I'm only in Texas! Hope you can put it to use. By the way, the woolen thread was imported from England. Ain't that somethin'?'"

James paused as if to catch his breath, then opened his mouth, hesitated, and said abruptly, "From Emelye." He looked at Elizabeth. Did he realize she had seen the words, "with all my love," in Emelye's closing? In a way she felt envious, for Emelye's gift to James was every bit as thoughtful as hers, and required far greater sacrifice. Moreover, his awe at seeing that scarf with its striking insignia—surely obvious to all who observed him—reminded her that the part of James's life she had chosen not to share was deeply meaningful to him. And he shared this part with Emelye. Just now she could not help feeling a bit envious for this as well.

A silence had descended upon the room, for everyone loved Emelye, and regretted that her heart was about to be broken. For Geneva, the gift had done what the sum of Emelye's many letters or her high school graduation picture or even the snapshot in her WASP flight suit had failed to do: transformed Emelye from the skinny young girl who walked away from her four years ago, with ankles wobbling above her first pair of high-heeled shoes, into a young woman of no small accomplishment. Perhaps Emelye's childhood fantasies had blossomed into love—who was Geneva to say otherwise? She felt guilty for her hardness when she dismissed Emelye's feelings for James in order to reassure Elizabeth. Abruptly she sniffed, missing her daughter with a sharpness she seldom experienced anymore, and wishing she could be around to comfort her when the time arrived. Sensing her mood, Tony slipped an arm around her shoulders.

"I thought someone said we were to have a champagne toast," said Edward spiritedly, from his wing chair. Merton, stationed just outside the door in his butler's uniform, rolled in the trolley with champagne and goblets, then popped the cork, a pinched look on his face.

James continued thinking of Emelye. He felt mean for all his impatience, treating her like a pesky kid sister. He forgave her everything, even her senior prom—that guy Cateau approaching him belligerently, rheumy-eyed from drinking on the sly; the only thing stopping him from taking a swing, James's air force cadet uniform. He was awestruck by the lengths Emelye had gone to since then, just to please him, even joining the WASPs and risking her life flying an airplane. The scarf had brought it all home. He'd die if anything happened to her. He began searching his mind for a way to soften the blow that Elizabeth's letter would bring.

CHAPTER 49

James was called back to base very early in the morning on Boxing Day, the final day of his leave canceled. Though he would not be briefed until he arrived at Bassingbourn, he told Elizabeth that he suspected he was to be sent on a sortie to France, where the Allied Forces had begun to attack German launching sites for deadly V-1 rockets aimed at London. Elizabeth thought with irony: what prompted James's return to Bassingbourn today may well save Father's life when he returned to London tomorrow.

Waving goodbye as his train steamed out of Bodmin Station, she saw herself a fortnight hence, bidding farewell to her new husband for whom she had willingly given up her virginity, while knowing she could be widowed before the soreness healed. *Godspeed, darling James,* she thought, pressing her fingers to her lips and throwing him a kiss.

"Dear Emelye, I'm afraid there is no easy way to tell you this. I do not know how anyone can be as happy as I am, yet at the same time, can feel as torn. You see, James and I...."

So began Elizabeth's letter to Emelye a short time later, up in the dormer attic bedroom. She felt surrounded by ghosts. There was the dressing table bench with its frilly skirt, where Emelye sat as Elizabeth brushed her long golden hair, admiring her for knowing precisely what she wanted when she grew up: to marry James. There was the bed Emelye occupied and the pillow where her head lay as she confided her misery at living in England, and her secret plan to move to Houston and live with James's family, to the one person she was certain would understand and respect her feelings. "*...what a relief, he* *hasn't found a girlfriend in England. Whenever he writes (never as often as I'd like, though I realize he's very busy), I comb his letters for any sign....*"

In the afternoon James telephoned. He sounded in a great hurry. There was a lot of noise in the background, and his voice was muffled, as though he had his hand cupped over the mouthpiece. "I've been thinking, rather than writing to Emelye at Avenger Field, it might be better to send the letter in care of my mother in Houston. I'll cable Mom and ask her to give it to Emelye when she comes home next month, after she finishes her training."

"But then Emelye won't find out until after we're married," Elizabeth pointed out. Somehow it seemed deceitful not to inform her until then.

"Hold on," said James, upon which he carried on a brief exchange with another flyer, or so she presumed, which ended with, "Yeah, go on, I'll be right behind you." Returning to the line, he said, "I know, but I still think it's better. I've been around guys who got 'Dear John' letters from home. It's real hard to keep going. I know this isn't the same thing, but I'd like to save Emelye's pride. Besides, Mother will—you know—help her as much as she can."

Elizabeth imagined Emelye's fellows clustered about her shoulders as she read her letter. How mortifying it would be! And what if it so distracted her next time she went up in a plane, she had a dreadful accident? "It's very kind of you to think of that," she said, feeling humbled that James's discernment was sharper than hers.

"I gotta go. I'll be in touch. Meantime, you'll find out what we have to do to get married, right?"

"Yes. The Registrar's office should be open tomorrow."

Their wedding ceremony was to be quite modest, the two of them standing before the local Registrar, with only Elizabeth's immediate family present. Father had expressed displeasure that they refused a traditional church wedding at St. Petroc's. Yet, in deference to Emelye, they wanted as little fuss as possible. Besides, Elizabeth was disillusioned by the Church's milk-toasty views on the war. She had not attended chapel since she entered university. It would seem disingenuous to seek the Church's blessing on her marriage.

The next morning, when Elizabeth approached the postbox with her letter to Emelye, she held on to the envelope for a prolonged moment, imagining Emelye's beautiful face as she read it, the open expression so natural to her closing up, hardening, as she realized her sister had betrayed her. Would Emelye ever forgive her? Or, would there be a permanent fissure in their family, as deep and indelible as the scar on Elizabeth's leg? Finally she forced herself to post the letter, her fingers propelled by the knowledge that Willa would cushion the blow it delivered. Yet, she wondered as the hatch clamped shut: what would Willa think of having such a burden placed on her shoulders? For that matter, what would Willa think of having Elizabeth as a daughter-in-law, when she would surely prefer Emelye? As she turned to go, she felt that she had surrendered some part of her integrity. Her spirits plunged.

In the next few days there were many things to be done, not least of which was to find a suitable wedding garment. A local shopping trip with Geneva ended in disappointment. They fared no better after a protracted journey by rail to Exeter, and traveling to London was out of the question. Geneva's wedding gown was too large for Elizabeth, and the design of its bodice offered no hope for alteration, according to Mrs. Greaves. Geneva tried to persuade Elizabeth to wear her good white wool suit, though it would need to be cut down so drastically that Geneva could never wear it again. Elizabeth loathed the idea of ruining Geneva's handsome frock, especially when new clothing was so hard to come by. Besides, when she stood before the full-length mirror in the double-breasted jacket and slim skirt with kick pleats, her thin, black-stockinged legs poking out, she felt she rather resembled a ram standing on a hillside.

"There's always my good burgundy velvet with the ivory lace collar."

Geneva grimaced. "Burgundy, for your wedding? You ought to wear something white," she protested. Then she gave Elizabeth a teasing look. "At least I assume you should." Mrs. Greaves, standing ready with the pin cushion and measuring tape, tittered like a school girl.

Elizabeth reddened. "Oh, bother! Who cares about a silly tradition?" she cried, and flung herself up the stairs to her room. From behind, she heard Geneva query, "Must you take everything so seriously? Bring the dress down so that I can take it to the dry cleaners."

Elizabeth knew that Geneva believed her testiness resulted from her guilt over injuring Emelye's feelings. Though this was partially correct, since composing the letter she had been haunted also by the certainty that Emelye would make James a far better wife than she. Making James happy would be Emelye's chief aim in life; her own paltry sacrifice was shameful by comparison.

On Thursday morning, January 6th, Elizabeth awoke at half past seven, feeling out of sorts. All through the night she had tossed and turned, and now her head felt heavy upon her shoulders. Apparently she had disturbed Bertrand's sleep, for he had retreated from the end of her bed and resettled on Emelye's bed. James would arrive around noon, and after lunch they would go into Bodmin and apply for a special license to marry within twenty-four hours—a mere formality in their case. The ceremony had already been scheduled: half-past four on Friday afternoon, in the Registrar's office.

Elizabeth rose, put on her robe and slippers, went to the dormer window and flung open the blackout curtains, then curled up on the window seat and gazed dispiritedly at the sorrowing winter morning. Here and there were globs of melting snow, as lackluster as soiled linen. A soft rain was falling. The sky was so heavy and gray, you could not see as far as the meadows stretching beyond Clearharbour. Inevitably, her glance fell on the wet hulk of the Anderson shelter, beneath the bare, bony limbs of the double sycamore tree. It seemed one could never look far without being confronted by some grim reminder of the war.

Just two mornings from now—her thoughts went on—she would wake up with James's fine athletic body stretched out next to hers in bed. By then, he would have seen her scar in its entirety, at close range. And…even…kissed it. More and more she dreaded watching him bring his lips to that most private of all places on her body. It made her feel subject to James's will in a way that was humiliating. *How dare he?* She thought suddenly, then caught her breath and blinked. It was frightening how abruptly her anger had risen: her late mother's most disturbing trait emerging in her. She had never imagined being angry at James over anything, and especially something so petty—twisting his words, spoken out of love. This, too, was her mother's way, she despaired.

Now she felt sick inside, as if she had sullied her relationship with James. Oh, what was the matter with her? Geneva was right when she accused her of taking things too seriously. She had been cooped up too long by the weather, probably, had spent too much time analyzing things. *I must get out or I shall go mad,* she thought. Hurriedly she dressed, slipped downstairs and took her hat and coat from the peg in the hallway. Geneva was sitting at the kitchen table with several Ministry of Food recipe pamphlets spread out before her, listening to Freddie Grisewood's *The Kitchen Front* on the wireless. Elizabeth could hear his unctuous voice dispensing advice. It sickened her more. From the hallway, she called to Geneva, "I'm going out for a while." Then she picked up an umbrella and hurried through the door before Geneva had time to question her.

The trip to Fowey took much longer than usual. The bus—like all others in England at present—was ancient and dilapidated. It rattled and shook violently as it rumbled along neglected highways, dodging potholes. The passengers bobbed and listed continually in their seats. *God in Heaven, will this war ever be over?* Elizabeth wondered, her composure in danger of cutting loose and hurling off like a runaway kite in the wind.

At Ready Money Cove, she pulled her coat collar up about her neck, and pinned her cap fast to her head, to keep it from sailing across St. Austell Bay. She climbed gingerly up a slippery path till she reached a more or less flat ridge, then, recovering her breath, she gazed out at the sea crashing wildly against the slate boulders. Only out the corner of her left eye could she see the rude war-time iron fence strung across the mouth of the cove. Feeling a sense of peace overtake her at last—coming here was just what she needed!—she shut her eyes, savoring the furious sound of the sea pounding her ears, and the damp sting of the rain on her face. How she loved this place! And who could guess how long it would be, before she returned, if ever? Since James proposed, she had realized as never before how dear to her was her homeland. Why was it that every blessing, every good thing in life, always came at an exorbitant price?

She went on standing there, lost in her ruminations, unaware of the minutes ticking by.

CHAPTER 50

When James arrived at Clearharbour shortly before one o'clock, he was nearly an hour late. His buddies had thrown him a bachelor party last night, at the Eagle in Cambridge. He remembered them standing around the piano, singing songs that got raunchier as the evening wore on; remembered burning his name into the low ceiling: just one among many names of aircrew members appearing there—American and British—some with other information added, such as where they were from, or the date they were there. Some of the fellows were probably dead by now, he thought, and as he guided the candle to form his name in smoky, ghostly lines, he imagined himself coming back someday, after the war, to see if his name was still there.

That was about all he remembered. When he dragged himself to a sitting position at five this morning, he blinked and swayed on his hips, thankful this was not his wedding day. He laid down again, and wound up oversleeping.

"Elizabeth left here before nine o'clock. I don't know where she went—it was raining," Geneva told him with a look of bewilderment. She led him to the kitchen. There was a pot of soup waiting on the stove and a loaf of Auntie Nell's dark-grained homemade bread on the table. The table was set for three.

Given the length of time Elizabeth had been away, James had a feeling she'd taken a bus to Ready Money Cove. That she was still not home an hour after he was due to arrive worried him. Of course, maybe she'd meant to get back earlier, but the buses were running late; nothing in civilian life ever ran on schedule during a war. So far, they had plenty of time to get to the Registrar's office.

Geneva tried to get him to sit down and eat, but he was too nervous. He waited an hour, pacing up and down before the kitchen window, keeping his eye on the driveway. After that he couldn't stand it anymore. He was going after Elizabeth. But the Registrar's office closed at four, and either way he went to Fowey, by rail or by bus, would take too long. "May I borrow your Rover?" he asked Geneva.

"You wouldn't get to Bodmin on what's left in the tank," she warned.

He considered this. "I'll get some petrol from the barracks up the street."

Geneva wasn't sure if he meant he would steal the petrol outright, or get it on the pretense that he needed it for official use. She handed him the car key. "Be careful. The streets will be slick."

By now, Geneva was pretty sure that Elizabeth intended to back out of the wedding, and she felt sick at heart. She didn't want Elizabeth to marry James unless she really wanted to; but she loved James so much, she couldn't bear to see him hurt. *"Please, God, make this come out right,"* she prayed.

All the way to Fowey James was on the lookout for a bus traveling back toward Bodmin, or maybe one pulled off the road with a flat tire, or with the bonnet up, smoke billowing out. He kept telling himself Elizabeth had some good reason for going out in the rain this morning and not coming back on time, other than that she dreaded the errand they were supposed to do together today; but his stomach was in knots regardless.

In little more than an hour he had left the Rover in the car park, and was hiking along the path overhung with bare and wintry tree branches, to Ready Money Cove. Once there he quickly spotted Elizabeth, standing on a high bluff, facing the sea: dressed all in black, her shoulders hunched against the wind, her collar turned up and her hands thrust deep inside her coat pockets; her figure so slight, she seemed in danger of blowing out to sea. For a while he stood there gazing at her. She seemed so remote from him, he felt like the young boy who idolized her, reasoning that he could never bring himself high enough to reach her. Had he been right, after all? he asked himself, fear taking a grip on him. But then, probably she was just freezing right now; yes, that must be it. She had just come up here to be alone and to reflect for a while—there was nothing unusual about that—and time got away from her. *She loves me!* He wished he had worn his full-length coat, then he could go up there and wrap her inside it with him.

There was no use calling out, for she wouldn't hear him. He climbed up to where she stood, taking the same craggy path she must have taken, grabbing himself a couple of times as his feet nearly slid out from under him on the slick rocks.

Elizabeth didn't realize he was there until he closed his arms around her from behind. When she jerked around in surprise, he saw that she had been crying. His heart collapsed: she was having second thoughts about marrying him. He remembered how he had to coax her; how she struggled to make up her mind. But then, having done so, she seemed so happy, so sure. Till today. What was it that made her so ambivalent toward him, when all he wanted was to give her everything? He had a sudden urge to master her, to force her to feel the same about him all the time.

"James, how did you—?" Elizabeth began, but he took her chin, and his mouth covered hers. She would never have said that James was a brutal man, and yet he was kissing her as he had never done before, desperately, invasively, his free hand finding its way inside her coat and trembling around her breast. She could feel the concentrated hardness below his waist, pressing against her. She leaned into him, her eyes blurred with longing. She wanted this, and more. She had a sudden, dizzying awareness of what having sex would be like.

Elizabeth's eager response brought James a swift feeling of triumph. He forced himself to loosen his grip on her, but he would not leave her alone again, not for a minute, not until they got up from the marriage bed, not until his leave was over. God, he wished the war would end! "Let's go, we've got just enough time to make it," he said. She nodded. They scrambled down from the ridge.

He wasn't trying to be romantic when he scooped her up and carried her to the car park. There just wasn't enough time left for her halting steps. She knew this. Again, she yielded to him, slipping her arm about his neck.

By the time they got to the car park and climbed into the Rover, he had explained about the party last night, which so slowed him down this morning, he missed the train he intended to catch and had to wait for another; and how it was that he was driving Geneva's car. "I'm so sorry, I didn't realize the time," she said. "I just—just had to get away."

"Why were you crying?" he forced himself to ask; he was terrified of her answer. She only shrugged. "Are you alright now?" he asked, his voice tender.

She squeezed his hand and smiled. "Yes, now that you're here. I think some-how I knew that you would *know*, and would come."

He returned her smile, ashamed of himself for failing to realize things were bound to turn out this way, when they knew each other so completely, when each could only be completed by the other. "Tomorrow night, we'll take the train to Boscastle—there's a small hotel that's supposed to be nice. I got us a room for two nights. I have to be back on base by Sunday night."

"Yes, fine. It's very pretty in Boscastle," she said, thinking of the eight days that the calendar—to which they would soon become enslaved—had deemed 'safe.' Longer than they needed.

Yet, he went on to say, "And I'll be getting a small increase in pay. I'll apply to live off-base. As soon as you get back, will you look into housing in Cambridge? Something furnished, if possible. We could move in right away."

"Alright," she said. Yet she had not anticipated moving from her room in Clough Hall quite so soon. In fact, since James was subject to being transferred to another base at any time, she had rather hoped she might be allowed to keep her room indefinitely. When James had a pass, they would find a place to be alone together. Not that it would be easy, since most hotels were billeting troops. Of course, she had not looked into the regulations for married students at Newnham College, for when she left for the holiday, the possibility that she might be married when she returned had not become real. Everything had been so rushed! And now, she thought sadly, she would return to her beloved room in Clough Hall just in order to clear out her things, then move in with James. No longer would she be a part of the college life that she had come to enjoy. She would exist on the periphery, a married woman. She and James would be together night after night, those eight 's's on the calendar grid soon displaced by forbidding 'x's. James's invasive kiss still felt imprinted on her lips. With what remnants of self-restraint would they force themselves apart after such a kiss? she wondered with dread. She would worry constantly about becoming pregnant; that is, when she wasn't feeling guilty for not wanting James's children.

Elizabeth realized that she had only truly envisioned being married to James in Texas, where everything would be different, just one enormous compromise, the price of being with the man she loved, for she did love him, desperately. But now, she saw her life in England—what was left of it—being disassembled piece by piece, beginning Monday next. She gazed out the window, trembling.

As the Rover sped along the wet streets of Fowey—the only civilian vehicle in sight—James began to wonder if he could trust Elizabeth's passion when they kissed at Ready Money Cove—after all, he had virtually overpowered her. And then later, why could she not tell him why she was crying? He needed some sign that marriage to him was really what she wanted. He reached inside his pocket and pulled out the small packet with her wedding ring.

"Here, see what you think of this."

When Elizabeth opened the packet and saw the ring—several thin strands of gold with a small bar connecting them—she had the sensation she was about to touch a hot stove burner. Marriage was circular, like this ring, with no end. Forever. One could not afford a mistake. "It's very pretty," she said, staring at it, feeling a hammering in her temples. *Marrying James would not be a mistake, surely; but I am not ready. Is it so wrong simply not to be ready?*

Between watching the road and glancing her way, James couldn't be sure what Elizabeth was thinking. "It's made from a brooch of Geneva's. I didn't want you to have to wear a cigar band until after the war, like a lot of brides do; and she offered."

"Oh yes. How very clever. Eh—thank you, James," she said dully.

He could not stop pressing. "Try it on, see if it fits. If not, we can have it sized in Bodmin, pick it up tomorrow."

"Oh? Well, alright," she said reluctantly. Quickly she slipped the ring on her finger and immediately off again. "It's fine," she said, though in truth she was not sure. It felt very heavy on her finger. She refolded the packet round it. With a faint smile, her mouth dry, she handed it back, and watched him slip it into his pocket. *I'm not ready.* Her breathing was shallow.

They drove a little farther and came to a roundabout. James looked both ways. An old taxi cab trundled by. He switched gears, then entered the circle. Neither of them spoke. *I cannot do this.*

As they emerged from the roundabout, she turned. "James, pull over and stop, please," she said.

He glanced at her. *It's over,* he thought. His heartbeat was a death rattle for all the ideals which had been building over his lifetime; for his belief in the future, that the best was waiting to happen. *He was in a plane, speeding nose-down toward the earth in a billow of flames and smoke.* He pulled over and switched off the engine. He stared ahead and waited for Elizabeth to speak.

"James, I can't—" she began, then she started to sob. He waited. When she recovered enough to look at him again, she saw a tear rolling down his cheek.

"I don't know what it is. I love you, but I can't face being married. Perhaps it's that I never imagined myself getting married before you asked me, and now—"

"We could wait...awhile," he offered, his voice constricted. He continued staring ahead.

For a few moments she hesitated, her newfound resolve unsteadied by his generosity. Perhaps if they could wait until after the war. Yet, pray, what if she felt the same as she felt now? Already she dreaded moving to Texas. Would it be fair to ask him to wait, when she was not at all sure she would feel any less reluctant? After all, she loved him deeply now, yet she was not ready to marry him. What difference could be made by the passage of time? She was shaking her head. "I—I'm sorry, James. Please, forgive me."

Even as she spoke the words, she knew that he never would. He turned to look at her, like a harmless animal who has been shot, looks up with recognition at the person holding the gun.

"We passed a bus halt not far back. Take me there. I shall get home alright."

James started the engine. The streets were dangerously slick, and when he turned the car round, rather too abruptly, it swerved out of control. Had there been other vehicles in their path, they would have smashed into one. Elizabeth caught her breath and glanced at him. His profile was stony. She hated this for him; the indignity of the swerving automobile seemed to add cruelly to the indignity he had suffered from her. And tonight, he must face the friends who gave him a send-off last night. Who would save his pride, as he would have saved Emelye's?

He put the car right again. His jaw set, he pressed the accelerator. They sped forward. Soon he pulled to a stop across from the bus halt. Elizabeth turned to him once again. "I'm so dreadfully sorry. You did not deserve this. You are everything that's fine in a—"

She reached out and touched his hand. Glancing at her, he withdrew it and looked ahead.

She opened the door and stepped out. She felt his cold gaze upon her as she passed in front of the car. She walked over to sit on the end of a wet bench, vaguely realizing she had left her umbrella behind at Ready Money Cove. She watched the Rover pass by. She could hardly believe she had sent James away and she knew she had given up her only chance of the kind of happiness she would have had with him, that she would never love another man.

At length she saw a grubby, ramshackle bus ambling forward. She rose and waved her hand, but it didn't stop, for it was already full. When it passed her by, belching a plume of black smoke in her direction, she cried, "Oh damn, damn, damn! Damn the war, damn it to hell. I wish God would strike me dead right here!"

She sat down to wait for the next one.

CHAPTER 51

In Lent term at Cambridge, the ground was white with snow; the bare tree branches glistened with ice and the rivers were frozen. The cold wind knifed down the pavement before Elizabeth as she made her solemn way from Clough Hall to university lectures and back again, wrapped in her heavy wool coat and muffler, boots, cap and gloves. Inside she felt as still as death, as if the blood in her veins was frozen like the rivers, yet would not thaw even in Spring.

Everywhere she looked, she was forced to see James: now he was waiting for her at the foot of the stairs; now, sitting with her at their garden table, his creative spirit roused and stirring him to interpret what he saw through his art; now he was stepping away from the Clough Memorial gates, waving farewell, the taste of his lips still on hers, *'till next time'* a sweet refrain that neither need voice for the other to hear.

Elizabeth's room, once treasured, had lost its charm: her punishment for having placed it higher than James in importance. She removed his drawing from her wall—*he would not want it hanging there,* she thought—and placed it, with no small amount of reverence, inside a drawer. No wall on the face of the earth had ever looked so bare, she would think as she lay in bed at night, staring at its blankness by the meager light of the coal fire. Likewise, her Frenchman's cross and humble Shaker doll, that once seemed to epitomize the promise of a rewarding life, now seemed to mock her cowardice in failing to take a bold step forward.

The most humbling part of Elizabeth's return was facing her fellow residents. Even if they overlooked her lifeless demeanor, James's failure to appear made it obvious that they had broken up. With the exception of Millicent, whom she was very grateful to see again after the disastrous holiday, and to whom she confided the truth, she felt that everyone was speculating about her ill-fated romance: *"She couldn't hold him, I daresay; handsome as he was, and a flying officer...."* She approached her pigeon hole each day with flickering hope: *"Dear Elizabeth, I forgive you, and will always care."* Had she been a fool to obey her overpowering instincts? She was not sure that she would ever know—perhaps she did not deserve to know. Yet she longed for James's forgiveness.

Much to Miss Welsford's dismay, she resigned from the Informal Club without ever having presented a poem. For a while she continued writing verse, only now it was dark in tone. Sometimes she returned to earlier poems to alter them, so that they befitted the way things had turned out. Gradually she sickened of writing verse. She considered disposing of the leather-bound volume in which her poems were written, but then it was a gift from her aunt and uncle—often she had imagined them choosing it with great care—so how could she? She placed it at the back of a drawer.

One day as she sat quietly fixing colored rags on to camouflage netting—the warwork she had been assigned—she found herself almost wishing she would be called up. At least if she were working in some munitions or aircraft factory, she might escape her memories. But it would be just her luck to wind up being in some small way involved in building Lancasters. Then she would be condemned daily to remember James on his bicycle that idyllic afternoon in Ely, looking up as one passed over. No, she could never escape her memories, and neither could she overcome her aversion to being more involved in the war effort than she was at this moment.

Then, on the 28th of February, 1944, came a letter from her sister. Emelye had celebrated her twentieth birthday on the 22nd. It was too soon for this to be a thank-you for the note of congratulations Elizabeth sent, her spirits lifting momentarily as she posted it: *at least Emelye need never learn I betrayed her.* Yet, as she carried the letter upstairs, she began to fear that James may have neglected to inform his mother that the wedding was off, in time to prevent her delivering Elizabeth's Boxing Day letter. *And so I've forfeited Emelye's love after all, and for nothing. It serves me right.*

Inside her room, she unsealed the letter, dated simply, "Valentine's Day":

"Dear Elizabeth, GUESS WHAT! James has asked me to marry him!"

The shock went straight to Elizabeth's knees. She sank down on the edge of her bed, the words swimming before her. "There I was, expecting a thank-you note for the neck scarf, and bingo! WOW! You should have seen me, dancing a jig around the sleeping bay, kissing his letter till it was covered in lipstick."

In fact, Elizabeth could see her sister vividly: the bubbly ingenue whose every happy thought ended with an exclamation point, covering a marriage proposal with lipstick prints. *Oh James, was it so necessary to punish me, that you would make an unwitting accomplice of Emelye?* she agonized. Yet, could it be, he felt rather that if he was to be denied the one thing in life he wanted more than any other, then Emelye was surely deserving of it, and therefore marrying her was a supreme act of unselfishness?

It suddenly occurred to her that apparently James had felt no obligation to inform Emelye of his failed romance with her sister. That seemed terribly disingenuous, and besides, was he not concerned that someone else may tell her?

Emelye continued, "I'm not sure I'll believe it's real until we're standing at the altar! Which we'll be doing at four o'clock in the afternoon on Saturday, May 6th, at St. Petroc's Church. A USAAF pilot who ferries B-17's overseas has agreed to fly me over for the wedding. (That's one great benefit of being in the WASP. There ain't many, I'm finding out.) Hopefully Serena can come with me, and we're going to see about booking passage for Willa and Rodney on a Liberty ship."

Now Elizabeth could not help but wonder if James had chosen to marry Emelye in the very place she had rejected, further driving home his wish to punish her. Yet he certainly could not go all the way home to be married, and Father would most surely have urged that they marry in St. Petroc's Church.

"We've got just about everybody involved. Aunt Nellie is in charge of the reception. Daddy's choosing the music. I'm to be given the diamond ring that belonged to James's grandmother. I'll wear Mother's wedding dress, and Mrs. Greaves is making a jacket to go over it, from Grandmother's wedding lace."

Elizabeth was amazed at all the activity set spinning among the family, without her knowing. It seemed that the details of planning a wedding which she had found so difficult, had posed no problem for Emelye, even though she was thousands of miles away from where the vows would be exchanged.

"Elizabeth, from the time we were children, you alone understood how I felt about James. I can't tell you how much that always meant to me. As you know, there were times when the only thing that got me through the misery of living in England was believing that one day I would marry him, and would be happy from the moment we said, "I do," for the rest of my life. And it's because you knew and understood before anyone else, more than the fact that you are my sister, that I want you to be my maid of honor."

Oh, but Elizabeth could not bear to attend the wedding, let alone, participate in it! Yet, how could she not, without serious injury to Emelye's feelings?

Then the answer occurred: the 6th of May was shortly before exams. It would be impossible for her to make a trip to Bodmin that close to the end of term. Thank God for the murderous 'Mays'!

"I guess that's it, except, I'd like for everyone in the bridal party to wear a pastel-colored dress. As soon as you get this, call Mother and let her know what color you'll wear. She'll try and get matching ribbons for your bouquet.

"Well, I'm about to take my finals here, and I've got studying to do. So I'll close. By the time you receive this, I'll (hopefully) have graduated in class 43-W-9 of the WASP, and be in Houston on leave. I report to Love Field in Dallas on March 15th. From there I'll be ferrying planes to the East Coast, both before and after the wedding. Ain't that somethin'? Love and Kisses, Em."

Elizabeth would have telephoned Geneva in any case, for she hoped that she had spoken with James and could fill in some of the blanks left by Emelye's letter. Not least of which was the reason for James's haste in proposing to Emelye after she broke their engagement—judging by the date of Emelye's letter, he could not have waited as long as a month—and his apparent intention to keep from her the fact that she was not his first choice.

"The cable from Emelye was the first I heard about it," Geneva said. She sounded weary, and she admitted that she had been worrying a lot. Obviously she felt caught in the middle of the whole situation, and she resented it. "I called James immediately," she added.

"Oh yes—? And what did he say?"

"The only thing I could extract from him was his promise to be faithful to Emelye, and to do all he could to make her happy. He said that he cares for her very much. Knowing James as I do, I'm sure that I can take him at his word."

"So I gather, you didn't urge him to tell Emelye the truth?"

"Why burst her bubble now?" Geneva retorted. "Again, if I didn't think James would be a good husband, I'd do all I could to save her from marrying him," she added, then after a pause she went on, "but you know, Elizabeth, being madly in love in the beginning doesn't mean a marriage will be happy. It's mostly just working things out one day at a time.

"I think they'll do that. I think they are—" she paused "—well suited."

Elizabeth had always believed Emelye and James were well suited, and yet, hearing it from Geneva was hurtful. All the while she showed her support and encouragement when Elizabeth was considering marriage to James, had she secretly feared that the marriage would turn out badly?

Elizabeth thought of the family heirloom that James would slip on Emelye's finger, and immediately cringed at the memory of hastily slipping the ring he had made for her on and off, as if she feared it might contaminate her. "I am sure James's parents are happy about the way things turned out," she remarked.

For a few moments Geneva was silent, thinking of Willa's letter that came in this morning's post, and realizing how astute was Elizabeth's reasoning. She said with diplomacy, "You have to understand, Emelye is like a daughter to her and Rodney. But they would have been happy for you and James, had things worked out…"

But not *as* happy, Elizabeth thought soberly.

"…and in time, they would have come to love you as their own. When you have children, their happiness is all you really care about," Geneva said. She was eager to get past the subject of Elizabeth and James, for it was on her mind constantly, and she feared that if this preoccupation continued, she would wind up letting the truth slip out in front of Emelye when she came over to be married. She asked, "Did Emelye ask you to be her maid of honor?"

"Yes, but I simply shan't be able to," Elizabeth said quickly, then explained about May exams. "Besides, I think the atmosphere would be quite strained if I were there, and it wouldn't be fair to Emelye, or anyone else."

Geneva agreed. "It's going to be enough of a strain just worrying about the children letting the secret out," she said, then she could not resist adding petulantly, "I'd give anything if they hadn't known about you and James."

In other words, if I had not announced I was to marry James when I wasn't sure, Elizabeth thought, feeling chastised. Yet she had been sure then! "I don't really think the boys paid much attention, but Elvira certainly did," she admitted.

"As a matter of fact, I'm putting Elvira in charge of keeping the boys quiet," Geneva said. "Having a role to play will keep her mind focused."

At this moment Elizabeth was too miserable to appreciate her little sister's notorious histrionics as much as usual. She checked her watch. She had ten minutes to get to Ridley Hall, for Bertrand Russell's lecture. The professor had just returned to Trinity College after a long sabbatical in America. Elizabeth intended to raise her hand and ask him to state the philosophical basis for reversing his position on the war. A huge crowd was expected, however, so there was no guarantee that she'd be called upon.

"I'm afraid I must ring off for now, but I—oh, I'm really sorry to have put everyone through all this," she apologized.

"It's alright," said Geneva. Yet her voice lacked the sincerity one could always count on when she accepted an apology. *It seems that I am always ruining things for other people,* Elizabeth despaired.

Elizabeth's letter of apology to Emelye—"I'm so sorry. If the wedding were any other time"—was pre-empted by a cable from her sister. Once again, the war had intervened: the wedding date had been moved up to March 25th, all military leaves in April and beyond having been canceled due to a major build-up of Allied troops. Elizabeth had been hearing about this "major build-up." What did it mean? Perhaps the Allies would soon put an end to the war. If so, then, thanks be to God.

Yet, March 25th fell shortly after the conclusion of Lent term, during a period when Elizabeth would be at home. With dread she realized that she could hardly refuse to be in Emelye's wedding now.

CHAPTER 52

Elizabeth desperately hoped that as soon as James learned she was to be in the wedding, he would recognize that in spite of the awkwardness she would feel, she had no choice but to agree to do so if his secret was to be left intact, and write a note acknowledging her effort on his behalf.

Yet James did not write. As the days went by Elizabeth was surprised to find that silence was the cruelest form of punishment: crueler than screaming, as her mother used to do, because at least then one earned the right to feel angry; one's bruised feelings had something to defend against. Silence drove one first to confusion, then to self-examination, then inevitably to self-doubt, and back again.

Finally, a week before the wedding, leaving him just enough time to reply, Elizabeth wrote to James: "Never forget that I care deeply for you, and for Emelye, and genuinely believe you will be happy. I shall always respect your wish to spare Emelye from knowing about us. Do please write and say that we can meet on your wedding day as friends. Yours always—"

James did not reply. On Friday, March 24th, with great reluctance, Elizabeth boarded the two o'clock train to London. Willa and Rodney had arrived at Clearharbour early in the week; Father met their ship and accompanied them home. Serena and Emelye arrived yesterday, as did James. For the first time ever, Elizabeth took comfort in anticipating the inevitable delays in war-time travel. She would arrive at Clearharbour quite late, missing the wedding rehearsal. If she was very, very lucky, perhaps the entire household would be abed.

She found a seat by the window and looked out at the passing scenery. Winter's brittle back had finally broken. The trees were bursting mutinously into the most vibrant, shimmering shades of green: great shaggy fists wagged victoriously against the blue sky. Daffodils and snowdrops and anemones were springing up in legions, in the fields and along the sloping banks of rivers that, once again, had been released to spill and tumble down their familiar course. It was a season truly befitting a wedding celebration: the beginning of a shared life. Elizabeth vowed to pray daily, for the remainder of her life, for the happiness of Emelye and James.

Night fell as the train approached the outskirts of London; the windows were shrouded in black. From there, it was as if they were traveling through an endless tunnel. A dim blue light shone up and down the corridor to keep passengers from stumbling over their feet.

At King's Cross, Elizabeth hastened through the crowd of soldiers and civilians, then switched to the underground and traveled to Paddington Station, where for more than an hour she stood waiting for a train to Bodmin—there were far fewer benches and chairs than could accommodate all the people waiting. She imagined James as he had made this journey at Christmas, his hopes high that she would give him the answer he so desired when he arrived. Fear of having made a drastic mistake seized her once again. If only she had accepted James's offer for more time…yet, would it have made any difference? How many years would pass before she ceased asking herself this question?

Elizabeth was exhausted, and her neck and back ached from the tension building steadily for weeks. Once out of London, she yielded to the soporific sound and vibration of the train, as it trundled and swayed down the tracks; she dozed fitfully for the remainder of the journey. Shortly before ten, the conductor moved down the dim blue aisle like a ghost, to announce quietly that Bodmin station would be the next stop. She came fully awake at once, every muscle braced as though for a physical attack.

Inevitably, inside the station she found herself gazing round, with racing heart, hoping against hope that the reason James failed to reply to her note was that he intended to meet her train: *"I forgive you, and we'll always be friends."* But there was no sign of him among the few weary people about—how foolish to think he might have come. He had no intention of making things easy.

She soon found the jingle was unavailable at the moment, and hiring it would involve a protracted wait. She considered. Home was not too awfully far from here, though it was all uphill. At least she had on sensible Oxfords. So she would go on foot. In moments she was stepping outside, being utterly swallowed up in darkness, the light of the moon in no more evidence than James. Suitcase in hand, a small radius lit before her by her torch, she made her way carefully along the pavement. Within less than half an hour she was walking up the Clearharbour drive.

Dogs barking; people chattering. *I ought to have left Cambridge two hours later,* Elizabeth thought in dismay as she opened the door to the light-locked conservatory. She paused momentarily, to gather herself. Usually it was cheering to cross over and open the door into the hall, and see the light shining. Not tonight. What if James happened to be standing there? Yet, thankfully the hall was empty. She was hanging her coat on a peg when Emelye burst from the sitting room and cried, "Elizabeth!" She smothered her in a hug. Elizabeth peered over her sister's shoulder, fearing James may have followed her.

"I thought you'd never get here! Let me just look at you!" They released each other and linked hands. For the first time in almost five years, the two young women took a long look at each other. Even though Elizabeth had seen pictures of Emelye over the years since she returned to America to live, she was unprepared for the degree to which she'd grown into the promise of her figure. Dressed simply in a checked gingham shirt, draped slacks, shiny brown loafers and white socks, she had a fresh-scrubbed, suntanned vibrancy that was consummately American. There was a smattering of freckles over her nose, and her brown eyes were luminous. Her hair color was lighter than Elizabeth remembered. She wore it combed back from her face and caught with a wide red band. The length of it fell in thick loose curls about her shoulders. Her waist was small and her hips and breasts were shapely, like Geneva's. It was easy to envision Emelye wearing her mother's wedding gown.

"You just missed James," Emelye said. "He and his buddies are spending the night at the George and Dragon Hotel." She rolled her eyes. "Probably won't be much sleeping. Anyway, I won't see him again till I walk down the aisle," she said with eagerness. Elizabeth was so relieved to be spared facing James for a little longer, she felt quite giddy. Of course, a postponement only gave her more time to dread the inevitable.

"Oh Elizabeth, I've never been so happy in my life!" Emelye cried, and hugged her fiercely again. Breathing in the sweet coconut scent of Emelye's freshly-washed hair brought back the memory of her as a child, emerging from the shower and plunging through the door of the bath, the scent of damp hair and dusting powder filling the bedroom they shared. Elizabeth realized suddenly just how fragile were her sister's emotions now. Having experienced something almost too good to be true, any small threat to its veracity would be shattering. She must protect her at all costs. She had never loved Emelye more tenderly than in that moment. "And I am ever so happy for you!" she said.

Elizabeth was soon being hastened into the sitting room where everyone was having drinks and talking. Her heart skipped a beat when Willa and Rodney approached, yet each greeted her with broad, Texas-style warmth, meeting her eyes levelly, trying to put her at ease. Overall, Willa had changed very little. Her figure was still slender and stately. She had, naturally, accrued some gray streaks in her hair, which she wore kicked up in soft curls in back, with the front swept up in a swirl and pinned on top of her head. There were tiny wrinkles about her mouth and eyes. Pretty, tilted eyes, looking deeply into one. James's eyes. Elizabeth realized as never before how remarkably James favored his mother.

Rodney was a bit more stout than Elizabeth remembered, and he, too, was graying, which seemed incompatible with his boyish face. How very fitting that the two couples whose friendship had endured for so many years, would soon have a blood tie established between them. And of course, grandchildren would follow. For the first time, Elizabeth grasped the consequence to James's family of her wish not to have children. Had they married, she would have set the gravestone on the Younger family line. And suddenly, not only James's reason for marrying Emelye, but his haste in doing so, seemed obvious: Every time he went up in an airplane, there was a chance he would not come down alive.

She could not have stood long with Rodney and Willa without her feelings of awkwardness returning, so she was not displeased to feel Bertrand circling her ankles. She picked him up. "There's a good fellow," she crooned, hugging him close. She excused herself to the kitchen to pour her cat a saucer of milk.

Inevitably, Serena was to sleep in the attic bedroom with Elizabeth and Emelye, Geneva having arranged for a cot to be brought up. Just as well, Elizabeth thought. It would probably be less awkward, having Serena there. Yet no sooner were they gathered in the room than it became apparent that the two friends were determined to spend the night chattering like school girls at a pajama party. Serena's hair was in pin curls and tied up with a net; her face was glossy with cold cream. She sat on the bed, legs akimbo, inhaling deeply from one cigarette after another, and flicking ashes into a small tray which sat in the crook of her thighs.

Pretty soon, she opened the prickly topic of sex with a round of slightly vulgar stories—probably exaggerated—that seemed designed to frighten Emelye as her wedding night approached. Emelye did not appear to take Serena seriously. She was no doubt accustomed to a bit of ragging now and then from her best friend.

Presently Serena handed Emelye a gift box, from which Emelye hurriedly extracted a sheer pink nightie, trimmed in black lace. Emelye was thrilled. She held it before her and waltzed round the room, breasts bobbing inside her flannel pajama top. "Where did you find this?" she asked.

Exactly what Elizabeth was wondering. Surely pre-war articles as eye-catching as this had long since disappeared from the shelves, even in American shops. "I've had it since I lived in Manhattan. I spent every dime I made, as you well know. I never got around to wearing this."

To Elizabeth Emelye said, "You knew that Serena was a Rockette? Dead center in the chorus line. You should have seen her high kicks! No one could match her." Elizabeth felt annoyed. Why must Emelye always boast about Serena? She had been doing so since they were children.

Serena looked down, tapping her cigarette against the tray, oblivious of the fact that she was stinking up the room. To her credit, she said, "You could have done just as well, Sis, if you had come up there." She cut her dark eyes provocatively. "Could have had a helluva good time, too. Hey, why don't you put the gown on and model it for us?"

"Not a chance! I'm saving this for James." Emelye said, with a high giggle that betrayed her nervousness.

"Knowing my brother, you won't be needing it much," said Serena.

Elizabeth's cheeks were burning. She did not want to hear trivial stories of James's conquests in years past, nor did she want to think of what lay ahead for Emelye and James beginning tomorrow night. Rather more abruptly than she intended, she reached for her pillow and started toward the door. Serena eyed her curiously.

"Where are you going?" Emelye asked.

"I'm rather tired. I think I'll just bed down in Chris's extra."

"Alright," Emelye said agreeably, then looked at Serena. "Elizabeth studies all the time, so no wonder she's tired. She's brilliant, you know. She'll probably be a college professor one day."

Embarrassed, Elizabeth said, "If I were brilliant, I wouldn't have to study so hard." They hugged each other goodnight. Emelye's breasts felt soft and feminine as they pressed against Elizabeth. James would probably prefer—no. She was not going to start imagining that.

"Sleep tight," said Serena, her sexy contralto voice dividing the second word into two languid syllables, rising then falling. Elizabeth imagined her saying this to her lover in the wee morning hours, right after having sex. Then she thought, horrified, *Now who's preoccupied with sex?*

"Oh, wait a minute!" Emelye said. "I almost forgot. I was going to ask you to do my hair for the wedding tomorrow."

Elizabeth was amazed. "But I've no experience styling hair." She caught herself just in time to avoid saying that her friend Millicent styled her hair for her first night out with James at Cambridge. Her cheeks grew hot. How easy it would be to slip over the next twenty-four hours! She must take care.

To Serena Emelye said dreamily, "When Elizabeth and I were kids, she used to brush my hair a hundred strokes every night." She turned back to Elizabeth. "I've thought of that so many times. Please, it would mean so much to me!"

It seemed to Elizabeth that Emelye was determined to infuse her wedding day with every possible sentiment. How could one refuse her? "Alright, but be prepared to redo it, if it doesn't turn out."

After the bedroom door was shut behind Elizabeth, Emelye turned to Serena, her eyes glistening with tears. "There's something so sad about her, it breaks my heart. I wish she could find someone as good as James, and fall in love."

Serena had already discovered she was unable to form close attachments with the opposite sex, that she quickly grew bored and anxious when men grew serious about her. Thus she was uncomfortable when others showed real emotion on the subject of love. She screwed up her face. "My brother, that creep?" she gasped.

Emelye threw a pillow at her.

CHAPTER 53

Shortly after three o'clock on Saturday afternoon, with Geneva and Grandmother and Serena the bridesmaid gathered round, Emelye sat before her mother's dressing table mirror wearing a coral-colored chenille house robe over her petticoat and stockings, a modest amount of rouge on her cheeks, and petal pink lipstick. Elizabeth stood behind Emelye, trying to focus her concentration on styling her long silky hair in spite of being painfully aware of the minutes ticking by. The house was off-limits for James today—one of those incomprehensible customs from which, admittedly, Elizabeth benefitted. Yet soon she would be forced to face him at last....

Geneva glanced nervously at the clock on the chimneypiece: ten after three. Elvira, Emelye's flower girl, was supposed to be dressed and in here by three. Yet she had vanished mysteriously, and Mrs. Greaves had been dispatched to find her. Elvira was usually punctual, as she liked emulating professional stage actors, who must always be on time. What on earth could she be up to?

Finally, at a quarter past, Elvira flung herself through the door. Everyone turned to look. "Wherever have you been, child?" inquired Cynthia, who wore a cloud of lavender chiffon around her neck to conceal an increasing number of wrinkles. Elvira wore peach organza, a color which paled beneath the heightened color of her cheeks.

"I couldn't find my right shoe, you see, and had to search through all the cupboards. Can you imagine where I found it? Under the bed," she said, with a lift of her brow and a flip of her hands.

What mischief had she been up to? Elizabeth wondered. That she was covering a secret was written all over her face. She hadn't had sufficient time to get into character before making her appearance.

Soon everyone had forgotten about Elvira and returned their attention to the bride. Thankfully Elizabeth need do little more than follow Emelye's instructions; the back portion of her luxurious hair was easily twirled under in a crescent that dipped between her shoulders. From there, Elizabeth fashioned a deep wave over her forehead, then swept up each side, looping two large sausage curls round her fingers and pinning them firmly on top.

Emelye turned from the mirror and clasped Elizabeth's hands. "It's perfect! I love you," she said, smiling warmly.

Not for anything would Elizabeth have traded Emelye's last three words. For the moment, they even salved her conscience for hurting James.

Now Emelye stepped into her wedding gown. Her mother fastened the long row of tiny covered buttons up the back, then Emelye slipped her slender arms through the long sleeves of the *point de gaze* lace jacket.

As Geneva fastened the three buttons down the front, Willa stood ready with Emelye's headdress, which would complete the bridal ensemble. The headdress was one of many things that Willa had procured in Houston for the occasion, along with Elvira's peach organza dress, and Elizabeth's mint green taffeta with ankle-length skirt of deep flounces—all thanks to Kaplan's-Ben Hur. Willa sent the wedding announcements, and had Emelye's wedding ring polished and sized. And through all these preparations, she felt guilty for wanting this marriage so much. Not that she had promoted the idea, for all her wishing. James's proposal to Emelye surprised her as much as everyone else. Lord, was it hard to write that letter to Geneva afterward! She must have started over ten times. Yet, she just had to say something. She doubted she could have ever felt close to Elizabeth. First of all, she would not have been able to carry on a decent conversation with someone as well educated as she was. As she worried over somehow revealing her ignorance, her tongue would sharpen in defense, and she'd wind up owing Elizabeth an apology. Obviously, marrying a highbrow was not a problem for James. But, bringing Elizabeth to live in Texas? Willa couldn't see it. People would have considered her a snob. So when James cabled her that Elizabeth had broken the engagement, she felt a little relieved. Not that she wasn't crushed for him, however. Willa knew her son. He never did anything by half measures. Elizabeth would be the one and only real love of his life.

Geneva was reaching for the wreath of silk flowers and seed pearls with the long, delicate wedding veil of soft netting attached. She placed it on Emelye's head and clasped it firmly on each side: the final touch. She stood back a little and gazed at her daughter. It seemed that Emelye's body had taken on an ethereal glow. She had transcended this time and place, and all who stood around her: the Virgin Mary with a host of votive candles burning at her feet. *My baby. My only, only child.* She could not have hoped for a better man to join her daughter at the altar today. Yet knowing James did not love Emelye as she believed he did, she was torn, and felt sometimes as if she were offering up an innocent lamb. *God, if I have done wrong, I pray you will redeem my sin; I pray you will put your love for Emelye into James's heart. Amen.* Geneva kissed her daughter's cheeks.

Emelye gripped her hands. "Thanks for everything, Mom. I love you," she said with feeling, and after a lengthy pause in which her eyes grew misty, she went on, "and I'm sorry I hurt you one time, but I've tried real hard to make you proud of me." Geneva nodded; she could not speak.

Now Emelye held out her arms. "How do I look?" Everyone swooned and applauded. Elizabeth thought of her burgundy dress with the ivory lace collar. How little she had been willing to put into her marriage ceremony with James. *This is right!* She thought. Then she glanced at the clock. Half-past three. Her sense of dread returned.

Emelye led the group downstairs to the front hall where Tony stood gazing up at his daughter with moist eyes. He fully ascribed to Geneva's practical view of the marriage between Emelye and James, for they were far better suited to each other than Elizabeth and James. Therefore, he felt no sense of unease about their future. How he loved Emelye! All the years she had lived away had never weakened the bond between them, perhaps because they'd written each other so often, and he had looked closely between the lines of effusive teenage vernacular and found plenty of signs that she was maturing into a fine and responsible young woman. Now, he felt an overwhelming sense of pride. He was the father of the most beautiful bride that had ever walked down the aisle of St. Petroc's Church. This was like his first night with Geneva in Ambleside: a time both surreal and sacred, that could never be repeated.

Andy and Chris stood on either side of Tony. Andy had been bribed—there was no other word for it—to keep his mouth shut, and behave like a gentleman all through the weekend. And now he savored the fact that half a crown would be awarded to him if he succeeded, and he would. Half a crown! He would save his money until after the war, when one could buy anything one wanted, and spend it all on sweets.

Chris was confused. He had been told that Emelye was to marry James, rather than Elizabeth, but when he asked his mother why, all she said was, "Elizabeth just isn't ready to get married, and please don't talk about it to anyone. Period." Last night, before bed, Elvira said, "Remember not to tell anyone about Elizabeth and James. PROMISE."

"But why?"

"None of your business. Besides, you're too young to understand," she said grandly, raising herself to her full height and summoning her most queenly stare.

Now Chris watched Emelye coming down the stairs, with Elizabeth behind her. Elizabeth was all dressed up, obviously as ready as anyone. Chris decided to question Father, who had not been around when he was given instructions.

He tugged on Father's hand. "Why doesn't Elizabeth marry with James?"

Everyone on the stairs, including Emelye, heard the question, saw Tony look down at his son in surprise. Behind Emelye, Elizabeth and Geneva glanced at each other in despair.

It was the greatest moment of Elvira's life. She would improvise, of course, and the one word she needed had secretly been provided her less than an hour ago. Projecting her voice so that everyone would be sure to hear, she stated: "Because, Chris, they're friends. And friends can't marry each other. You have to be in love."

Everyone laughed at the irony in the statement, a good many of the laughs masking a sense of relief.

He never actually said, I love you, thought Emelye uneasily, not in his letter proposing marriage or any letter afterward, not even face-to-face over the past couple of days, not in so many words, at least. *But there's more than one way of saying those three words. And there has been no shortage of kisses, some of them sweet and gentle, some of them down right—He loves me, I know he does. Why else would he ask me to marry him? We're going to be happy, gloriously happy....*

They were outside now, in the shimmering sunshine, the stiff breeze lifting Emelye's bridal veil and floating it on the air like a thin curtain over an open window on a blustery day. Serena managed to gather it up, her arms arched high in the air. "Hey, it's easier than dealing with a parachute," she said, giggling as it swirled about her seizing hands. How sexy she looked, thought Elizabeth, even in petal pink satin with a sweetheart neckline and puffed sleeves, and a pile of curls on top of her head. It struck her that Serena would never look suitable as a bride, for she was far too glamourous for any groom.

Soon they were boarding the horse-drawn bridal wagon that would convey them to the church. Outfitted with four wooden benches and festooned with white bunting and bows and flowers, this was a joint project of Grandmother and Auntie Nell.

Elizabeth gazed at her sister admiringly as the wagon rolled slowly down the streets of Bodmin towards Church Square. Along the way, pedestrians stopped in their tracks, captivated by the bride; some whistled, others cheered. Emelye sat with the virginal dignity of a princess during a royal visit, and indeed, she was soon lifting her hand to wave at them, working both sides of the street, seeming to intuit their hunger for pageantry in this long, relentlessly drab war.

Minutes later, Bach's majestic *Kommst du nun, Jesu* chorale surged up from the mighty St. Petroc's pipe organ, with the clean, clear, elongated notes of a solo trumpet floating above: Father's choice for Emelye's wedding march. Elizabeth stood at the foot of the long central aisle, her knees wobbling as she waited her turn. Ahead of her, Serena stepped off with confidence, and glided towards the high chancel steps, beside which her brother awaited his bride.

Now Serena was halfway down; it was time for Elizabeth to go. *If my legs buckle today, James will not hasten to my rescue*—. As she stepped forward, her hands trembling round her bouquet of daisies, she glanced at the vicar—shorter than James by a head—then lifted her eyes slightly. She allowed nothing into her peripheral vision beyond the shoulder and lapel of James's dress uniform. Oh, but she felt his eyes upon her every step; felt she was burning in the heat of his stare. At last she paused, within two feet of James, ready to turn off to the left and take her place next to Serena. After bowing her head to the cross, she was suddenly compelled to look at James, to face down her dread. He had never stood straighter, nor held his chest higher, had never looked more handsome or noble. He could have been the model for a statue honoring all the soldiers of all the wars ever fought in the history of mankind. And cold as a statue's eyes were his, as they caught and held hers. She quickly looked away, imagined James's fighter plane soaring through the sky above the ocean, the book of Spenserian sonnets discarded and tumbling down, its pages torn, its spine broken as it turned and twisted in the air, tumbling down, down, then plunging into the sea.

Elizabeth found herself facing Serena, whose eyes narrowed with recognition: *She knows everything.* Perhaps she had been told; but no, given her sharp instincts, she probably drew her own conclusion. Fearing Serena now, Elizabeth looked away and took her place.

A theatrical pause, and then the organ pipes exploded with an arpeggio worthy of signaling a procession to heaven. Geneva rose along with everyone else to watch Emelye float down the aisle on Tony's arm, smiling brilliantly, confidently, clutching her bouquet of white lilies and gladioli. As she passed, the reflected colors of the great stained glass windows splayed over her white gown like a rainbow. Geneva caught her breath; her tears spilled. Edward clasped her hand and held it fast. Seeing this, Elizabeth was filled with love for her grandfather, and with gratitude that she would not be leaving him to move to Texas.

She would have given anything to see the expression on James's face as he watched his bride coming towards him, but she dare not look. *Love Emelye*, her heart commanded him. She offered her prayer for their happiness. Then as the vicar commenced the service, she focused her eyes upon his white surplice and priestly stole.

Afterward, walking beside James's best man, a USAAF officer whom she had never met and whose eyes she avoided, Elizabeth followed the newlyweds from the church and down between two columns of officers in white gloves and gleaming shoes, standing at attention, their chests thrown out. Were these, along with James's best man, the same comrades-in-arm who toasted him at the Eagle on the night before he left to be married to her? Was their presence here today a way of salvaging his injured pride?

James assisted his bride aboard the two-seat, horse-drawn wedding carriage, festooned in white, then climbed in after her. As they settled in their seats, the ever-precocious breeze caught the wedding veil and twirled it high in the air. Gathering it down, James anchored it behind Emelye's knees. Then, as Elizabeth watched—she would have turned away, but there was no warning—James, smiling, reached his arm round Emelye's waist and kissed her with such ardor that those looking on were moved to cheer. *He loves her,* Elizabeth thought, with a bolt of awareness. She felt at once grateful and miserable that he had found love for Emelye locked away in his heart: the answer to her prayer. As Emelye's hands swept up to clutch his chest, her wedding diamond was caught by a ray of dying sunlight, creating a sudden, blinding beam, like a bright star burning out.

CHAPTER 54

After the towering arches of the St. Petroc's nave, with light sifting softly through high holy windows, the reception hall in the Bodmin Public Rooms seemed low and cramped to Elizabeth; and the bright ceiling lights seemed harsh and carnival-like. The peppy background music of the small military band ensemble was jarring to the senses, striking up within minutes after one had been borne from the church on Bach's majestic wing. Yet, Auntie Nell's long refreshments table, done up with pristine white linens from the Brookhurst cupboards and great silver urns of spring flowers, lent a certain dignity to the setting. She had even somehow managed to transport a beautiful two-tiered wedding cake which she'd made, from her kitchen at Camellia Cottage. The ingredients were obtained through a stockpiling of her coupons plus those of Grandmother and Geneva, which began immediately the engagement was announced. "There won't be any cardboard cake with satin icing for *my* niece," swore Auntie Nell. Thanks to Father, the champagne flowed.

After the bride and groom were toasted, the pictures taken and the cake served, the band played the wedding waltz. Elizabeth sat on the sidelines holding a plate with a square of wedding cake which she felt almost criminal for wasting as she watched Emelye and James, all her imaginings down the years of what a handsome couple they would be made manifest in the vision before her. Emelye had dispensed with her headdress and wedding veil. Her blond hair was exposed in all its abundance, swinging to the rhythm of their twirling steps. She looked up at James with adoring, trusting eyes, and James smiled down at her. Elizabeth read his thoughts: *You are mine, and I will take care of you forever.* She was rent through with jealousy. How long would it take for her to be at peace with what she had forfeited? How long before her prayers for the couple's happiness would not be tinged with regret?

As the wedding dance ended and another waltz began, Tony and Geneva joined in. Tony was in constant pain, but was determined to simply bear up until this night was over, rather than rely on his cane and thereby draw attention to himself. Besides, since the war began, he and Geneva had rarely danced together, and he was not about to squander this opportunity. They still had the old magic, by Jove! He knew it from the moment he took her in his arms. Of course, tomorrow he would pay the price, just as he always did after a bit of coaching when a dance was to be performed in a play at the *William & Mary*: lying in bed with his knee elevated, a bottle of Aspro nearby. Damn and blast! Why could he not have injured some other part of his body? Still—he reminded himself—he was fortunate to have survived that bombing in one piece, and damned lucky to be doing what he was doing right now, no matter how painful it was. Thanks be to God, the highly secret Operation Overlord—the Allies' greatest hope—was just beyond the horizon. If it could be brought off successfully, the war may very well be over in a matter of months, and then there would be no more injuries; no more deaths. Tony suddenly felt flush with anticipation. He smiled down adoringly at Geneva, the love of his life, as they waltzed round the floor....

Along with others, Elizabeth soon lost herself in the spectacle of her parents dancing. Their crisp style, their flawlessly synchronized movements, marked them unmistakably as professionals. It was easy to imagine how, long ago, they had been caught up in the romance of their dazzling presence on stage, and fell in love; how easy it would have been for Father to be lured away from the young woman to whom he had pledged his love, and who was far away and isolated from his glamourous life as a performer.

By the time the band progressed from waltzes to fox trots, practically everyone was dancing. Auntie Nell and Uncle Morey were two jolly barrels pivoting round and round. Elizabeth was heartened to see her grandparents out on the floor as well. Grandfather was looking very well indeed, in his dress suit of deep blue. His face had lost that gaunt look which characterized it at Christmas, and he had regained some of the weight he'd lost. Elizabeth believed that he would live for a good many more years, and she was determined to spend as much time with him as possible.

Naturally, every eligible young man in the room was showering attention on Serena, and one of her most ardent admirers appeared to be Jerome Owsley, who had accompanied his father Kenneth to the wedding. Elizabeth had not seen the Owsleys since the war began, for she seldom went up to London. She calculated Jerome's age to be around sixteen. He was already quite a handsome young man, with finely-hewn patrician features. He wore his straight reddish blond hair a bit longer than was stylish; hence, overall, he looked somewhat theatrical. Like his mother, he had alluring eyes with long lashes, and from all evidence as he and Serena engaged in conversation—that Serena was four years his senior seemed of no consequence to either of them—he was as much a charmer as his father. Which may prove unfortunate, if ever he married. According to Father, his parents were separated once again, due to Kenneth's perennial skirt-chasing. Helena was currently touring military posts in Europe with a troupe of entertainers led by Bob Hope.

The air came alive with jitterbug music, causing an exodus of older couples from the dance floor. Elizabeth saw Jerome catch Serena's hand and lead her out to dance. Then she lost sight of them, and found herself staring at James and Emelye. Emelye's image as a bride possessing grace and dignity was soon shattered: her wedding dress was hiked above her knees, and her shapely hips swung to the music. James—no slouch himself—flung her out, wrist-length, and back again; hiked her up on one hip, then the other, her white-slippered feet tucked under her; plunged her body like a sword through his parted legs, the back of her hair brushing the floor; then brought her to her feet again, and twirled her round and round, her beautiful long legs with slender ankles coiling, uncoiling, like a figure skater's. On and on, their bodies thrilled to the rhythm. James was grinning. Elizabeth had never seen him look so carefree, so completely at ease. It was as if he and Emelye had grown up dancing together. Now that she thought about it, perhaps they had.

I could not have danced with him, she thought sadly. It came to her that, at last, she was truly bidding James farewell.

At half past ten o'clock, Emelye changed into her traveling suit, and the wedding party and many of the guests proceeded, on foot, the short distance to Bodmin Station. From here the newlyweds would embark on their honeymoon in a shower of wedding rice. Inevitably the train was behind schedule, and there was an anticlimactic wait. High on champagne, the party was quite noisy and gay by now. With a discreet wave of farewell to Grandmother, Elizabeth seized a chance to slip away from the group. Walking home would not be easy in high-heeled dress sandals. Still, she was determined to be on her way, alone with her thoughts.

As she walked along, her steps guided by dim torch light below and a full moon and scattering of stars above, she considered whether to spend the night in Chris's room, and avoid encountering Serena, or return to her attic bed-room, where Serena would sleep a few feet away. How she loathed the thought of Serena questioning her about James. Could she be convincing in her denial? And if not, what then? Elizabeth did not know what Serena was capable of. Would she confront her brother, angrily, with the truth? Or, tell Emelye she had been lied to?

Or if not, might she, at some point, reveal the truth unintentionally?

At home, Elizabeth climbed the stairs and paused in indecision at the door of Chris's room. At length she realized that if she hid in there, she would prob-ably confirm Serena's intuition. She proceeded to the attic room.

For a long while, she lay wide awake on her pillow, staring up at the ceiling. In spite of all efforts, her imagination leapt ahead to the wedding night that would commence a few hours from now. Would Emelye excuse herself to the bath, and emerge in her sheer pink and black lace nightie? *"Knowing my brother, you won't be needing it much."* She remembered James's passion at Ready Money Cove, and her eager response. Her face felt hot—oh, stop it!

She turned on her stomach and drove her hands underneath her pillow. The end of one finger brushed the sharp corner of what she quickly realized was an envelope. She switched on the bedside lamp and pulled it out. Her name was scrawled across the front in James's hand. For some while, she could only stare at it in dread. Finally, it came to her that if she had slept in Chris's room, Ser-ena might very well have discovered it before she did.

She unsealed the envelope. At the top was today's date.

"Elizabeth—

Today I lay down my life for Emelye. She deserves nothing less. But she will never have my heart. You will carry it with you, to your grave.

—James."

PART IV

1944–1945

CHAPTER 55

It was around five o'clock on an evening in late September. Emelye was sitting alone at the kitchen table, slicing tomatoes and cucumbers on a cutting board, while Willa went into the front hall to answer the telephone. A pot of pinto beans was simmering on the stove, giving the kitchen that familiar gassy, onion-y smell, and a pan of corn bread was mixed and waiting for the oven to warm up. A small oscillating fan whirred on the ceramic tile counter. It still seemed like summertime in Houston. Through the screen door Emelye could see the big pecan tree in the back yard, its limbs weighted with ripening pecans that she and Willa would be gathering from the ground in a month or so.

Emelye still loved Willa's kitchen better than any other room in the house. It had never changed except in color scheme—several years ago Rodney and James painted the walls pale yellow, and Willa put up new café curtains on the window and the door glass, a pattern of yellow pears on a white background. Emelye was sitting at the same porcelain-topped table that had been in here forever. Thanks to Serena, who was clowning around one night and accidentally dropped a skillet, there was a small chip on one edge, where the cast iron showed through. The kitchen table was where all meals were eaten in this household, except when there was company for dinner and they ate in the dining room on the good china. It was also where you got a good talking to if you were in trouble. Serena, mostly. James, rarely—he was a college man by the time Emelye moved here. The only occasion she could remember was when he announced he was joining the USAAF. And that lecture didn't do any good, because he was determined. Emelye hated the thought of him leaving, but she had never been so proud of anyone in her life. As far as she was concerned, James had become twice the hero that he was before. She vowed to write him often, and she reasoned that being away might make him miss her just a little. Living under the same roof with James had not prompted him to fall in love with her, as she had hoped.

Emelye never caused any trouble—she was always afraid of being sent home to England—except that time when she broke her date with Larry Cateau for the senior prom. She would have risked anything if it meant a chance to be with James, especially once he was away in training. As she sat here across from Willa, she feared she would be forbidden to go to the prom with James. But after a short lecture, Willa said, "You'll have to live with the consequences of what you've done. Meantime, I want you to write your parents about it." And so, reluctantly, Emelye obeyed. But in truth she just felt so relieved that she'd be dancing with James at the prom, nothing else mattered.

Larry enlisted in the Army right after graduation, and she'd never heard anything of him since. Had he been killed in combat, like so many others? She'd probably never know, because his mother moved away from the Heights soon after he left. Willa heard about it at Kaplan's-Ben Hur. Willa was right. Hardly a day went by when Emelye did not think of Larry and feel guilty. Given the conversation they were having when the telephone rang just now, she felt especially ashamed. Guy would have never stood up a girl….

Pretty soon Emelye gathered from what she overheard that it was Rodney calling, to say he'd be late, that Mr. and Mrs. Kelso were coming in to sign an earnest money contract. Emelye knew the house the couple had been looking at, a pleasant two-story brick with a big front porch, over on Harvard Street. Back in high school days, when she first came to live here, Rodney would sometimes offer to show her and James and Serena a house he'd just listed. Serena expressed no interest, and James was usually too busy, between college courses and his part-time job at Yale Pharmacy. But Emelye loved walking around the bare rooms, imagining what the house would look like with new wallpaper and rugs and curtains, and just the right furniture. If she liked the house, she'd imagine living there with James someday, caring for him and their children. Of course, she never told this to Rodney, but she always gave him her opinion on the selling points of houses he showed her. Rodney always listened, which made her feel important. Now that she was living here again, and had a lot of time on her hands, she often went with him on house tours. She felt a thrill of anticipation about the Kelsos putting down earnest money. Rodney said they had three kids and a dog. Mr. Kelso had just been promoted to accounting manager at Foley's.

Willa came back into the kitchen. She was wearing her white pinafore apron with strawberries embroidered on the pocket. She tightened the sash around her waist. "Rodney says for us to go on and eat and just keep his plate warm, he'll be home around eight," she said—probably the sort of instruction repeated more than any other by a real estate broker to his wife. She lifted the lid off the beans, tested one for doneness, then turned off the fire. She opened the oven and slid the pan of cornbread in, then, with a glance at the kitchen wall clock—shaped like a teapot—she turned to Emelye. "Now, where were we?" she said, then frowned. "Oh yes, you were telling me about Nell's first little boy, dying—"

Emelye sighed. "It was the Spanish Influenza, during the First World War. He wasn't much more than a baby. I didn't hear about it until the first time I went to Camellia Cottage, and Guy showed me Gerry's picture," she said. Just thinking about that happy day made Emelye's throat thicken up. She would never forget how uneasy she felt when she hugged her big burly cousin good-bye the day she sailed away from England all those years later, knowing he would be off to the war in a few weeks. Then he made it nearly five years, most of them stationed over in Egypt, only to wind up being killed at Arromanches in the Normandy invasion. Whoever dreamed up the phrase, 'war is hell,' wasn't kidding. Guy was the sweetest boy in the world, and he wanted to spend his life helping others. Even the games they played as children were a way to act out helping people. He was buried in a cemetery right there at Arromanches, along with the others killed in his regiment. Aunt Nellie and Uncle Morey would not even be able to visit his grave until the war was over.

Emelye found out about Guy's death just a few hours after the doctor at Love Field confirmed that she and James were expecting a child. Immediately she thought, by golly, if this baby is a boy, we'll name him after Guy. James would be all for the idea, she was sure, and she really wanted to write her aunt and uncle, and tell them so, because it might make them feel a little better. But until she was sure James knew about the baby, she wasn't going to write to anyone else about it. And it may be months before she was sure he knew because at that point he was en route to a new assignment in France, at something of an outpost. There were many of these, where the Allies had driven out the Germans, and Allied troops occupied tents that had been occupied by German troops just a few weeks earlier. James said the way things were going, he probably wouldn't be staying in one place for very long, from now till the end of the war. He had recently completed transition training for the new P-51 Mustang, a long-range aircraft equipped with a powerful Rolls-Royce engine, and the new airplane of choice for escorting bombers into Germany. Every few months, some new plane came off the assembly line, better than the last. It seemed the USAAF was determined that James learn how to fly every one of them. He was always enthusiastic about learning to fly a new plane, and she was happy for him, and proud. But now that she was expecting, all she could think of was the dangers James faced every time he went up in a plane.

What if he ran out of luck, like Guy, and did not live to see his child?

As she reached for a tomato and started to slice it—that was three now, and ought to be plenty—the doorbell rang.

Willa and Emelye looked at each other, alarmed: who would be stopping by, this close to supper time? Emelye could not find her voice. Willa hesitated for a moment or two, lifting her hands then letting them fall at her sides. "I'll get it," she said, her words scarcely more than a whisper. She took a deep breath and went to the door.

Time stood still in the kitchen. The oscillating fan breathed cool air on Emelye's face, then drew it away, and brought it back again. Presently she heard Willa say, "Yes, thank you. No, it won't be necessary." Never had two short phrases been more fraught with meaning. And the amount of time that passed before the front door finally clicked shut, followed by dead silence, made Eme-lye slowly put down her paring knife, rise to her feet, and grip the edge of the table, the blood beating in her temples.

As she walked down the long hall, from the kitchen toward the front door, the hardwood floor seemed to tilt beneath her feet. At the other end, just in front of the stairway, stood Willa, the light from the transom shining down on her white apron. She held a Western Union envelope at arm's length, as if she was afraid it might explode in her hands. And—it was funny how the mind would note certain things at certain times—Emelye saw, too, the blue star in the front window as she passed by the living room, that signified a soldier lived here. A soldier who was alive, fighting for his country. Willa handed the envelope to Emelye. "It's for you," she said, her voice husky.

They looked at each other. Emelye unsealed the envelope. Then Willa was standing behind her, with her hand on Emelye's shoulder, and they were reading: "Regret to inform you…report received states your husband First Lieutenant Sidney James Younger missing in action in France…."

Emelye felt Willa's hand slide heavily down her back. She turned and guided her shocked mother-in-law to Rodney's easy chair in the living room. She lifted her feet up on the ottoman. "How can they have lost him we never call him Sidney," Willa said, the words rushing out on one breath. Emelye agreed there was something ominous about the appearance of James's first name, which was never used except on official documents. It made his plight seem hopeless. Yet, she knew that there was hope, that 'missing' was a temporary state, apt to change any minute to 'found,' maybe had already changed, though of course there was another possibility for change, to another word, beginning a different phrase—

"My God, look at you!" Willa cried. She rose and grabbed Emelye's elbows, led her to the couch and ordered her to lie down and take deep breaths. As a matter of fact, now that Emelye thought about it, her heart was beating pretty fast and her face was burning, a sign of elevated blood pressure, something that every expectant mother was warned to avoid. Willa was easing a pillow under her head. Then, before Emelye was fully aware she had left, she was back again with a moist cool face cloth, bathing her forehead.

"There now. The last thing we need is for anything to happen to you and the baby, so just try and relax—" Willa said, with an attempt to appear calm, though she didn't feel calm at all.

"I'd a lot rather James be missing in France, than Germany. His chances are at least a hundred times better," Emelye said, remembering the front page of the newspaper after the Liberation, the grainy picture of Eisenhower parading triumphantly through the Paris streets in the back of a convertible, in a shower of confetti and streamers. Since then, the whole country was crawling with Allied ground forces, moving in a tight line toward the Netherlands and Germany, where Emelye hoped to God they'd kill every last one of the Nazis, and their mothers and their widows and their firstborn sons. She squeezed Willa's hand. "I'm alright now, thanks."

After Willa's initial response of numbing shock, her very next reaction was anger. How could God let this happen, after all her years of praying for James's safe return the first thing every morning and the last thing every night, and several hundred times in between, *Damn it to hell, he is my only son!*—Then she thought of Nell, and felt contrite, and was thankful that there was something solid to hope for, that James was in France, not Germany. Missing, not Killed. Thankful that Emelye was here to remind her. She suddenly thought to call Rodney and went to the phone, wondering, *Oh Lord, how will I tell him this?*

It seemed to Emelye that the worst thing about an MIA telegram was that it usually meant prolonged waiting and wondering, for all the loved ones on the receiving end, and always meant you had absolutely no control over the situation. There was nothing Emelye hated more than being powerless. It was like being in the back of a truck, bound and gagged, in the seediest part of London, when she was six. It was like being thrown in the attic closet at St. Michael's School, and hearing the key turn in the door.

And maybe that's how James was feeling, too, she thought now. *Please, God, don't let James think he won't be found, that he has been abandoned. I love him so much, he's the best man in the world, he is my everything, oh God, let him be found!*

She tried to imagine James's circumstances. His last letter, written near the end of August, said that he'd been "pulled out on a special reconnaissance duty." So presumably he was not attached to a squadron when he went down, but was alone. He might be harder to locate. And…she reasoned…with the end of this God-forsaken war within view, and everyone desperate to reach the finish line, how much time and effort would the USAAF have at their disposal, to search for one missing pilot? What if James was hurt really bad? Bleeding? Without proper medical attention, he could die before they found him, she realized. And then, on top of everything else, she remembered that James may not know that a miracle occurred during one of those five days and nights of their honeymoon. He made no mention in his August letter of having received her letter saying they were expecting. *God, don't let him die without knowing he's going to be a father.*

Abruptly Emelye sat up and stared into space, a prickly feeling beneath her ears and goose bumps rising on her forearms. Maybe all that time she spent in the WASP was for a purpose she didn't know about.

Willa came in. "Rodney's canceling his appointment, and coming home. He wants us all to be together," she said, and her voice caught. *Please, God—*

"What are you doing, sitting up?"

"I'm going over there, to help find James," said Emelye.

CHAPTER 56

Just how to help locate James occurred to Emelye within moments after she realized it was her destiny to do it, and it wasn't all that complicated. She would simply present herself at the Eighth Air Force headquarters in Bushy Park, politely ask what was being done, and just keep asking until she was certain that the search for James was ongoing. Then she'd stick around until he was found and brought back to England. How could they look a soldier's pregnant wife straight in the eye, after she traveled thousands of miles, and say they just didn't have the time or the manpower to keep looking? But if they did manage to weasel out of it, she would look to her father to take it from there. On the eve of her wedding, she had discovered—purely by accident—that he worked in espionage for the British government.

Emelye and Serena had landed at the RAF base in Norwich, England two days early, and spent one night in London before traveling by rail to Bodmin. Serena spent the night at a hotel with John Stockton, the pilot who flew them over. Emelye slept on a cot in the basement of her parents' home on Norfolk Square. In the middle of the night, she was awakened by the sound of her father's voice, next door in the scullery. She listened with growing amazement as she gathered he was talking on the telephone, helping to get some high official safely out of Occupied France and across the channel by ferry. She could not imagine her father, a creative artist to his very soul, involved in clandestine activities. But then, just hours earlier, she had seen first-hand the bombed-out, patched-up, bleeding city where he lived. She supposed he was just doing his bit in the war, like everybody else. The next morning, she admitted to him that she had eavesdropped. For a moment, he looked as if he had been "caught out," as the British say. Then, in a leaden voice, tinged with irony, he said, "We'll just let it be our little secret, agreed?"

"Does Mother know?" she persisted.

"Not much more than you do," he said, and changed the subject.

She had never breathed a word of this to anyone, and until tonight she had never thought she might benefit from his connections and his expertise.

Of course, the first thing was to get overseas, and quickly.

She placed a long distance telephone call to Nancy Herkemer, her former commanding officer at Love Field. Nancy was more than willing to help. If Emelye could get to Dallas, she would find her a ride to the East Coast. Talking to Nancy made Emelye miss the WASP so much, a lump swelled in her throat. Those women could always be depended on to get things done, and no excuses. It was little wonder most of the men in the Air Force—not to mention the U.S. Congress—found them a threat to their egos. Pretty soon, however, Nancy thought of an obstacle that Emelye had overlooked for the moment: She had resigned her commission when she learned she was pregnant. "You won't have clearance, here, or on any other base," Nancy pointed out. Emelye's heart sank in defeat; however, Nancy quickly formulated a solution: Emelye was to send a telegram to her U.S. Congressman. Mention her service as a ferry pilot, but don't overdo it, in case he was among the majority who voted against making the WASP an official branch of the Army Air Force; emphasize James's contribution to the war effort, volunteering to fight with the Allied Forces even before the U.S. entered the war, "and above all, don't mention your pregnancy."

After hanging up from the call to Nancy, Emelye jotted all this down on the telephone message pad, then looked up to see her in-laws standing side by side in the hall, and looking worried. Rodney had not even been home long enough to hang up his hat and remove his suit jacket. He opened his mouth to speak, but she headed him off. "I gotta place a call to Serena," she said.

Serena was stationed at Las Vegas AFB, flying the B-26 Marauder, which was used as a target tug for training Flying Fortress gun crews. Once Emelye's call went through, she had to wait for Serena to be summoned to the telephone. Just hearing the shrill zinging of planes taking off in the background returned Emelye's thoughts to the day she made her first solo flight in a T-6 Texan, her eyes glued to the strip of runway in front of her, her whole arm shaking as she released the brakes then pushed the throttle full on, praying that she hadn't overlooked anything on that check list—.

"Hey, Em, everything okay down there?" Serena sounded out of breath, and anxious about a long distance call from home in the middle of the day.

Hearing the news that James was MIA and that Emelye was going over to help find him, Serena paused to absorb the shock, then swore at the top of her lungs what idiots they had in the Air Force, losing her brother; they couldn't find their way through a hole in the wall. "You can't go over there, pregnant. He's my brother. I'll go," she swore.

Usually Emelye was thankful for Serena's take-charge attitude. There had been plenty of times when she devised some scheme to get them what they both wanted. But just now, it made her so angry she could barely control herself. "You can go to hell, for all I care. He's my husband, and I'm going."

"My folks won't let you," Serena snapped.

"They can't stop me," Emelye retorted, glancing toward their perplexed faces. "Now, shut up and listen. I need some help."

Serena calmed down and listened then, which gave Emelye a heady feeling of confidence and self-possession. When she finished explaining the situation, Serena promised to talk to John Stockton about giving her a ride from New Jersey. John was still ferrying planes overseas from Englewood AFB. Emelye drew a mental line, connecting all the points of her journey. "I guess I'm covered, then," she said, her head spinning. She glanced at her watch. Less than an hour had passed since she opened the telegram about James and the world was tilted on its axis.

"Atta girl, Emelye, I know you can do it!" Serena said with spirit; then more slowly, she added, "I love you, Sis; you know that, don't you?" Serena rarely said *I love you*. Emelye, whose emotions were never far from the surface, dare not reply for fear the thin shell of her composure would crumble. Until now, she had not realized just how thin it was. She'd be no use to James if she was an emotional wreck.

When Emelye hung up the telephone, she sniffed the air. "Something's burning."

"Oh Lord, it's the corn bread," Willa cried. She hurried to the kitchen, grabbed a pot holder and removed the smoking pan from the oven, thinking how sick she was of corn bread and pinto beans; once the war was over she would never again be caught dead—*Oh damn it to hell, where is my boy?* She put down the pan of charred bread with a great clatter, and burst into tears.

In the hall, Rodney told Emelye with quiet firmness, "I'm going with you."

It was the last thing she wanted. If she traveled alone, she could sweet talk the soldiers she encountered from one check point to another, to help speed things along. Having her fifty year old father-in-law at her side would cramp her style. Besides, Emelye knew that if Rodney was around, she would be tempted to rely on him to do her thinking. This was the biggest risk she had ever taken in her life. She had never felt so brave, or self-reliant. "I appreciate that, Rodney, but I know what military bases are like," she argued. "If two of us go, it will take twice as long." She studied his stony expression, his jaw rigid with determination. She could have wept for the pain she knew he was feeling. "It could make a difference to James," she pleaded.

Slowly, Rodney hung his hat on the hall tree, removed his jacket and loosened his tie. "I'll be happy to help you with that telegram," he said without looking at Emelye.

Rodney phrased her request with the kind of careful diplomacy that always made people eager to do what he asked, and was partly responsible for his success as a real estate broker. Within twenty-four hours, the Congressman replied warmly to Emelye, wishing her the best of luck.

Three nights later, sometime after dark, Emelye went out to sit in the wicker love seat on the front porch. Ordinarily she wasn't the kind of person who sat around reflecting on things. But this was the first time she had slowed down since the telegram came, and she needed to think about what was ahead. The blue star hovered in the window, and the blackout curtains were drawn like a stage prop behind it. Up above, a harvest moon was shining with a steady benevolence that made you believe God was in his heaven and all was right with the world. Except all was not right with the world. She'd be leaving early tomorrow morning, and in two more days she would be climbing through the hatch into the belly of a B-17. She remembered the first time she stood on the ground at Avenger Field, watching a B-17 take off from an air strip and roar into the clouds. She was thrilled by the power of those huge uplifted wings and that long, tapering body; it seemed all the bombs in the German arsenal combined could never bring it down. Yet, she soon learned that in order to accommodate the added weight when transporting 4,000 pounds of bombs, the B-17 had to be as light as possible. Therefore it was made of thin metal, easily penetrated by enemy fire, which was one reason a complement of small fighter planes ran interference on missions into enemy territory.

Inevitably, she wound up asking herself the question she'd been avoiding for three days: was it really fair to force the child in her womb to take that trip with her in a bomber, minus its cargo and its escort? Yet it was too late to back out. And James needed her. *Please, God, get us safely there,* she prayed. It was at least comforting to know that her father would be waiting in London: "Come ahead. Shall do all I can to help. Godspeed," said his cable.

The screen door opened, and Rodney came out and sat down beside her, the wicker squeaking under his weight. "If you need me at any time, for anything at all, I'll get over there somehow," he said gravely, without facing her.

Emelye realized Rodney was allowing for the fact there might be bad news waiting when she got overseas. "I'll remember that," she said gratefully. "But if anything—" she swallowed down the fear swelling in her throat—"happened to James, Willa would need you to be right here with her. She's all bluster, Rodney; you're her real strength, you know that."

For a while they were both silent, alone with their thoughts. As Rodney looked out over Heights Boulevard under the soft moonlight, he could distinguish the dark silhouettes of the neighboring houses. How peaceful it was. Just like it used to be years ago, with rarely an automobile passing by—not because of gas rationing as it was now, but because few people owned automobiles then. He remembered sitting out here late at night sometimes, shortly after James was born. He remembered feeling his heart would burst with gratitude for his blessings: a wife he was crazy about, and a brand new healthy son sleeping upstairs in his crib. In fact, it was about this time of year. *James will be twenty-three years old next month*, Rodney realized suddenly, and all at once he wanted to take a swing at somebody, something. Only twenty-three! Rodney had done his duty to his country, in the First World War, and he remembered very well that what made it all worthwhile, for him and every other soldier, was the belief that their generation would be the last to make that kind of sacrifice. How naive he had been, as he sat out here on those nights after James was born, not to imagine that his son would grow up just in time to fight another war....

He just had to believe that James would survive this. In a husky voice, he said to Emelye, "You know, I really believe that somewhere out there, James is alright. Hanging on. It isn't just wishful thinking, either. James has plenty of common sense. And he's strong, and stubborn. It's hard to get the best of people like James. You just can't do it, that's all." His voice peaked in the middle of the last sentence, then drifted off in a whisper.

Emelye's eyes were swimming. She took Rodney's hand in hers. "I know it. You're right. He's fine. We just gotta be sure he isn't left waiting out there in vain. He deserves better than that."

Rodney sniffed, and patted her hand. How large and warm his hand felt, Emelye thought, how comforting. Suddenly she wished she could just keep holding it, all the way over to England.

After a while, Rodney said, "James is one lucky man, being married to you." *And I hope he realizes it,* he thought uneasily, because he was not really sure how his son felt about the wonderful girl he had married. Rodney had never known James to be as tight-lipped as he had become since Elizabeth jilted him. He wouldn't let anybody in on his thoughts or feelings. Didn't want anybody's advice. He and Willa were both worried about how things would turn out between James and Emelye, when the war was over and they really settled into married life. His mind was suddenly overtaken by a tragic image: Emelye as his son's widow, carrying on with their child, never knowing he married her while loving someone else. "I'm going inside now," he said abruptly.

Around midnight, Emelye sat on her bed, packing the small alligator leather suitcase her parents had given her when she sailed away from England. After folding a maternity-size flannel gown and putting it into the case, she paused, moving her hands along the small mound of her abdomen. At nearly six months along, she wasn't showing very much. She figured this was owing to the fact that the WASP demanded its members stay in the top physical condition they developed in training, and the fact that this was her first baby. She closed her eyes, recapturing the feeling of James's hands moving tenderly over her body, during their honeymoon. He had to teach her how to love him. She didn't know what to do, whether to just lie still and be done to, or be more—well, maybe the word was *daring.* Like she supposed Serena was with men, though she never went into details. By the end of the week, Emelye had caught on pretty good as a pupil, and she and James were going places she never expected to go.

Emelye could not remember a day in her life when she had not awoken with love for James in her heart. The fact that he actually loved her back—oh yes, after that honeymoon week, she would never doubt it again—still seemed the greatest miracle that could ever happen. She was determined to be the best wife in the world—.

How easily her thoughts had leapt into the future. *But what if we have no future?* She wondered uneasily. *No. If I was not meant to find James, and bring him back, safe and sound, then why has everything fallen into place so perfectly?* She touched her swollen belly and spoke aloud to her child. "We gotta go, Sugar. Daddy needs us."

Geneva opened her eyes and glanced at her bedside clock: 6:30. She'd been awake all night, well as a matter of fact she had not slept much for the past three nights, since Tony telephoned with the upsetting news that James was

MIA, and to say that Emelye was making arrangements to travel to England and that he would keep her informed. She'd spent most of her time near the telephone, keeping her own prayer vigil for James, and also for poor Willa and Rodney; she had already cabled them her love.

This was the day that Emelye would depart on her journey. Well, just barely. It was twelve-thirty a.m. in Houston—no, one-thirty. They were on war time: one hour ahead. Was Emelye lying awake at this very moment, too wound up to sleep?

She would wait until seven o'clock. By then someone ought to be within hearing distance of the telephone in the lounge at Clough Hall, and could tell Elizabeth her mother was on the line....

By the time Elizabeth reached the telephone she felt quite certain her father had been hurt or perhaps killed in a blast, this time his luck running out. Hearing instead that James had come to harm was doubly shocking, for she had not once even considered this possibility. Geneva's voice sounded dull with fatigue and worry. "Frankly I wonder what good Emelye can do, coming all the way over here—your father's using his connections to help—but I admire her for trying, bless her heart. You've just been on my mind so much since it happened. I felt you'd want to know, so that you could be praying," she said.

Elizabeth peered out the mullioned window at morning shadows on dewy grass, her eyes blurred in despair. If anything happened to James, she could not bear it. She could not live with the fact that in her selfishness she had denied him the one thing that would have brought him happiness for the brief time left to him on this earth: to be with her. *She was slipping the ring he had made specially for her, on and off her finger....* "Of course I shall pray! I should never have forgiven you, if you had not let me know. Oh, Geneva, how dreadful," she cried, and her voice broke.

Afterward as she groped her way up the stairs, tears spilling from her eyes, she passed Millicent, coming down. "What is it?" she asked worriedly.

"James has been reported MIA. Oh, Millicent, what shall I do if anything happens to him?" she sobbed. She continued up the stairs. Millicent stared at her retreating figure. *Foolish girl, look how much you care for him still! What could have got into you, breaking up with him? You haven't had a happy moment since.*

Upstairs Elizabeth sank to her knees beside her bed and folded her hands together. She prayed aloud, her voice coming in choked spasms. Finally she rose to her feet, blew her nose, and sat down at her desk. She wished that James could know she was praying for him, and would be doing so constantly, until he was rescued. She found herself staring at the drawer where she kept his letters—there were nearly fifty in all, from the beginning. She had carefully placed them in the drawer, arranging them in chronological order, with the most recent one on top. It was her way of registering in her mind and heart that, while their romance was over, and must be put aside, she would treasure the memory forever. She had not opened the drawer since then. Perhaps it was wrong, but just now she longed to touch the letters again, to feel a connection with James. Slowly she opened the drawer, her heart pounding….

She lifted the stack of letters, realizing abruptly that the one on top—James's letter written in late November of last year, suggesting they travel to Bodmin together, at Christmas—was missing. Panic rising, she quickly went through the others. She found the missing letter on the bottom of the stack, and for a moment or two, she felt weak with relief. But it should have been on top. Had someone sneaked into her room and gone through her things? Granted, she often left her door unlocked. But who would have done such a thing? And for what reason? No, it was preposterous—

Yet…there was that day in April when her grandmother Francine surprised her by paying a call. Suffering a deep bronchial cough, and looking pale and unhealthy, she said she believed that she had not long to live, and wished to tell Elizabeth goodbye. All the while, she puffed away on one cigarette after another. Feeling a sense of pity for the ill woman, and admittedly, a sense of gratitude for the unexpected opportunity to ask her all those questions she had stored up for most of her life, Elizabeth defied her father by talking with her.

As they parted, her grandmother said, "There is no need to tell your father that we have talked. *D'accord?* After all, he resents me, and will only be cross with you. I should not want to think that I have come between you and your father, just for having a little talk about your mother."

Elizabeth promised to honor her grandmother's wish, knowing, of course, that it served her own best interest as well. The last thing she wanted to do was bring down Father's wrath.

Except for Father's adamant claim that her grandmother was not to be trusted, there was no reason to suspect she had poked round her room. In any case—she remembered now—her grandmother had not even entered Clough Hall beforehand, but waited outside on a garden bench while someone found Elizabeth to say she was here.

No doubt she'd simply made an error in arranging James's letters, probably because she was distracted by heartache at the time. She placed the letter on top where it belonged, then closed her eyes and slowly moved her fingers along the lines of her name and address, written in his hand. *James, James, hear my heart calling yours and know that I care....*

CHAPTER 57

On my honor, I will do my best to do my duty to God and my country and to obey the Scout law. To help other people at all times. To keep myself physically strong....

James lay swathed in bandages on a narrow cot that was rank with body odor and hair oil. The long room in which he lay smelled of the rotting apples heaped in one corner. A few feet from his cot was a huge gaping stone hearth. In front of this was a long wooden table with a candle burning in the center. And at the far end of the room was a rough wood plank door. The door was open halfway, exposing darkness on the other side, as if this place were at the edge of all creation, and only a vacuum existed beyond it.

A thick-waisted woman, dark-haired, dressed fully in black, stood before the hearth watching James with small black eyes, her arms folded under her bosom. He knew somehow that the two were not supposed to converse but he did not know how he knew this or why they were not supposed to. He lay still, struggling to keep straight the sequence of events that brought him here so that later he could report back to the Scoutmaster—But he could not discipline his mind to stop *"...daydreaming. It's his only problem, Mr. Younger. He is a very smart boy!"*

"His mother and I are very proud...."

"Of course, daydreaming is not unusual for a boy in the sixth grade. I'm sure he'll outgrow it, and one day he'll be a great success...."

...and do my duty to God and my country...and keep myself physically strong...and do a good turn to someone every day.

James had tested his limits and found he was able to wiggle his toes on both feet. He could not lift his right arm at all. He could lift his left arm, but no more than a few inches, and there was a throbbing behind his eyes that grew worse every time his mind returned to the sequence of events and struggled to remember the order, starting from the very beginning, the dilemma suddenly facing him: should he circle around and try to come in closer, and maybe he'd get lucky and hit a clear patch and get some pictures? Or, go back before it was too late? He couldn't risk a radio transmission from where he was. How many times could he circle and go lower, and still have enough fuel to get back to base? Down below, massed together through the camouflage of trees, were the long stream-lined uniform shapes. Forty-six foot, fourteen-ton rockets, each with a one-ton warhead, they struck at a speed over four times that of sound and could not be stopped once they were launched. Fingers of fog were beginning to swirl around them. There wasn't much time. He would try once more—

"Soldier, what is your name?" A woman asked in broken English. She was the first English-speaking person he had encountered since he was brought here. He turned his face very slightly in the direction of her voice. The woman's figure seemed fluid, and there was light all around her, as if she were an apparition. James could not trust his eyes; they were like two round balls, moving without coordination. Regaining his vision was essential, or they would put him behind a desk. "*Son, if I had 20/20 vision and your physique, you can bet your ass I'd be taking that bus to Cimarron AFB right along with you, instead of sitting behind this desk.*" James would rather be dead than behind a—

The woman's impertinent voice: "You've been brought to a safe house. But it's risky, you know? Where is your dog tag? How do we know you are not a German spy, wearing a stolen jacket with an Eighth Air Force patch, eh? And who is 'your friend Elizabeth' who gave you the little book? Odd for a flying officer to carry a book of poems in his jacket—"

The poems. Yes, now as the woman floated away, he remembered: an hour and seventeen minutes from zero, bearing 210 degrees south-southwest. Flames shooting from one engine; black smoke mushrooming through the fog. Pressing the pocket of his jacket, beneath his heart, to be sure the Spenser volume was there, the last thing he did before descending into the fog: a stringed puppet, blind as to what awaited him below. *On my honor I will do my best to do my duty to God and my country…* and remember 49 degrees, 15 minutes by 1 degree, 5 minutes.

Floating down in the density of fog: *Sir, First Lieutenant Younger reporting. Sir, you won't believe this, the mother of all V-2 storage sites, not too far from Rouen. Enough V-2's to wipe London off the face of the earth, Sir—*Abruptly

James opened his eyes to a blurred vision of a dimly lit room. A man stood next to his cot, speaking to him in French. Slowly, James focused his vision. It was getting better now. Yet nothing was as he remembered. The ceiling in this room was very low, with exposed rafters. The air was still and musty. A lantern with smoked-up glass, emitting very little light, hung from the center rafter. Hulking wooden vats were lined up next to the walls. Where was the open hearth and long table, and the lady who stood watching as they carried him in a few minutes ago? Or, had he been daydreaming? Safe house. No children allowed. Couldn't stay in one for long. Too dangerous. They might have to move you before the Hudson came to fly you back.

So they had moved him….

The Frenchman had a scar running diagonally down one cheek, and his right arm ended in a stub at the elbow. With his left hand, he thrust a small pan toward James. James stared at him, bewildered. The man shrugged, put the pan on the cot next to James, and turned away. Only then did James know what the pan was for, and suddenly he had to pee so bad, he felt he might explode. His hand trembling, he fumbled for the pan and shifted his weight to the right side, a shockwave of pain racking him, the smell of burning in his nostrils…

…as he felt the blade slice down his right thigh; then he was hanging upside down, entangled in the ganglia of his own strings, the ground far below, his arms flailing, reaching for the knife strapped around his leg. Missing, reaching again. *The Air Force is the most prestigious branch of the U.S. Army. Only the best and the brightest go to flight school and the best of these become fighter pilots.*

"Classmates and teachers remember James, who was voted 'Senior Favorite' in the class of 1939, and was Captain of the track team. He graduated third in his class…." The best and brightest missing, reaching again.

He was staggering down a narrow dirt road in the dark, 49 15 1 5, *On my honor I will do my best to do my duty to God and my country…*and remember, 49 15 1 5. One foot struck something hard as granite and he stumbled and fell forward, landing spread-eagled on the body of Christ, their foreheads touching, the blood from their wounds, mingling. For a prolonged moment they looked into each other's eyes. And he knew that he'd been given the chance to see what death was like. It was simpler than he thought, just to find yourself suddenly relieved of duty, that was all, and then you didn't have to worry about making everyone proud by being the best fighter pilot and earning another merit badge so the Scoutmaster would shake your father's hand and then everyone say the Pledge of Allegiance to the Flag. *"We can always rely on James* *to do what is expected of him, and more. He intends to finish his engineering degree when he comes home after the war."* In death you were free to walk on, without worrying about your future or what you left undone, the pictures not taken, because none of it mattered after all, the mother of all V-2 storage sites, 49 15 1 5, because where you were now there were no wars: now he knew this was the physical manifestation of Elizabeth's ideal—

Someone was shaking a torch light in his face. The heat from the torch was scorching, like heat rising from a skillet on the fire. James struggled to lift his right hand and push it away, but his hand wouldn't move; it trembled all the way up his arm. "—Eh? Speak up, soldier." A woman's voice, sharp, brusque, different from the other woman's. English with a heavy French accent. He could not see her for the hot torch light burning his eyes. "How can we help you to get home, if you refuse to talk to us? Perhaps you don't remember anything, eh?" A long pause. He uttered his name, rank and serial number. "Yes, we already know that. But if you won't tell us more, we cannot help you get home. You want to go home, don't you? Oh well. We will try again in a day or two." The torch light moved away. Clacking footsteps on narrow heels, the short steps of a small person. Angry steps, impatient.

It was then James realized it was not the torch light that had burned him. He was burning with fever. *I can't save us. The mother of all storage sites.* He struggled to go back to where he was, recapture that feeling that he had been freed by death from responsibility…and *All, all are sleeping, sleeping, sleeping on the hill.* What happened when you died had nothing to do with going to church, ten years of perfect attendance medals from Sunday School, serving as an acolyte and lighting the candles on the altar on Sundays; they were like stair steps, he always thought, lighting the way to the cross…

…it was dawn, the sky just beginning to light up behind the little church up on the hill, and the light reflecting off the colored windows. *All, all are sleeping….* He was rolling past on the flat hay-strewn bed of a wagon that bumped along a rutted road, holding his breath and tensing his muscles to absorb the painful jostling. He saw a bearded priest in a long black frock and black, squarish hat, walking up the steps toward the door of the church, the wind blowing his frock around his ankles. The whole scene seemed to belong in a world apart from the one in which James lived. You wouldn't know there was a war going on right in the neighborhood. He was possessed of an urge to climb out of the wagon and become a part of this world, escaping the other. Yet when he tried to lift himself, every bone in his body seemed to stab the one connected to it, like soldiers battling with swords; and he fell back, his breath heaving. As the view slowly passed from his sight, James tried to imprint on his mind that stone church with colored windows outlined against the blushing sky, and the figure of the priest approaching it. A tear ran down his cheek. Someday he would make a drawing of this and give it to Elizabeth, only he would add the poem's cemetery, to show—But no. He had tossed out his drawing pad and set of pastels on the day he wrote Emelye, asking her to marry him. *On my honor I will do my best to take care of Emelye....*

He woke up. His fevered body felt bolted down to the cot; his head was throbbing. *To keep myself physically strong.* Again, the room was lantern-lit. He focused his eyes. It took longer than the time before when his eyes were getting better, or was that time before only a daydream? A man he had not seen before was leaning back in a wooden chair, his legs parted, nearby the bed. His clothes, ragged and soiled, hung loosely on him. His thin yellowish-gray hair hung around his collar, and the hair on the sides was hooked around his ears. His yellowish beard hung in dirty clots against his chest. His body reeked of filth and alcohol, as if he had drunk so much it was oozing through the filthy pores of his skin.

He had a small volume open in his rough hands. James narrowed his eyes, his heart leaping as he recognized the binding. It was the Spenser.

The sight brought James alert. His stomach roiled in fury. When he raised up to grab the book, his right thigh felt like raw meat being fed through a grinder. He moaned in pain and collapsed again, gasping. He had to get the Spenser—

The man closed the book and looked across at James's face. His eyes were rheumy and bloodshot. He reached down and picked up a bottle from the floor. He took a drink, his eyes still on James, the brown liquid running down his chin. He belched loudly, and put the bottle down again.

Now he rose, uttering a phrase that seemed both vulgar and threatening. The chair fell backward and clattered on the floor. His eyes bright and a leer on his face that laid bare his few, rotting teeth, the man made as if to hand the book to James. When James lifted his hand to seize it, he snatched it away, and bellowed with laughter. Spittle flew from between his teeth. He slapped the book on his thigh.

He came close to James's chest, narrowed his eyes and spoke again, his tone low and vicious. He raised himself to his full height, drew his arm to his chest, and struck James hard across the face with his knuckles, then rammed a fist into his side. James let out an anguished cry. The room spun before his eyes. The man took the lantern and walked out, leaving James in the dark.

He knew now that they were going to kill him, that all his thoughts and imaginings as he lay here had been a rehearsal of his death.

... To help other people at all times.... 49 15 1 5...49 15 1 5...*A V-2 rocket is hurling undetected through the cloak of the stratosphere, the fate of its target already sealed. Closer and closer it comes to London. There will be no warning at all; not a sound. Then another is being launched, and still another....*

CHAPTER 58

Emelye rode through London in a dilapidated, fume-saturated taxi, the scent of charred wood and shell dust in her nostrils. Her white-haired driver was forced to detour time and again around streets that were taped off due to broken gas or water mains, or craters too deep to drive over. Past one bombed-out building after another they went, the detours often forcing on them the tragic sight of some family's possessions—or what was left of them—stacked at the curb in front of a heap of bricks and cement and shattered glass: fragments remaining of their used-to-be home. Though it was Sunday afternoon, and light rain was falling off and on, civil work crews soldiered away with their shovels and hammers and saws. It must have been dispiriting to know there had been no German loss of life or limb in all this destruction. The latest round of enemy attacks were carried out by thousands of pilotless V-1 buzz bombs.

Emelye asked herself if things were really any worse today than when she spent the night here on her way to Bodmin for her wedding. She was ashamed to realize that she had been too happy then, and too wrapped up in herself, to fully appreciate the misery surrounding her. She remembered posing with Serena in front of one of the many war posters at Piccadilly Circus while a photographer from *Picture Post* magazine took a picture of them: two young women in sleek Santiago Blues with silver wings on their lapels, smiling broadly on a sunny day. Feeling impervious to harm. A feeling opposite to this overtook her now: *I cannot save my husband.* Digging her fingernails into the worn, brittle edge of the taxi seat that seemed to epitomize as much as anything else how long and relentless and wearying the war had become, she willed herself into a positive frame of mind. Daddy had promised to do all he could to locate James and bring him safely home, and she'd never known him to fail. Everything would be fine. She patted her tummy and willed her child to know this, too.

When the taxi finally stopped at the curb at No. 12 Norfolk Square, her father was leaning on his cane in the doorway. Last time she saw him, on the glorious day when he walked her down the aisle of St. Petroc's Church, he was as handsome and robust as ever. Yet now his familiar brown sweater with sleeve patches hung loosely on his frame. His face had grown thin; his dark eyes were sunken in deep wells of fatigue. His smile as he waved at her was pale and lackluster. Could it be that living in a city under siege for four long years had finally exhausted him, both in body and spirit? *Just when I need him the most,* she thought with regret, then felt unspeakably selfish.

Emelye was wearing a full-length, double-breasted coat, so it wasn't until Tony caught her in a long, affectionate hug that he became aware of her swollen belly. *Oh my God, she's pregnant! Pregnant, and she's come all this way. And no certainty she can be of any help, now that she's here.* He released her, but held her hands fast. "Shame on you, you ought at least to have told me about the baby," he scolded her. He could not quite manage to keep the tenderness from his voice. This would be his first grandchild.

Emelye blushed. That her father had guessed her secret by physical touch was a little disconcerting. "I wanted to be sure that James had gotten my letter about the baby, before I wrote to you and Mother. And then—" She paused, her eyes suddenly choked with tears. "Have you heard anything, Daddy?"

Tony had gathered quite a lot of information in fact, but all of it led to still more questions, only one of which Emelye might—if they were very lucky—be able to dispose of. "Not much, I'm afraid," he said honestly. Emelye's countenance dropped. He lifted her chin and looked into her deep brown eyes; saw the child who was counting on her father to put everything to rights. It broke his heart. "Still, it's early yet. Come, let's ring up your mother to say you've arrived—she has been worried. Then we'll have a long talk."

Emelye followed her father into the sitting room, where the furnishings that were too large and heavy to be moved to the basement had been left in place and shrouded with dust covers. A telephone sat on the dusty walnut floor, with an old gooseneck lamp nearby, its globe lit. The ply board covering the deep windows and door glass shut out all natural light. She remembered a letter from Daddy a very long time ago, that after the second time the windows blew in—on the night he was nearly killed by a bomb—he stopped having the glass replaced.

Before Emelye knew it, he was telling her mother she had some important news. Then, with a lift of his brow, he handed her the receiver.

She resisted the urge to fix him with a cold stare. "Hi, Mom! Yes ma'am, I am. I just wanted to be sure James knew before I wrote to you—" she paused as her throat closed up—"but it hasn't worked out that way."

There was a long moment of silence on the other end. "And you risked coming all the way over here?" her mother demanded, as if it were the craziest thing imaginable.

"Mom, remember, I piloted planes for two months before I even knew I was pregnant."

"But you didn't go overseas, into a country under attack," she persisted. "Besides, all those hours in a plane with no bathroom! That's very foolish, and especially in your third trimester." Emelye was amazed at how quickly her mother arrived at her figures, almost as though she'd been imagining every day since the wedding that her daughter was expecting. Though she was not about to give her mother the satisfaction of knowing it, coming over, she barely made it to Greenland where they stopped to refuel, and by the time they landed at Norwich, she was desperate again to find a toilet.

"Listen, I want you to promise me that when you've finished your business in London, you'll come stay with me until after the baby is born. I won't have you making a trip all the way back to the States."

Again, Emelye was amazed at how quickly her mother drew a conclusion. She had not thought that far ahead. "We can talk about that later, Mom. Right now all I can think about is finding James and getting him back over here."

When Emelye handed the receiver back to her father, he promised her mother he'd 'look after Emelye.' As if she were a child. After a pause, he added, "I love you, too," and winked at Emelye. All at once she found herself imagining growing old with James, the two of them just as loving and affectionate as their parents were. It gave her a warm, buttery feeling inside. All she had to do was get him safely home….

Downstairs in the kitchen, Emelye sat at the huge wooden table while her father poured tea into thin porcelain cups with mismatched saucers, long ago discarded from the upstairs rooms. He had procured a tin of H&P Thin Captain's Biscuits—which he remembered that Emelye used to like. Touched by his thoughtfulness, she removed a couple of them from the tin and placed them on her saucer. Right now she was too keyed up to eat a bite.

Emelye noticed the row of knobs and tiny red signal flags on the kitchen wall, which corresponded to the bell pulls in the upstairs rooms. It occurred to her now that, until the war, her father was always on the other end of those signal flags. "It must be hard to live like this, year after year," she remarked.

Replacing the lonely tea kettle on the big iron stove with enough black iron burners to cook a royal banquet, he said, "One grows accustomed." The stoicism in his voice was not lost on Emelye. How spoiled and coddled Americans must seem, living in their safe homes, with relatively few inconveniences.

As her father sat down, Emelye caught a glimpse of the grim tightening of his jaw. "Daddy, does Mother know you're in pain?" she asked worriedly.

His eyes darted toward hers in a way that answered her question before he spoke. "No need causing a fuss," he said, "it's just the weather—so raw and damp lately. A little sunshine, and I'll be much the better. Now, here's what we have learned so far...."

Upon receiving Emelye's telegram, Tony had hastened to Eighth Air Force Headquarters. There he was directed to one Colonel Holbrook, who had been assigned to handle James's case. It seemed to Tony from the colonel's report that the Air Force had been thorough in their search for James. They had recovered the burned-out remains of his P-38, miles from the course where he was to have concentrated his reconnaissance efforts. Fortunately he had been able to bail out, and his survival kit was missing from the plane. "But this was over a fortnight ago, and all efforts to locate him have failed," he told Emelye. "He didn't turn up in any of the field hospitals."

Emelye remembered Rodney saying that James had plenty of common sense, and that he was strong and stubborn, and no one could get the best of him. This bolstered her now, and she repeated the words to her father.

"Yes, of course that's all to the good," he said, his expression tender. "Hopefully by now he has been picked up by Allied sympathizers, but keep in mind, he could just as well have fallen into the hands of German collaborators. The Free French are still ferreting them out."

He could not have known the demoralizing effect of those words on Emelye. She had never allowed herself to dwell on the possibility that James had fallen into the hands of the enemy, let alone, voice it. It was as if not doing so could keep it from becoming reality. She nodded uneasily.

Tony went on to explain that after consulting with Colonel Holbrook, he got the SOE involved. American pilots were occasionally sent over to bring back parties being aided by the Free French, or to make air drops of food and supplies, so fortunately there was a good line of communication open. Yesterday morning, he received word about an unidentified pilot with multiple injuries, being put up just outside a small village near Grenvilliers. The pilot was around six feet tall, with brown hair—a promising description, indeed. "Every pilot carries a small regulation picture, in case he has to bail out of his plane, and new identity papers have to be made up for him," he said. "This pilot's photo was delivered to me just a few hours ago."

Emelye's eyes lit up. Here they were on the brink of finding James, and her father waited all this time to say so. "Why didn't you tell me?"

He shook his head. "Grenvilliers is far from where James's plane went down, and therefore it is unlikely to be him. Besides, part of the photo is torn away; and what remains is badly wrinkled, especially round the facial features. In spite of all efforts, I haven't been able to make anything of it."

"If it's James I'll know it," Emelye said, her heart racing.

"Sit tight, and I'll fetch it," he told her, and walked out of the kitchen.

No sooner had her father left than she heard a telephone ring softly, but from here she couldn't tell if it was the one upstairs in the sitting room or the special phone at his basement desk. He was gone for a long while after it stopped ringing, and all she could think was that they'd found James, and when he came back into the kitchen he would be grinning from ear to ear.

Unfortunately, when he returned his expression was unchanged.

Placing the photo before her, he said, "The pilot in this photograph was found by a farmer and his son passing by one early morning on their way to the fields. He was badly injured, slumped over a large stone crucifix which had been toppled along the roadside—you remember the crucifixes, don't you, when we traveled through France?" Emelye remembered only the wooden cross left behind by the French cyclist, which Elizabeth took as her own. She nodded anyway. "Apparently the pilot stumbled over the crucifix in the dark, perhaps while trying to find his way to help. There was a considerable amount of blood on the crucifix."

Imagining James—for of course, Emelye could not help hoping that the pilot really was he—out in the middle of nowhere, badly hurt and seeking help, made Emelye want to leap out of her chair and hasten to where he was—

"This was roughly twenty-five miles southeast of Rouen. Apparently the farmers laid him in the back of their wagon, and took him to a place where they knew there would be access to at least minimal first aid.

"At that point—or so I gather—our agents took over, and tried to identify him. No luck. And the young man doesn't speak—perhaps he is incapable. I don't know. But as you can imagine, they are suspicious."

To Emelye's dismay, she could not identify the mysterious pilot's photo with any certainty, even when her father placed her wedding photograph with

James beside it, for the sake of comparison—something he admitted having done a number of times before she arrived. Having lived in the same house-hold with James for years; having laid beside him, both of them naked, for a whole honeymoon week, she felt she ought to know every single feature of his face, by heart. Yet she did not. *Already I'm failing him,* she thought drearily.

She shook her head. "I just can't be sure, Daddy."

A pained look crossed her father's face. "Alright," he said.

"Why hasn't the Air Force sent someone to see if it's James?" she asked.

Tony took in a breath. "I'm afraid that's the sticky part. You see, since James was not attached to a squadron when he went down, few know him, except men from his former squadron. They are all scattered now. And more than a few are dead. The Air Force can't spare the time or manpower to track down someone who might remember James well enough to make a positive identifi-cation, relieve him of his duties, and send him over there. At least, not at present. The best Holbrook could promise was to get someone over 'should an opportunity arise,' as he put it."

And so it was far worse than Emelye's greatest fear. The reluctance on the part of Air Force officials was so reasonable, there was no way to argue her case. James had never mentioned in his letters to her—or, perhaps he did not know—that many of his comrades-in-arm had lost their lives in the line of duty. Maybe some of them had stood in those proud columns outside St. Pet-roc's Church when they got married. The next step she had anticipated after the Air Force's refusal to go on searching—calling on her father's connec-tions—had already been taken. And maybe she was just muddled from exhaus-tion, but it seemed now the two sources she had counted on for help were just going around in circles. And all the while, James was badly wounded, his fate in limbo. What if he was bleeding internally? He might even be dying—

Her father was saying, "I admit I had some hope you would know for cer-tain if the pilot in the photo is James. Still. I shall go and have a look in the morning, weather permitting. I just got a call confirming the arrangements."

At first, Emelye was so overjoyed that she could already see herself standing on a windy air strip at some RAF base, watching a small aircraft touch down with James inside. She was holding his hand as they carried him on a stretcher through the hospital door, her father on the other side.

Then her eyes fell on the cane looped around the back of his chair, and all her expectations imploded. "Daddy, you can't go over there, the shape you're in. Besides, you said that there were still a lot of German collaborators running loose. I bet they'd love to get someone important like you in their sights."

"If the weather is sufficiently improved for the trip to go off on schedule, then very likely my leg will also be improved. So it often happens," he told her. In truth, even if his leg were improved, it was still subject to buckling at any moment. The area round Grenvilliers had suffered heavy bombardment. Many villages were destroyed; the main roads were impassable. His best bet was to round up a bicycle in Paris as a means of transportation out there. He didn't want Emelye to know all this, however. With a wry smile, he added, "And it would be nice to believe I am as important to the cause as you are convinced that I am, but I'm afraid I'm merely one of many, just doing the little bit he can," he assured her.

The more Emelye thought about it, the more unfair it seemed for him to place himself in danger on her behalf. "Daddy, what about Mother? And the children? I couldn't live with myself if I caused them to lose you," she said. How long ago it seemed that she assured her in-laws she would go only so far as London. Had she really believed it then? Or, had she always somehow known that it would come to this? "I'm going myself," she declared.

The mere idea caused Tony to bring a shaky hand to his forehead. "I couldn't possibly let you take that kind of risk. You have no idea how chaotic things are over there—villages burned out, road signs down, people wandering about, lost, in a daze, many of them desperate enough to steal, murder, to do most anything. No. It's quite out of the question."

"Listen Daddy. The way I see it, everyone is taking a risk over here, every day. Just getting out of bed in the morning is a risk, and going back to bed at night, too. I have no more right to safety than the next person."

He threw her a cold glance. "Perhaps not, but the baby you're carrying certainly has."

He was right. She had not bargained for putting her child through this particular risk. Still, after considering things carefully, she leaned across the table and put her hand on his. "Daddy, let me put it another way. If this pilot turns out to be James, well, it's pretty evident that he's bad off. What if—" she took in a breath, forced out the words, "—if he's dying? Daddy, I want to see him. More to the point, I want him to see me, to touch my belly and feel that child in there, know that he has a son, or a daughter, coming after him." *It's a boy,* she thought suddenly, *I know it is. And he'll be named Guy West Younger.* A thrill of anticipation went through her, transcending everything else for the moment.

"And Daddy, if I don't make it back—I'm sure that I will, but if I don't—well, there's no one depending on me at home."

Father and daughter took a long, measuring look at each other. Emelye could not be sure what her father's response would be to the commitment she could hardly believe she had made. He could easily put a stop to her going over there. Without his help, she could not do it. Maybe just a part of her really hoped that he would spare her.

A woeful feeling overtook Tony as he slowly admitted to himself that he was not equal to making this journey; he had the morbid sense of having lost forever some capability essential to his manhood. Well there was no use pitying himself. His daughter was grown now, and a damned sight more courageous than even he had expected. He had no right to keep her from her husband's side. It would take all night to get her even halfway prepared, but by golly—

Still, the agents on the other side of the channel were not going to like dealing with an amateur, Tony thought now, which led him to think of numerous other drawbacks. "You can't speak a word of French," he said discouragingly.

"*S'il vous plait. Merci beaucoup.* You told me when we went over there on vacation that those were the essentials, remember."

"But they won't be enough," he protested. Not to mention, she sounded like a Southern belle.

"You can teach me more."

"And you've never handled a firearm."

"Oh yes I have. I carried one in my plane, in the WASP. We had to be able to defend ourselves. I logged more than 700 miles, and I always had a gun within easy reach." She did not tell him that, holding the gun for the first time at the firing range in training, she found it terrifying; obscene in its raw, unmitigated power. She did not tell him that she refused to load the gun she carried in her plane, for fear she would injure herself.

Tony gave her a helpless look. "Your mother will never forgive me."

"I'll make a deal with you, Daddy. You don't tell her I'm going over there, and I won't tell her how much pain you're in."

CHAPTER 59

By five minutes before ten o'clock on Monday morning, Emelye was seated at a sunny table at *Marceau's,* a sidewalk café on *Avenue St. Germain* where she was to meet her contact, a woman whose code name was "Bridget." *"Ten o'clock sharp. Be on time. She will not wait for you,"* her father warned. After three hours' sleep, she felt as much in a fog as the tiny air strip about a mile from the Hippodrome where the plane had touched down and left her, to make her way into the city on foot. A copy of the French newspaper *L'Humanité* lay open before her as instructed; a cup of coffee—for which she paid the exorbitant price of fifty *centimes*—sat untouched, by her own choice. Apparently the coffee in Paris that her parents used to rave about was a casualty of the war. The saccharin tablet, provided in place of sugar, only worsened the vile flavor. Her flight bag was stuffed with chocolate bars and dollar bills and cigarettes—in case she needed to ask a favor—plus a Michelin street guide to Paris, which had already saved her neck this morning as she navigated the confusing streets. Her brain was still reeling from the crash course in espionage that had consumed most of last night and for which there was no textbook, just a constant barrage of instructions, most dispensed by her father as they came to his mind rather than in any specific order. *"Above all, do not deviate from my instructions in any way,"* he urged her at least a dozen times.

Over a month had passed since those Germans who once walked around the city like proud roosters were hurried into prisoner of war trucks by French soldiers, their hands in the air. It didn't look like anyone had had time to clean up. Stone building fronts, with their extravagant carving around windows and doors, were covered with grime and soot. The streets were filthy, and confetti and streamers from the victory parade were banked up against the curbs along with crisp autumn leaves. Sand bags were still heaped up here and there in the streets, where the French had fought it out with clusters of diehard German snipers. There was a huge tank still parked in front of one building she passed. She couldn't tell whether it was German or French. It looked like its occupants just climbed out and walked away.

Emelye checked her watch. One minute past the hour. Well, just one minute wasn't anything to worry about. In spite of her efforts to appear cool and dispassionate, she feared anxiety was written all over her face.

So far the café tables were empty except for her. But now two small men in faded neck scarves, dingy shirts and scruffy caps, walked in and sat down three tables over, each of them noting her presence with a curious glance. A waiter approached them with menus. One of the men shook his head, then ordered something in French. When the waiter walked away, the two men lit up cigarettes and began talking in earnest, gesturing with their hands. Maybe they were part of the Free French, discussing some important mission in coded language. On the other hand, maybe they were German collaborators. Emelye's hand moved down to the deep pocket of her coat where her father's impossibly small Browning .380 revolver, fully loaded, was stowed. Silly. The last thing she could imagine was needing a gun. The SOE agent was to get her from Paris to the little village where James—she hoped with all her heart it was James—lay injured, dreaming of going home. Daddy was sitting by the telephone in the basement, with direct service to Paris. She had the number memorized. All she had to do was avoid deviating from instructions in any way....

A matronly woman walked by carrying a shopping bag with a small bulge at the bottom—maybe she'd been lucky enough to buy a loaf of bread. Emelye had seen the long lines in front of the shops as she wandered the streets this morning. The shelves behind the windows were nearly bare, so it was pretty obvious most of the shoppers in the queue would walk away empty-handed. Now the woman paused, her eyes sweeping the café tables. Emelye's heart raced. Could it be? Yet, surely Bridget would not be matronly. The woman pivoted around, and walked into a little shop across the street with patriotic flags and books in the windows, and big photos of DeGaulle and Leclerc. Emelye let out her breath. A few seconds later she rose from her chair and checked the red awning for the name of the café, fearing she'd somehow misread it and wound up in the wrong place—but no, there it was: *Marceau's* in faded gold letters. Relieved, she returned to her table. The two men went on talking and gesturing. Pigeons gathered and pecked at crumbs on the pavement, making their guttural noise.

The next time Emelye checked her watch it was seven minutes after ten. *"Above all, do not deviate from my instructions in any way."* Unfortunately, it had not occurred to her to ask what she was to do if Bridget deviated from instructions. What would it mean? That she had gotten caught in the snare of German collaborators? Suddenly all this was beginning to seem unreal. She was back at home in the Heights, having a bizarre dream, and would wake up in a few minutes, realizing with wild relief that there had been no telegram saying James was MIA....

By ten-fifteen, Emelye had begun to wonder if she ought to search for a public telephone to call her father. Yet, what if Bridget showed up while she was gone? *"She will not wait for you."* And so she continued to sit, long columns of indecipherable French words staring up at her from *L'Humanité*. The tables were beginning to fill.

At five-till-eleven, a short woman with a tidy figure approached her table and sat down so swiftly she seemed to have appeared out of thin air. She was dressed smartly, in a waist length purple jacket with a self-belt and wide lapels, a black blouse with a large bow in front, and a slim black skirt. On her head was a felt hat with the brim turned down in front and a black net veil covering her forehead and eyes. Emelye's heart was beating so rapidly she could hardly sit still. The woman did not look directly at her, instead gazing toward the street. In a rather husky voice that seemed odd for one so daintily built, she said, "I see you found a French newspaper, Andrea." Andrea was Emelye's code name, and Bridget's words were in accordance with the script. Emelye was so relieved that her mind went blank. Several awkward moments passed before she stumbled over her lines. "Ah—ah yes, but one has trouble finding British newspapers." She hoped to God her British accent was convincing.

Apparently it was, because Bridget moved her chair a little closer and lit a cigarette. As she did so, Emelye got a whiff of the stale lipstick spread thickly on the woman's lips. She noticed prominent bluish veins beneath the thin skin of her hands. *"Bridget is first-rate, the best agent we've got in France. We're damned lucky she's available—and willing—to help us."* Emelye had envisioned someone young, nimble as an acrobat. This woman had to be in her fifties, at least. But then, Daddy was nearly fifty and less than nimble given his injured leg, and it didn't keep him from being involved in espionage.

Rather than the two of them leaving from *Marceau's*, as Emelye had been told they would, Bridget advised her to be standing on the southwest corner of *boulevard du Montparnasse* and *L'Université* at noon. A gray Citroën would approach and stop at the curb. She was to open the back door and climb inside. The party who would drive them was a doctor, Bridget said, then abruptly rose from the table and walked away.

Emelye felt encouraged. According to her father, with train service interrupted and few motor vehicles available, the French people depended almost entirely on bicycles, no matter how far the distance they must travel. Until now, it was open to question just how she and Bridget would reach James, let alone, transport him safely from there to the airstrip where a Hudson aircraft would be dispatched to wait for their arrival. And obviously, it could be vital for James to be examined by a doctor, before he was moved. Emelye could only presume that the doctor, like Bridget, was an SOE agent.

Now I see why Daddy sang the woman's praises, Emelye thought, though the puzzling deviations from what she'd been told to expect nagged at her. Right now, the most important thing was to find her way to the intersection where Bridget said to wait. Then maybe she could locate a public telephone nearby without a long queue in front of it. It wouldn't hurt to just let Daddy know she had made contact with Bridget, tell him of the deviations, and ask if everything sounded on the up-and-up.

She pulled out the Michelin to study it, realizing abruptly that she needed to use the restroom. Hours had passed since she squatted in the deserted field on her way into town. Men in Paris were provided urinals along the boulevards that reminded her of newspaper kiosks. You could see the backs of their trouser legs as they relieved themselves, which she found absolutely mortifying. Even if they had such things for women, she wouldn't be caught dead in one. She hastened inside the café to find the door marked, *Toilette*. The tiny chamber proved to be as grimy as the Paris streets. She was soon glad for the few tissues in her handbag. The toilet paper provided was nothing more than squares of newspaper, strung on a piece of wire. Newspaper! How much further could people be reduced by the war just in their ordinary, daily lives? The soap provided was, well, more like a rock. She couldn't get any lather worked up, and felt like her hands were dirtier than they were when she walked in.

It took Emelye nearly an hour to make her way to *boulevard du Montparnasse* because she had to keep stopping to refer to the map, which unfortunately did not save her from a couple of time-consuming wrong turns. Once she found the street, she passed two public telephones—one without a single person in line—but she wouldn't stop because by then she was worried about being late.

As it turned out, she arrived at the designated spot on time, then waited twenty minutes before the Citroën finally pulled up to the curb. While she was relieved that the two agents hadn't stood her up, she was now more uneasy than ever. She should have telephoned Daddy while she still had the chance. From now on she would be completely cut off from him. She peered cautiously through the window in the passenger door, to be sure Bridget was inside. If not, then she would turn on her heel and go to the nearest telephone. The woman sitting there wore a parrot green sweater, a brown skirt and dark glasses. Short, bleached curls peeked out from under her brown beret. She was facing ahead. Emelye felt uncertain. "Bridget?"

With a quick glance, she said, "But of course, who else? Get in!"

Emelye opened the rear door, stepped up on the running board, and slipped inside.

Besides creating confusion, Bridget's change of clothes struck Emelye as odd. Of course, maybe she had ripped or soiled the outfit she was wearing earlier; or maybe she was just vain, and wanted to show that she had a larger wardrobe than most women in Paris—those drab matrons standing in line at the shops with their bread tickets, for instance. But where had she gotten such nice clothing? Maybe she just had a flair for fashion, and was particularly good at making over her pre-war frocks.

From inside, the Citroën looked pretty old. The seat covers were badly worn; there was a faint smell of rusting metal overall, and an odor of stale cigarette smoke that seemed to be absorbed deep down in the upholstery; no doubt it had been accumulating for years. Bridget and the doctor were puffing away, adding to it, which made Emelye grateful the windows were open. In the floor near her feet was a large metal can smelling of petrol. A smart idea, bringing extra fuel. Daddy warned there was no telling how many detours they would be forced to take, around areas that had sustained heavy bombardment.

The Citroën moved out into traffic consisting mostly of bicycles, many of them towing carts. There were some horse-drawn vehicles, too, and a few dilapidated trucks—some with odd-looking tanks hitched to the back, like small trailers. All of which made Emelye feel especially fortunate for the doctor's automobile. Now that they were on their way, she felt a thrill of anticipation like she used to feel as a child, in that moment when she'd climbed the ladder to the top of the sliding board and peered down, just before plunging.

At first she thought her companions unfriendly, for they ignored the fact that she was there. But then she recalled her father saying that no agent knew the true identity of another, that it was risky to exchange more than the information needed to get the job done. For instance, they had been told that "Andrea" was a member of the British ATA—the counterpart of the American

WASP—who had gone out a few times with First Lieutenant Younger when they were both stationed at Bassingbourn. Emelye was to stick to that story and tell them nothing more.

The doctor had hulking shoulders and a thick-muscled neck that reminded Emelye of a bull dog. As he drove, he would turn his head now and then so that she caught a brief glimpse of his profile. He always wore a scowl, as if he did not appreciate having his day interrupted to make this journey.

Soon Bridget and the doctor began quite a lengthy discourse in French, a veil of cigarette smoke between them. What were they talking about? Emelye wondered, trying to pick up at least a few of those cognates her father had told her to listen for. It was no use. They spoke far too rapidly.

On the outskirts of Paris they approached a fork in the road where a large tree with fire red leaves stood out dramatically between the two tongs. A sign with an arrow pointing left read, "Versailles"; an arrow pointing right, "Rouen." Emelye knew that the village where they were headed was located in the general direction of Rouen. What would it mean if the doctor turned instead towards Versailles? That he was mixed up? Or, heading the wrong way on purpose because he was really a German spy and she was about to be handed over to the enemy? She thought nervously of all the 'deviations' she hadn't been able to tell her father about. She held her breath and gripped the edge of her seat. When they reached the fork and veered off to the right, toward Rouen, she was so relieved that her knees began to shake. *What's the matter with me?* Ridiculous to imagine she'd fallen into the clutches of German collaborators. What would they want with her?

For a pretty good distance, Emelye didn't see many signs of the war, though once, in the offing, she spotted the neat rows of triangular tents of an Allied encampment. This was comforting, though Daddy warned that only in case of an emergency was she to blow her cover for military officials, because they would just send her home "post-haste," to get her out of their hair. Less than a mile further, a long column of majestic Lombardy poplars stood perpendicular to the road, their branches, delicate as lace fans, throwing uniform shadows on the ground below. It was nice to know the war had not destroyed these stately trees.

Soon, far back on what was apparently a vast piece of property bordered by the poplars, the broad corner of a three-story house with a steep mansard roof, a formidable chimney, and shuttered windows became visible. As the Citroën sped on, Emelye gradually gained a full view of the massive house front. Maybe she should not have been shocked to discover the opposite end had been blown to bits, but she was. All that was left was a charred ruin with a twin chimney poking up from the rubble like a spear. She could not help feeling sad. It was as if she had known this house, had climbed its stairs and looked out its windows at the poplars. Seldom did she give a thought to Brookhurst. It was just part of all she wanted to escape while growing up. But now she found herself so grateful it had been spared by this war, and her grandparents too, that her eyes stung.

She went on half-listening to Bridget and the doctor, noting that they had begun to speak sharply to each other, like two lovers quarreling. Maybe the staccato rhythm meant they were discussing the obstacles before them: for instance, what to do if the doctor found the pilot was injured in such a way that he could not be moved—a troubling possibility that Emelye and her father had discussed last night, yet with no ready solution. If it proved to be the case, there was no telling how long it would take them to get back to England. She started to voice this concern, but then maybe Bridget and the doctor wouldn't appreciate her quizzing them.

It wasn't long before they began to encounter roads marked off with yellow tape, warning of un-defused bombs in the vicinity. Daddy had told her to expect this. The doctor would throw the Citroën into reverse gear and turn his head to look through the rearview mirror, his meaty arm draped over the seat. He would seem to stare right through her, his fat face pinched up, his eyes little angry flames. Once, they approached a crossroad with a seemingly endless caravan of Allied troops passing by. The doctor's thick neck turned red, and he swore bitterly, clapping his fist on the steering wheel. Emelye wondered defensively: *Have you forgotten what they've done for you?*

Eventually, the doctor pulled over and yanked the extra petrol can from the back floor. This was met with surprising annoyance on Bridget's part. It was the only time that she outdid the doctor in a torrent of angry words.

Had she counted on the original tank of gas lasting a lot longer than it had? Was she afraid they would wind up stranded out in the middle of nowhere? Emelye could not resist saying worriedly, "I sure hope we'll have enough." The remark was met with silence. When the tank was refilled, the doctor returned the empty can to its place without so much as a glance toward Emelye.

As they traveled on, so often did they make wide loops around impassable roads that before long Emelye was completely disoriented. The farther they went, the more numerous the ruined villages along the way, some of them so tiny and isolated that she wondered bitterly, what was the point of destroying them? A string of rude houses and small barns lined up on either side of a narrow road, charred to smithereens; apple orchards left with the fruit dropped to the ground, rotting. Occasionally they passed a group of refugees, their belongings heaped on the back of a horse-drawn cart, with sometimes an ancient, proud-looking matriarch, or maybe a younger woman heavy with child, seated beside the driver as the others traveled on foot: several generations of a family, all displaced. Emelye felt awful for them. They were much worse off than those who lost their homes in London, where all sorts of social service bureaus were in place to help people out. Would this war ever end? she wondered miserably.

Around four o'clock, with the sunlight dimming and the shadows lengthening, they drove through the remains of still one more deserted village, pretty soon closing in on a hunched old man with a long gray beard in a faded plaid shirt and a beat-up hat. With the aid of a walking stick, he was striding boldly down the center of the road, turning his head from side to side as if surveying the ruins around him. He had probably made this walk every day of his life, Emelye thought, greeting his friends along the way, some on foot like he was, some waving from their doorways. How lonely he must be, if not in shock. Suddenly the doctor started honking the horn. Maybe the man was hard of hearing, maybe just stubborn, but he ignored the noise. The doctor gunned the motor and started to pass him. Maybe he didn't know the man was going to swerve to the left when he did, but that's what happened. As the man's left side was thrown against the Citroën's right front fender with a great thump, Emelye's hands flew to her mouth in horror. But the doctor just sped forward. Anxiously, Emelye looked behind them, and there in the dust lay the man on his side, one hand groping the air. Emelye found her voice. "Stop, he's hurt," she demanded, gripping the back of the car seat. The doctor sped on. Bridget calmly turned to gaze at Emelye. "*Stupide!* That will teach him not to walk down the center of the road, eh?"

Emelye turned back and watched the man until she could no longer make out his figure heaped in the road. No one came to help him.

When she turned to face ahead, the road was a blurred strip before her. She felt sick to her very bones, and her heart was hammering so violently that she wondered Bridget and the doctor could not hear it. Who were these people? She could not accept that the agent her father respected so highly could be that cold to another human being, and that a doctor would not even stop to render aid after knocking down an old man in the street.—*Or, is he really a doctor? Now that I think about it, where is his satchel?* She let her hand slide over the gun, deep down in her pocket. But there was not much hope of holding two obviously fearless, experienced, people at bay when her hands were shaking so hard, she would be doing good to retrieve the gun, much less hold it steady. Besides, what would she demand they do? Stop and let her out in the middle of nowhere? Return her to Paris, leaving James to fend for himself? If it was to James they were truly headed, *Please, God....*

On they drove, deeper and deeper into the darkening countryside.

CHAPTER 60

A few minutes later, Emelye heard a low rumble in the distance. She and Bridget looked around. Far behind, thunderclouds were assembling like a pack of wild dogs that had picked up their scent. Bridget uttered an angry oath. Emelye thought of the old man. If he was still lying in the street when the storm broke, he would get thoroughly drenched, and probably wind up with pneumonia. She felt awful for him.

Ever since that unfortunate encounter, she had been speculating about what her companions were really up to. If they were only posing as SOE agents, and really working for the Germans, then surely her father was their target. He could say all he wanted to about not being important, but people who were not important didn't have phones in their basement with direct service to Paris. So, why hadn't they called it quits when they learned he was sending some amateur to identify the pilot? None of it made sense unless they really were doing their jobs, and just happened to be utterly ruthless when someone got in their way. Even a harmless old man. No. Regardless of how many times Emelye considered that possibility, she could not accept it.

Eventually, at a point where the road curved off to the right, they passed a village down in a hollow on the left. The village appeared to have miraculously escaped from harm. At its edge, on a gentle rise, and separated from the village by a long band of Lombardy poplars, stood a little church with a lane winding up to the door, its bell tower perched high above the entrance, as if proud to say it was here. What a peaceful, heartening sight. Emelye could pull the gun, and demand that her companions stop the car and let her out. She could probably find help in getting back to Paris from that village, especially with her supply of chocolate bars and cigarettes to ease the way. Yet on the other hand, where would that leave James? *Oh God, what if it isn't even him?* James may have been found, may be on his way back to England right now; all the while, here she was out on some wild-goose chase with two criminals—

The thunder rumbled again. It was louder now, and more menacing. The storm was edging closer. Bridget and the doctor had grown subdued; the atmosphere seemed charged with anticipation. Abruptly, Bridget raised her hand and pointed to the left, remarking to the doctor. Within a few yards he turned left onto a dirt road, not much wider than a footpath, and overhung with a thick fringe of trees that all but quenched out the fading daylight. The Citroën headlamps flashed on. As far as Emelye could see down the road, there were just trees and tangled, overgrown brush. A great place for a safe house? Or a perfect place to murder someone and leave them? She closed her fingers around the pocket holding the gun, her hands quaking. *God in heaven, make my hands be still!*

A few yards down the road, the doctor brought the Citroën to a stop and turned off the ignition. All was silent. Emelye felt paralyzed inside, as if her heart had gone dead with the engine. Without taking her eyes off her companions, she began to slowly ease the gun toward the pocket opening. *Just one shot in the back of each neck; you can do it.* Bridget took a drag on her cigarette, then looked around at Emelye. She was still wearing her sunglasses, but Emelye was too distracted to puzzle out the reason why. Her ears were pounding. She had a fleeting thought that her blood pressure must be sky high. "Come, hurry up. With any luck, your airman friend is inside," Bridget said, gesturing her head toward Emelye's right. *It is a trick. One very quick glance, that's all, and be ready*—Yet when she looked, she was amazed to find she could just make out the long side of a building, almost entirely hidden among the trees. Bridget opened the door and stepped out, tamping her cigarette under her foot. *It could still be a trick.* Emelye reached for her flight bag. "You may as well leave that in the car," said Bridget shortly.

Why the interest in her flight bag? Was there someone else around who would search it while the three of them were inside the house? For what—money? Documents? A firearm? "I—I think I'll just take it along," she said. She noticed Bridget glance significantly at the doctor, but she did not catch his reaction. She and Bridget opened their doors and stepped out on the ground, but the doctor remained behind the wheel. "Isn't he coming?" Emelye asked.

"If we need him."

Meaning what? Emelye wondered. That the pilot might not be James? If not, would they just abandon the injured pilot like they abandoned the old man in the—

"Hurry up!" Bridget glanced up at the sky again, uttered an oath.

Emelye followed her, zigzagging through the labyrinth of skinny trees and brush, her knees wobbling. Soon the building came into full view—maybe a house, or an inn. It was two-story, built of timber and something that resembled stucco, only more primitive-looking. Upstairs and down, the window shutters were closed, with boards nailed across them. There was a door in the center and a very small porch, suggesting they were entering on the back side. A long board was propped next to the door, and there were brackets on each side of the door frame. "Safe" house. *She was being pushed inside. The door was closing behind her. She could hear the board being fitted in the brackets....*

They stepped upon the porch. Bridget rapped hard on the door. No answer. She called out, rapped again. Finally came the sound of movement from within, and the door opened slightly. A weathered-looking man peered out through bloodshot eyes. Seeing Bridget, he opened the door wider and mumbled a slurred greeting. The man reeked with the combined odors of body filth and strong whisky. Stepping through the door, Bridget cried, *"Ivrogne!"* After uttering a long string of angry phrases, she repeated, *"Ivrogne!"* Reluctantly Emelye passed inside, sensing the man's bloodshot eyes moving up and down her figure. She kept her free hand down near her coat pocket. She was beginning to feel more confident about handling the gun. Outside the thunder continued. If the injured pilot proved to be James, and Bridget and her comrades were legitimate—*Please, God!*—they might have to wait out the storm before moving him. And all the while, darkness was gathering. Maybe that was why Bridget was frustrated that it was about to start raining. It would be black as pitch around here at night.

They had entered a large room with a huge open hearth, like the mouth of a cave; in the center stood a long table with a lantern burning on top. Weaving on his feet, the man swept up the lantern and led them across the floor to a doorway, spouting off in drunken French as he went. The floor was made of wood planks, rough and dry, like a theatre stage in disrepair. Once the man stepped through the doorway, the glow of the lantern plunged abruptly, and Emelye realized he was descending a flight of stairs. The last thing she wanted was to go down those stairs. But at least she was behind the others. It was a good sign they weren't trying to hem her in. Nonetheless, once Bridget had passed through, she had a fleeting urge to slam the door shut and run like hell.

Now she was through the doorway, swinging her free hand up from her pocket and gripping the stair rail. It, too, was rough and dry. She found herself drawing her fingers back instinctively, for fear of splinters. The stairway was narrow. The air was cool and musty going down.

At the bottom of the stairs was a narrow passage with huge wooden vats lined up on high shelves on either side. With the lantern weaving in the drunken hand, it seemed like the walls were moving; as if they were groping their way through a Halloween fun house. At the end was a door. When the man opened the door, it squealed on its hinges. The hair stood up on the back of Emelye's neck. The man led them inside what was apparently the main part of a cellar. With the dim glow of the lantern, you couldn't see anything but shadowy shapes like boxes and crates, heaped up around the edges of the room. The air smelled cloyingly sweet, like overripe fruit. *It is a trick. I am going to die here.*

Then, in the far corner, Emelye spotted a man's figure lying on a cot, his body covered with a dark-colored blanket, his bandaged head facing the wall. All her hopes—gathering force not just since the night she refused to let that MIA telegram intimidate her, but since she was a little girl on Heights Boulevard, beating out her hero's footsteps—were coiled up inside her like a spring. *I have come to take you home.* She was vaguely aware that Bridget had dropped behind her, and the drunkard was hanging the lantern on the nearby wall. *Please, God, let it be James....*

Then she was putting down her flight bag and reaching out to touch his shoulder. It trembled beneath her hand, which made her think of a frightened animal, an animal who has been harmed. Had someone—"James? James? Is it you?" He did not respond. She nudged his shoulder a little harder. He flinched and moaned, then slowly turned his head toward her. He seemed to be struggling to open his eyes, and he was shivering so hard his teeth were chattering. She felt uncertain. There was a lot of grizzled hair on his face—she had never seen James unshaven—and his mouth was so parched, it seemed a shrunken hole in the growth of hair. But it just might be James's nose and forehead, she thought, and as his eyes finally fluttered open and narrowed on her, she was sure it was James. It wasn't his eye color—there wasn't enough light to be sure of that—but the slight upward tilt at the outer edges: Willa's eyes.

It was all Emelye could do to keep from crying out with joy and gathering him in her arms. Yet she remembered her cover. She touched his brow. It was burning like fire. She was about to tell Bridget to bring the doctor when she heard her say in an odd, caressing tone, "You would hardly recognize your handsome husband now, eh?"

Husband. A chill went up Emelye's spine. Glancing around, she found herself gazing, for the first time, into Bridget's naked face. Her eyes were hard, her chin, lifted defiantly. Emelye felt a queer sense of recognition.

Bridget's mouth curled into a feline smile. "So you finally recognize me, eh? We will send your father a little souvenir, Emelye. Then he will know that after many years of waiting, I met his *other* daughter once again, and what a pity, he was not around to protect her."

CHAPTER 61

As James lay there in darkness, his eyelids warm and heavy, he recalled a lesson in art class long ago, where they filled a sheet of drawing paper with horizontal lines, using every color in the box of crayons. Next they covered all those colors with solid black crayon, so that it looked like a black wax rectangle. Finally, using a scissor blade, they carefully etched a design through the black. Everywhere the blade etched, the colors came through.

James felt he was now seeing his own true colors, as if the scissoring of a lock of Emelye's hair—the act by the woman clearly orchestrated and somehow even more demoralizing to witness than the swift blow wielded by the drunkard that pitched Emelye to the floor just moments earlier—had etched the design of his character through the dark. If he had not been so selfish as to marry Emelye, she would be safe at home right now, rather than lying just out of his reach in this godforsaken hole.

Hearing his name called, then turning to see Emelye materialize through the blur of feverish eyes, he had thought he was dreaming. It took his mind a little time to absorb the fact that she had actually come all the way over here and found him, when even the Air Force had apparently given up. Then he wondered: How had she known where he was? And how had she managed to get over here? It seemed obvious the woman and the drunkard were in league with the Germans, but how had Emelye fallen into their hands?

By now James had tried to awaken her several times, but his voice was little more than a whisper, and failed to stir her. In between, he alternated between chastising himself, and trying to puzzle out all the questions in his mind, the most pressing of which was, what would happen now?

The woman who brought Emelye down here had a serious grudge against her father, for some reason. And her remark about sending Tony a souvenir convinced James that he and Emelye had about five seconds to live. But then, to his shock, the woman and the drunkard walked out without finishing the job. That would tend to suggest someone else was coming behind them. To interrogate Emelye, find out where her father was, so they could have him murdered? Was it only a matter of time before a group of thugs stormed in? James knew about some of the techniques of getting people to talk, and they were not pretty. And what about when they finished? Still, what was the meaning of the lock of hair? he wondered, his mind running up against a wall. His inability to figure things out frustrated him. If he had not been hurt, he would have had all the pieces put together by now. In any case, their only hope of survival was that Emelye could get out and go for help. And admittedly, her chances were slim. That the woman and the drunkard had not even bothered tying up Emelye suggested this place was sealed pretty tight. James didn't mind dying so much, but he could hardly bear the fact that Emelye would lose her life because of him.

"Wake up!" he cried desperately. Emelye did not stir.

James had forced himself to face the fact that, if they somehow survived, the only decent thing for him to do was to admit to Emelye he had married her for every reason except the most important one, and offer her a divorce. *Divorce.* The word shamed him to his bone marrow. His parents may never forgive him, but he would just have to live with that. What was important, Emelye would probably be spared the stigma of being a divorced woman. No doubt many couples who married in haste while overseas would part ways one day when the boys went home after the war. And anyway, folks would be too busy rebuilding their own lives to dwell on Emelye's. He would go somewhere far away. And pretty soon she would find somebody who loved her like she deserved to be loved—"Emelye, hon, wake up will you?" he pleaded. Just the effort to make himself heard started him shivering again and exhausted him so utterly, he felt he could never expend that much energy again.

Just give me a few more minutes, Daddy, it seems like I just went to bed—

When James heard her soft moaning, a sense of hope rallied him. He raised up slightly. "Emelye, wake up! We gotta get out of here." He collapsed again, dizzy, catching his breath.

Alright, I'm coming, Daddy—. Emelye opened her eyes in the pitch dark. She groped for the lamp by the bed, wondered why her mouth was gritty inside. "Daddy, turn on the light!"

"No, Hon, it's James, and there is no light."

Emelye was confused. She had seen Bridget before. But where? When? Still, they'd found James, and—

When Emelye tried to raise up, pain barreled through her head and down the left side of her neck, recalling the blow from behind her left shoulder. "Oh God, it hurts!" She grabbed her forehead and lay her head down again, ever-so-carefully, on the cold stone floor. She lay still, catching her breath, realizing abruptly where the grit in her mouth came from, and that a tooth had ripped the inside of her mouth and left a piece of raw skin flapping. She licked her lips and tasted blood.

"I know, and I'm sorry," James said, guilt taking a swipe at him.

"What happened to Bridget?"

"The woman? She and the drunk are gone, but I doubt they're finished with us. Listen, if you can just find your way upstairs through the dark, you may be able to see better up there. I don't know. And maybe there's a way out of this place. Did you pass a little church, coming here? Up on a hill?"

Emelye was still trying to get things straight. Bridget led her into a trap. "Someone hit me—who hit me?"

"The drunk man," James said hurriedly. He wished to God she'd just get up, they didn't have all—

"Did the doctor come?"

"Doctor? You've gotta doctor on the way here?"

"No. I guess I only thought I did," Emelye said slowly. "Oh boy, I really messed up. I should have telephoned—"

"Tell me later, Baby," said James. He asked her again about the church.

She struggled to remember. "I…yes, in a little village. It wasn't even—"

"Good! I'm never sure what I've dreamed and what really happened. But I saw a priest there. If you can somehow get to him, ask for help. But for God's sake, be careful." James's breath was heaving from exertion.

"James, I've got a gun!" Emelye cried. The words exploded in her head. She grabbed her forehead again, moaning.

That they had a gun at their disposal seemed to James too good to be true. But apparently the woman had already thought of this. "No, they took your flight bag with them."

"It wasn't in there," she said dizzily, then realized her hip was resting on the firearm. "Oh God, I fell on it. I've been lying right on it all this time. It could have gone off and killed the baby!"

A baby. James's mind spun.

"Just give me a minute, let me see if I can get up, oh James, it's so confounded dark in here, and my head!"

A baby. It changed everything. He longed to hold Emelye, and it probably served him right that there was no time. "Oh, Honey, a baby!" He thought back to the way Emelye fell when the man struck her. Not face down, but on her side. He didn't know whether that was better, or worse. What if the baby was hurt, or even dead? For that he would never forgive himself. *A baby.*

Emelye was not going anywhere until James put his hand on her belly and felt their child growing there. Very carefully, she lifted her hip away from the gun. She felt a stab of pain there, and she would not have been surprised to discover a bruise in that spot, in the exact shape of the Browning. Wincing, she dragged herself in the direction of James's voice. When finally she felt the edge of the cot against her hands, her head was throbbing so hard she was not sure she could stand on her feet. There were spots before her eyes. Panting hard, she laid her head on the edge of the cot. She wondered if she had a concussion. She had no idea what that would feel like.

James could hear her heavy, uneven breaths. *Emelye's hands were tied behind her. A man was holding her head under water. Jerking it up.* "Em, for God's sake, you need to go for help *now.* I don't know how long—"

"Here, reach out your hand," she interrupted. She raised up and groped in mid-air until she felt the edge of James's quivering hand. She grabbed it. Pain shot like a missile from there to his shoulder. "Watch it!" he cried through clenched teeth. He caught his breath. "Something's broken, my shoulder maybe, I don't know."

"Sorry, sweetie," she said. She edged closer. The stench of dried blood came from his body, mingled with the nauseating odor of filthy bed linens. God. Poor James. That he was so neglected infuriated her. She wondered when was the last time his wounds were dressed. Now she gently pressed his hand against her belly.

A baby. My baby. James didn't realize he was crying until he felt a hot tear slip down from his eye. His voice choked with tenderness, he said, "I love you." Whether he was speaking to the child so warm there against his hand, or to the mother who carried it, he did not know; but he felt an abundance of love he thought he'd never feel again after losing Elizabeth. *Everything has changed.*

He was panting hard and his heart was beating rapidly. He laid back again. "Go on, and don't hesitate to use that gun. Don't come back, unless you find help, and even if you do, be sure it's safe before you come anywhere near this place," he said. Then he told her what to report about the V-2 storage site in case he didn't make it; with every day that passed he struggled harder to remember the coordinates, and he hoped he had told them to her correctly.

"But James—"

"Hurry up!"

"Alright, but don't think for a moment I'd come all the way over here and leave you behind; that's crazy!" *I love you*, he had said. Regardless of her pain, she was giddy with joy. She could live on those three words forever.

On her way out she must have banged into every box and crate in that room before her hand finally brushed against a door latch. With irony she recalled putting her torch inside her flight bag this morning as the sun burned through the fog. She stood there dizzily, holding her head, then she fiddled with the latch until it opened. "At least I've found the way out of this dungeon," she told James.

"That's my girl," he said faintly.

Given all they were up against, it seemed ridiculous to be thrilled that she had pleased him in this small way. Yet she could not help it. Mrs. James Younger. "*I love you*," he had said. Just in these past few minutes she had experienced everything she ever wanted from marriage to James. She would devote the rest of her life to pleasing him.

The next part of the journey was through a narrow passage so that it was relatively easy to span the distance and find the rough wood of the stair rail on the other end. As she stepped up, she heard a wild skittering noise, which sent a shiver up her spine and made her wonder how many rodents were living in this place where James had been dumped. Soon she was groping her way up the stairs. She had no idea how many there were. She did not realize she had reached the top until her foot swung up into thin air and she stumbled through the doorway. Once she regained her balance it occurred to her that Bridget and the doctor may well have left the drunk man behind, to be sure she and James didn't get away while they were gone to—what? Her mind drew a blank, and then it registered: they had gone to search for petrol. My God, they were going to burn the place down with James and her locked up inside.

Realizing that the drunkard could be lurking in the darkness, ready to spring on her, frightened Emelye so that for a few moments she stood immobile, a death grip on the gun, listening for the sound of breathing. *His rough hand was closing around her throat....* With what little breath she was able to get past her terror, she sniffed the air all around for his filthy alcohol stench. All she smelled was rotting apples. She waited. Nothing happened. At last she let out her breath.

There was a little light coming in through chinks in the shutters on this level, but it was nearly dark outside so she couldn't see much better up here than she could down in the basement.

She could hear the thunder rumbling again. Was the storm closer? If not, then surely only a little time had passed since Bridget—no. "His *other* daughter...." Emelye's mind was poised on the verge of a long-ago memory, but the only image before her was that of Elizabeth leaning her head against a door, listening. What did that have to do with anything? Damn it, who was that woman? Maybe Daddy could figure it out. That is, if she and James ever got a chance to tell him about her.

She kept one hand pressed on her head and listened for voices outside, or a car motor running, anything. She could hear nothing except the insistent rumble of thunder. It seemed to reverberate in her head and down the side of her neck. She simply had to put mind over matter and keep going.

She made her way to one window. When she touched it she felt the palm of her hand slice open. Stupid! Why hadn't it occurred to her there may be broken glass? She brought her skirt hem to the cut and held it there tightly. She had no idea how long or deep the cut was. And to think, she'd taken care to avoid getting a splinter in her finger when she first got to this place. After a few moments she took the gun and tapped around to find out where the rest of the glass was. Eventually she made the unfortunate discovery that the shutter latch was not on the inside. If she could figure out exactly where the latch was on the outside, she could just shoot a hole through it maybe, and then somehow push the shutter hard enough to loosen the board nailed to it. But what if Bridget and her friend were right out there? *They had returned with the petrol, and were outlining the building with a stream of it.* It would be better to be up above them where they couldn't reach her so easily, and overpower her; where maybe she could get a shot at them. She had to find the stairs and somehow climb them without breaking her neck. As she groped around, holding her head, trying to sharpen her eyes to pick up the shape of a stairway, she realized that if her geography was correct, the front of this building was not all that far from the main road. If she was high up, she might be seen from the road by someone who would help. That is, if she was lucky enough anyone would happen to pass by in time. No one was likely to be walking up the road after dark. Or in the rain.

It wasn't long before the stairway found her. She bumped into the rail with her right elbow, and pain flashed through her arm. She cried out, then rubbed her elbow a little, held her forehead tightly for a moment, like you would restrain a naughty child, then made her way up, gripping the rail.

Pretty soon she was standing in front of a window, licking salty sweat from above her mouth. Till now she had not even realized she was burning up inside her coat. She unbuttoned it and threw it on the floor, then used the butt of the Browning to break out what glass remained in the window. She could feel blood trickling from the wound on her palm down over her wrist. Damn it! She pressed her palm against her skirt for a few moments, remembering there were band-aids in her flight bag. She stood back, held the gun with both hands, winced hard and fired at roughly the center of the shutters. Her hands kicked back on her wrists, and her head seemed to teeter on her shoulders, like a loose rock on a cliff. And a lot of good that did, she thought bitterly when she peeked through the hole. She could use up all her ammunition, shooting holes through the shutter, without accomplishing anything. With any luck, maybe all this wood was rotten, though. She stood back, raised her foot and kicked the exposed piece of shutter with the thick heel of her shoe. It may as well have been a wall.

Suddenly, for the first time, Emelye felt totally helpless. Anger engulfed her. "Damn it to hell, you son-of-a-bitch! Get the hell out of my way!" she cried, kicking harder and harder, violence unleashing within her, blow after blow after blow. "Get the hell out—

A louver cracked. Bolstered now, she kicked some more. Another one cracked. She poked her hand through and pushed, swearing at the louver to get the hell out of her way. She finally had a hole big enough to force her arm through. She kept nudging on the cross board until the nails finally gave way. She heard the board drop down and hit the ground. She stood back, panting with exhaustion, both her arms trembling. She reached out again and groped around for the latch. When her shaky fingers finally reached it, she could tell it was rusted hard. Her fingers trembled helplessly on it. "Damn you to hell!" she cried. She remembered her blood pressure. She could almost hear Rodney's gentle voice: *"Calm down, just work with it a little, that's all. It'll give."* And that's what she did, until her fingers were raw. But it finally opened just a bit, and with more nudging, a little more, until it gave completely. She could not have said whether it was her sense of relief, or her awareness of having come through for James, that gave her tired arms the jolt of energy needed to fling the shutters wide open. She leaned out and gazed up at the leaden sky, breathing deeply of the pungent air.

She was amazed at how close the road was—much closer than she calculated, surely no more than thirty yards from here. If she were not expecting a
baby, she would jump clear to the ground and run for help. Instead she yelled
from the window, "Help me!" again and again, each time adding the polite,
"*S'il vous plait.*" She'd go on yelling until someone came: a cart load with a
family walking alongside, an old man walking by with a stick, anybody; and if
Bridget and her friend appeared, she had plenty of ammunition left and she
was not a bit afraid to empty it right into them.

The wind picked up and the trees began to sway. Far in the distance, lightning had begun its wild dance in the sky.

After a few minutes, the rain flooded down. Emelye felt a warm wet trickling down the inside of her leg. She had not even realized she had to go to the
bathroom. She could no more stop it than she could stop the rain. She went on
calling for help.

CHAPTER 62

✿

Elizabeth was on her way to a tutorial when Geneva telephoned to report that Emelye and James had somehow fallen into the clutches of Francine Tremont.

"*Somehow.*" As she stood rigid, listening, she was seized by the memory of her furtive visit with her grandmother last spring, and her recent discovery that James's final letter to her at Cambridge had been misplaced. How quickly she had dismissed her suspicion that her grandmother secretly entered her room and searched her desk drawers. *This is all my fault.* Her grip on the notebook in her hand tightened so hard, the spiral binding dug into her fingers. She could not find her voice. Geneva quickly went on to assure her that the couple were safe now, back in England, "though your father says that James is badly hurt—some broken ribs, a sprained shoulder and a deep gash in one thigh. The farmers who rescued him after his plane went down took him to some country doctor who sewed it up. But after Francine intervened, he was neglected, and the wound became infected."

"*When the doctors told me I have not long to live, I knew I had to see my granddaughter before I die. You are all I have left, ma chère....*"

Elizabeth felt quite faint and had to lower herself onto the nearby bench.

"Elizabeth, are you there?"

"Ah, yes," she managed to say.

"The army doctors took James into surgery immediately, to clean out the wound and re-stitch it," Geneva told her. "He's on the mend now, except for his vision, unfortunately—he suffered a mild concussion. He is being fitted with glasses, and of course he'll be given a desk job for the duration of the war."

As little as James had discussed his duties with Elizabeth when they were together, she knew that he was proud to be among the ranks of flyers. She recalled the double column of uniformed airmen outside St. Petroc's on his wedding day. She tried to envision him behind a desk, stacked with official papers, whereupon his verse came back to her with a sting: *"I can do the work of dull men, who draw their lines straight—"* Forced to sit behind a desk, James would be miserable. And she had clipped his wings.

She thought of dear, brave Emelye, who put her own life at risk to save him. "And Emelye suffered no injuries, I hope?" she asked fearfully.

"No, thank God!" said Geneva, and her voice cracked. "Dr. Rand gave her a thorough checking-out as soon as she got to London. Tony's bringing her home this weekend, and she has promised to stay till the baby's born.

"Oh yes—I forgot to tell you, Emelye is pregnant."

Again, Elizabeth was struck mute. Emelye would rejoice in giving James the treasure that she had wished above all to withhold from him. She could not quite manage to feel happy for them, as they deserved, but she was deeply thankful the child had not been harmed by her treachery. At last, obeying an impulse, she added, "Please tell Father that I shall be coming home also. I—there is something I must tell him." Quickly she rang off.

Skipping the tutorial, she went up to her room and sat trembling on the edge of her bed. As she reflected on the brief conversation, she was struck by the fact that Geneva had spoken the name Francine Tremont as if she were simply a common enemy, not unlike Hitler or Mussolini, dismissing the fact that she was Elizabeth's grandmother, that the same blood ran through their veins. Yet Elizabeth had never felt so indelibly marked as a Tremont. She imagined her mother's white Mercedes crashing through her smiling image in all the family photographs taken since Father married Geneva. She had always been haunted by a feeling that she didn't quite belong in their family. She believed it was her guilt for having betrayed her father that set her apart. Now she realized her separateness was far deeper and more fundamental: as a Tremont, she could never bring anything except tragedy to those she loved. Thanks be to God, she was the last in their blood line, for the world would be far better off without them. Her instinct to avoid children had been right, at least.

By the time Elizabeth left for Bodmin on Friday, she was determined to confess to her father not only her clandestine visit with her grandmother, but her earlier betrayal of him, which had led to her compulsion to question the woman. Perhaps he would be more understanding; perhaps less. At least she would have finally got it all off her chest. *Essay on the Qualities of Moral Courage, by Elizabeth Selby....Personal risk is inherent in an act of moral courage. In the case of one individual's betrayal of another, for instance, only through full con-*

fession of the guilty party to the party who has been betrayed can the shadows looming between the two parties be vanquished. Yet the guilty party runs the risk of the permanent dissolution of the relationship....

As the train sped along, she began to wonder if she might somehow get out to visit Grandfather tomorrow. Since suffering the stroke two years ago, he had never really regained his general equilibrium. As time went by, the penmanship in his letters to her was ever more shaky; he was ever more preoccupied with his health. He always claimed that seeing her was good for him. It would be nice to think she could at least help him some, by coming home, when she was sure to do a great deal of harm otherwise. Yet suddenly she wondered: What would become of Grandfather if she and Father wound up so deeply estranged, they were no longer on speaking terms? What if it so upset him, he suffered another stroke? Still one more tragedy at the hand of a Tremont.

So then for now she must spare her father the full truth. She felt no relief, as she had felt previously when she narrowly passed up the opportunity to confess the crime which grew more and more ancient yet never diminished in her heart. All she felt was despair.

Elizabeth walked from Bodmin station to Clearharbour with heavy steps. Why had she blurted out to Geneva that she was coming home? It would have been so much easier to simply write a letter to Father, detailing her grandmother's visit, and offering her apologies. Yet...more cowardly....

Tony and Emelye and Geneva were sitting around the kitchen table, absorbed in discussing all that happened in France, when the dogs began to bark in the hallway. "Must be Elizabeth," Tony said brightly. He reached for his walking stick and went out to greet her. They had not seen each other since last summer, and he had missed her. Always during such long separations, memories of his sprightly little girl in London warmed his heart, eclipsing the grief she had caused him in more recent years. Whenever he was about to see Elizabeth once again, the image in his mind was of the child hurrying towards him, leaping into his arms. How he longed to have his Lizzie back again!

Geneva had said Elizabeth wanted to talk with him. *She has found a young man and fallen in love again,* he thought jubilantly. But when he met her on the drive and saw her troubled countenance, he knew he was mistaken. He hugged her lovingly, thinking how much thinner her slight figure had become since the war began. He looked into her face. "What is it, Darling?"

His eyes were so tender and concerned that Elizabeth started to cry. This was how much he cared for her, and yet she always wound up hurting him. He stroked her hands until she had composed herself. Then, filled with dread, she began, "I'm afraid I'm partly to blame for what happened to James and Eme-lye."

At the mention of her grandmother's visit, his face became immobile; his eyes, forbidding. His body stiffened. When she was finished, he said in a voice that quavered with disdain, "I'm astonished at you, and very disappointed. Francine obviously used your own mother's tactics to get inside your room at Clough Hall. And you didn't look hard enough to see through it! Plus the fact that I forbade you to talk to her, for any reason—

"Well! I think you had better come inside and repeat this to Emelye." He reached for her suitcase and walked unevenly ahead of her. She stood still, too bruised to put one foot in front of the other.

In a few steps, he paused and turned to her. "You know, sometimes I think you overlook the fact that there's a war going on, just because you are against it.

"But the rest of us are fighting like hell, and would appreciate a little help by your just speaking out when something seems a bit out of the ordinary. But perhaps you're just too high-minded." Even as he spoke, he knew his words were mean-spirited, and that he would later regret them. Still, look what she had very nearly cost them!

Elizabeth watched her father turn again, and proceed into the house. As she followed him, slowly and at some distance, she could hardly imagine that less than an hour ago she was weighing the consequences of a full confession. He would never get it from her now, not for anything, she thought.

In that moment she hated him.

CHAPTER 63

During her tearful confession out on the drive, Elizabeth barely alluded to the early part of her conversation with her grandmother before rushing into the part that had resulted in disaster for Emelye and James. Now, sitting around the kitchen table with Father and Geneva and Emelye, Bertrand curled up on her knees, she endeavored to tell her story in detail from the beginning. There were exchanges early on that she was determined Father and Geneva should be aware of. "My grandmother seemed very much open to talking about my mother—" she began.

"Really, I do wish you wouldn't refer to that woman as your 'grandmother,'" Geneva said hotly, "your only real grandmother is Cynthia."

Elizabeth was startled. Rarely did Geneva lift her voice to interrupt when someone else was speaking; obviously she was unnerved by Father's announcement upon entering the kitchen: "I'm afraid Elizabeth was an unwitting accomplice to Francine." While she knew her ties to her maternal grandmother were as strong as any in her life—woefully so—she did not pause to argue the point with Geneva. Feeling scattered, she said, "Alright. Where was I?"

"You told us your—told us Francine was willing to talk to you about your mother," Emelye said gently. She wore a loose pink cotton dress and white wool cardigan that Elizabeth recognized as belonging to Geneva. In spite of the purplish swelling on her jaw, and an overall soreness in her neck and left shoulder that prevented her from turning her head too far in that direction, Emelye maintained the placid look of the expectant mother. So far she did not appear to condemn her sister's behavior, regardless of the consequences. Apparently Emelye had taken to heart Father's word, 'unwitting.' Such was her generosity.

"Yes, thanks. I did not tell her that my mother was quite bitter at the end of her life—she surely knew this, and besides, I did not want to lead her into speaking unfairly of Father," Elizabeth said. Her eyes drifted to his face, seeking evidence of gratitude, or at least a little softening. Yet it remained fixed in displeasure. She despised herself for her pitiful need to win his favor again, even while resenting him. She went on, "I simply told her I had often wondered what my mother was like as a child: Was she naughty, or was she a good little girl? She said, rather defensively, 'Well of course Jane was good, and very, very clever. I adored her.'"

Elizabeth looked from Father to Geneva. Did either of them realize the significance of that answer, that if it was truthful, it might well give credence to her mother's claim that Father's love affair with Geneva had changed her, made her hateful? Neither seemed to, so perhaps her grandmother was lying. Or, perhaps her mother's bitterness seemed too far in the past for Father and Geneva to be concerned about it. It would never be that far in the past for Elizabeth. "I asked, then why had she moved so far away that she could never see her?

"She told me, had she stayed in England, William would have given her no peace."

Father and Geneva exchanged a glance and Geneva's mouth opened slightly, then closed. Elizabeth had no idea what the exchange meant.

"I asked why she had not visited me in hospital, after the auto crash," she continued, turning to her father for whose benefit she had raised the question, since he had made a point of her neglect on numerous occasions. "She said that she had meant to, but her companion was called back to Paris due to a business emergency. They had to leave straightaway. She said she telephoned the hospital in Exeter and asked the nurse in my ward to convey her apologies."

"That's an outright lie!" Tony swore, outraged. "If she really wanted to see you, what was to keep her from staying on a day or two? Surely she was capable of getting herself back to Paris. Did you ask her that?"

Elizabeth dropped her eyes, then looked up again. "I didn't think of it," she apologized. "It was then she asked about you."

"Alright. Go on," he said with a disgruntled sigh.

Elizabeth looked at Emelye and Geneva. "She wanted to know if Father was staying in London, keeping the theatre open. I told her that he was. She said, surely he found time to do his duty for the war effort. I said yes, but I didn't know exactly what he did, that he didn't talk about it," she said, then with a glance at her father she added, "I must say, I don't see how she could have made much of that remark."

"I shall tell you how," he said. "Francine was working under cover for the Germans when she became an SOE agent towards the end of 1943. She probably spotted me at a recruitment meeting, or perhaps a training center. Likely, when she called on you at Cambridge, it was by way of finding some clue as to my current base of operations. Case closed."

Mrs. Greaves managed to come in and out of the kitchen often enough to follow the discussion. Now she interrupted to say, "And I'm sure it was me own fault for lettin' 'er know where to find Miss Elizabeth."

Elizabeth stared at her in puzzlement.

With a glance at Mrs. Greaves, Geneva told her, "Not necessarily. It could have been one of the children. People occasionally call and ask for you. It isn't any secret where you are."

"I'm sure it was me own self," Mrs. Greaves said lugubriously as she refilled the tea cups. Geneva went on peering at Elizabeth, shaking her head in a way that said, 'never mind.' As time went by, Geneva had noticed Mrs. Greaves developing a fatalistic streak. She had also become a little absent-minded. Tony agreed with her that the dear old woman really ought to retire—they'd provided a pension for her—but as he pointed out, with Clifton away at the war, she needed to stay busy. Besides, everyone in the family adored her.

After Mrs. Greaves left the room, Elizabeth turned to Emelye and admitted, "My—Francine remembered having met 'my American sister.' She wondered if you were studying at Cambridge also. I told her you had moved back to the States before the war, and you had recently married your childhood sweetheart. Then I...suppose I made my worst error. I told her he was a flying officer, stationed in France, and that you were a ferry pilot over in the States."

Tony looked at Emelye, one eyebrow raised.

"That was pretty much the gist of the conversation," Elizabeth concluded, somewhat relieved that it was all out. She explained that on the chimneypiece in her room at Clough Hall she kept various photos of her family, including a fetching snapshot of Emelye in her flight suit, taken at Avenger Field. There was also the picture of Emelye and James on their wedding day, she told them. She did not say that she felt compelled to keep this photo in plain view, as a reminder she mustn't dwell on all that she had forfeited by breaking up with James, but must pray daily for his happiness with Emelye. "She would have seen those photos if she came into my room. And of course, all my letters…from the family…were in my desk," she said, with a quick glance at Father.

Now Elizabeth asked the question she may have asked when Geneva telephoned, had she not been so shaken. "I say, have they apprehended my—my grandmother?" She gave Geneva a pleading look which said, *I can hardly escape who I am, now can I?*

"Oh yes. They were interrogating her within hours after the deed, and her partner, as well," Father said.

"I didn't realize she had a partner."

"Francine could not have accomplished anything alone; she was a little 'nobody,'" he said dismissively. "But her partner had connections all the way up to the German high command. He was driving the car when Emelye was abducted from Paris, posing as a doctor. His real name was Jean Toffte."

Noticing Elizabeth's look of confusion, Emelye now told her the details of her harrowing day beginning in Paris, and how she eventually called for help from the window of the house in the country where she and James were being held captive. Elizabeth was awestruck by the sheer physical feats Emelye had accomplished—and while pregnant. It seemed a miracle the child was not harmed.

Tony said, "Together, Francine and Toffte had aided in the capture and death of a number of fugitives. They were among the last of the hold-outs in France, and they were assigned to being sure the Allies didn't find that V-2 storage site. Francine probably got a damned sight more information than she bargained for, from poking round your room, though none of it could have proved useful until this injured pilot turned up mysteriously, and no sign of his plane. Was he flying reconnaissance? Had he found the storage site and radioed back? Or, was he a spy? They couldn't get anything out of him. If they had tortured him, he might have died. They put him under guard until they could find out more."

Elizabeth was endeavoring to follow all this. "But if they couldn't identify him, how did they know the pilot was related to you?" she asked.

"That was where Francine came in—I don't believe she was the first to know about the pilot. But after they intercepted my inquiry, she quickly put two and two together. She saw her chance to get rid of me, which may have raised her status a bit, though I'm sure her personal desire for revenge was much stronger. She knew bloody well I'd come over there to identify my son-in-law."

"See, Daddy was going over, but I wouldn't let him because he was having such pain in his leg," Emelye explained.

"I'm much better now," Tony said, with a contrite look at Geneva.

"And I'm thankful I didn't know about all this until it was over," said Geneva.

"I'm pretty sure that explains the delay in Paris," Tony continued. "As soon as they learned I was sending someone else over, Toffte was ready to call off the whole thing. He feared it was a trap. But Francine was not so ready to give up. So, posing as 'Bridget,' she went so far as to keep the appointment with 'Andrea,' my substitute, in Paris, to find out if she was anyone important. Instead she found herself sitting across from Emelye."

"And recognized her from her pictures in my room," Elizabeth reasoned.

"Precisely. So, here was James's wife, and my daughter into the bargain, ripe for the picking."

"I imagine her mouth was watering," Geneva said coldly.

"Francine had to find Toffte and convince him to help," said Tony.

"And I don't think he was just pretending to be annoyed," said Emelye. "I don't think he wanted anything to do with her scheme."

"No doubt he recognized Francine's agenda had become personal. That, of course, will prove the undoing of an agent every time, double or not."

"But you know, I still don't see how they linked this pilot with Daddy, unless they got James's dog tag," Emelye said, "and if they had the dog tag, it seems like they would have put it in the box they confiscated, with James's brass and the lock of my hair. Those wings and lieutenant bars could have belonged to any American pilot. What better way to prove they had killed us both than to send the dog tag?"

"What box?" Elizabeth asked.

"A little package they'd put together, to send to Daddy after the fact. It included a lock of my hair which Francine took while I was lying on the floor unconscious—James saw her remove a pair of scissors from her pocket and clip it off."

Imagining her sister lying there innocently as her grandmother collected a specimen of her hair gave Elizabeth an unsettled feeling. Somehow the term, 'premeditated murder' had never seemed quite so evil as it did now.

Tony shrugged. "Remember, Francine and Toffte were not working alone, and by that time the dog tag may have been in someone else's hands," he said. Yet in fact, as far as he knew, James's dog tag had never been recovered by either side. The confiscated box came into his hands even before Emelye was sent home to Norfolk Square from the base at Dover, and what should be right on top but a volume of Spenser's poetry with an inscription from Elizabeth on the fly leaf? At the time he had no way of deducting that it was by way of this volume that Francine had identified the pilot as James, because the inscription included only her first name and 'Bodmin, Cornwall, August, 1938.' But now that he knew Francine had a look at James's letters to Elizabeth, it was pretty obvious how it all added up for her. Naturally he did not tell Emelye the volume was in the box, and he was inclined to get rid of it lest she somehow find out one day. Yet, it was indirectly involved in the identification of one of Germany's largest V-2 storage sites, not to mention the prosecution of a group of double agents. So it was valuable in a historical sense. He slipped it into a box of books stored in the basement, and deferred making a decision.

"But how could they be sure you would die, if they just left you trapped in there?" Elizabeth was asking.

"It seems they intended to burn the place down, as soon as they located some more petrol," said Emelye.

Elizabeth brought a trembling hand to her forehead.

Emelye quickly reassured her, "But of course, lucky for us, it started raining hard—I mean, it was like the storm that day when we were all over there, remember? And that Frenchman waited it out in our car, and he stank so bad."

...And left his wooden cross behind, unfinished, Elizabeth thought, remembering those mysterious dark eyes, probing hers. She had a strange, prescient feeling....

"Anyway, it wasn't long after the rain stopped that a family of refugees passed by with all their belongings on the back of a cart. I didn't think I'd ever get across to them what I needed. But I managed to get the father to bring his lantern and break into the house. I took him down to the cellar where James was. He had this big surprised look on his face. He sent his wife to the nearby village, to get help, and she brought back the priest. He could speak a little English, thank God."

"I see," Elizabeth said quietly. After a moment she asked, "What will they do with my grandmother now?"

Tony considered telling her only that Francine had already been executed: a tidy way of putting it. As frustrated with her as he was, he did not have the heart to tell her the gruesome details of how the Free French dealt with German collaborators—making an example of them, shaving their heads and parading them barefoot through the streets of Paris with people taunting them, spitting at them along the way. Still, he could not spare her indefinitely from the details of what lay at the end of that humiliating journey. The press were always there. "The Resistance moves quickly in the case of German collaborators. Two days ago, Francine was hanged alongside her partner."

The image of her grandmother hanging from a rope, her neck broken, her feet dangling in the air, was immediate and overpowering. Elizabeth could not speak.

"And we can thank God the Tremonts can't bring any more grief to us or anyone else," said Geneva.

"Are you sure?" Elizabeth burst out. She fled from the table and up the stairs, hugging Bertrand to her breast.

CHAPTER 64

In the middle of November James was fitted with prescription lenses for reading. He had no trouble with distance; it was things up close he couldn't see. He reported for duty back at his old base—Grafton Underwood—where he sat behind a desk, processing papers for troops being transferred in and out. Though he felt a sense of longing every time he heard an airplane engine firing up outside, he didn't mind being grounded as much as he would have expected, knowing the war couldn't last much longer and pretty soon he and Emelye would be going back to Texas, with their baby. Emelye was so sure they were going to have a boy, she wouldn't even choose a girl's name. He went along with her, imagined buying Guy a toy truck and a red wagon and an electric train someday, and teaching him to swim in White Oak Bayou where his dad had taught him. He felt fortunate to have survived to raise his child; Emelye had brought him a reason to live when she came over to France to rescue him.

The Air Force had sent a doctor and one attendant to pick them up from that house in the woods. Securing his broken bones with splints, they wrapped him up like a mummy, fastened him to a litter, and carried him out, his jacket draped over him. With that jacket riding there against his heart, and Emelye walking alongside, he began to wonder if by some slim chance the drunken guard had replaced the Spenser volume in the breast pocket. He was selfish enough to want it back; it was all he had left of Elizabeth. Still, now that everything had changed, it would be a disaster if Emelye discovered he'd been carrying it with him when he crashed. At the hospital in Dover he asked a nurse to check the breast pocket. As she ran her fingers down inside it, then, with nurse-like efficiency, checked every other pocket as well, he wondered where he could have her put the volume that Emelye wouldn't find it. Under the mattress?

That all the pockets were empty came as no real surprise. It was probably for the best, he told himself. But he felt a sense of loss so acute that hot tears glazed his eyes, and he quickly looked away so the nurse wouldn't see.

One day Tony came down from London to see how he was getting along, and while there he told him that Elizabeth was partly responsible for his capture by enemy agents.

James's mind was still a little fuzzy, and he had a hard time following his father-in-law's explanation. Something about Elizabeth having been duped by her vicious grandmother, when Tony had warned her time and again to avoid the woman. When it was over, James said, "Well I'm sure Elizabeth didn't mean any harm."

"Yes, she feels dreadful about it. Still, it's rather unfortunate she didn't have more foresight to begin with," Tony said stiffly. James wondered why he apparently couldn't forgive an honest mistake. The truth was that if Elizabeth had been his wife, he would never have volunteered for that particular mission because he knew how dangerous it was. So, who was to blame? But he could not say this to Tony, so he just let the remark stand.

Only after Tony left, when James was thinking things over, did it sink in that Elizabeth had not disposed of his letters. Again, he felt a stab of loss: he had torn up the letters she wrote to him before he married Emelye. He had tossed them in a trash can on top of the quote from Aristotle. *All my love,* said the card. Yet, what did it prove that she kept his letters? That she cared for him despite the fact she'd broken their engagement? He already knew that; and in one of his clear moments when he lay in the dark basement on his cot, in so much pain the only part of him he could exercise at all was his mind, he came to realize his mistake in rushing Elizabeth into marriage. If he hadn't been so worried about losing his life from one day to the next, he would have obeyed the instinct that kept telling him to take it easy, and eventually she would have been ready. Alright. Could it be that she hoped somehow—no. He wouldn't allow himself to think about that, not with Emelye carrying his child.

Since marrying Emelye, James had known that he would inevitably come face-to-face with Elizabeth again while in England—if not at Clearharbour one weekend when they both showed up there, then certainly on holidays when the whole Selby family gathered. He couldn't appear to be going out of his way to ignore her, because then Emelye would wonder why they weren't friends anymore. He especially dreaded the upcoming Christmas holiday at

Brookhurst, where just a year ago he and Elizabeth announced their engagement.

He was relieved when Emelye wrote that the gathering would be at Clearharbour this year. As she explained, "At this point, Mother doesn't think I ought to go anywhere in a wagon—or a sleigh, if there's snow on the ground—so Uncle Morey and Aunt Nellie will meet my grandparents at St. Tudy and they'll all travel from there to Bodmin on the train." More than anything, James was thankful to be spared a sleigh ride through the snow-covered countryside.

Luckily when his train arrived late on Christmas Eve, Elizabeth had already gone up to bed. On Christmas day there were so many people in the house, it was easy enough for him to avoid her. He was aware that she felt as awkward as he did. Now and then from across the room their eyes would meet; and just for a moment his heart would puff up like a cloud. She was usually the first to avert her eyes. If there was one thing he was burning to say to her each time this happened, it was that he wasn't angry anymore; sad for the way things turned out, but not angry because he had realized his part in it.

When James left Clearharbour around ten o'clock in the morning on Boxing Day and headed back to base, he had a nagging headache and he was shaking. This could have been from the strain, but then he still had plenty of after-effects from his injuries, and this included frequent headaches and the shakes. At any rate, he felt relieved it was all over and that as far as he could see, he and Elizabeth had not given themselves away to Emelye.

Within a few minutes after he got back, he was told he had a telephone call. Emelye was on the line. Her grandfather had suffered a fatal heart attack.

She said her grandmother had reported that they were in the library by the fireside when it occurred. The clock had just struck two. Lord Edward was reading the *Times*, while Abraham and Sarah lounged at his feet. She was sitting across from him, embroidering a crib sheet for her first great-grandchild. She heard a rustle of newspaper, followed by a gasp, and looked up to see him clutching his chest as if it had exploded inside him.

The news didn't seem quite real to James. A few hours ago when he left for Bodmin station, Lord Edward shook his hand and said he and Lady Cynthia would be leaving shortly for Brookhurst, to be there in time to preside over the Boxing Day luncheon for the servants. "A pretty bleak affair at this point," he admitted. "Let us all hope that before next Christmas, the world will be at peace. Godspeed, James."

"Well, I'm sorry. I guess it's fortunate he didn't suffer much," James said carefully, not really sure how Emelye was taking all this.

"That's what I keep telling Mother; she's real upset. I guess he must have been kind of like a father to her, though I never realized."

Only then did James stop to think of Elizabeth. She must be devastated. And he could do nothing to comfort her, he thought with regret. The old anger rose in him again for a moment: as he could have, had she married him.

Lord Edward was already in retirement when James first met him, and as far as he knew, he didn't lead an active life outside Brookhurst. Attending his funeral at St. Petroc's Church, he discovered the gentleman was much better known in the community than he would have thought. There were several hundred people in attendance, a mixture of what the British called, 'the gentry,' and those who were old and leathery-looking, and plainspoken. Many who paid their respects to the family seemed to be acquainted with Morey West, and it was apparent they had known Lord Edward way back when he operated his tin mining company. Often James overheard people remarking on some generous deed he had done for them in the past. He found himself thinking about his dad, how he was always doing something for others, always helping his community. Suddenly he missed him with a sharpness he seldom experienced, and he felt bad for judging him sometimes. Dad had always done the best he could for his kids. It gave James a nice feeling to think of his son growing up knowing his grandfather Rodney Younger. He could hardly wait to get back to Texas.

By now Emelye had grown large carrying the baby, and she was not very steady on her feet. As the family stood in a circle above the grave, in their heavy coats and gloves and mufflers, James held a protective arm around her. Yet he could not help peering across at Elizabeth's solemn face, so pale in its frame of a black woolen scarf, and her red-rimmed eyes. He sensed that, regardless of being surrounded by her family, she was experiencing her loss all alone. At least a dozen times since he arrived this morning, he had felt tempted to reach out and hold her, to say that he knew how much it hurt, losing her grandfather. But he knew they'd both be better off if he kept his distance. All at once, he had a strong feeling that one day soon Elizabeth would go far away, cutting herself off from her family. He felt panicked; he wanted to know where she was all the time, in spite of the fact she would never be his again. Maybe he ought to try and talk to her: *Please, don't go away!*

He remembered himself, and looked down at Emelye. The wind blew a stray tendril of blond hair across her face. She pushed it back. He drew her a little closer. She smiled up at him trustingly, bringing to mind how completely she had trusted him on their wedding night and how the knowledge that she'd always counted on his loving her, how there had never been anyone else for her, had made him flush with a tenderness he hadn't known was there.

He recalled that at the base in Dover, an Air Force colonel conducted an interview to get Emelye's story. Yet he warned her that in order to protect the integrity of the SOE, she was not to divulge what happened in France to any-one else—in particular, the press. So the official records reflected that James bailed out of his plane, was temporarily MIA, and in due time was rescued by the Air Force. James was credited with pinpointing the V-2 storage site, and received a promotion to Captain. Emelye received no accolades for her courage and determination, even though without it, that vital information would have died with him. "It doesn't matter," she told him when he said he thought it was wrong, "all I cared about was getting you safely home."

As he went on standing there with his arm around her, he feared again that she might someday find out about him and Elizabeth. He would never love Emelye as he loved Elizabeth, but he couldn't bear the thought that she might suffer the injury of finding it out, and lose her trust in him.

A few days after her grandfather's funeral, Elizabeth sat curled up in the dormer window seat of her room at Clearharbour, stroking her cat and look-ing out upon the bare double sycamore tree with dead leaves heaped round it, and the crude hump of the Anderson shelter nearby: a dull and sorrowful scene that extended beyond to the meadows, shrouded in mist. She fancied the Cornish landscape was mourning the death of a man who had loved it so much, he could seldom tear himself away from it. The last time she had Grand-father all to herself was that weekend she came home to make her confession. She would never forget how happy he looked when he came out on the steps to greet her. For the next few hours she basked in his love, and it cheered her immeasurably after the bruising she'd received from her father. She had come to comfort him, yet wound up being comforted. They hugged each other tightly before she left, and she told him that she loved him ever so much. She would take nothing for those few hours, and ironically, she would not have had them except for the dismal errand that brought her home.

The question she'd flung at her family in the Clearharbour kitchen came back to her now. She had a queer feeling that the window in which she sat had become a ledge. With her beloved grandfather gone there was nothing to keep her from figuratively jumping off, moving far away from Father and his family so that she could bring them no further grief. She thought ahead. In a few months she would sit the Tripos. Then where would she go? From the beginning, her course of study had been preparing her for a future of more study—philosophy went round in circles; a new question rode the coattails of every answer—and her next logical step would be to apply for a teaching fellowship. She supposed that, rather than applying at Cambridge, she may well find a place in some university located so far away that she would seldom be expected to return. Scotland, perhaps? Or Ireland? Yet now she asked herself a question she'd been fending off for some time: was a future surrounded by books really for her?

Oh, how the prospect used to send a thrill up her spine: Miss Selby, a wise old don, her feet slippered, her hair braid trailing down her back, would sit in her room far into the night, debating some variation on the age-old questions of *what is truth?* or *what is the nature of good?* with a handful of enthusiastic women lounging in chairs and on the floor, the fingers of each warming a glass of sherry. When the coal fire died down, she would despatch the young women to their beds, knowing she had encouraged them just a little more towards the liberation of independent minds.

Yet as the war trudged on she had begun to question the value of accruing vast quantities of existential knowledge in a world in which the use of force was so often the first resort in resolving disagreements. Increasingly, through the clamor of debate she wished for silence and meditation; through the endless maze of questions, she wished for answers that could not be unraveled. Often she thought of Fr. Ogilvie, whose study of philosophy eventually led him down a new path, toward holy orders. It was unfortunate she never asked him what had prompted him to change his direction. She longed for the sense of peace that pervaded his spirit, and she feared she would not find it along her present route, no matter how far away from home she might go.

CHAPTER 65

❀

Elizabeth was absorbed in preparation for the Tripos when a letter came from her father, informing her that her grandfather's affairs had been settled, and he had set aside legacies of £750 for each of his grandchildren. While she had given no thought to the settling of her grandfather's estate, and never imagined she might benefit from it, it seemed to have taken an awfully long time. Perhaps the war somehow slowed down routine legal processes. "I have already transferred your share into your account at Barclay's Bank. I would advise that rather than spending it a little at a time, you save it for some meaningful investment. Still, it's yours...."

Meaningful investment. She resented her father's inference that without his help she would not conclude that the use of her grandfather's generous gift deserved serious consideration.

Admittedly, Elizabeth had little appreciation for the value of money, for she had never had any of her own. Not that she was extravagant—Father never complained that she overspent. How far would the sum of £750 go? She had some vague sense that it may prove a means for her to leave her family behind and make a fresh start somewhere far away: a meaningful investment. Yet she wondered if it was right to use Grandfather's money to do something which would undoubtedly break his heart, were he alive. For now, she was too busy to give the matter further thought.

When her exams were over, she packed up her things to move out of her room at Clough Hall. Her eyes circled the bare chimneypiece, the gaping bookshelves, the empty wall space above her desk where, for a short time, was framed the heart and soul of Cambridge. Even if she had become disenchanted towards the end, she had done a deal of living here in this room. Leaving it made her sad. *Someday I shall have another room of my own,* she thought. But how, and where? This she still did not know. She had decided not to apply at any university.

Elizabeth regretted moving back to Clearharbour even temporarily. For one thing, Emelye and her baby son Guy had occupied the dormer attic room since he was born, and the buttery served as Elizabeth's room. Unfortunately in the buttery, one was distracted from morning till night by noise coming from the kitchen—dishes clattering, children running in and out banging the door, Mrs. Greaves chattering to herself when there was no one else to talk to. Still, she could certainly manage the inconvenience until she arrived at some decision about her future, or until the war was over and her sister and family returned to the States—whichever came first. She had done far worse to her sister and nephew than she could ever make up to them. And Guy was very sweet, a pleasure to be around actually. The first time she held him—during Easter break—she was a little nervous, wondering if she would be changed by the experience, if some latent maternal instinct would emerge and fill her with longing. The fact that it did not seemed to justify her decision not to marry James, if not her decision to break off with him at the last moment. Nothing could justify that. No, what Elizabeth really minded about living at Clearharbour was being about when James came for visits. He was awarded many weekend passes nowadays, which he spent at Clearharbour. Since the Christmas holiday—the memory of which would haunt every future Christmas because of the death of Grandfather—she had managed to avoid being at home when James was there, but now she would be trapped.

It occurred to Elizabeth that she might speak to Grandmother about moving to Brookhurst for a little while; her letters often alluded to her loneliness, and her sense that her life had become as aimless as in that period long ago when she had ceased to manage stage talent, but had not yet returned to Grandfather. Still, it would be all too easy to become complacent at Brookhurst, as her grandmother's companion, and put off the inevitable decision about her future.

To Elizabeth's surprise, she returned home to find Emelye and Guy had moved downstairs to the buttery, in deference to her. "But you needn't have done," Elizabeth chided her, sorry to be robbed of this one small chance to make a sacrifice for them. Guy lay contentedly in his mother's arms, wearing a pale blue shirt and booties that doubtless had been passed down from Chris or Andy. As Elizabeth kissed his forehead and cuddled his cheek tenderly, it occurred to her that guilt for having betrayed Father had now reached down into her relationship with still one more generation, like an infection, unchecked, will continue to work its way deeper and deeper into the tissue.

"Never mind," said Emelye. "It's really more convenient. I won't be running up and down the stairs all day long for a fresh diaper, or something else I discovered I need. And the wash room is nearby, which is a blessing. Wait till you have a child one day, and you'll know what I mean."

They looked at each other. Elizabeth would never have a child.

So Elizabeth reclaimed the attic bedroom. Yet she felt ill at ease somehow as she put away her things, as if the room itself were telling her she ought not to remain for long.

She had been home but a week when victory in Europe was finally declared—for at least a month the shops had been selling flags and bunting and banners emblazoned with portraits of King George, in anticipation, and Father had stocked up at the Selfridge's flag department. Geneva and the children packed up to take the first available train to London the following day. Grandmother would journey there as well. Emelye and Guy would travel to Grafton Underwood, to celebrate with James.

Elizabeth would remain alone at Clearharbour. She felt a profound sense of relief and thankfulness that the war was over. Yet she felt that she had no right to join in all the celebrations. She resolved to spend her time in a vigil of prayer that this war would fulfill the broken promise of the First World War: that it would truly be the war to end all wars. Otherwise she intended to take advantage of the blessedly quiet household, and spend a lot of time thinking.

Emelye and Guy left before Elizabeth came down the next morning. She was still so exhausted from exams that she slept longer and harder than usual. She felt somehow bereft that she hadn't been on hand to hug her sister and baby nephew goodbye, even though they would return in a few days. After a cup of tea, she stood in the hall in her robe and slippers, waiting to say farewell to the others.

Soon Andy came down, toting his leather suitcase. He had grown considerably taller in the past year and his face had slimmed down. Next year he would enter Eton, Father's alma mater. He was still pretty mischievous, and Geneva worried he would get into his share of trouble there. Andy, of course, could hardly wait to go away from home. As Elizabeth hugged her brother's gangling figure, his pocket jingled with coins. He admitted he intended to spend all his savings on sweets in London. She had not the heart to tell him that, just because the war was over, sweets would no more magically appear in the shops than petrol would magically fill the empty tanks of automobiles. Nor would he believe her. "I love you," she said suddenly, feeling a little sad that he was grow-ing up so fast.

Now down the stairs came Chris, who paused to beg Elizabeth to go with them to London. "It won't seem right if you're not there with us, Sis," he said, his brows furrowed gravely. With his sweet, soulful dark eyes gazing at her, it was hard to resist his appeal. It occurred to her that Chris would grow up to be a very persuasive individual, because his sincerity shone through so brightly. "I need to be alone for a few days, rest up from school. I shall be waiting for you to come back and tell me all about it," she said. Hugging him close, she had a disconcerting notion that she had spoken falsely, that she wouldn't be here when he returned. *How ridiculous. Where would I go?*

Elvira practically knocked Chris down, speeding by with the large portman-teau that had been located only after a painstaking, torch-led expedition through the crowded attic. As she neared the age of thirteen, her figure was beginning to blossom into feminine curves. Not that she showed any sign that she was aware of these changes. According to Geneva, she took no notice of boys. Not surprisingly, Elvira was taking along several elaborate costumes to wear in London, in case she was invited to fancy dress balls—the reason for the outsized piece of luggage. As Elizabeth helped her pack these most treasured articles last night, she said that she was "enormously grateful" that the war was over, for now, in just two years' time when Chris went away to Eton, there would be nothing to keep her and her mother from moving up to London where she would undertake the study of drama, and become "an actor on the legitimate stage," as she put it rather grandly.

How lovely to feel so certain about your destiny, Elizabeth thought. Then all at once she felt scared inside: That was exactly her reaction many years ago, when Emelye stated clearly what she expected to attain in her future. And still she did not know what her future held. Hugging Elvira closely, she said, "Take care, my dear." In her heart she added, *"Do grow up and play all those roles you want to play. I love you."* When they released each other, Elvira demanded, "Why are your eyes wet?"

"Are they? Perhaps I've a cold coming on," Elizabeth said, and sniffed.

"D'you know, I can already summon tears at will. An actor must be able to, you know. Give me just a moment, and I'll show you—" She turned away—

"Pray, don't! I don't want to see you cry," said Elizabeth desperately, turning her round again, patting her freckled cheeks. *I don't want it to be the last thing I remember,* she thought, for in that very same moment it came to her with cer-tainty that she would not be here when her family returned.

When Elizabeth looked up, Geneva was coming down the stairs, wearing a smart but weary tailored brown dress with long, cuff-less sleeves and deep patch pockets. Geneva's hair had grown out considerably of late, and there was a flounce of faded red curls bouncing beneath the wide brim of her matching brown hat.

When their eyes met, Geneva caught the revelatory look on Elizabeth's face. *She's going to break off all relations with Tony,* she realized. She had worried and prayed hard about this for as long as she could remember, and especially since the day she came home from Cambridge to tell them she had talked to Francine, paving the way for the woman's treachery. She must talk to Tony as soon as they got to London. Put her foot down. When they returned—

"Hurry up, Mummy!" Elvira cried from the door, "We'll miss our train."

Geneva was hugging Elizabeth, kissing her. "I love you," she whispered.

"You too," said Elizabeth. Again their eyes met.

"We'll see you in a few days," Geneva said. With all her heart, she wanted to add, *"And we'll get everything worked out, I promise. Things will be different."* But who could guess how much Tony would be willing to divulge about Jane, even now?

"Righto. Godspeed," said Elizabeth, with a curious tone of finality that made Geneva feel compelled to put down her suitcase and stay home. But Tony was waiting. They owed each other this celebration together.

"A few days," Geneva could not help repeating.

When the family was gone, Mrs. Greaves came up from behind. With a great sigh, she said, "Well, Miss Elizabeth, now I can get a few things doan, can't I? Shall I pour you another cup of tea?"

"Not just yet. I think I'll go back to my room and lie down for a while."

As Mrs. Greaves returned to the kitchen, Elizabeth noticed her stiff gait. More and more she suffered from arthritis. Her fingers were so gnarled she could no longer manage needle and thread. Poor dear woman. "Oh Mrs. Greaves—I'm so glad Clifton will be coming home now."

Mrs. Greaves paused and turned around, her face all lit up, her eyes wide and luminous behind her glasses. She opened her mouth to speak. Her hands flew up. "Oh, I can't talk about it or I'll be adrivelin' and asnivelin' rest of day, won't get me work doan." She hurried out.

Bertrand was making figure eights around Elizabeth's ankles. She picked him up and hugged him close, then climbed the stairs to her room. She stretched out on her bed, opened her arms wide, closed her eyes and lay very still, in an effort to open herself to the knowledge of where God was calling her.

Yet she fell asleep almost at once, Bertrand curled up at her feet, warming them.

When she awoke and opened her eyes, she found herself staring at the shelf across the room, where the plain Shaker doll stood next to the Frenchman's primitive wooden cross. She continued staring at the two articles for quite a long time, her mind strangely at peace. Eventually she picked up an earlier train of thought and turned it over in her mind: *On the other hand, if I were to use Grandfather's money to go to a place we once enjoyed together....*

Elizabeth felt a tingling beneath her ears. The first thing to do, of course, was go to the library and check out every available book on the subject; yes, and perhaps go to Exeter, or even up to London, to find more...

...but no, that would just be a way of putting off the inevitable.

It was only to Barclay's Bank that she must hasten. She went in to have her bath and get dressed. It would soon be eleven o'clock.

In the afternoon Elizabeth sat down at her desk with pen and paper. The struggle began at once about what to put into her letter to Father and Geneva: Should she bare her soul about the torture in her mind and heart since that day long ago when she betrayed her father? Or would they consider her cowardly for doing so in a farewell note which they would receive long after she was gone?

Of course they would. If she told the truth, she had no choice but to remain and face the consequences. And, to be fair, perhaps that was what she ought to do. Yet resistance welled up in her. She knew in her heart that now was the time to go, that if she did not go now, she never would.

She sat back. How extraordinary to realize that, whereas she had always thought she could never really be free unless she told the truth, her only hope for freedom now was in not telling. So in the end Father's feelings were to be spared. Perhaps to spare him was an act of moral courage, after all: she must live the rest of her life with the knowledge of what she had done, and could never experience the unburdening of a confession. Yet there was one consolation. She could never again bring harm to those whom she loved.

She saw clearly now that her destiny had been sealed in Dartmoor Forest: she must not only leave her family behind, but break all ties with them.

She stood up and gazed round the room. She must travel light, for the distance was great. And there were things that must be dealt with before she left. The hardest thing would be to burn James's letters. She thought of Emelye, her baby in her arms, her face radiant with the knowledge that she had everything she had ever wished for. As far away as Elizabeth went, she could still be the means of Emelye's destruction if those letters wound up in her hands, particularly the ones written while Elizabeth was at Cambridge, though long before that they had suggested, in the sweetest and most timid language, that James hoped one day she would be more than his friend.

Before she knew it she was setting a match to the fireplace wood and waiting for the flames to leap and curl round it. Then, heart pounding with dread, she opened the cupboard and withdrew James's letters from the far back corner of the top shelf.

As she knelt by the fire and slowly released each one from her fingers, she dared not look at the writing in James's hand, for if she did, his face as she declared she could not marry him would be emblazoned on her mind. If she did, she could not go through with this.

Rather, she kept before her like a guiding light the image of Emelye holding her beloved child. This, and the image of herself a few hours from now, emerging from the leafy bower of sycamores along the Clearharbour drive with her suitcase in hand, and turning her face towards America.

Clearharbour
The final book in the *Clearharbour Trilogy*
will be published in 2007
Visit the author's website at:
www.suzannepagemorris.com

978-0-595-67752-8
0-595-67752-5